DESTINY

ZOMBIE RULES BOOK 4

DAVID ACHORD

SEVERED PRESS
HOBART

DESTINY

ISBN: 978-1-925342-67-3

CHAPTER 1 – WINTER

The snow was coming down in thick, sticky flakes, but I didn't let it spoil my fun. There were four of them. I happened upon them living in a veterinary clinic.

Let me explain. Since the pandemic, a little over two years ago now, these zombies, whatever you want to call them, have been evolving, in a manner of speaking. I thought they'd eventually die off. I had a long-winded explanation of why and told it to anyone who would listen. Boy was I wrong. Oh, a lot of them did die, but a lot of them didn't.

Somehow, they'd started – well, I don't know if it's the proper word to use, but they began evolving.

During the first year, I spotted a couple of them squat down and drink water out of a rain-filled pothole. Up until then, nobody had seen them ingest anything other than living flesh. They'd also stopped decomposing. Instead, their skin was healing, sort of. It wasn't a normal type of healing. The skin turned into a spider web of ugly, blackish scars. So, they were healing, just not like normal humans. They still smelled awful, like a mixture of rancid meat and baby shit.

It didn't stop with their injuries healing. They've begun to communicate with each other. Nothing but grunts and gestures, at least, for now. They've started to work together in teams too, and last but certainly not least, their body mechanics had rejuvenated; they could run now. Oh, they'd never win any Olympic medals. If you can imagine a drunken oaf wearing high heels trying to run, that's kind of what they looked like. But still, if they caught you…

And now, in the third year of this apocalypse, I was running into groups of them nesting together. I assumed the nesting was a basic primal need, coupled with the need for their body to rest and recuperate.

It was both fascinating and scary.

So, on this cold December day, I decided to go out and do some scavenging. I needed to get out, I needed space. Kelly wanted to go, she usually did, but today I told her bluntly she needed to stay at home. She didn't like it, but she didn't object. I'd had yet another dream about Julie and my kids. It put me in a bad mood and the only thing I wanted at the moment was to be alone.

Scavenging, we did it whenever we could. The list of our needs was forever endless. Fuel, ammunition, medicine, toilet paper, food, you name it we needed it. Scavenging was not an easy endeavor. You had to pick an area, recon it, and then clear the structure of any threats. Only after you'd successfully achieved those objectives could you begin your search. And even then the rewards were few. Almost all edible products had been eaten within the first month of the outbreak, and that was about three years ago. Every once in a while, I'd get lucky and find a sealed container of some type of freeze dried item, but that was rare.

I started out early and drove to an area in south Nashville that I'd been systematically searching. Completely finishing Trousdale Road was my objective today. It was a nice street for scavenging purposes, on one side of the road were residential houses and the other side was occupied by various commercial and retail businesses.

About the time I'd started searching, the snow started. Lightly at first, but it got progressively thicker as the day wore on. I managed to search six houses before breaking for lunch, which consisted of some smoked venison and hard tack. I ate in the comfort of my truck. It was deathly quiet, no animal noises, not even wind blowing. The snowfall was muting everything. As I ate, I realized I was looking at a gutted pharmacy that I'd once searched with Julie and Fred.

It seemed like so long ago.

"I sure miss you guys," I muttered. I sat there for several minutes, thinking about them. At some point, I realized I was making myself even more depressed than usual and shook off the thoughts. Finishing lunch, I wiped my hands and face with a rag and dug out a pair of binoculars from the console.

"Let's see if anyone has decided to join me," I muttered again, and took a long scan of the area, again. It was an ingrained habit now, like a feral animal, always checking my surroundings for any possible threats. The only thing that caught my eye was a veterinary clinic. The glass entry door had been broken out. It wasn't like that the last time I was in this neck of the woods. Curious, I decided to check it out.

As I said earlier, those things stink. Get a few of them together and the odor is even more prevalent. That's what it was like when I got to within a few feet of the entrance. There was a big rock laying a couple of feet inside the doorway. Interesting.

Who threw that rock? Was it another human survivor, scavenging like me? Or, there was another possibility; have those things relearned the rudimentary use of tools? I didn't know. Maybe it was time to capture another one and do some tests.

Whoever or whatever had done it, I considered them a threat and exercised due caution. I was well armed; currently, I had four different weapons. I had my trusty Kimber model 1911 Custom Carry holstered on my hip. It was a forty-five caliber and since I had limited ammo for it, I only used it when I had to. I had a Mossberg twelve gauge pump shotgun sitting in the passenger seat, I had ample ammo for it, but it was loud. My Marlin Bullpup twenty-two caliber rifle with subsonic ammunition was my second most favorite. I was pretty accurate with it in ranges under fifty feet and it barely made any noise. My last weapon was my favorite; my trusty machete, currently sticking out of my backpack. It was no samurai sword, but I'd managed to put a pretty sharp edge on it.

I stood at the entrance and took a whiff, trying to estimate how many were inside based on the severity of the odor. There were a few, definitely more than one, but I didn't care. Using the barrel of the Bullpup, I tapped on the aluminum door frame, whistled and backed up quickly. I didn't have to wait long. Two of them exited immediately, and after a moment two more filtered out. I shot the first one in the head and then took off running. The others dumbly followed. Out running them was pretty easy for me, I was on the track team in high school back when I was a scrawny sixteen-year-old kid. I was bigger now, but I was still pretty fast.

I put some distance between us, about thirty feet always worked for me, stopped, and picked off a second one with the rifle before carefully laying it down and retrieving my machete. There were two left, both of them women. I used my most enticing come hither smile to coax them closer.

The sound the blade made as I buried it in her neck was very satisfying, almost orgasmic. I had to make sure I severed the spinal cord, otherwise it was a wasted blow. I got the blade free just as the last one came upon me. Whirling in a circle, I torqued the blade completely through the last one's neck, decapitating her. It felt wonderful. Her head rolled off and fell to the ground as I deftly stepped back and admired my handy work. It was fun, exhilarating, and I found myself smiling.

"I wonder how many of you nasty things I've killed." The head stared back at me with lifeless black eyes. I started walking back toward the clinic when I heard a snarling noise behind me. Turning quickly, I saw it was the women with the gash in her neck. She was dirty, rather bloated, maybe from overeating, hell I didn't know, and wearing a heavily soiled wedding dress that no doubt used to be white. She hissed like a snake and even wiggled her black tongue at me as she feebly tried to move. I walked over to her and squatted, just out of her reach.

"Well, my pleasantly plump wanton bride, it looks like it's just the two of us." Her limbs flailed as she tried to crawl. I looked up at the dull dreary sky and stood there, letting the heavy snowfall hit me on my face.

"I've got to tell you how I love you always, I think of it on gray mornings with death." She stared at me blankly. "It's the beginning of a beautiful poem called Morning, have you ever heard of it?" She stopped snarling now and looked at me with those zombie black eyes. There was no emotion there, only a primal hostility.

"No? How about a little Emily Dickinson; A little snow was here and there, disseminated in her hair." She continued staring, silent with the exception of ragged panting, which caused black goo to spray out of the gash in her neck like a miniature oil well.

"For some reason, I've always liked her poems." I spotted a rather large diamond ring affixed to her left ring finger. It was grimy and little bits of rotted flesh was stuck to it, but even so, it was still an impressive rock.

"I see you have your wedding ring, so at least you got married before turning. Was it everything you'd hoped for? Did you know, unlike you, Emily was a spinster when she died?" Only one of her arms seemed to be working, even so, she managed to wiggle her fat body toward me. I took a step back.

"So, how did you turn, darling? Was it your husband who infected you? Was one of your bridesmaids sick, but attended the wedding anyway so as not to let you down? Maybe it was the lecherous uncle who stuck his tongue down your throat when he gave you a kiss?" I squatted down and held her in place with my machete as I looked closer at her ring.

"Did you know the belief that a diamond is a rare gem and a symbol of wealth and esteem is nothing more than a successful advertising strategy created by a corporation who happened to have owned most of the diamond mines in Africa?" The zombie bride retorted with a snarl that sounded like wood grating against rough sandpaper.

"In fact, there is no religious basis for a diamond whatsoever. Furthermore, there is a dirty little secret about the diamond industry that's often ignored." She gave me another blank look. I nodded as if she'd begged me to explain.

"They're called conflict diamonds and the profits derived were used to fund civil wars and contributed to various forms of human rights abuse.

"Heh, I can see by your expression you're thinking about the Kimberly Process, which supposedly solved the problem with the distribution and sale of conflict diamonds, but it didn't work." I received yet another raspy snarl and she tried to grab me again.

"Yeah, I understand what you're saying, nobody likes a Mister-Know-It-All. It's a character flaw I have. I've been doing better, but sometimes I can't help myself." I looked around again at her friends, who were now truly dead.

"Do you know how much I enjoy killing you infected shit-birds? It's become an outlet for me, a way of venting my frustrations and the rage I have for how life has turned out. Oh, I know what you're thinking, why don't I do something more constructive, like maybe write some poetry?" She snarled again and I replied with a scoff.

"To tell you the truth, I'd rather do this. You see, I have no fear of dying anymore, and now that my wife and kids are gone..." I didn't finish the sentence and stared at the bride.

"I bet you were a beautiful woman once." She wasn't beautiful anymore. Her lips had rotted away, or maybe they had been bitten off, several teeth were chipped or missing, her long blonde hair was matted and large chunks were missing, and her face was a patchwork of discolored scars and torn skin. I stood, put my boot on the back of her head to keep her steady, and brought the machete down. Satisfied she was really dead now, I used her soiled dress to clean the goo off of my blade.

It was quiet once again. Nothing was stirring. I stood silently in the parking lot, alone with my feelings, looking at the dead, watching them slowly being covered by the snow, wondering if they had regained any human emotions. Did they have an understanding of what'd happened to them? If so, were they outraged, sad, indifferent? Did they get angry or frightened? I didn't know.

I started to walk away, but as an afterthought, I walked back and retrieved the ring. I had to use the serrated blade on my pocket knife to cut it off, but she didn't mind, she had no use for it anymore. I used some snow to clean most of the gore off and looked at it in admiration a moment before putting it in my pocket.

"Maybe Kelly will like it." Indeed, she would, but I wasn't sure I'd ever give it to her. The implications of giving a woman a diamond ring were clear, even now.

I walked back to the clinic and went inside. The building was empty, no additional zombies. Sadly, there was nothing left inside that could be put to use. No medicine, not even any dog food. I looked over their nest as long as I could without heaving chunks. They'd found blankets, doggie blankets I guess, and piled them on the floor in the kennel. As I suspected, their digestive systems were working again; there were piles of turds in every corner. It was disgusting. I painted the FEMA symbol on the front wall and in the triangle where you were supposed to notate hazards, I wrote 'zombie turds!'

I kept it up all day, moving from one business to the next. The results weren't remarkable, but I found some stuff we could use, like used rolls of toilet paper, small cakes of soap, a bottle of ibuprofen, but nothing really special. Well, in one business, a consignment store, there was a bunch of women's clothing. I realized I had no idea what size Kelly wore, made a guess of it, and grabbed a dozen pair of vintage Levis denim jeans. The snowfall continued throughout the day and every time I exited a building my truck had a thick covering.

"Damn, it's really coming down," I announced, a little too loudly, even if there wasn't anyone around. Admonishing myself, I got back to work. I'd encountered no other zombies, which I guess I should have been thankful for.

The last business, a dance studio yielded an eight-pack of paper towels stored under the sink in the back room, virtually a treasure. I put the rolls in a plastic trash bag before tossing them in the truck and took another look at the sky. It seemed to be a deeper shade of gray than a few minutes ago.

"Those roads are going to get worse," I said to nobody as I checked my watch. It was time to head home. I jotted down the locations I'd searched and the results on one of my ever present notepads. It was a habit of mine. My grandmother once told me that as soon as I learned how to write I started taking notes. I got teased about it over the years, but for some reason whenever I wrote something down it helped me memorize it better.

I'd tossed the notepad onto the passenger seat and it fell open to some other pages in the front of the pad. Picking it back up, I read it over. They were notes of possible plans of action in order to find my abducted children. I'd read them over dozens of times, adding an idea every time I read them until I couldn't think of anything else. None of them had panned out. I was no closer today of finding them than I was when I first found out they'd been taken. Throwing the notepad to the backseat, I put the truck in drive.

Kelly eyed me quizzically when I walked in, trying to gauge my mood. I gave her a tight hug and a kiss. The ring stayed in my pocket though.

"Feeling better?" she asked.

"Yeah, thanks for being patient with me."

We discussed our day over dinner. I told her about the nest I found, glossed over my killing spree, and showed her the clothes. She in turn told me about the vegetables in the greenhouse that had ripened, the antics of the chickens in our coop, and how Shithead, our pet donkey, had followed her around all day. We chatted some more as we cleaned up the kitchen and then she coyly laid out some blankets and pillows on the floor of the den. I threw a couple of logs in the fireplace, stoked it with the poker, and then we helped each other out of our clothes.

I watched the shimmering firelight dance in her eyes as she locked her ankles around my waist, meeting my rhythmic thrusts. She liked eye contact, not that I'm complaining. There was nothing especially outrageous about our sex life. She liked to kiss, preferred missionary, and intense eye contact when she orgasmed. It was perfectly fine with me.

When we had worked ourselves into a near state of exhaustion, I kissed her passionately, rolled off and lay on my back. We'd both worked up quite a sweat. The fireplace did a good job of keeping the den warm. Kelly rolled to her side and snuggled up against me. I stared at the ceiling quietly.

"You look like you're deep in thought," she said. I didn't respond. "Are you thinking about Julie?" she asked. While I thought of Julie quite often, at this particular moment she was the furthest thing from my mind. I turned my head and glanced over at her.

"No, of course not," I said.

"But you still think about her." Her tone wasn't accusatory, but it still sounded like it bothered her.

"Yes, I do," I responded. I wasn't trying to hurt her feelings, but I saw no reason to lie about it. It had only been a couple of months since her death and I missed her terribly.

"Do you remember when we first met?" she asked.

"Sure," I replied. "It was on March sixth, almost two years ago." I remembered the exact date was because it was the day before Julie's birthday.

"When we decided to leave Birmingham, I was scared to death. None of us really knew anything about guns or shooting, and then for the last twenty miles we somehow attracted that horde of zombies. I was convinced we were going to run out of gas and be trapped. But, you guys killed them all. You saved our lives."

"Yeah, that was a good day."

"When I first saw you I thought, oh my. You were this tall, muscular blonde with the cutest baby blue eyes. And that scar on the side of your face made you look ruggedly handsome."

"I certainly remember the next day. You gave me an extra-long hug, right in front of Julie."

Kelly giggled. "I couldn't help myself." She became quiet then and softly stroked my chest. It felt good, relaxing.

"Do you regret being with me?" she suddenly asked. It came out quietly, almost a whisper, but still I could sense a note of apprehension. I rolled to my side and faced her. She looked at me questioningly with her dark smoldering eyes. We'd never talked about this before, so I guess the conversation was overdue.

Marc and Ward, our two psychologist buddies, might question the fact that Kelly and I had hooked up so soon after Julie's death. They probably would tell me I had not allowed myself time to grieve. But I had never asked for their opinion.

"Not for a minute," I replied and continued looking at her while I stroked her dark hair. We filled a void; two lonely people who needed each other on cold dark nights. We never discussed the how's and why's of how we became lovers, we simply accepted the inevitability of it. I rolled on my back again and stared at the ceiling, watching the flickering shadows.

"I never loved Terry," she said softly. I remembered her brief affair with my friend, Corporal Terry Alexander. He had been hooked up with Andie when she and Terry had their fling. As in all affairs, it didn't turn out so well.

"What about your ex-fiancé?" I asked. She shook her head slightly.

"I loved him once. I probably would have mourned him a lot more if he hadn't dumped me for another woman back before." That's how we referred to it now. Simply before. We never said 'before the outbreak,' or 'before the world went to hell.' Now, we simply referred to it as 'before.' I put my arm around her and cupped one of her sweaty breasts as she wiggled closer to me.

"I've not thought of him in a long time," she added, and paused a moment.

"Halloween."

"What?"

"Halloween night, we got drunk on a bottle of wine we'd found, made love, and then you told me you loved me. Did you mean it?" I lay there quietly for a long minute. It was true, I said it, but did I really mean it?

"I think so," I finally said.

Kelly sighed. "Okay. It was a nice birthday present, by the way."

"Your birthday is on Halloween?" I asked. She nodded. "I'm sorry, I had no idea. How old are you?"

"Twenty-three." I sat there in silence, wondering if I could really love her if I had not even taken the time to learn when her birthday was. Thankfully, she changed the subject.

"So, if you're not thinking of Julie, what are you thinking of?"

I got up and walked over to the desk, retrieved a wrinkled piece of paper and sat back down beside her. She sat up and took it out of my hand.

"What is it?" she asked as she looked at the paper.

"Do you remember the Marine corporal I told you about? The one who helped me escape?"

"The bulldog? Yeah, what about her?"

I pointed at the paper. "She wrote that."

"So, what is it?" she repeated.

"It's a series of chess moves, but they don't make much sense."

"Why not?"

"Bulldog was very good, but predictable. She was what you would call a traditional player. When she played white, she always used a particular opening style named after a famous chess master. But this," I pointed at the paper, "this is something totally different, and some of them aren't even valid chess moves." Kelly reached for the paper and looked it over.

"Are you any good?" she asked.

"Felix and I used to play all the time. His father taught us how when were about nine or ten. We would play for hours." At the mention of his name, Kelly grimaced.

"That punk was a two-faced piece of shit. I still can't believe he was your best friend."

"Yeah, well, he wasn't always a piece of shit," I replied quietly. I thought back to the days before, when he and I were thick as thieves. We were huge chess enthusiasts until he got a PlayStation on his twelfth birthday, which quickly took the place of chess.

It reminded me, Christmas was in two days. I'd not gotten any type of present for Kelly and had no idea if I should or what I should get her. Should I give her the ring?

"I know how to play a little," she said, breaking me out of my reverie.

"What? Oh. Well, there used to be a chess set at the old homestead. If the snow's not too deep, we'll head over there tomorrow and get it. We need to check things out and feed the cows anyway."

"Okay, it leads me to a question."

"Fire away."

"Those clothes you brought home, while I appreciate the gesture, they aren't my size. Would you be offended if I got a load of Julie's clothes to wear?" she asked. "I mean, I'm maybe an inch taller than her, but I think most of her stuff will fit me."

"I don't see why not," I responded noncommittally. I mean, after all, I reasoned, Julie was dead. All of them were dead. Perhaps my kids were dead too. Every time I thought of it, it was like someone was twisting a knife blade in my gut. I shook it off and set Bulldog's paper back on the desk.

"Are you finished with it?" Kelly asked. I nodded.

"Good, now come here," she said huskily and pulled me back on top of her.

CHAPTER 2 – SNOW

The snow seemed deeper than this time last year. Back before, the only place in Tennessee with regular snowfall in the winter was on the Cumberland Plateau. Nashville usually got only a couple of inches, with a rare year of several inches. When that happened, people freaked out. It virtually shut down the entire city until it melted off. I guess the reduced carbon footprint was the cause. I had kept meticulous notes ever since moving in with Rick, but I'd neglected to record weather statistics. It didn't seem relevant somehow, but I vowed to start. Kelly watched as I stuck a yardstick in the snow.

"How much?" she asked.

"Nine inches," I replied.

"Wow, I think that's about what I got last night," she said. When she grinned mischievously, I realized she wasn't talking about the snow. I scoffed.

"I'd say we need to work on your estimation of length." She giggled and groped me playfully.

"So, how's your leg doing in this cold weather?" I asked. She subconsciously reached down and rubbed her thigh. She'd cut it pretty good a few months ago and it wasn't yet fully healed. It was the only flaw in her long, sexy legs.

"It's a little stiff," she replied.

"Okay, why don't you get out of the cold, I'm going to ski over to the farm. I should be back in about three hours."

"I want to go," Kelly pleaded. I gave her a sidelong look.

"Are you sure? It's about a half mile away, including going uphill for the last part." She nodded defiantly, as if I were issuing a challenge. I wasn't. In fact, I was thinking she was going to be a burden, but I kept my opinion to myself.

"Okay, let's get the skis."

The pristine snow blanketed everything. It was only broken up by an occasional animal track, but that was it. No vehicle tracks, no ski tracks, no two-legged tracks. It was a good sign.

I'd never skied before until finding several sets in a house on Concord Road. The previous owners even had ski boots in my size. It took a little bit of practice to get it right, but since then I always looked forward to the winter and heavy snowfall.

I took the lead and broke trail, keeping a nice slow pace so Kelly could keep up and I could keep an eye on our surroundings. Even so, we were both breathing heavily when we reached the crest of the hill where the old homestead stood. I looked around while we caught our breaths. Kelly had her parka zipped up where it was covering most of her face. She unzipped it, looked around, and gestured at our surroundings.

"The snow is beautiful, isn't it?" she asked. "It's so peaceful and serene."

"Yeah," I answered as I looked at the old homestead. The soldiers had put quite a few bullet holes through the front of it and broke out the windows. I didn't find that aspect peaceful and serene; it was depressing. I pointed at the metal shutters Rick and I had mounted way back when.

"Why weren't those closed?"

"We never had a chance," Kelly replied. "Konya was shot while he was standing right there," she said, pointing to a spot near the front door. She had watched helplessly as Konya was murdered by an unknown sniper, and later watched Terry bleed to death in the barn.

I nodded in understanding as I stepped out of the skis and caught her rubbing her thigh.

"How's it feeling?"

"It's okay," she responded between breaths. Since we'd hooked up, I'd noticed she seldom complained about anything as opposed to Julie, who vented a lot. I'd grown used to it, it certainly helped me figure out what she was thinking, but silence was nice.

"How about you standing by and keeping watch? I'll check out the house and the barn." She nodded gratefully.

The old home was built almost a hundred years ago and had withstood the test of time. But, when the group of Marines had raided it, they shot it up pretty good, allowing inclement weather to seep in and do her number. I found the chess set easily, put it in my backpack, and looked around. There wasn't anything else of value left. We'd done a thorough job of getting everything moved before the bad weather had set in. I often thought about burning it to the ground in an attempt to erase the memories that haunted my dreams.

The barn was still in reasonably good shape. Rowdy's tour bus was parked beside it, at the moment it was nothing more than a large rectangular mound in the thick snow. I had plans for it, but it was going to wait until warmer weather. I motioned to Kelly and we headed toward the main house.

The main house was not far away, only a couple of hundred yards, sitting on another small hill. It was once owned by a married couple named Henry Riggins and his wife Susan, whose maiden name was Parsons. The Parsons family had settled in this area at the turn of the nineteenth century and the farm had been in the family ever since.

The Riggins home was very nice once, a lot of square footage and luxurious amenities. But now, it was in much poorer shape than the old homestead. The Marines had treated it like they were assaulting a Taliban bunker; there were holes everywhere and they even used C-4 to blow the heavy steel door. The resulting blast caused quite a bit of structural damage. Part of the roof had collapsed since the last time we were here.

"How'd that happen?" Kelly asked.

"I'd say the heavy snow fall was the proverbial straw that broke the camel's back."

"Well, that sucks. Is it safe to go inside?"

"From the way the roof fell in, I think we can get into some sections. All of Julie's clothes are in the master bedroom." I pointed. "If the hallway is accessible, I think we can low crawl through the main entrance and get inside."

"I'll do it," Kelly said. "You keep watch this time." I looked over at her questioningly.

"I'm smaller than you," she continued, "it'll be easier for me to crawl around. Besides, I know what clothes to get, you don't." I think I must have frowned or something, because she put her hands on her hips. "Are you saying I can't do it?" she asked. I shrugged and gestured toward the door. She stepped out of her skis and headed in.

She made a couple of trips but had to stop when our backpacks were stuffed. Her cheeks were a rosy red and she was winded, but she was smiling cheerfully.

"I didn't realize she had so many clothes," she said.

I grunted in agreement. Whenever Julie and I'd gone scavenging, she'd always loaded up on clothing, more clothes than she could ever hope to wear.

"We'll come back with a truck after the streets thaw out," I said and pointed at the field. A herd of cows had spotted us and were making their way toward us as quickly as the deep snow would let them.

"Alright, we need to get some hay out." I hated to think how many calves had frozen to death already. Unfortunately, there was little I could do about it under the present circumstances. They followed us as I went over to one of the large round hay bales and removed the protective tarps. They didn't wait for me to finish and the bull practically pushed me aside to get to it.

"They've lost some weight, but they still have some fat on them, that's good." Kelly nodded in understanding. I looked around and surveyed everything I could see. There were so many things that needed to be done; I could think of a dozen right off the top of my head. Unfortunately, there was only so much Kelly and I could do in a day.

"Oh well, I suppose we need to head back and take care of our home chores." Kelly agreed with me and we started skiing back the way we'd came. When we reached the homestead, I stopped and gestured toward the bridge.

"Go wait down there, please. I want to visit." Kelly looked at me in concern. "It'll only be a few minutes." She nodded and skied down the hill while I made my way over to the mound. Rick's mound. With the exception of my grandmother and my two kids, it was the place where everyone I had ever loved was buried.

"Hi everyone," I said quietly. "It's been a few days. Lots of snow and ice this winter, but I guess y'all already know that." I paused and glanced down the hill at Kelly. She was standing beside the bridge, leaning over the railing staring down into the not yet frozen water, her hot breath forming a halo of fog around her head.

"Andie, don't be mad, but I've been pretty neglectful with the journal. I promise I'll update it tonight." I paused again. Try as I might, I couldn't seem to think of anything meaningful to say.

"Julie, don't think for a minute I've forgotten about the kids." I sighed deeply, the tears were coming. "But I don't know the first place to look for them." My voice was cracking now and I had to take several deep breaths.

"I've been thinking something over and I'm going to give it a try, see what you guys think. Kelly doesn't know it yet, but we're going to reestablish friendly relations with the school group. Now I know what y'all are thinking, they're not worth it, but they may know something. If there is any possibility they have any involvement whatsoever with the Marines killing y'all, I'm going to find out. And trust me, if they were, I'll kill them all."

I stood there patiently for a full ten minutes, waiting to see if any of them would speak to me today. I was met with silence. Not even the crows were cawing. Nope, nobody was going to speak to me today.

"When it gets warm, I'll see what I can do about some gravestones." With nothing else to say, I nodded a goodbye and skied down the hill toward Kelly.

CHAPTER 3 – JOURNAL ENTRY: FEBRUARY 21ST, 3 A.Z.

Winter is proceeding with about as much excitement as rust eating through an old Detroit car. Though it hasn't been easy, Kelly and I are making do and not irritating each other too much.

We've managed to keep the livestock fed and watered. I wasn't able to save all of the newborn calves though; we lost ten that I know of.

And, thanks to our foresight, we have enough wood to keep the stoves in the greenhouse going and the plants from freezing.

We, as in Kelly and I, spent Christmas by ourselves. I fixed up a small tree, we decorated it and then exchanged gifts. I gave her some scented bath oils and candles I'd found and she gave me some disposable razor blades. Sitting here writing it down, it doesn't seem like much, but I was happy with it.

At about the end of January, there was yet another huge snowstorm and although it was nice and sunny today, we're going to need a few days of consistently warm weather to thaw everything out. I'm hoping March will have some warmer days. It'd certainly help.

Kelly and I pass the time pretty much the same way Julie and I passed time back during our first winter together. We do as many chores as we can, train, read books, play cards, play chess and play with each other.

I took her hunting yesterday. I'd seen frequent deer tracks around the old homestead and thought it'd be a good training lesson. We headed out before daylight and set up in the barn's loft. It was an eight-point buck with thick, gnarly antlers. He had a scrape along his flank and was walking with a pretty bad limp. I don't know how he had survived this far into the winter. Kelly took careful aim and shot him squarely in the heart. I tried to tell her we had done the old boy a favor but it didn't stop her from crying. I wasn't mad. She's a kind-hearted person; an admirable character trait.

When it comes to food, water, livestock, ammo, fuel, and all the other basic items, we won't starve, but we don't have an abundant supply. This is due to the recent attack by those damned Marines and the looting by others that followed. Conservation is the rule, now more than ever. We compensate by sharing everything we can; food, bathwater, the same dinner plate, you name it.

It's hit or miss with fuel. Sometimes we find gas that's still good, sometimes it's contaminated with water or just plain bad. When that happens, it causes problems with our engines which translates into a few hours of flushing the fuel lines and start all over again.

All in all, we're surviving. I still remember the first winter, after Rick had died in his sleep. I was extremely lonely, at least until I found Julie. In that regard, Kelly has been great and it is because of her that I've kept my sanity. We both have our nightmares though, so I guess it's good we're there for each other.

I must admit though, the only time I'm really happy is when I'm killing zombies. I like to get up close and personal with them. When I'm in killing mode, I don't think about how much I miss my wife, my friends, and my kids most of all.

I anguish over them constantly. Are they still alive, and if they are, are they being treated well or are they being treated like lab rats? It tears at my soul more than anything else ever has.

I need to stop writing now. – Zach.

CHAPTER 4 – TONYA'S SCHOOL

"You've never said what you thought of all of those zombies on the railroad tracks," Kelly said as we played a game of chess by candlelight.

"I have an idea," I responded, "but I don't know how valid it is." She looked at me questioningly. "Well, it goes something like this. I think they were collectively migrating south for the winter."

"Really?" she asked incredulously. I nodded. "But we've seen them frozen solid and then come back to life when they thaw out."

I shrugged. "It doesn't mean they enjoy freezing. It might also mean they're searching for food. They're thinking again, not at an advanced level, at least not yet, but they're thinking." I watched as she moved a pawn forward instead of moving her knight out of danger. I momentarily debated whether or not to cut her some slack before taking it with my bishop.

"Shit," she muttered under her breath. "So, if they're thinking again, are they going to come back?"

It was a good question. "I don't know, but I'd say it's possible, especially if they're looking for new food sources." I watched in mild amusement as she advanced another pawn.

"Why'd you do that?" I asked.

"To try to – I'm not sure. To keep your bishop from moving, I think. Was it wrong?"

"I'll mate in three moves. Do you see it?" Kelly furrowed her brow and stared at the chessboard for a full five minutes.

"Okay, I think I do," she finally said.

"Play it out then." I watched as she started moving the pieces.

"What are we going to do when they come back?" she asked as she moved my queen to the final position and looked up at me, wondering if she had done it correctly. I nodded approvingly.

"If you're referring to the zombies, since there are just the two of us, whenever we encounter large numbers, we're going to avoid them and run in the opposite direction. We don't have the strength of numbers, nor do we have enough ammunition." I instantly thought about my escapade at the veterinary clinic and chose not to tell her about it.

"In the meantime, we're going to have to use what's left of the cold weather to our advantage."

"How so?"

"We're going to do as much exploring and scavenging as we possibly can. When it warms up, we'll probably have to start restricting our travels and stay close to the farm." She frowned.

"What?" I asked.

"Oh, I agree, but I hate going into strange houses. We always see the same things: family pets that've starved to death, people who've killed themselves, and zombies of course." She paused a moment and I thought she was going to tear up. "I wish we had a dog or a cat," she said sadly and looked at me. "What about everyone at the school?"

"Honestly? I'm leery of them."

"I guess it's just the two of us then," she said. Her tone was matter-of-fact, but I knew what she was thinking.

"You want more social interaction."

"I suppose," she said with a sigh. "I mean, yes. I'm not a loner, Zach. I like being around other people."

I nodded in understanding. Humans were social creatures after all. I was the same way at one time and wondered at what specific point did I stop wanting to be around other people. Those two frumpy psychologists would have a heyday exploring the issue I bet. I reached across the chess board and caressed her hand.

"I think the roads are clear enough to drive on. How about this, after we feed all of the critters in the morning, we take a ride. Maybe see if we can find Bo and Penny." Her eyes lit up.

"That'd be nice," she said with a smile. "I'd love to see Rhonda and her kids too," she added.

I nodded slowly before responding. "Yeah, I'd like to as well, but I'm not so sure how Tonya will greet us." Kelly's smile left her, but she didn't protest. I reset the chessboard.

"There's only one way to find out I suppose, we'll go over there tomorrow and test the waters, alright?" Kelly's smile returned.

"I think that'd be nice." She got up and went into the kitchen, returning a moment later with a glass of water.

"You didn't say anything about the Marines. Do you really think Colonel Coltrane and his people will come back?" I nodded.

"In one respect, I hope they're far, far away. That would negate them coming back to look for me."

"And me," Kelly added. I shook my head.

"They think they killed everyone else, including you. So, if they come back, it'll either be to take me prisoner again, or kill me outright. We have to be cautious." I may be immune, but I sincerely doubted they'd let me live after everything that had happened, and if they found out about Kelly, it was possible they'd kill her merely on general principle.

She nodded thoughtfully as she mulled over what I said and looked at me.

"If they're far away, that means…"

"That the chances of ever seeing my kids again are pretty remote," I finished. She nodded slightly. "Yeah. I think about it constantly, just in case you're wondering."

"I know," she said quietly. "I didn't mean to bring it up, I'm sorry."

""Don't be," I replied. "One day something is going to happen. I'll have an epiphany, and I'll figure out how to get my kids back."

"*We'll* figure out how to get them back," she admonished. I offered a smile.

"You got that right. Alright," I said, changing the subject. "Final game of the night. I'm going to be black and play without bishops. Let's see how you do. Oh, let's make a wager on it."

"What kind of wager?" she asked.

"How about, the winner gets to have their way with the loser," I said as I eyed her. This brought another smile to her face, which is what I was hoping for.

Kelly drove, allowing me to keep watch and she slowed to a crawl as we neared the school. The fencing was supplemented with additional strands of barbed wire and it looked like they were starting to build a wall, which was a good sign. I directed her to stop when she turned in the entrance. The gate was standing open. So much for the reinforced fencing. Kelly pointed.

"What is that?" I looked at what she was pointing at and nodded in understanding. They had found a large boiler somewhere and relocated it to the side of the building. There were various weld patches, pipes leading to and from it, and a large partially enclosed fire pit was under it. Fog was emanating from around the boiler and the smoke stack from the fire pit had a thick plume rising in the air.

"Well I'll be. It looks like they've put together a steam-powered heating system. Damn, that's impressive," I admitted.

"Should we go in?" she asked.

"I'm not sure. I would've thought they'd at least have a guard on duty," I said, shaking my head in disapproval. Kelly suddenly gave a short gasp as the door to the bus suddenly opened and a man peered out.

"I guess he's the guard. Boy, nothing can get past him," I quipped sarcastically and gave him a halfhearted wave. He nodded, stepped out of the bus and stretched. He was a rather homely looking man, perhaps in his early thirties but already starting to look older than his years. He sported a long beard with wisps of gray starting to peek out, and even longer hair of the same color scheme tied in a ponytail and sticking out of a farmer's hat. My immediate thought was that I was going to get Kelly to give me a trim as soon as we got home. He was wearing a heavy canvas duster, which made it hard to judge his size, but I guessed him to be rather bony.

"Good morning," I said when he walked up to our truck.

"Good morning," he replied. "You two must be Zach and Kelly." I nodded and stuck my hand out through the open window.

"I've seen you before, but we've never officially met." He offered his left hand, and when he did so, the rifle that was slung over his right shoulder slipped off and fell to the asphalt with a disturbing clank.

"Gosh dang it," he muttered, set the rifle against the door of my truck and then offered his hand again.

"My name's Floyd." He gestured at his right hand, which was tucked into his jacket pocket. "Excuse the handshake, I injured my right arm a while back and it doesn't work so good anymore."

"How's everything going, Floyd?"

"Not too bad," he said and looked around before continuing in a lower voice. "Tonya is a slave driver, but I must admit, we've made some really good improvements around here. Are you guys coming to visit?"

I paused a moment before answering. "Kelly really wants to see Rhonda. But, I think given the current situation with Tonya, I'll hang outside here with you." Floyd grunted.

"Yeah, I've heard the story. Tonya is pretty opinionated, that's for sure." He looked back at the school. "How about this, I'll go check with her and see what she has to say."

"Well, I appreciate that, Floyd."

"Sure, I'll be right back." We watched in silence as he walked into the school.

"What?" Kelly asked. "You've got that look of scorn on your face."

"He left his guard post," I said disdainfully and pointed at the open bus door. "Hell, he even left his rifle. They should have some means of the guard being able to communicate with people inside the school. They either don't have it set up or Floyd was just looking for a reason to get out of the cold." Kelly snickered.

"I take it you don't approve."

"You got that right," I said contemptuously. "Remember Terry relentlessly tutoring Tommy and Joe about a guard's general orders? The first general order is to never leave your post until you're properly relieved."

"Yeah, I remember that. He's probably turning over in his grave right now."

"Yep."

Our conversation was cut short when one of the front entry doors swung open. Marc came jogging out as fast as his stubby little legs would allow him.

"Hi, you two," he said exuberantly. His hair had gone without a trim as well and he was even sporting a full beard. We got out of the truck and Marc insisted on hugging each of us. Ward came outside at about that time and insisted on joining in.

"How've you two been?" I asked.

"It's been okay, Zach. It's been cold as everything, but we've been okay." I nodded in understanding. Our conversation was interrupted by Tonya walking out of the front door. The docs' mood changed abruptly, as if they'd been caught doing something wrong. Tonya and I eyed each other. Her hair was almost fully gray now, I guess she didn't bother with coloring it anymore, and it was cut in a short butch style. I actually think she'd gained weight since the last time I'd seen her, which was not easy to do nowadays. She stared for another second or two before speaking.

"What's everyone doing standing out here in the cold? Come inside, for God's sake." She turned and walked back in without waiting for a reply. Kelly looked at me with a small, hopeful smile.

"Well, if that wasn't an invitation, I don't know what is," Marc said with a big grin and led us into the cafeteria, which was where everyone invariably congregated.

"I've got a kettle of water on the stove and was going to fix everyone some hot tea. Would you two like some?" Ward asked.

"It sounds good," I responded. Kelly ignored him and ran to the far end of the cafeteria where Rhonda was. I watched as the two of them embraced. Rhonda's hair was still the same strawberry blonde color but about an inch or two longer than the last time I saw her. Her weight was about the same, as was everyone else. I guess they were doing good, food wise.

I looked over the others. Everyone looked about the same and there were two strangers sitting at the far end of the cafeteria chatting with Gus while Tonya sat across from them, her back to me. They appeared to be about my age, perhaps a year or two older. One of them eyed me curiously as he toyed with an empty coffee mug. They were probably telling them about me and I could only imagine what the two of them were saying. The other one barely glanced at me but instead had an intense interest in Kelly and ogled her shamelessly.

I grabbed a chair and sat, watching them casually. It was difficult to believe my friends and family had been murdered while these people sat here in the comfort of this school in blissful ignorance. Marc pulled up a chair, sat, and patted my leg.

"Damn, Zach, it's so good to see the two of you. How've you been?" he asked.

"I miss my kids, Marc," I answered with equal quietness. My answer was guarded. I hoped that it would provoke some kind of informational response, but if Marc knew anything he was keeping a good poker face. I kept at it.

"But otherwise, we've done okay. I've got a lot of hard work ahead of me when the weather warms up. Those people just about destroyed everything." Ward hurried in with a tray of cups filled with steaming tea. I nodded in thanks and took a couple of sips before continuing.

"You know, I'm somewhat surprised those goons didn't pay you guys a visit as well." Ward had distributed the tea and came back to sit with us. I watched them casually, but intensely as Marc repeated what I'd said. There was no outward reaction, but they also avoided making eye contact with me.

The distant whistling of a tea kettle interrupted our conversation. Ward jumped up.

"One day, I'll find a big, two gallon kettle," he said with a grin and hurried back into the kitchen. He came back a moment later with the kettle and held it up.

"Who wants a refill?" he asked loudly. There was a chorus of responses. I nodded gratefully as he refilled my cup first. The tea bags were soggy now, but we reused them anyway. It was brackish and tasted like green tea about three years past the expiration date. As I took another sip, I looked up and saw Tonya standing. She purposely walked toward us and sat down on the other side of the table. Ward hurriedly placed a new teabag in her cup and poured hot water in.

"Have any of you seen Bo or Penny?" I asked. They all shook their heads.

"Ward and I went down to the horse farm just before the first snowfall," Marc said. "But nobody was around."

"What about Johnny and his crew?" My question drew some sidelong looks. Johnny was friends with Chet. Unfortunately, Chet and several other people were killed when their tanker truck overturned and exploded during a fuel run. The ones who were left, Johnny and two of his friends, were an unlikeable sort and everyone generally avoided them.

"I saw them driving down Franklin Road back in November," Tonya said, "but I don't think they're living in that big old house anymore. They certainly didn't bother to stop and chat."

"We went by there yesterday," Marc said. "Nobody answered our knocks, but we didn't go inside."

"There was a grave in the backyard," Ward added. "We couldn't tell how long it'd been there, but it wasn't there in November." I nodded in silence and sipped my tea, casually wondering which one of them had died.

"Oh, I almost forgot," I said, looking at Tonya. "A while back, Benny loaned me a couple of books. I've got them in the truck and figured you'd like to have them back. I'll bring them in before we leave." Tonya was looking right at me when I said it, but she didn't acknowledge it. Oh well, I'll give the books to their guard, if he was awake. She broke her attention from me and looked down at the far end of the cafeteria where Kelly was. She was playing with the little girls and laughing happily.

"It looks like they're all happy to see each other," she observed.

"Those kids have really grown," I commented, which of course made me start thinking about my children. Tonya stood abruptly.

"Walk with me, Zach. I'd like to show you some of the improvements we've made."

"Sure." I stood and followed her toward the kitchen. She pointed at one of the kitchen's ovens.

"That doesn't look like a commercial gas oven," I commented.

"We yanked it out and I made a wood burning one out of scrap steel," she said and continued pointing out things as we walked. They had indeed made several improvements. They had two latrines, male and female, which had been reworked for post-apocalyptic use, as were a lot of other small things, like sand buckets hanging on the wall every twenty feet or so, which I assumed were fire buckets. They had heavy tarps hanging over windows for blackout purposes. There were even candle holders here and there with crayons stuck in them.

"Those things burn just like candles and we have hundreds of them," she commented. We eventually made our way outside. Tonya pointed out a new greenhouse and chicken coop.

"We finished those before all of the snow and then we got this." She walked over to the boiler.

"As you can see, we diverted the creek over here so we have a water source close by. The boiler converts water to steam which serves to heat the entire school. I have plans of making it a power source as well."

"Very impressive," I said and meant it.

"We've still a long way to go, but I think you have to admit we've made considerable progress. I'd like to have running water throughout. Perhaps this summer we can make it happen." I nodded in understanding. She went on to explain how they found the boiler and the effort it took to load it up and haul it back.

"I'd like to make a few more modifications, but I think we've done a decent job. What do you think?" she asked and eyed me expectantly.

"I must agree. You guys have done a lot." She nodded at the compliment and turned back toward the boiler. I watched her as she checked the gauges, clucked her tongue and opened the firebox door.

"That damned Floyd let the temperature drop again," she quipped stiffly as she threw in a couple of logs. She shut the door, rubbed her hands together, and continued to stare at the firebox. I withheld comment about the stack of unseasoned, green wood lying on the ground nearby. Tonya turned toward me.

"It's time the two of us talked, don't you think?" she said. I eyed her suspiciously. She was right. We needed to clear the air. Whether or not it ended with me cutting her throat was still undecided. She had a revolver holstered on her waist, but I was sure if she tried to go for it I could get to her first. She turned toward me, casually but deliberately.

"I still hold you responsible for my little brother's death," she declared.

"Yes, I know." I made steady eye contact in an attempt to figure out what she was thinking, but she was showing no emotion. I decided to stir the pot a little.

"So, tell me, Tonya, if we came to you and Benny first and presented you with the facts, what exactly would you have done?"

"We would have dealt with it," she said after a long pause.

"What does that mean exactly?" I pressed. "Be more specific." I waited for her to answer, but her only response was to break eye contact for a moment and recheck the gauges on the boiler.

"I'm going to speculate here. If we had come to you first, you would have probably given him a good scolding with a few empty threats and that would have been the extent of it. Eventually, he would have found someone else to rape, torture, and murder. You know it, and I know it." She continued staring pointedly at me for a long moment before speaking.

"I'm not saying you're wrong, but it was wrong of all of you to exclude me from the decision-making process which ended in his death." I nodded in mock understanding. The truth was, I didn't give a shit what she thought about it. Her brother was an evil piece of trash and deserved what Fred did to him. I thought that was the end of it, but she continued pressing the issue.

"I'd like to ask you something, are you to be held to the same standard that you and Fred held my little brother to?"

"I've never raped anyone," I responded quickly, icily.

"Oh, I believe that. But, you've killed. You've killed more people than Anthony, I'm betting."

"And if someone threatens or brings harm to my loved ones, I'll kill again," I responded in a deeper tone. I felt myself clenching my teeth. "But comparing me to your little brother, a piece of shit psychopath, is out of line. I consider it an insult."

"Oh, you do?" she retorted. I didn't bother responding. Instead, I stared at her hard, my hand edging closer to the lock blade knife in my pants pocket.

"Alright, point taken," she finally conceded. I could have said more, much more, but as far as I was concerned, what was done was done. Besides, I had an ulterior motive for even socializing with these people and it wouldn't do any good to get into a confrontation with her. At least, not yet.

"Do you think we were involved in the deaths of everyone?" she suddenly asked.

"I hope that you weren't," I responded quietly. If I knew for a certainty they were, I was most assuredly going to retaliate. I wondered if she sensed it.

"We didn't," she responded pointedly. "You know there was no way we could have stopped them even if we knew what that damned colonel was up to, right?" I didn't answer. Tonya took a deep breath. "When we found out what had happened, we were all devastated. If we had tried to stop them, they would have killed all of us. No doubt in my mind, they would have killed us."

I slowly nodded, she was right. I didn't want her to be right, for some reason I wanted her and the rest of them to be culpable and I wasn't sure why. Maybe I'd talk it over with Kelly.

"What happened to Benny?" I asked with her same suddenness. Her mouth tightened.

"Zombies got him when we were searching for the boiler." That was it. No other explanation. I didn't push it. I liked Benny, but I had other things on my mind.

"I want to make something else clear," she said, breaking me out of reverie.

"Yes?"

"The school is mine," she asserted. I arched an eyebrow. "I know you started the plan, but I've taken it and developed it. Even you have to admit that much."

In fact, I didn't want to admit it at all. They were homeless when we allowed them to live here, and that little fact seemed to have been lost in history. But, what was I going to do, tell them it's mine and they had to leave? The truth was, I didn't need the school and I was pretty sure I didn't need them.

"Fair enough," I replied. She folded her arms as if she'd just made a significant conquest.

"While we're making things clear, perhaps there are some things I need to make clear as well," I said. Her expression was wary now, suspicious.

"I have roughly fifteen hundred acres which belong to me. That includes everything on it. So, if I see any of my cattle where they shouldn't be, I'll consider it rustling and will take appropriate measures." Her eyes narrowed.

"What are you talking about?" I pointed across the street where the radio tower stood and the field surrounding it.

"As we drove up, I saw six cows with yellow and orange colored ear tags. Those are mine. The Parsons, those were the people who originally owned the farm, they've been using those tags for years. Nobody else around here uses that color scheme. Those are my cattle."

Tonya frowned. "We got those when we thought you were dead."

I scoffed. "And when you found out I was still alive, you didn't load them up and bring them back, now did you." Tonya stared out across the street.

"We need those cows," she quipped, as if that were a satisfactory explanation.

"Tonya, you are a very intelligent, driven woman, I admire that. Hell, I wish we were friends, I could learn a lot from you. You want to establish boundaries, I get it," I said, "but it's a two-way street." I pointed again.

"Don't encroach on my boundaries again or there will be consequences." She looked at me icily. I returned her stare. "I don't think I need to spell it out, you know what I'm capable of." I paused a moment.

"So, do you have anything worthy to trade for them or should I load them up and take them back home with me?"

Tonya suddenly broke out into a chuckle. "I'm sure I can come up with something. If I may ask, how in the hell are you and Kelly going to be able to manage fifteen hundred acres on your own?"

"I can handle it," I retorted. Tonya chuckled again.

"I suppose you can at that."

"None of the horses have blankets on," Kelly observed. After leaving the school, we drove down to the once magnificent horse farm located at the Franklin Pike intersection. "They're going to freeze to death."

"It's a common misconception that horses need blankets in the winter. As long as you let them grow their winter coats, they're fine." I gestured at the horses and counted twenty-eight of them. "They've got nice thick coats, but there used to be over a hundred horses out here. I don't see anywhere near that number. Let's go take a look."

The horse stalls were open, but they'd not been mucked in quite some time. On the other hand, all of the tack and saddles had been neatly stored. I loaded up some of it.

"Are you going to take any of the horses?" I shook my head. "We could use a few," she said.

"Yeah, we'll pick up a couple more later, but not right now." I looked around the barn. There were a few farm tools I could use, but held off and instead spotted a trailer. I pointed at it. "I've been toying with an idea having to do with golf cart batteries and that trailer will come in handy for hauling them. We'll come back for it later. Right now, let's see if we can find Bo and Penny."

We headed back down Franklin Pike and I soon took a series of side roads.

"Where are we going?" Tonya asked.

"Bo's house," I replied.

"I thought he lived at the horse farm?" she asked with a small amount of confusion in her tone.

"He did, but he also had a small farm in a community called Duplex."

"Duplex?"

"Yeah. I've no idea why it was named that, but for obvious reasons, he didn't tell anybody where it is."

We made it there twenty minutes later. The entrance to his home was a long, winding gravel driveway that had sections washed out. It was a bumpy ride. I stopped a decent distance away from the house and tapped on the horn. There was no response from the house.

"It's not looking too good," Kelly said apprehensively. I nodded.

"Alright, let's clear the house." She started to open the truck door but I stopped her. "If they're in there, they might have gotten attacked or something. If they've turned, you can't hesitate, okay?"

She nodded nervously and exited the truck. It was a small house and we cleared it easily. There was nobody home.

"You're becoming pretty good at this stuff," I commented. Kelly looked at me.

"Really?"

"Yeah, much better than the first time when we went into Cool Springs Mall."

"That means a lot, coming from you," she said with a heartwarming smile. "I must admit, I was scared to death that day. I thought at any minute I was going to hurl chunks, but you made me feel safe." She smiled and I grunted.

"Alright, enough mushy stuff." She nudged me as I looked around. "Someone's been living here."

"Did you see the bedroom in back?" Kelly asked. I frowned, not knowing what she was pointing out. "Oh, Zach, how short your memory is. Didn't you see the changing table and the crib?" I straightened in realization. "Yeah, Penny's given birth." She waved a hand around. "But it looks like they're gone now. Where in the world did they go?"

I sighed. "I've no idea. They've bugged out, but I've no idea why or where they went. This is weird."

We searched the house thoroughly for any clue that might've let us know what was going on with them. We found nothing.

"What do you think?" she asked.

"Well, the house is spotlessly clean and it's been prepped for winter. The water pipes have been drained and there's even some antifreeze in the toilet bowl."

"Yeah, and there's no food, not even any rotting food." Kelly looked around. "I think they plan on coming back someday, but where the hell did they go?"

It was the question of the day, and we had no answer.

"Why don't we leave a note?" Kelly suggested. It was better than nothing. I wrote a couple of sentences but Kelly felt my brevity was inadequate and added a several more paragraphs. Thinking of nothing else, we secured the house and headed home.

CHAPTER 5 – BATTERIES

The cart barn was kind of inappropriately named. It was actually the ground floor of a private country club located on Franklin Pike. It had two commercial steel roll-up garage doors, but no windows. When we popped one of the doors open, two infected things lunged out at us. I backed up quickly, drew my sidearm, and made short work of them.

"Golfers," I grumbled sarcastically. Kelly giggled and Floyd looked at me with surprise.

"You're mighty quick with that gun."

"I had a good teacher." He nodded in admiration and peered inside cautiously.

"You must be talking about that gunslinger friend of yours. Ward talks about him all the time."

"Yeah, that was Fred. He was quick as lightning." I wish he hadn't have mentioned him. I missed Fred almost as much as I missed Julie. He and Rick had profound impacts on my life and they were both long gone. Thankfully, he changed the subject.

"It's dark as all get out in there," he observed. He was right, there was absolutely no ambient lighting.

"Yeah, this isn't going to be easy. Just because we've made a bunch of noise out here, it doesn't mean these two are the only ones left." I used my flashlight and shone it inside. The garage was full of golf carts, neatly parked and plugged into their individual chargers. It was a good sign. If I was correct, the batteries had been all charged up back before.

"Alright you two, this is going to be a slow tedious process." I looked at Floyd. "I'm thinking Kelly stands watch out here and the two of us clear this place out."

"I'm behind you all the way," Floyd said with a straight face.

"Yeah, fine, just don't shoot me in the ass by accident," I replied. "Kelly will take it very personally."

It took us over an hour to clear every nook and cranny. It was time consuming and took a lot of energy, so afterward we took a lunch break consisting of a couple of cans of pork and beans.

"Floyd, tell us a little bit about yourself," I suggested. He shrugged as he wolfed down some beans.

"Well, it's a typical story I guess you'd say. I wasn't married and didn't have no kids, but I came from a large family. We all lived in Marshall County on the family farm. My big brother was a decorated veteran of Desert Storm. When he came home, he took over his father-in-law's car dealership in Shelbyville. Some of the family worked there and the rest of us ran the farm." He ate some more and his face darkened.

"All of them are gone. Some of them got sick and died, some of them got sick and turned into them zombies. My brother did the deed and killed all of them, but then he got infected somehow and I had to kill him." Finishing his lunch, he leaned back against the rock wall lining the cart path. A slight breeze was blowing from the west and the sun was bright in the sky now. It was pleasant, but still cool enough to require a light jacket.

"So, I was making a go of it by myself."

"You didn't have a wife or a sweetheart?" Kelly asked. Floyd shook his head.

"There were a couple of gals here and there, but nothing special. I ain't the most handsome guy out there, so I didn't never attract very many women. Anyway, back this last spring I'm working a field with a disk harrow and got too close to a utility pole. I caught a guide wire and it somehow got wrapped around me and the tractor and trapped my arm. I got the tractor stopped, but damned if I could work my arm out of the cable. It was tighter than Dick's hatband and had cut the circulation off. I sat there for about seven or eight hours, totally helpless. It was getting dark and I was getting scared. Then, God smiled upon me, I guess. The pole finally snapped in two and it gave me enough slack to get my arm out, but the damage was done." He motioned at his right arm. "I can wiggle it a little bit and flex my fingers a little, but it doesn't work no more."

"That must have been rough," Kelly said sadly. Floyd nodded ruefully.

"Yeah, you might say that. If that wasn't bad enough, my dog died during all of it. He was my buddy and all I had left in the world. I was pretty depressed and convinced myself I wasn't going to be able to survive on my own with only one arm. I'd heard those radio transmissions a few times and made a decision. I loaded up, hopped in my car and made my way to the school." He chuckled.

"That Tonya, she can be a real bitch, but I got to say, she's probably the smartest woman I've ever met." He paused a moment and cleared his throat. "They've told me some stories about Tonya's little brother, but I'd like to hear it from the horse's mouth, if you don't mind."

I told him the entire story while we worked. The batteries were big and heavy, and with Floyd's bad arm I did most of the lifting and loading. Kelly kept watch with a pair of binoculars.

"So, he was a real life serial killer?" Floyd asked when I was finished with the story.

"Yep."

"Damn," he said in quiet amazement. I looked over the trailer.

"Well, Floyd, I don't think we can load up any more batteries without the tires bursting."

"I'd say you're right. What are you going to do with all them things?" he asked as I began tightening down the loading straps.

"I'm going to hook them up to a solar energy set up we have and increase our power storage." Floyd looked at me in wonder, like I was talking about alchemy or something just as magical.

"You can do that?" he asked. I nodded. Floyd slapped his thigh. "You're something else, Zach."

"I'm a survivor, Floyd," I said. "Just like you."

"You was just sixteen when all this stuff started, right?" I nodded. "Well, how in the hell did a teenage kid all by himself manage to survive?" I smiled.

"Well, it all started with that same teenage kid and a man named Rick Sanders."

I spent the next hour regaling the two of them with stories about my friend, Rick. We laughed together at Rick's antics and even Floyd misted up a bit when I told of how he died.

"I would have been right proud to have known him, I believe," he said.

"I think he would have liked you as well."

We sat there enjoying the sunshine, talking about life. We had a good view of a portion of the golf course and there were several horses grazing. I chuckled and pointed.

"Well, I'll be. Those are Bo's horses. At least now we know they haven't been eaten." After a while, I looked at my watch and suggested heading back when Floyd suddenly frowned.

"What's wrong?" Kelly asked.

"Well," Floyd replied haltingly, "Tonya told me if I was going to skip out on the day's chores I shouldn't come back home empty handed. She's likely to give me all kinds of grief."

I sympathized and thought it over. Kelly piped up.

"Why don't we go check out the kitchen in this place? I bet they have some expensive commercial cookware. The pots and pans at the school look like they've seen better days." I looked over at Kelly and then at Floyd. His face lit up in hopeful expectation.

As soon as I popped open the front door, we were greeted by seven of the stinkers. They stumbled over each other in their effort to get to us, which made it easy. I shot three of them before Floyd got a shot. He had trouble reloading and Kelly helped him out while I took a closer look at the ones we'd just killed.

"Any differences?" Kelly asked.

"Not really. These look emaciated, like they hadn't eaten anything in a while." There were two more in the cooler along with a corpse that appeared to have been chewed on extensively.

"I guess when they turned, their brain couldn't figure out how to open the door," Floyd remarked. He was probably right on the money. It was an inconsequential bit of information, but I was still going to jot it down when I got home.

"You know, I'm glad we're interacting with the school people again," Kelly said. We were lying under the blankets in front of the fireplace. It had become our favorite nocturnal spot.

"There's something I need to tell you," I replied after a moment. I felt Kelly's head move and sensed her staring at me. I told her of my suspicions. She listened in silence as I explained everything. She analyzed it, probed me with questions, analyzed some more, and finally shook her head.

"I don't know, Zach," she said. "I mean, all you have right now is a gut feeling, but nothing concrete."

"True, and that's why I want to find out the truth."

"Why didn't you tell me sooner?" she asked.

"I didn't want you to slip up and say something unintentionally," I explained. "Tonya would figure it out in a second."

"You underestimate me, Zach," she said with a huff. I agreed by snuggling closer to her.

"You're right, I do underestimate you."

"I'm glad you're finally seeing that." There was a smugness in her tone which caused me to chuckle.

"I should have seen it sooner. There are a lot of things I should have seen sooner." I kissed her for emphasis. It seemed to have the right effect.

"So, what do you want me to do?" she asked.

"I think Rhonda may be the key," I said. "She's a good-hearted person. Like you. When you think the time is right, ask her about it. I think she'll tell you the truth."

"Mmm, I'm not so sure," she responded.

"Why do you say that?"

"After talking with her, I've found out she and Tonya have become quite close. Since her little brother and daughter-in-law are dead, Rhonda has become somewhat of a surrogate daughter to her. I think I'd have a better shot with Floyd." I frowned.

"Why do you say that?"

"You've seen the way he's been ogling me." In fact, I had. I'd debated on whether or not to have a little talk with him about it, but decided it was harmless and ignored it.

"So, you're suggesting that if you do a little flirting with Floyd he'll tell you all of his secrets?" I asked. Kelly chuckled.

"Yep, men are like that."

She made a good point.

CHAPTER 6 – STRANGERS

I had no idea who they were, but they were sitting in the middle of Murfreesboro Pike near an old abandoned amphitheater. We'd apparently spotted each other at the same time because the driver reacted the exact same way I did, he stopped and waited. Kelly was in the passenger seat, eyeing them with a compact pair of binoculars.

We were well into the first week of March and were still waking up to cold mornings. Although we had a warm spell toward the end of February which gave most of the roads a good thaw, it was cold this morning. The thermometer read twenty degrees when I fed the cows, so Kelly and I opted to take advantage and go on a scavenging mission. Rule number five, the cold slows them down, still held true.

"Interesting," Kelly remarked. I glanced over.

"How so?"

"They're SUV is clean and even looks like it has a fresh coat of wax. He's got some oversize tires on it too. I bet it's a four-wheel-drive."

"Okay, how about the people?"

"I only see two of them, a man and a woman." She continued staring. "I'd say they're in their twenties, and maybe Hispanic." She dropped the binoculars and frowned. "Or maybe something else, I'm not sure." I grunted in acknowledgement. They were about two hundred yards from us, well within range.

"Is either of them pointing a rifle at us?" I asked. I already knew the answer, but I wanted her to start thinking tactically under situations like this one.

"Nope, I don't see any guns. The passenger is looking at us with binoculars. I don't see their breaths, so they have the heater running and the windows rolled up."

I nodded silently in surprised acknowledgement. That was something I hadn't noticed and it was a pretty good observation. The fact that they had their windows closed meant they were limiting their sense of sound. Not a big deal back a few years ago, but now it was unwise. I looked at her in admiration. I probably should have praised her or something, but for some reason I didn't.

"What do you want to do?" she asked. I put the truck into drive.

"We're not here to make friends," I said gruffly. "We're going to avoid them and move on." Kelly continued watching them as I turned down a side street into a subdivision. I made a series of turns, entered a driveway and cut across a couple of backyards.

"They started to follow us, but I don't see them anymore," she said. I gave a curt nod. Feeling confident we had lost them, I crisscrossed through various subdivisions and started looking for houses or businesses that might yield something of value.

"These neighborhoods are all beginning to look the same," Kelly said and gestured around at the subdivision we were currently in. "It's amazing how much things can change in just a couple of years."

I agreed. The yards were no longer plush with thick fescue grass, they were mostly a mixture of weeds with lots of dead patches and the telltale signs of mole infestation. Broken tree limbs and trash was everywhere, windows were broken out, cars were wrecked or vandalized, and there were a lot of houses that were now nothing more than burned-out remains.

"How in the world did all of these houses burn down? Did people do it?" Kelly asked.

"People, a natural gas leak, lightning strike, it could have been anything."

"Such a shame," she murmured. I agreed with a silent nod.

We went through the routine all morning. Many of the homes had their front doors standing open. It was a good indicator they had already been searched. Nevertheless, we found a dead-end street where all of the houses appeared to be untouched. I pointed at the last house.

"Do you see how the driveway goes around to the back of the house and there's access to another street?" Kelly nodded. "That'll be our escape route if someone blocks the street."

"Okay."

Kelly and I worked diligently clearing each house. Most were either vacant or contained only corpses. After three years, the foul stench of decomposition was only a faint whiff now, unless we walked into a house with zombies still inside.

It wasn't until one of the last houses we entered that we encountered one. Actually, it was two, a man and a woman. They were trapped in a closet under the stairs and were easy to kill.

"I bet they've been stuck in that closet the whole time," Kelly opined and eyed them curiously.

"Oh, that's so gross," she blurted. "They've been eating off of each other."

"Yep, I believe you're right."

It took her a second or two until the reality of it sunk in and she started gagging. I shooed her outside and finished searching the house. Unfortunately, there was nothing of value in this house. In fact, the rewards were very few. The only big treasure we found was a foot locker filled with some nice woodworking tools and a one pound plastic container of Folgers coffee.

"It's still sealed," I exclaimed when I showed it to her. "So, it should still be fresh, sort of."

"Wonderful," she said and then gestured at the tools. "Those must be old. Do you know how to use them?"

"I'm no expert, but I can learn."

"Maybe we can learn together, right?"

"Of course."

"Not a bad haul, huh?" Kelly asked.

"No, not bad at all," I responded. In addition to the tools and coffee, we'd found some toothpaste, a package of dental floss, and a couple of boxes of baking soda.

"Are you glad I'm with you?" she asked.

"You mean here with me scavenging?" I asked.

"You usually only do this yourself." I grabbed her by the waist and pulled her tight.

"Yes, I'm glad you're with me."

"No more Lone Ranger bullshit then?"

"No more Lone Ranger bullshit," I agreed. She smiled and kissed me.

"Okay, Kemosabe, let's drain some gas tanks and move on."

"Where to?" she asked. I shrugged.

"I think we're going to need to concentrate more in the rural areas and country farm houses. My gut tells me that's going to be the best chances of finding ammo. We have to be careful though."

"Okay, let's do it," she said with a smile.

We were able to siphon out somewhere around ten gallons from a couple of cars. Kelly poured in a bottle of Heet while I looked over a map and pointed out an area on Hobson Pike near the Wilson County line.

"This area is only a couple of miles away. I bet there're some farms around."

We exited the neighborhood and back onto a main road. We'd only traveled maybe twenty yards when Kelly gasped and pointed. The black SUV was stopped down the road, the two occupants sitting there staring at us.

"They're starting to really irritate me," I muttered. Kelly retrieved the binoculars from the console and looked them over.

"They have binoculars now. The dude is checking us out and the woman just waved at me." Kelly suddenly inhaled. "He's holding up a microphone." I frowned before turning on our CB radio. I had no idea what channel they'd be on, so opted for nineteen. I made a show of holding up the microphone and pushed the talk button.

"Can you hear me?"

"Most definitely, man." The response was in a thickly accented voice.

"Why are you following us?" I demanded.

"Perhaps it is you who is following us," he responded in a cheerful, almost mocking voice. "Do you intend us harm?"

"If you think we're following you, I'll put your mind at rest right now. Goodbye." I put the microphone back on the hook and drove away in the opposite direction. Kelly looked over her shoulder as I sped off, drove through some yards, and exited the subdivision on a back street.

"They're following." I glanced in the rearview mirror and felt my jaw muscles tightening. I sped up at about the time he spoke on the radio again.

"Please stop, señor. I was only kidding with you. We want to talk with you."

I spotted a small knot of cars piled together at an intersection. The way they were all jammed together reminded me of an incident a couple of years ago when Rick and I were being followed. There was a gap between a few of the cars, but you had to zigzag through it at a slow speed. I drove through it, whipped the truck around and stopped about fifty yards away. I grabbed the microphone as I put the truck in park.

"If you want to talk, start talking, but if you come through that pile of cars you're a dead man."

I opened the truck door and stuck the muzzle of my rifle out. Kelly nervously followed my lead and did the same.

"I've got the front," I said hurriedly. "Keep an eye on our six." I watched her turn around out of the corner of my eye. Directing my attention to the pile of cars, I watched as the SUV quickly braked and stopped on the other side.

"Are you pointing a gun at us, man?" he asked over the radio in a somewhat annoyed tone. I grabbed the mike.

"I want you to answer my original question, why are you following us?"

"We only wanted to make new friends," he said.

"You have a strange way of doing it," I replied and continued before he had a chance to say anything else. "But it doesn't matter. We're not looking for friends, so turn around and drive away."

There was no further chatter on the radio. After a long minute, he backed up and drove away. I got back in the truck and slammed the door. Those two had angered me. Kelly must have sensed my mood and was quiet now. The two of us rode in silence for a couple of miles before I stopped suddenly.

"Look," I said, pointing at an older ranch style house with a large prefab metal building in the back.

"I bet there might be some goodies in there," I said as I eased down the driveway.

We cleared the house and building in silence. Kelly was still unusually quiet, probably due to my outburst earlier, but I had better things to do at the moment than have a little group therapy session.

"Alright, let's see what we can find," I said. Kelly didn't acknowledge, which made me start thinking maybe I'd said something critical toward her without even realizing it. I'd figure it out later.

Neither the house nor the shed yielded any ammunition or firearms, but apparently the homeowner, the gentlemen who had hung himself from a crossbeam in the shed, was an electrician. He had a little of everything relating to the field. I waved a hand at it all.

"I think we can use some of this stuff." While I was looking over the equipment, Kelly pulled a tarp off of something and gasped. I walked over to what she'd discovered.

"I haven't ever seen one of those in real life," I said. It was a snowmobile. Snowmobiles were practically nonexistent in the south. After all, there was no need for them.

"I think it's the first one I've ever seen too," Kelly said.

"Not much use for them around here back before, but we can sure use one now. I hope it runs. Let's start loading this stuff."

We didn't have room for everything, so I concentrated only on stuff I thought we could use to upgrade our power grid. After loading up the snowmobile, I checked my watch. Kelly looked at me, but didn't say anything.

"Alright, we've been here thirty minutes," I said. "That's our limit, and the truck is full. What do you say we head home?" Kelly nodded in agreement and got in the truck.

I was normally the quiet one, I could listen for hours while Kelly would prattle on and on about everything under the sun, but when she was quiet it always meant something was wrong. I knew she wasn't sick so that could only mean I'd done something. There was a time when I ignored her until she got it out of her system, but she'd grown on me lately, although I never admitted it.

"Is there something bothering you?" I finally asked. Her typical first response was nothing was wrong, but after a little bit of prodding, it came out.

"You know, it'd be nice if we had some friends," she said a little testily. "I'm not saying those two are prime candidates, but still..." her voice trailed off at the end. I didn't respond and thought about it as I drove. She was a social person, like all humans. I, on the other hand, had convinced lately convinced myself I didn't need anyone, like Henry David Thoreau, the quintessential misanthrope. Well, I had myself mostly convinced. Besides, Thoreau had a secret craving for people to love and accept his literary works.

Okay, yeah, I really liked having Kelly with me. She was pretty, sexy, loved sex, and was pleasant company, and I was slowly coming to realize she was quite smart, but I damn sure didn't need anyone else. I mean, who needed friends, right?

We turned into our driveway as the sun was disappearing beyond the horizon. It was getting dark enough to use the headlights as Kelly jumped out and unlocked the heavy steel gate. I drove through, stopped and waited as she locked it and jumped back into the truck. When I parked, we sat there in silence a moment.

"Those two seemed sketchy," I finally said. She didn't respond. "I mean, look at the way they made contact, it seemed strange to me."

"Well, I'd say after you threatened to kill them we can pretty much write them off." She got out of the truck and walked into the dark house before I had a chance to respond.

It was completely dark when I had everything unloaded. Kelly had the fire going and dinner ready. She and I ate a quiet dinner of ground chuck and mixed vegetables. We shared the same plate and beverage glass with candlelight for illumination. The lack of conversation continued.

"This is the last of the fresh meat," I commented. "We have some smoked meat, but maybe I ought to butcher a cow tomorrow." Kelly responded with an unintelligible mumble.

I knew this was the part of a relationship where I was supposed to communicate and work out an amicable solution, but I wasn't sure I cared about any kind of an amicable solution. I mean, I didn't need any friends, and neither did Kelly. She had me.

After dinner the two of us cleaned up the kitchen, mostly in continued silence.

"I'm going to check outside," I muttered. I saw a slight nod, but that was the only acknowledgement. I made the last rounds, ensuring everything was secure and there was no unknown threat, no hidden enemy lying in wait to attack us in the night. Locking the three deadbolts, I added some wood into the fireplace and watched as the flames took hold.

"Do you want to play some chess?" I asked. Kelly shook her head.

"I think I'd rather lie by the fire tonight, okay?"

"Sure," I replied.

We brushed our teeth together, undressed, and got under the covers. In spite of the tension in the air, it seemed natural when we worked our bodies together into a spoon. I had my arm draped over her and she stroked it lovingly. I made several attempts to say something, but could get no further than a sigh. Kelly squeezed my arm.

"If you've got something to say, please just say it."

"I've got trust issues," I finally said. "I don't know how much you remember, but it started with Macie's boyfriend, Jason. He and his friends tried to ambush and kill me."

"Julie told me about that. But, you killed them, right?"

"Yeah, they were stupid and didn't stand a chance, but Andie's uncle, the captain, he came very close to killing me. Felix, my best friend at one time, turned on me. Colonel Coltrane abducted me, had everyone killed and kidnapped my children. And those people at the school, they act like I'm nothing more than a guest and seem to have totally forgotten I'm the one who came up with the original concept of the school and gave them a place to live."

"I understand, Zach, but there's something you're not seeing."

"What's that?"

"We need to rebuild," she said. She rolled around to where she was now facing me.

"Think about it. There's only so much the two of us can do. Look at how much Tonya has accomplished with the group of people she has. A couple of psychologists, Floyd the crippled farmer, Rhonda was a nanny back in the day, she has no special skills. Gus, who knows what the hell he did, but it couldn't have been anything special, right? So, with just a few ordinary people she's accomplished wonders." She gently reached out and stroked my face. "You did the same thing, you know. Back when everyone was still alive, you all accomplished a hell of a lot."

She gazed at me with her dark sultry eyes. I felt my blood pressure rising as I pulled the blanket off of me and stood, feeling the sudden need to do something. I grabbed the poker and jabbed it at the burning logs. A spray of sparks erupted. Kelly stood and put the screen back in place before an ember set our blankets on fire. I put the poker back in the rack and placed both my hands on the mantel. The fire was warm against my torso. She pressed her body against my back and wrapped her arms around me.

"What's troubling you?" she asked quietly. I sighed heavily.

"We lost, Kelly. Everybody in our group is dead and my kids are God only knows where. We lost." I continued gripping the mantel tightly. "For all I know, when Colonel Coltrane had me locked up in that shitty little room, my kids were probably at the end of the hallway in another shitty little room and not only was I totally oblivious, I was powerless to do anything."

"But, it wasn't your fault."

"Yes, it was," I responded gruffly and turned around to face her. She tried to draw me close, but I held her at arm's length. "But you don't understand."

"Explain it to me then."

"Alright, it's very simple really. I was arrogant, a know-it-all, and that arrogance blinded me. I did it with Andie's uncle. I did it with the colonel and my supposed best friend, Felix. That's a bad record if you ask me. Now, it's over. This isn't some kind of damn zombie movie where the plot ends with everyone living happily ever after. Our plight has taken its course. The only thing we have left is to try and survive for a few more years and not die a horrible death. Don't you get it? The only thing we're doing these days is existing, we're not living. What is our endgame, have you ever asked yourself that?" Kelly stared at me in silence.

"I can answer for you, there is no endgame. There is no win. There's nothing for us. One day, you may start having a pain that just won't go away. Eventually, you'll figure out its cancer. One day, I'll have a farming accident, or I'll be ambushed, or maybe while I'm tending to the crops the zombies will get me.

"We're living under a fallacy, a mistaken belief that there is a happy place awaiting us. A light at the end of the tunnel and all that bullshit. It doesn't exist."

"Wow," Kelly said quietly. I turned back toward the fire. After a minute, Kelly pressed herself against me again. "Whether you think you can or you think you can't, you're probably right. Henry Ford said that, I think." She continued holding me and we stood like that for several minutes. In spite of myself, I chuckled.

"You amaze me sometimes with your insight." She responded with a tighter squeeze and I sighed again.

"I can't help but think you'd be happier living back at the school."

"You'd be wrong," she replied. "Besides, you need me."

"Yes I do," I admitted quietly. "We need each other."

CHAPTER 7 – UNEXPECTED VISITORS

After my blowup the previous night, Kelly calmed me down with her tender ministrations and I ended up promising her I'd do everything I could to carve out a happy life for ourselves, which meant she won the argument.I grunted to myself thinking that one over and started sorting out the electrical equipment.

As I laid everything out, I was trying to plan out how I was going to upgrade our solar power grid, but I was distracted. By Kelly, of course. I remembered an episode of one of those scripted reality shows, the one with the ducks and all of the men with their long beards. There was a scene with the patriarch of the family in which he said all women have quirks and if you could put up with said quirks you'd have a happy relationship.

Kelly's quirks were talking and sex. She loved to talk about anything under the sun and she loved sex. Sometimes she liked to have a conversation while we were having sex, but thank goodness it was only rarely. Any issue we encountered, any problem, any disagreement, invariably led to a long, mostly one-sided discussion, followed by lots of sex.

They were quirks I could put up with.

My thoughts were interrupted by an unfamiliar truck pulling a cattle trailer making its way up the drive. I grabbed my shotgun and was about to take cover behind my own truck when I recognized the occupants, Tonya, Ward and Gus, I relaxed a little and set my weapon down, although I wasn't so sure I wanted them anywhere around my property.

Floyd had been relegated to ride in the bed of their truck and although it was a sunny March day, it was still quite chilly. The thermometer was hovering at forty and I could see he was cold and miserable.

"This is a surprise," I said when they exited. I briefly wondered why they had a new truck, but decided I didn't give a shit. Ward walked up and shook my hand, grinned foolishly and grabbed me in a hug.

"We've missed our old friends and thought we'd visit," he replied with a grin. Yeah, I thought, and y'all just happened to bring a truck hauling a cattle trailer. I gestured at Floyd.

"You look pretty miserable," I said.

"I'm a might cold," he replied through chattering teeth. Gus scoffed at Floyd's perceived softness. Kelly stuck her head out of the door at about that time and I motioned at her.

"Go on inside with Kelly and she'll fix you a cup of good old fashioned stale coffee."

Floyd nodded thankfully. She smiled warmly as he walked up, hugged him and led him inside while chatting it up. For a second, I experienced a pang of something, and when I realized it was jealousy it surprised the hell out of me. Before I could decipher my thoughts, I was interrupted.

"What are you doing over here?" Tonya asked as she looked over the electrical supplies laid out on the ground. I gave her a look, and then decided I wouldn't be giving away any of my secrets.

"I'm going to upgrade our solar power grid," I replied. She looked around and spotted the solar panels mounted on the roof. I watched as her eyes followed the conduits to a concrete block enclosure on the side of the house.

"Do you mind if I have a look?" she asked. I shrugged and led her to the enclosure.

"The enclosure is weatherproof but vented," I said, pointing at the eaves. "All of the wiring is protected with conduits and the batteries are on a raised platform." She looked over the set up carefully. I was proud of it, but I saw her frowning.

"Do you see something wrong?" I asked.

"It's not a bad set up, but you have the wrong type of charge controller for these batteries and you need a shunt at this junction," she replied while pointing at the grid panel. She turned and looked at me questioningly. "How much experience do you have with solar power and electricity, if you don't mind me asking?"

I shrugged. "Not much. I've read a couple of books." She nodded in seeming understanding. "It works well enough," I said defensively.

"Zach, for a novice you've done some good work. But, let me tell you something. I have a bachelor's degree in both electrical and nuclear engineering, along with a master's and doctorate in nuclear engineering. I've written so many treatises on alternative energy it'd make your head spin. You may be incredibly smart, but on my worst day, when it comes to this field of expertise I can run circles around you."

"I believe you," I said simply. I figured the next thing she was going to brag about was that her dick was bigger than mine, and if it were indeed true, Kelly was going to be devastated.

"So, let's talk business," she said. I looked at her quizzically. Here it comes.

"We need more cattle, she said plainly. "If you want to work out a trade, I'll help you set up a power grid system that'll increase your efficiency and storage capacity." She pointed at the breaker panel. "You're going to want a surge protector on that panel. I have all of the equipment you'll need back at the school, plus, I'll throw in some additional solar panels we found. They're used, but they're the latest generation and in good shape."

I rubbed my face as I thought it over. "Beef cattle or dairy cattle?" Her eyes narrowed.

"There's a difference?"

"You might say that. Floyd knows the difference and one of the things he'll tell you is that dairy cattle require more maintenance. They need milking twice a day, whether you use the milk or not."

Tonya frowned. "I didn't know that." I didn't tell her about the cream separator we'd found but weren't using, otherwise she'd probably want that thrown in with the deal. I continued.

"There's a way around it, but I'll let Floyd explain all that." I thought for another minute as we walked back outside. The truth of the matter was I had too many cows to keep up with. I looked at the cattle trailer they'd brought with them. "Alright, a dozen head for now. If I like the way y'all are taking care of them, I'll give you a dozen more in a couple of months."

"Sounds agreeable," she said after a minute and held out her hand. I looked at her stubby outstretched paw. I didn't want to touch her. Hell, I didn't like the woman, but I shook on it anyway.

"How'd it go with Floyd?" I asked as we shared a dinner plate.

"Well, if I had to guess, I'd say he's smitten with me," Kelly replied. When I looked at her she giggled. "I caught him staring at my breasts a couple of times." Once again, I felt that pang of jealously. It irritated me. I thought I had my feelings for her firmly and narrowly defined. But, when she mentioned Floyd ogling her, I found myself staring at them as well. She was wearing a button-down flannel shirt with a few of the buttons seductively left undone. I've seen her breasts many times, but even so, her cleavage was very alluring. I forced myself to focus.

"Did he have anything to say?" She shook her head.

"Before I had a chance to ask him any direct questions, dumbass Gus invited himself inside and drank most of the coffee while talking about sports." She rolled her eyes. "Why in the world he thought baseball would interest either of us is beyond me."

"It figures," I muttered.

"Yeah, he kept me from asking any prying questions, but I think if I can get Floyd alone again he'll tell me anything I want to know. So anyway, how'd it go with Tonya?"

"I have reluctantly conceded she knows more than me about electricity and she's going to help upgrade our power grid. In return, we're going to give them some cows."

"Is it going to be a good deal?" she asked. I nodded between bites.

"Yeah, we have too many cows for us to handle as it is. Besides, it couldn't hurt to be nice to them, right?" Kelly expressed her approval by leaning over and kissing me on the cheek, causing me to look down the front of her shirt.

"I think we got the better deal," she said. "And as for Floyd, I'll have him telling me all of their little secrets in no time." She punctuated her declaration with a cheerful grin.

"Alright, I have an idea which may help you along."

"Oh, yeah? What?"

"Well, it involves Floyd, you, and me."

CHAPTER 8 – JORGE

In truth, I was anxious. Floyd admitted his marksmanship skills were somewhat limited due to his bad arm and Kelly is, well, a girly-girl. Don't get me wrong, I'm very appreciative of her femininity and I'm not bashing women in general. Hell, Julie and Andie were excellent marksmen, markswomen, sharpshooters, whatever the proper term. Mac was a pretty good shot and I even had Macie making headshots at two hundred yards with scoped sights. But, when we executed Operation Bell Road last year, shooting all of those zombies had stressed Kelly greatly. She said she still thought of them as humans. And of course, there was the deer she killed which caused her to cry afterward. Now, she was acting as my backup, armed with the Remington model 700 sniper rifle that used to belong to Rowdy. This time, she may actually have to shoot a real human.

That's why I was anxious. It had nothing to do with Kelly wearing one of those bras that pushed her boobs up and out, causing them to strain the fabric on her already tight-fitting tee shirt, and that she and Floyd were sitting alone together in a parked car, all by themselves and hidden among many other abandoned cars. Nope. It had nothing to do with that at all. Don't think I didn't notice her unzipping her jacket as soon as they hopped in the truck, revealing said tight-fitting tee shirt.

I'd been thinking about it constantly for the past three days now. After burying Julie, it took perhaps two days before Kelly and I started sleeping together. It wasn't an act of love. It was nothing more than two lonely people sharing themselves on a cold lonely night. I told myself that was all it would ever be, even though I told her I loved her a month later.

I hadn't repeated it because I didn't really believe it. It was the wine talking. We drank a whole bottle and I hardly ever drank. But now, in spite of how I may have felt in the past, I realized I was actually developing strong feelings for her. Much stronger than I thought was possible. Anybody else would have felt elation at having such an epiphany. All it did for me was confuse the hell out of me. I sighed heavily, scratched myself, and reached for the microphone.

"Ready?" I asked curtly. I was answered by a microphone click. I responded with two clicks and switched to channel nineteen. "Is the gentleman with the raggedy black SUV listening?"

I was parked at the same location where we'd originally spotted them. The odds of encountering them again weren't good, but I had no other idea of how to make contact with them. I originally was going to use the radio tower, but the generator was out of diesel and needed maintenance. I opted to save the fuel for my farm implements.

I waited a minute and repeated my broadcast. There was no answer. I did this for almost an hour and was about to give up when I finally got a response.

"Don't be making fun of my ride, man." It was him, his accent was unmistakable.

"How are you this morning?" I asked pleasantly.

"Doing so-so, man. How about you?"

"Pretty much the same," I replied. "I'm parked near the location where we first saw each other and I've got a thermos of hot coffee. Why don't you join me and we can talk?"

"Okay, man, just don't be pointing a gun at me this time." It took about ten minutes before the black SUV came into view, and I'll be damn if there wasn't a fresh coat of wax on it. Even the tires looked like they had been wiped down and were glistening.

I got out, leaving my rifle and shotgun sitting in the truck and walked out carrying a thermos and two cups. Oh, I still had my beloved Kimber holstered on my hip, I wasn't totally trusting after all.

He turned off his vehicle and exited a moment later. He wasn't a big guy, maybe five-nine, lean, dark black hair with accompanying eyes, clean shaven, hell, he was clean all over. Even his Chuck Taylors were pristine looking.

"Buenos Dias," he said.

"Hello," I replied. "My Spanish is limited."

"No problem, man," he replied while holding out his hand. "My name is Jorge and my English is better than most Americans." I couldn't help but smile as I shook hands with him.

"His name's Jorge but he prefers it to be pronounced George." After meeting Jorge, Kelly and Floyd followed me back home. I glanced at them quite a bit in the rearview mirror and couldn't help but notice there was a lot of smiling and laughing going on between the two of them. When we got home, we had lunch together and even used separate plates for the occasion.

"What's his girlfriend's name?" Kelly asked. I shook my head.

"It's his little sister, Maria. He's twenty-four and she's twenty. Their father is still alive too. The mother got infected. He had a girlfriend, but she was killed." I finished my lunch and pushed my plate away. "And, most importantly, he said Maria is still a virgin and I should not get any ideas about her." Kelly burst out laughing, so Floyd immediately joined in. We sat at the table enjoying our stale coffee while I continued.

"So, there are three of them altogether; Jorge, his father Josue, and Maria. They have a small farm consisting of five acres on a dead end street near Smith Springs Road."

"How did they survive?" Floyd asked.

"They blocked their road by turning a couple of buses over at the end of the street. That kept the roaming gangs out, and for some reason Josue had a lot of bear traps. They used them to trap zombies, making it easier to kill them. They've lived off of their gardening, hunting, and scavenging." I shrugged. "No different from the rest of us, I suppose, at least, for some of us." For some reason, I thought of the cannibals I had encountered a while back. "Oh, Jorge said there's a UPS hub a couple of miles from his house that he wants us to help clear it and salvage."

"That sounds promising," Floyd remarked.

"Yeah. Anyway," I continued, "it was a pleasant meeting, and to borrow a phrase from the late great Bernie the Beekeeper, I have opened the vestibule of barter by giving them a jug of honey." Floyd stared at me questioningly, but I didn't bother to explain. I was ready for him to leave, so I stood and stretched.

"Well, Floyd, we have a lot to do before sundown. I bet Tonya has some work waiting for you as well." Floyd realized he was being kicked out and looked crestfallen.

"Yeah, I guess I better get back." He stood slowly and struggled to put his jacket on. Kelly jumped up and helped him get his bad arm into the sleeve, glancing at me and winking. The two of us walked him outside. He stopped momentarily, turning toward us.

"I appreciate y'all inviting me to join in, today," he said, glancing a little bashfully at Kelly. "I had a really nice time and I'm glad we didn't have to shoot nobody."

"We appreciate you helping us," I replied and absently put an arm around Kelly's shoulders.

"Oh, I meant to say something earlier," he said. "I spotted a group of zombies wandering down the Interstate yesterday, about a dozen of them. We didn't do nothing with them. They didn't see us and kept on walking."

I nodded. "I appreciate that. I guess with the temperatures beginning to warm up, they're starting to become active again."

We waved at him cheerfully as he drove away. Kelly pressed against me as we waved.

"You owe me big time," she exclaimed.

CHAPTER 9 – CODE

"Well, it's official," Kelly said as we watched Floyd drive down the road and out of sight. "He's definitely got a crush on me." I eyed her.

"Oh, yeah?"

"Definitely."

"Did you get anything out of him?"

"Yep," she replied, but with a little hint of apprehension in her voice. "We should sit down first." She led the way as we went back inside and sat at the kitchen table. She took her time and refreshed our coffee.

"Okay, they told him everything and he believes they were being truthful because he was told the same story by different people at different times."

"Sounds like he was testing them to see if he was being bullshitted or not," I reasoned. Kelly nodded. "Smart man."

"Yep. He said he wanted to make sure he wasn't hitching his wagon on with a group of people who'd sell out their friends."

"Alright, sounds reasonable. What else did he say?"

"On that day back in September, they were visited by the Marines."

"I knew it," I growled. I felt my blood rising and started to stand, but Kelly put a gentle hand on my arm, causing me to sit back down.

"Let me finish, sweetheart." She waited for me to calm down before continuing. "They told Floyd the Marines came to the school, questioned them, and then basically held them prisoner for about four hours. Apparently, the colonel came back to the school and told them not to worry and that they were taking your kids into protective custody but didn't mention anything else they had done. They waited two days before going to your house. When they saw the carnage, they figured everyone had been killed, including you and me."

I nodded. It sort of made sense, but there were still a lot of unanswered questions. Like, among other things, why didn't they take the time and effort to bury the dead?

"So, why did they keep it a big secret?" I asked. "Did Floyd say?"

"Yeah, he said when they found out you were alive, Tonya and the others were worried to death you would hold them responsible, so they decided to stick with the story that they knew nothing. She told everyone about the conversation the two of you had and that she told you the truth. Some of them were worried you'd retaliate, but Marc and Ward told them you're an honorable man and wouldn't harm them." She paused, waiting to see my reaction.

I drummed my fingers on the kitchen table, trying to keep my anger in check. Kelly kept stroking my arm, watching me with concern. I quickly finished my coffee, barely noticing that I'd burned my tongue. Kelly continued.

"For what it's worth, Floyd said they told him you were a cold-blooded killer and he should keep his distance from you, but once he met you he knew it wasn't true." I looked at her.

"And Rhonda went along with this as well? She thinks I'm a cold-blooded killer too?" I asked. She nodded.

"I don't think she believes it, but she's always been a follower." After a couple of minutes, Kelly stopped stroking my arm and squeezed it gently.

"What do you think?"

"Well, it's a lot to think about," I said. "I must admit, I never thought Rhonda would think so badly of me."

"If you want my opinion, I think they were caught in the middle, so to speak, and had to go along or suffer the consequences."

"Let's hope you're right." I paused for a moment before looking at her. "Do you think I'm a cold-blooded killer? Be honest." She returned my stare with one of her own.

"I know you've killed people. I don't know how many, but I know you've killed. But, I've never thought for a minute you're a cold-blooded psychopath."

"Thanks," I mumbled as I hugged her tightly. As I hugged her, I found myself hoping she'd never ask what the number was.

After dinner, we opted to snuggle on the couch and read. I had the service manual for the snowmobile while Kelly had a book of abridged Sherlock Holmes stories. After finishing with the manual, I stretched and kneaded the muscles in my neck.

"Which story are you reading?" I asked her.

"The Sign of the Four."

"Yeah, I like that one."

"Yeah, I love how he can figure out puzzles with only a few clues." She stretched and yawned. "But I think I'll finish it later. Do you want to go to bed?"

"Certainly."

I slept comfortably, but it didn't stop me from dreaming about Julie and the kids. I awoke the next morning with a wisp of a dream floating away. It disappeared before I could memorize it, saddening and frustrating me. Kelly had barely moved in the night. She was still snuggled up against me, breathing deeply.

Working my way out of bed, I washed up and dressed as quietly as I could. I tried not to wake Kelly, but that was like asking me to walk through a china shop and not break anything. She sat up and stretched before heading to the bathroom with her eyes barely open. It was a little chilly in the house, so I added a log to the fire, re-stoked the pot belly stove and put the kettle on it. While I waited, I picked up the book Kelly was reading last night. She had dog-eared a page and I read the chapter, remembering the scene and the dialog from when I had read it long ago. Kelly walked in the den and gave me a good morning kiss.

"Don't lose my place," she admonished in mock seriousness. I grunted. "You know, Sherlock got me thinking last night."

"About what?" I asked.

"Bulldog's chess moves. They're almost like some kind of code." I think the blood drained from my face as I stared at her. She saw it. "What?"

I quickly stood and walked over to the desk. Kelly joined me as I picked up the piece of paper. It was wrinkled and soiled now, but still legible.

"You are a fucking genius is what you are," I said to her.

"When you say fucking, are you using it as a noun or an adjective?" she asked with a mischievous grin.

"I suppose both," I replied with my own smile.

"It's really a code?" she asked. I nodded solemnly.

"I believe it is." I thought about Ruth. She didn't have a lot of respect among her fellow Marines, but I knew from our conversations and chess games she was a smart one. Very underestimated. The whistling of the tea kettle barely registered in my brain as I sat at the desk and opened one of my notepads.

I never viewed farm work as a laborious burden. I liked farming. I liked working the crops and the livestock. But, today it seemed to take forever to complete the chores, and as any farmer can attest to, when it comes to farm work you're never completely finished. Be that as it may, Kelly and I found a stopping point late in the afternoon and started toward home.

"What do you think about cooking something on the grill?" Kelly asked. "And I'll fix up a green bean casserole."

"It sounds wonderful. My stomach's been growling for the last hour."

"I've noticed," she joked.

I was looking forward to getting home, but we were suddenly stopped by the appearance of some rotten bastards trying to get through the fence on the south side.

"Where did you nasty things come from?" I asked rhetorically as we approached the fence line. The three of them were snarling and gnashed at me as I got close. One of them was actually drooling at the prospect of taking a bite out of me. The fence kept us apart, which meant I didn't need to waste ammunition. They looked pretty much the same as all of the other ones we'd seen lately.

"I'll take care of them," I said and stepped closer. I took the drooling one out first by taking the top of his head off with my machete. The second one leaned forward, burying the barbed wire into his skin as he tried to reach for me. I did a tomahawk chop on him, burying the machete all the way down to his furry unibrow. Then, before I could wrench the machete free, the third one backed off. He stared at me coldly with his black eyes before turning and shambling away.

"Oh, no you don't," I muttered. Kelly gasped as I used a fence post for leverage and climbed over. The third one turned his head as I landed and actually broke into an erratic run. He was having a hard time going in a straight line, looking much like a drunkard trying to flee from the police. I chased him down and swung at his neck. He went down in a clump. I landed a second blow to make sure he was done for and looked around anxiously. I didn't see any others around, but you could never be certain these days.

"It looks like we're not going home just yet," I lamented. It took us an hour to drag them down to the sinkhole and set them on fire. We were exhausted and dirty by the time we finally made it home. I got some charcoal going on the grill and washed up.

"I hope that's not a sign of what's coming," Kelly said as she washed up beside me.

"With the weather warming up, I think we can expect to start seeing them more frequently. We can't be doing stuff on our own, that's for sure. We'll have to stick together like peas and carrots."

"Fine by me," Kelly said with a smile. I walked up behind her and put my arms around her.

"I don't know why you like me," I said softly. Kelly stopped fixing the casserole and clasped my arms.

"I've always liked you, Zach. You're a good man." Her voice lowered to a murmur.

"I think there's something you should know though, I'm falling in love with you." She paused again. "Hell, who am I fooling, I'm already in love with you." She looked at me briefly before turning back to her casserole. It took me a long while to answer and I wrapped my arms tightly around her.

"I won't lie to you. I think about Julie frequently, probably more than I should, I guess. But, I have to say, lately you occupy my thoughts quite often. I find myself watching you while you sleep, or while you're brushing your hair, or while you're doing nothing more than reading a book. Am I in love with you? I don't know, Kelly. I'm all mixed up inside. I hope that makes sense."

"More than you realize," she said, turned and smiled at me. "Oh, I watch you when you sleep too," she added. I looked at her skeptically.

"You do not," I said. She continued smiling.

"Oh, yeah. Last night in fact. I watched you for about ten minutes and then I went into the den and figured out Bulldog's coded message." I think my jaw hit the floor. She giggled. "I was waiting to surprise you."

"Are you shitting me?" I implored.

"I shit you not," Kelly responded and retrieved one of my notepads out of a kitchen drawer. I started to reach for it but she jerked it away and grinned at me coyly. "Quid pro quo," she said teasingly. I frowned and she continued grinning.

"Okay, so what am I going to have to do?"

"After dinner I want a hot shower and then a full body massage, from head to toes, and I especially want my feet rubbed. You've never done that for me." She looked at me coyly, knowing I couldn't resist.

"Your wish is my command," I said with a flourish of my hand and snatched the notepad from her.

We ate dinner quietly as I read the product of her deciphering over and over, occasionally comparing it to Bulldog's scribbling.

"The last part is only three letters, CDC. Is that what I think it is?" I nodded.

"The Center for Disease Control, it has to be. They're in Atlanta." I jumped up and got an Atlas out of the desk drawer.

"I-24 is the best route," I muttered. "But, I've no doubt I'll have to make some detours here and there."

"When do we leave?" she asked. I continued looking at the map.

"Day after tomorrow. Don't worry, I'll get everything sorted for you before I go." Kelly responded by shaking her head pointedly.

"Don't even think about it, I'm going with you." I looked at her coldly, candidly.

"That's probably not a good idea, it'll in all likelihood get very ugly."

"Don't be stupid, you know I'm going." I was strongly inclined to be more forceful in my demand, but ultimately I knew better. I'd have to lock her in a closet or something to keep her from going. A part of me really wanted her with me, another part wasn't so certain.

"Alright, if you're sure."

"Of course I'm sure."

"Alright," I said again. "We have a lot to do." I thought a moment. "We'll take the Volvo, so we need to get it prepped."

"You take care of the truck and I'll get some stuff packed," Kelly said instantly. I grabbed her, kissed her, and held her tightly. It was sinking in slowly and I realized my pulse was racing. I finally knew where my kids were. At least, I hoped they were still there.

"You're shaking," Kelly said. She had her head against my chest. "And you're heart is going a hundred miles-per-hour."

"Yeah," I mumbled. I was anxious, very anxious. All of the what-if scenarios were flooding my mind. What if it was a trap? What if they'd gone to the CDC and have since left? What if they'd been horribly mutilated in the experiments? What if they'd been killed? I continued holding Kelly and forced myself to calm down.

"There's something I have to tell you." Kelly pulled her head back and looked at me.

"I've killed more people than you know about. In fact, I'm not certain I'd ever be comfortable telling you exactly how many."

"Okay," Kelly responded tentatively.

"The point I'm trying to make is once we get down there, I'm not going to hesitate to kill anyone who gets in my way. That includes anyone who even *looks* like they're going to get in my way. Maybe you shouldn't be a part of that."

"Fuck you, I'm going with you."

"Okay," I said. Can't say I didn't warn you, I thought, and hugged her again, tighter this time. After a long moment, she pulled away.

"We'll get everything ready tomorrow, but tonight I'm going to have my hot bath and massage."

"Okay," I replied, knowing there was going to more than a bath and massage involved, and no, I wasn't complaining.

My thoughts were preoccupied, which normally would have been an indicator of insanity. I mean, who in the hell would be preoccupied while in the middle of giving a full body massage to a beautiful, naked woman. Thankfully, by the time I got to her feet, she'd fallen sound asleep. I carefully got the blankets over us and I lay on my back, snuggled up next to her, thinking about my kids. I didn't remember falling asleep; the last conscious thought I remembered was I wanted to jump in the truck and leave that very minute.

As fate would have it, we didn't have to leave after all.

CHAPTER 10 – CHILDREN

I heard the noise of the vehicle before I actually saw it.

"Whoa, Hank," I whispered forcefully as I pulled on the reins and jumped off of Hank, hurriedly pulling my rifle from the scabbard. I took cover behind a tree and watched as a military Humvee came into view and slowly made its way up the driveway to my former residence.

Julie and I… I mean, Kelly and I had spent all of yesterday getting everything ready, and this morning I was making one final check around the farm before the two of us headed out. But, what I was seeing out there in front of me meant our mission was going to be postponed. They'd finally come back for me.

The scene was like a surreal image in a movie. The vehicle, a dirty military Humvee, approached slowly, inexorably. I couldn't feel anything below my waist, but my legs were steady. I made a concerted effort to control my breathing and keep my heart rate steady.

"I thought there'd be more," I muttered as I used the side of the tree as a brace to steady the fore stock and take aim. This was it. I was going to take out as many as I could before they got me. There had to be more of them. I wondered if there was another group moving in on Fred's house at the same time and hoped Kelly wasn't caught off guard. Jumping on Hank and hightailing back to the house would have been futile. If that was their plan, they were already there. Whatever her fate, I was going to kill as many as I could, and if I lived through this, I'd see what I could do.

They must have spotted me; the Humvee's tires barked in protest as the driver slammed on the brakes. There were definitely two of them sitting in the front seat and the backseat had passengers as well. As I was about to shoot through the windshield, the driver got out and raised her hands.

It was Ruth, AKA Corporal Bulldog. I'd recognize her anywhere. She wasn't looking so good. Her dirty combat uniform hung loosely on her, and her face bore the appearance of someone who'd not slept in a while. For a brief moment I felt sorry for her. She looked directly at me and waved tentatively. I held my position and waited, wondering if anyone was making a move to flank me, or perhaps they had a sniper out there somewhere and he was waiting for me to come out in the open for a clear shot.

All of these thoughts were rushing through my brain as I caressed the trigger, but suddenly, as I watched, something unbelievable happened. There was no controlling my heart rate now, it shot up like someone just popped me in the ass with a cattle prod. Two other people got out of the Humvee and as I kept watching, they helped two children get out.

My children.

I immediately took my finger off of the trigger and fought hard to settle myself. When my hands stopped shaking, I whistled for Hank, saddled up, and slowly made my way toward them, all the while holding the rifle at the ready. Stopping several feet away, I gave them the once over and peered inside the military vehicle. There were three assault rifles lying in the back seat along with some duffel bags stuffed in the cargo compartment.

"Hello, Zach," Ruth said nervously.

"Don't worry about the weapons, Zach." I looked over at the person who had spoken. It was Gunnery Sergeant Smithson. He was fatigued as well, but otherwise looked the same as I remembered. Maybe his hair was a little longer, but he was still clean shaven and his chiseled features seemed to indicate he was as fit as ever. "They're worthless at the moment. We're out of ammo."

"All of you step away from my children," I demanded coldly.

"But, Zach, we brought them back to you," Ruth responded.

"That's the only reason any of you are still alive," I said and then lowered my voice to a growl. "Now step away from my children." They did as I ordered. The three of them moved as one and stood together closely, Sergeant Smithson standing in front of Ruth protectively.

The kids, my kids, were oblivious of the tension in the air. The only thing they were paying attention to was Hank. I nudged him toward them. Hank, who was very gentle by nature, nickered softly and sniffed them. I kept my rifle pointed at the three of them.

"What now, Zach?" Major Parsons asked. I glanced at my children. Little Frederick was walking around pretty well, even if he had his arms outstretched like Frankenstein. A sense of pride rippled through me. Macie had not moved from the position where Ruth had set her down. She was looking around in wonder at all of the sights and seemed particularly fascinated by Hank. He nudged her curiously. She fell back and squealed in glee. It was hard work keeping my emotions in check at that moment.

"They've grown," I commented.

"We've taken good care of them," the major said.

"You better hope you have," I quickly retorted. Little Frederick looked at me curiously for a second before his attention again went to Hank. "They're not even sure who I am, thanks to you people. Tell me what's going on here."

"There's no need for all of this, Zach," Major Parsons contended. "Why don't we sit down like civilized adults and discussed this?"

"Are you going to make me kill you in front of my kids?" I rejoined as I stared at him in contempt. He dropped his eyes and stared at the ground.

"Let's hear it," I repeated. Ruth spoke up.

"After you escaped, Colonel Coltrane sent out search parties," she said. "When you weren't found, he wanted to come back here and wait on you, he knew you'd show up eventually, but he was ordered to relocate all of us to Atlanta." I stared at her shrewdly, trying to determine if she was telling the truth.

"By whom?"

"The President," Ruth answered.

"Where to in Atlanta?"

"The CDC," Sergeant Smithson added. "Up until two days ago it was operational."

"You said, *was*." The Sergeant nodded. "What happened?"

"About fifty thousand of those things is what happened," he muttered ruefully.

"The place was attacked and overrun," Ruth said. "It was horrible."

"It was one of those rules of yours, Zach," the Sergeant continued. "They're getting smart. We thought we had eliminated most of them, but those things fooled us. The only thing we could think of was they hid in abandoned buildings throughout the city and waited for the right moment." Sergeant Smithson sighed and continued.

"For weeks we'd watch in amusement as small groups of them tried to climb the fencing or attempt to push their way through the concrete barricades. Little did we know those things were actually probing and testing our defenses, looking for weak points." He paused a moment and looked at his companions.

"Long story short, one night they massed together and attacked us."

"What, like a coordinated attack?" I asked skeptically. The Sergeant nodded. It was hard to believe those things, who were nothing more than sub humans now, were able to do something like they said.

"What happened then?" I asked. He pointed at Ruth.

"Ruth was assigned guard duty for the kids. We ate dinner together and then she put them to bed. The two of us were hanging out together when the alarms were activated." His features darkened.

"Like I said, it was a mass attack. About six hours into it, it became obvious we were being overrun. So, we grabbed them and got the hell out of there." He pointed at Major Parsons. "I figured we needed the doc here, so I made him go with us." He then lowered his head a moment before raising it and looking me directly in the eye.

"Zach, on my word of honor, the three of us here had nothing to do with the death of your people." I stared at him balefully, dubious whether or not he was telling the truth. I'd get to the bottom of it, but it was a subject for another time. I gestured toward my kids.

"Where were my kids at when y'all were holding me captive?" I asked.

"They were being kept in another building," Major Parsons interjected. "Not far from where you were housed. They were not harmed, I can assure you."

I continued glaring at all of them. In contrast to Sergeant Smithson, the major had not shaved in a day or two. His uniform was cleaner, but all that told me was the two enlisted Marines were the ones doing all of the dirty work. He returned my stare with an arrogant one of his own. It angered me, I couldn't keep my emotions in check any longer. I walked up to him and kicked him in the testicles. I've no doubt it would have been a fifty yard punt if I had been kicking a football. Parsons gasped and doubled over in pain. Smithson moved toward me, but I stopped him by jabbing him in the gut with the barrel of my rifle. He backed away quickly with his hands raised.

"Easy, Zach. You may not like him, but he's the only doctor we have."

"You people kidnapped my kids and killed my friends!" I yelled so forcefully spit flew from my mouth. Ruth started to speak, but I cut her off with a look. I waited until I could speak without yelling.

"Y'all are going to tell me everything, but first things first, where is everyone else?"

"It's just us, Zach," Ruth said. "We honestly don't know if anyone else survived."

I kept a wary eye on them as I retrieved my walkie-talkie out of the saddle bag and called for Kelly. After a few tries, she answered.

"Where are you?" she asked.

"I'm at the Riggins house and I have company. Marine company. Check your surroundings and then get over here ASAP." I jammed the walkie into my pocket and watched as Major Parsons, who was on all fours, began vomiting. Little Frederick saw and started crying, which surprised me.

Kelly sped up the driveway in the big Volvo and actually slid sideways to a stop, spraying all of us with gravel. She leapt out of the truck like a super cop in an action movie, pointing her handgun wildly. It looked really cool, but the only problem was she had left the truck running and in gear. It was lurching forward, a couple of feet at a time. I gestured toward the truck. She hurriedly jumped back in, set the air brake, and shut it off. When she got herself sorted out, I had the three of them move away from the major's vomit and sat them down on the cold ground.

"Cover me a minute," I directed to Kelly, set my rifle down and searched the three of them. There were no hidden weapons, but I couldn't help but noticed when I was patting down Sergeant Smithson he was nothing but rock hard muscle. I'd have to be careful with him. I then grabbed their assault rifles and put them in the Volvo.

"So, tell us the whole story," I commanded. "Starting with the kidnapping."

"Our original mission order was only to snatch you and carry you to Fort Campbell," Sergeant Smithson said. "I was the NCOIC."

"What is NCOIC?" Kelly asked. "What does that mean?"

"Non-Commissioned Officer in Charge," Sergeant Smithson answered. Kelly nodded in seeming understanding. "Anyway, as you know, we pulled it off without a hitch, other than me having to pop you in the back of the head."

"Yeah, I had a headache for two days. I owe you for that one," I retorted. "Keep going."

"After we got back to Fort Campbell, we had a mission debriefing. That's when I found out you had kids and one of the other teams had grabbed them." He looked over at our dilapidated house. "And then, well, I guess you know what was talked about next. If that wasn't bad enough, we lost one of our own." I stared at them icily. I'm sure I didn't have to tell any of them I didn't care in the least that one of their fellow soldiers was killed. Hell, they all should have died.

"Who ordered the use of lethal force?" I asked. "Colonel Coltrane?" They nodded solemnly.

"Someone inside the house started shooting, that's how Lamance got it, and then it all went to hell," Ruth said quietly, almost in a whisper. She cautioned a glance at me. "It was a woman who started shooting. We found out later who it was."

"Who?" I asked. The two of them glanced at each other uncomfortably.

"We were told it was your wife." I didn't doubt them, it sounded like Julie. She wasn't timid to shoot if she felt threatened. I wondered who told them it was her, but decided to wait until later to ask.

"What happened after I escaped?" Smithson looked at me and his jaw muscles tightened.

"I won't sugarcoat it, Zach. Everyone was pissed that you killed Solonowski and wanted some payback."

"Killing me would have defeated the whole purpose of abducting me in the first place, wouldn't it?" I asked. Smithson grunted.

"Oh, we had orders to take you alive."

"I imagine if I were caught I had a good beating waiting on me." Smithson replied with a tight smile.

"We searched for you for two days," he said. "You were doing a pretty good job of hiding from us. Anyway, on the evening of the second day, Colonel Coltrane recalled everyone and issued the orders to relocate. He really wanted to find you too, but he had orders, and orders are orders. We packed up everything and left."

"So, the President is the one who gave the order to move to the CDC?" Kelly asked. The two NCOs nodded. Major Parsons was mostly unresponsive and sat there morosely, gingerly cupping his ball sack.

"And to take Zach's children?" There was a moment of silence, broken by Ruth clearing her throat.

"I won't bother with a long-winded explanation, but we're not sure POTUS was ever made aware of the children," she said and looked over at Major Parsons. "Right, sir?" He was still in pain as he looked at her, but slowly nodded his head in agreement.

"We knew we'd eventually relocate, we just didn't know when," Ruth said. "There've been groups working on a cure ever since the outbreak. Our group's primary mission was to travel around the eastern region, make contact with survivors and test them. There were other units similar to ours scattered around the country but everyone was ordered to relocate and consolidate."

"Go on," I urged. Major Parsons spoke up

"We were making progress."

"If you're thinking about saying something stupid like, my children were instrumental in your research, I'm going to cut your tongue out." The major made brief eye contact with me and quickly looked back down at the ground. I glared expectantly at the other two and motioned for them to keep talking.

"Three nights ago, the zombies attacked. We literally killed thousands of them, but there were too many." Sergeant Smithson paused and looked over at

Ruth. "Before that happened though, me and Ruth had talked about bugging out. We'd had enough. Things were all messed up and it wasn't getting any better. Colonel Coltrane's behavior became, well, what's the correct word—"

"Bizarre, odd, weird, contradictory, take your pick," Ruth added. Smithson nodded in agreement. Even Major Parsons nodded.

"Justin and I had been secretly planning on it. We had this Humvee already loaded up and ready to go."

"So, when it became obvious we were going to be overrun, we knew it was time to act." Ruth cast me a worried look. "I won't lie to you, Zach. Our original plan was for just the two of us to bug out. But, when the time came, I couldn't leave without the kids."

"She insisted on taking them," Smithson added. "She cares for them like they're her own." I looked over at Ruth, who was choked up now. Sergeant Smithson grabbed her hand and gave it a reassuring squeeze.

"I gotta tell you, going out into that mess with two little kids was definitely not what I had in mind, but Ruth was right. Leaving them there was out of the question."

"How did numbnuts here end up with you guys?" I asked.

"He saw us leaving, followed us, and demanded to know where we were going with the kids. I told him we were getting the hell out of there."

"They asked me to join them," Parsons added. "More like insisted, but I didn't argue."

"Yeah," Smithson said and shrugged. "He's a doctor, so I thought it'd be a good idea, even though our loadout was only enough for two people."

"Where were you going to go?" I asked.

"Here, Zach," Ruth said. "When we made the decision to take the kids with us, it was a no-brainer."

"If we got caught, we would have been shot for desertion. We started to do it several times, but something always came up and we aborted. It looked like it wasn't ever going to happen, but when those things attacked, I knew then we had to do it." He shrugged again. "Hell, I wasn't sure we were even going to make it off the premises, but they were all concentrated on the east side of the center."

"Sounds like a convenient story," I contended. Sergeant Smithson sighed.

"You've never been in the military, Zach. Duty and obedience to orders are beat into your brain all through boot camp. Going AWOL is almost as bad as renouncing God." He sighed again.

"So, like she said, we talked about it and we planned it all out, but never acted on it until that night." I thought it over for several minutes. They watched me in silence, unsure if they should say anything and opted to keep quiet.

"Alright," I finally said. "I'll give it to you guys, you brought my kids back." I looked pointedly at Major Parsons. "What you did to me was unforgivable, but I can live with it. But, I want to make something crystal clear. In a few minutes, Kelly and I are going to take my kids home. I'm going to feed them, give them a nice hot bath, and I'm going to check them from top to bottom. If I find one single thing wrong with them, one single injury, one single scar, one single mark, I'm going to kill you very slowly." It was a cool morning, but Major Parsons was now sweating profusely.

"I only drew blood a couple of times," he lamented. I stared at him a long minute and then looked over at Kelly.

"There is one other thing we need to tell you," Ruth said. Sergeant Smithson and Major Parsons looked at her sharply. She ignored them. "Janet, she's alive." I stared at her in disbelief.

"When the Colonel raided your house and after the gunfire died down, she was found in the basement, huddled over your kids. Colonel Coltrane gave her the option of going with him and caring for the kids. She agreed." I frowned and shook my head slowly. That woman had more lives than a pregnant cat.

"Why didn't you bring her with you then?" I asked.

"Because I don't like the bitch," Ruth said disdainfully.

"Ditto," Major Parsons muttered. I certainly understood the sentiment. I glanced at Kelly a second and made a decision.

"You two," I said, indicating the sergeant and corporal, "are free to go. Major Parsons is going to be a special guest for a while." I pointed in the direction of the old homestead. "Start walking that way." He slowly got to his feet and at first refused to move. "Either start walking, or else," I threatened. He walked.

I directed Major Parsons while I followed him on Hank and soon had him in the old barn. I pointed to the cage. "Welcome to your new home."

CHAPTER 11 – RECOGNITION

"How are they?" Kelly asked quietly as I came into the kitchen. When we got home, we fed them and then I bathed them while Kelly cleaned up.

"They're asleep," I responded just as quietly. I had them bundled up on the floor and the two of them feel asleep with Macie's arms around her big brother. It was heartwarming.

"I'm pretty sure he finally recognized me," I whispered. "But, I don't think Macie has any clue who I am."

"Do they have any injuries?"

"A couple of needle marks on their arms, which I expected, but otherwise they're in good shape." It was true. In fact, the two of them appeared very healthy and well-fed.

"That's good, right?" she asked. I shrugged. "Do you think they'll try to break that major out of the cage?" I shrugged again.

"They might, but I took their weapons and the fuel level on their Humvee is very low." I'd told them they could spend the night in the old homestead and we'd bring them breakfast in the morning, or they could leave. I doubted they'd leave. Even I knew Marines were fiercely loyal to their own and no matter how much they may have despised Major Parsons, they wouldn't abandon him.

Kelly and I bedded down in the den with my kids and they instinctively snuggled up against us. It was a wonderful feeling. Kelly fell asleep almost immediately. I stayed awake for over an hour, mulling over the events of the day. It was almost like an act of God that my children were back home. I had serious doubts about how we would have fared had we attempted to infiltrate the CDC and rescue my kids, so I counted myself grateful and said a silent prayer of thanks.

Major Parsons was still locked in the cage and it didn't look like he slept very well. He sat up and looked up at me sullenly as I entered the barn. I pulled up a bucket, the same bucket my buddy, Rowdy Yates, had sat on back when I was in that cage, and sat down. Opening my thermos, I poured myself a hot cup of coffee. It was stale, hell all coffee was stale these days, but even so I made a display out of enjoying it immensely.

"How was your night, Major?"

"It could have been better," he replied sullenly.

"I found needle marks on my children's arms."

"It was necessary for us to draw blood samples," he said defensively. "I told you that." I suppressed the impulse to throw my coffee in his face and instead stared at him coldly.

"I know what you're thinking," he continued, "but humanity depends on us finding a cure. I had orders." I didn't respond and instead continued staring at him while I drank.

"What are you going to do to me?" he finally asked. I let the silence linger while I finished the coffee and poured some more in the plastic cup.

It was a good question. Part of me wanted to take a knife to him and work on him nice and slow while he screamed in agony, but another part of me was indecisive. I pushed the thoughts aside for a moment and changed the subject.

"Do my kids have the same, what did you call it, antibodies? Do my kids have the same antibodies as I do?" His face brightened and he moved closer.

"Yes they do, sort of. Do you know what an antibody is?" he asked.

"Sort of," I answered.

"I'll give a simple explanation. An antibody is a y-shaped protein molecule produced by B cells. They're the body's primary immune defense. All humans have them, well most do. Now, an antigen is a foreign substance introduced into the human system that induces an immune response from the antibodies. Follow?" I nodded. "Yes, good. In your case, you and your kids have a unique antibody which is resistant to the virus. In addition, you have an antigen in your system which appears to make you completely immune."

"But my kids don't have the antigen." He shook his head.

"It was our belief that you were exposed somehow and your immune system responded accordingly. Your children apparently have not been exposed."

I thought about what he said and decided to tease him with a little information. I tapped the cage with my hand and told him the story about my encounter and the subsequent quarantine. He listened in fascination.

"So, you were exposed?" he asked.

"I got a little scratch on my finger and some of that damned black goo got in my mouth." I pointed at the scar on my finger. "I cauterized it as soon as I was able and then forced myself to vomit. Even so, within the next few hours I got sick."

"Could you tell me what your symptoms were, please?" he asked.

"Well, let's see. During the night, perhaps three hours after I was exposed, my pulse rate skyrocketed and I began running a high fever. I was feeling really anxious, antsy. At some point, I was in a delirium and was convinced spiders were crawling all over my skin. That lasted most of the night, but the fever broke at some point. My wife sat with me throughout the night and tended to me." She also took a lot of detailed notes that night. Some of the stuff she wrote was a little intimate, so I doubted I'd ever let him read them.

"Fascinating," he said.

"But I still got sick."

"Yes, that was to be expected, but you didn't turn." He frowned and shook his head before looking at me. "Are you certain this is the only time you were ever exposed?"

"I don't recall any other incidents," I answered. "But it could have happened unknowingly somehow." I thought about the time I was shot. I was out of sorts when that happened and it was several hours before I was rescued by Julie and Fred. I wondered if anything else had happened to me during that incident.

"I need to expose myself in order to test it," he muttered to himself.

"What was that, Major?" I asked. He was lost in thought for a moment before realizing I had asked him a question.

"Zach," he said in the tone of a question. I stared at him unemotionally. "We should go back to the CDC. You and me. The research team I was working with are a group of very intelligent doctors and scientists. With your help, we can create a vaccine and inoculate all survivors. We'd make history, Zach." I continued staring at him and didn't respond.

"Are you at least going to let me out of this cage?" he asked. I ignored his question and walked out. After shutting the barn door, I walked over to the old homestead. The two Marines were standing at the doorway watching me.

"How was your night? I imagine with all of those bullet holes and broken windows it was pretty cold."

"We had sleeping bags, and got a fire going," Sergeant Smithson answered. "But we had to keep watch since we had no weapons to defend ourselves. We didn't get much sleep."

"It was a nice home, once," I said quietly. He gestured toward the barn.

"How long do you intend on keeping him locked up in there?"

"How long would *you* keep him locked up?" I responded. They glanced at each other without answering. "You two look like shit. When's the last time you had a decent meal?"

"It's been a few days," Ruth answered. I nodded and took my backpack off. They both gasped when I pulled out a Tupperware container holding almost a dozen hard boiled eggs.

"Eat up," I said. I watched as Ruth hurriedly retrieved a container of salt from her rucksack and the two of them began eating. Ruth suddenly stopped and looked up.

"Would you mind if I gave some of these to Major Parsons?" she asked. I shrugged indifferently. She took that as a yes, grabbed a few and jogged into the barn.

"How are your kids?" Sergeant Smithson asked.

"They're doing okay. My son finally recognized me, but my daughter still has no idea who I am." I had been standing, in case they decided to bum rush me or something, but I slowly realized they weren't a threat, so I pulled up one of the chairs and sat.

"Do you have any kids?" I asked him. He shook his head.

"My teenage sweetheart dumped me back when I was in basic training. Since then I wasn't interested in getting serious with anyone. I'd been playing the field, figured when I turned thirty I'd find a woman and settle down, have kids, all that shit." I nodded in understanding. He had supplemented his eggs with some kind of packaged crackers and washed it all down with his canteen of water. I didn't tell him we had some fresh milk back at the house.

"If I'm reading your rank insignia correctly, you're a gunnery sergeant, right?" He nodded. "You seem a little young for that rank."

"Attrition," he replied with a shrug.

"How was the food supply down in Atlanta?" I asked.

"Lots of freeze dried food, MREs, the usual stuff," he replied. "They had some garden plots, but with the influx of people, they didn't produce near enough to keep up with demand, so fresh produce was a rare luxury." He pointed at the crumbled eggshells sitting on the floor of the porch. "So, you guys obviously have chickens." I nodded and pointed at the chicken coop I'd built a couple of years ago.

"After the house got shot up, we moved everything to our current location. We've got chickens, cattle, goats, rabbits, horses, jackasses, garden plots, a smokehouse, and a greenhouse. At one time we had three of them, but your buddies destroyed them for some reason."

"For what it's worth, I have no idea why he did it," he said while making a brief gesture at all of the bullet holes riddling the house. "Well, they were fired upon and Lamance was shot, which caused the Colonel to order them to open fire, but..." he struggled to find the right words. "It probably could have been handled differently."

"Yeah," I replied. "They shot up both houses, killed my friends, killed two of my horses, and our dogs," I said irately. "It could have been handled differently." I had some more to say about it, but I suddenly thought of what he said about Lamance.

"By the way, what'd you guys do with Lamance's body?"

"Ruth told me the Colonel said to leave it. When I found out, I wanted to come back down here and at least bury him, but the Colonel wouldn't allow it."

I suddenly got goose bumps. The bodies were burnt beyond recognition, so I relied only on a count, which, at the time, confirmed to me all of my friends and family had been murdered. But, if what he was saying was true? There should have been one extra body on that pile of burnt corpses. Three of the bodies were smaller, feminine, I assumed they were Julie, Jessica, and Andie. I cleared my throat.

"What size was Lamance?" I asked.

"He was about six foot, on the lean side, maybe one-seventy. Why?"

"Just wondering," I replied evasively. My brain was churning, trying to remember the exact details of when I found the bodies and when I finally worked up the strength to bury them. Kelly said she'd watched Terry die and saw Konya get shot. And Konya was missing his left thumb, but I was too distraught at the time I buried them, never thinking to pay attention to such a detail. But, nobody actually saw Fred get shot. Was he possibly still alive out there somewhere?

Smithson was looking at me curiously. I'm sure my body language was all over the place. I tried to relax.

"I want to know about you and Solonowski, what happened?" he suddenly asked. I told him the story of how I goaded the hotheaded Marine into attacking me. I also told him of Ruth's involvement. By the look on his face, I guessed Ruth had already told him.

"Did you really have to kill him?"

"Yes," I replied. "He wasn't going to simply allow me to walk out of there, now was he? The tests that s0-called doctor was performing on me were becoming more and more invasive. It was only a matter of time before he started doing things that were going to be irreversible." He was silent, mulling over what I said, but it was obvious he didn't like the fact that I killed one of his own, I could see it all over his face.

"Let me ask you something, big tough Marine, if you had been in my shoes wouldn't you have done everything you could to escape?" He looked at me somberly. After a moment, he responded.

"Alright, I guess I can see your point."

"But you don't like it I killed one of your soldiers."

"No, I don't." He was silent for a few minutes now. I waited until it got to the point where it was becoming a little awkward.

"Well, I've got a lot of work to do before sundown. Is there anything else you want to ask?"

"I've got a few, but right now the only thing I'm going to ask is for you to let the major go." I thought a moment, nodded, pulled the keys out of my pocket and tossed them over.

"Leave the keys in the barn," I said. He nodded curtly and I stood, causing him to stand as well.

"I have work to do," I said. "We generally eat dinner at six. You and Ruth are invited, not the major."

"Woothie!" Frederick shouted in baby talk and ran over to her as fast as his little legs would carry him. Ruth picked him up and hugged him before she realized I was glaring at her and put him down quickly. Macie was also making noises, but Ruth wisely did not go over to the couch where she was sitting. I directed them toward the kitchen and scooped Macie up in my arms.

"It's a shame that my own children are more excited to see you than me, don't you think?" They didn't answer. I had a few more remarks on the matter, held them back, and sat down at the head of the table. I sat with Macie on my lap, but she kept squirming and I finally relented and handed her off to Ruth. Thankfully, Frederick still liked me and had no problem sitting with me.

"Janet and I took turns with them. I cared for them the best that I could," she said defensively.

"Yeah," I retorted. "But you never told me they'd been taken." Ruth avoided eye contact and didn't respond. Kelly gave me a subtle look.

"Alright, I didn't invite you guys here just to interrogate you. Let's change the subject."

"Okay," the sergeant replied warily.

"I'd like to hear more about the CDC, if you don't mind." His expression changed then to a more thoughtful expression.

"I can tell you what we were told," he said.

"Sure."

"When the outbreak first started, the CDC personnel were caught with their pants down," Sergeant Smithson said. "They had protocols for almost every type of contingency, but they were overwhelmed by how quickly it spread and how violent the infected were. It was assumed all of their field teams either became infected or were wiped out."

"So, what'd they do?" I asked.

"Fortunately for them, their security staff were mostly retired military people and they reacted quickly. They locked down the facility and waited. They figured out, like everyone eventually did, the cold weather slows them down considerably. So, during the first winter, Atlanta had about a month and a half of freezing cold weather. They worked their asses off building fortifications." He gave a short, humorless chuckle.

"It worked, more or less, until those infected things organized and launched an offensive."

"Yeah," I said as I grabbed a notepad. "Can you be more specific about that?"

"Sure," he replied. "It started around sunset. Guard post three, which was on the east side, reported there was a large number massing together. The OIC..."

"OIC?" Kelly asked. Sergeant Smithson explained.

"The military uses acronyms for everything. The OIC is the officer in charge. He was manning the TOC. Oh, I'm sorry. The TOC is short for the Tactical Operations Center. So, the OIC, a REMF Captain..."

"REMF?"

"I'm sorry, Kelly. I'm too used to talking to fellow soldiers. A REMF is a derogatory term," he paused.

"It means Rear Echelon Mother Fucker," I said. "Someone that doesn't know anything about real soldiering."

"Yeah, exactly. So, this captain decided the guard was being overly dramatic and didn't put out an alert. By the time we realized something was up, they were attacking."

"How?" I asked.

"In human waves, or I'd guess you'd say in zombie waves," he replied. "It was so simplistic it was ingenious. Our defensive fortifications consisted of the fence, sandbags, concertina wire, and guards posted in armored vehicles. Everyone, me included, thought that was enough. After all, those things couldn't climb, use weapons or drive, or anything like that, which was true, but they thought up something entirely different. They simply walked up to the twelve foot tall fence and made a zombie ramp." I furrowed my brow as the sergeant explained.

"The front ranks would fall to the ground, the second rank followed, and so on. They effectively created a ramp for their companions to walk up and clear the fencing." I paused in my writing and looked at him skeptically.

"I'm not exaggerating, Zach. It was both scary and amazing to watch. Once they cleared the fence, they'd fall to the ground and start the process again. The inner perimeter between the fences and the building was only about twenty feet wide. They simply repeated the ramp building process, and within no time they were up to the third floor windows, which as I said, were totally unprotected.

We killed thousands of them, but killing them only aided in the ramp building process." He shook his head ruefully.

"We never in a million years would have guessed this strategy. Think about it. They sacrificed maybe a couple thousand of them so the other forty-eight thousand could get to us. Oh, and they used their heads as battering rams to break out the windows." I continued writing long after they had finished telling of the incident. When I finally stopped, I saw them staring at me intently.

"The major believes they instinctively knew what the CDC was and that was their reason for attacking it."

"I can't say I disagree." It made absolutely no sense how they knew, and yet they did. I changed the subject.

"Two questions: is the President really alive and did he really order me taken prisoner?"

"He's still alive," Smithson replied. "The colonel wasn't bullshitting about that. He's supposedly tucked away in one of those super-secret underground bunkers. As far as him giving the order to have you imprisoned, I have no idea, but there were daily radio communications with him." He pointed at Ruth and himself. "We weren't privy to what was discussed though. The major may know."

"Alright," I said, "fair enough. What about the research? What were they doing exactly?" Sergeant Smithson shrugged.

"You'd have to ask Major Parsons about all of that," Ruth replied. "All of their testing and research was done in the labs, and only a few people had access."

"Yeah," Sergeant Smithson replied levelly. "But, we went on a few missions where if we saw an infected person wandering around by itself, we'd go out and snatch it. I assume they were being used for their experiments. I don't have any idea what they did to them."

"So, were any of them cured?" The two of them continued staring at me, although I could see a hint of confusion now. I continued. "The infected subjects, were any of them cured?"

"I don't know," he answered. "Again, you'd have to ask the major." I kept my silence and sipped some coffee. The major had just told me they thought they had a cure, but he didn't inform these two. It seemed suspicious.

"The meal was awesome, Kelly," Sergeant Smithson said. Kelly smiled and thanked him. "And I must admit I've really enjoyed spending time with you guys, but I think we should be heading back."

"Yeah," Ruth added. "We really appreciate it." She then looked a little worried. "Would it be possible to fix a plate for Major Parsons?"

"Of course," Kelly said before I had a chance to respond. She got up and fixed a large plate, much more than I would have given him, especially considering how low our food supplies were.

"Where're you three going to go?" Kelly asked when she handed the plate to Ruth. Ruth looked at her worriedly.

"We have no idea," she replied.

"They're going to go wherever Major Parsons orders them to go," I said with a chuckle. "Isn't that right, Sergeant? I mean, the man may be a doctor, but he outranks you. If I had one, I'd bet a dollar he orders them to return to Atlanta and they'll foolishly obey him, right Sergeant?"

"I don't know about that," he replied with a disapproving stare. "If we go back to Atlanta, we're likely to be tried as deserters and shot."

I shrugged. "Good point. I'm sure y'all with think of something." I was ready for them to go and indicated as much by standing and staring. They took the hint.

After they left, I cleaned up the kids while Kelly cleaned the kitchen. Frederick couldn't keep his hands off of me and I smiled while he did things like pulling my hair and sticking his tiny fingers up my nose. Macie quietly stared at me in only a way a small child stares at big humans. I couldn't tell if she recognized me as her father, but that was okay. I had them back and life seemed pretty good, for a change.

I realized my face was hurting because I was smiling so much. After the warm bath, I had no problem getting them bedded down and they fell asleep within minutes.

"Well, that went better than I expected," I said. Kelly agreed. "I think I know a perfect way to end the night," I added teasingly.

"Yeah, about that, you're going to need to get them to sleep in their own bedroom, Dad," she said with a grin. "Otherwise, we won't be having much fun after dark, if you know what I mean."

"Good point."

I got up early and, to my surprise, the little guy was awake and staring at me. When we made eye contact, he gave me a big grin. I got him dressed, fixed the two of us a snack, left a note for Kelly, and soon we were riding along on Hank. Frederick was ecstatic and squealed in delight when Hank started walking.

The information they told me about Lamance got me thinking. Would one of my friends have survived? Nobody had actually confirmed Fred had died. Or Konya, for that matter. Kelly saw him get shot, true enough, but she didn't stick around to see if he survived or not. I'd already been all around the homestead and never saw anything indicating Konya had crawled away. The only thing left of him was an old blood stain on the front porch. It was a large, brown stain, indicating a lot of blood loss.

"I doubt he survived," I muttered. So, I rode over to where Fred was supposed to have been shot, which was a field where we had a large potato plot growing.

"Alright, big guy, if you'd been shot but didn't die, what would you have done?" I looked around. Supposedly, he was in this field. If I were injured, I think I would have tried to hide, maybe crawl somewhere that offered concealment.

I looked everywhere I could think of, but I found nothing. No lone boot lying in the weeds, no skeletal remains, nothing. That could've meant anything.

Maybe he was one of the burnt corpses, maybe coyotes dragged off the body. I simply didn't know and it was killing me.

Unfortunately, the farm work was pressing. The fair weather this past week was causing the grass to spring to life. The cows were happy for it, and soon it would lessen my workload, but right now it was still necessary to take the tarps off another large round hay bale.

"We're going to have a lot of hay to cut in a few months, you think you're ready to run a tractor?" Little Frederick grunted and made some kind of unintelligible response. I grinned. "The man you were named after would have had a lot of fun hanging out with you."

We made our way over to the old homestead at a leisure pace. The three of them were still there, sitting in some chairs in front of the house eating what appeared to be MREs. They watched expectantly as I rode up. I saw Ruth looking at the forty-five I had holstered on my belt, but she didn't comment. I dismounted from Hank with Frederick in my arm. Before I could tether him, he walked over to the Marines to check them out, and more importantly, see if perhaps they'd share something tasty. When I set Frederick down, he started waddling over toward Major Parsons. The Major had squatted down and held his arms out expectantly. I caught my boy quickly.

"No, Frederick. That man is evil," I said, pointing at the major, who actually looked hurt. I didn't care.

"Don't even think about touching him," I warned the man. He sat back down in his chair, crestfallen.

"Enjoying the morning sunshine?" I asked the other two. They nodded. I pulled up one of the chairs and sat down. "Why are y'all still here?"

"We were just discussing the situation when you rode up," Sergeant Smithson replied. I looked him over. He was freshly shaven again and saw me looking.

"Ruth is a master with a straight razor, you want her to give you a shave?" I grunted and shook my head.

"What's your first name, Justin?" I asked curiously. He nodded. "Justin, what have y'all decided?"

"Nothing yet," he replied while looking pointedly at Major Parsons. The major looked quite haggard; I hoped his balls were still sore. Their combat utilities were still grimy and I almost suggested they could use our washer, but stopped myself.

"Major, before you three head off into the wild blue yonder, I'd like to ask some more questions. Do you feel up to giving me some honest answers?" He waved his hand flippantly.

"I'll take that as a maybe. Well, let's see. Did you try to infect my kids to see how they'd respond?" He shook his head quickly, and then looked at the ground.

"We were going to, though."

"You son of a bitch," I growled. He looked up quickly.

"I vigorously objected, Zach. I kept them out of danger, you have my word on it." He looked at me pleadingly. "I've, no let me rephrase that, we've grown quite fond of your children, Zach."

"But you were in agreement to inject them with zombie juice though. How in the hell did you rationalize that?" He started to answer, but I cut him off and looked at the other two.

"Am I the only one who sees how warped this man's thinking is?" They didn't respond and refused to make eye contact. I shook my head. "Alright, since you're so fond of them, did you administer any proper inoculations?" The major's face lit up then.

"Oh, yes," he responded. "The CDC had a number of vaccinations stored." He looked around. "All of the children at the facility were inoculated. Tetanus, polio, all of the childhood diseases, they were vaccinated."

"How many kids are there?" I asked.

"Seven children under the age of eighteen," he answered. "I hope they're still alive," he added.

"And none of the others were immune?" I asked. Major Parsons shook his head. "Other than the woman we had found in Kentucky, but she's dead now." I paused and thought a minute.

"Do you guys think anyone else at the CDC survived?" My question was met by dour expressions.

"I don't think so, Zach," Justin replied slowly. "But anything's possible, I guess. By my estimation, we probably killed seventy-five percent of that invading force of those stinking things, and that wasn't near enough."

"The smell was ungodly," Ruth said while wrinkling her nose. "When we got the Humvee loaded, we had to shoot our way out. We had five hundred rounds of ammo and we used every bit of it."

"We should still go back and check," Major Parsons remarked. I looked at the other two as if to say, I told you so. They didn't bother to respond.

The four of us were silent now. Frederick was very talkative and had a hell of a conversation with Hank, who in turn listened patiently while he nibbled on a patch of grass, only twitching an ear occasionally.

"How did it begin, Major?" Major Parsons looked at me somberly.

"That's the million dollar question. It started somewhere in the Mideast. Cairo was supposed to have identified patient zero, but the information was very limited and questionable. The consensus is human-to-human contact was the way it spread, much like the flu. That's what patient zero complained of when he was admitted, flu-like symptoms." He held his hands up and shrugged.

"Other than that, we are still unsure of its genesis."

"Zach?" I looked over to see Ruth staring at me. "Is there an option available for us to stay here?" It took me by surprise.

"Why would you want to stay here?"

"Because we have nowhere else to go," she replied morosely. My first impulse was to tell them to get off of my farm, but I kept hearing what Kelly and I had discussed the other night.

"What about your family? Where were they, Oregon?" I asked. She frowned.

"We spoke with some people who had come from Fort Leonard Wood, Missouri. They advised the travel through that area was like traveling through hell." I thought it over. In fact, I'd been thinking this over ever since they'd arrived.

"Y'all have done more traveling than I have, so I can only advise you about the immediate area. I'd not recommend downtown Nashville. A sizeable portion is underwater. What's left has an overwhelming number of both zombies and rats. They're everywhere. The Nolensville, La Vergne, and Smyrna areas aren't too bad and there are very few people, but I can't say how many zombies are running around." I pointed south.

"Down that way is an area called College Grove and beyond that is a quaint city called Lewisburg. Lots of farmland. I've checked out some of it and there are plenty of farms which are vacant.

"Let's see, as I said, downtown Nashville is nasty, Old Hickory Lake is toxic, so I can only assume the Cumberland River is as well." I paused a moment. "I suppose I can work up a map."

Ruth looked at Justin and he cleared his throat. "Would you be opposed to helping us out until we get on our feet?"

I stared at the three of them a moment before looking out over the farm and fixing my eyes on the mound where everyone was buried. Maybe Fred was there, maybe he wasn't. Why I'd decided on Fred and not Konya or Terry, I didn't know. Kelly seemed to really believe they were all dead.

I sat there staring at it for a full two minutes thinking it over. At first I was going to say I needed to talk it over with Kelly, but I already knew what she was going to say.

"I suppose so," I finally answered.

CHAPTER 12 – JOURNAL ENTRY: MARCH 12TH, 3 A.Z.

I finally have good news to write into this journal. My children have been returned to me. After I had escaped from my imprisonment, my captors loaded up and relocated to the CDC in Atlanta, taking my children with me. So, yesterday, three of them showed up at the farm with my kids.

They had a big story of how the CDC had been overrun by zombies and they grabbed my kids and heroically escaped. I questioned them extensively about it. They believe it was a deliberate, planned attack by the zombies. The story seems plausible, but I'm naturally suspicious.

We discussed other things, specifically their actions concerning my family and me. I'll not take the time to write out the details. Suffice it to say, they have apologized for their actions and put the blame on poor judgement and blind obedience to orders. In addition, the three of them swear they were not in the group that had attacked my former home and murdered everyone.

They think I have naïvely accepted this explanation and have forgiven them. Not true. After talking it over with Kelly, we allowed them to stay on our farm. I have several things going on in my brain when it concerns them. Some of those ideas are forgiving in nature, others are vengeful. I'm really not sure how to proceed at the moment, but until I decide, I'd like to keep them close by where I'll have no trouble finding them. They've been staying at the old homestead for the past two days and have really cleaned it up and made several repairs. They salvaged some windows from a home somewhere and replaced several of the broken ones. I must grudgingly admit, I like their incentive and I've decided to start including them in the farm work.

The bottom line is my kids are back where they belong, with their father. Not with a group of strangers and being used as guinea pigs. I don't think it really hit me until the second night. After Kelly had dozed off, I sat up and watched my kids sleeping. They looked so innocent and peaceful. It had a profound effect on me and reawakened in me the belief and resolve to survive and make this world a better place for my family.

CHAPTER 13 – SATE

The little stinker had awakened before me, again, and he was very vocal about it. Kelly stirred, rolled over, and groaned.

"He's just like his father," she lamented as she sat up and stretched. "Up before the sun." Frederick screamed out something unintelligible, causing Kelly to groan again. "He's very loud, were you like that when you were a kid?" I chuckled and gave her a kiss.

"My grandmother said I was very quiet. I guess he takes after his mother in that respect." I crawled out of bed. "I'll take care of him."

"Are the Marines joining us for breakfast?" Kelly asked.

"I assume so," I responded. "I have a little surprise for them today."

"What's that?"

"I'm going to work their asses off. I've got a list for the major and you're going to keep Ruth busy. Sergeant Smithson is going to help me all day." Kelly chuckled.

"That's good. You and Justin need some quality time together." I frowned suddenly. That's not what I had in mind.

Little Frederick's morning singing, yelling, and general discourse about who knows what also succeeded in waking up his little sister. She looked at her big brother in irritation as she rubbed the sleep out of her eyes. She definitely was not a morning person, much like her mother. I herded the two of them into the bathroom, where Kelly was already waiting for us.

"Any chance of hot showers tonight?" Kelly asked as she rinsed out some wash cloths.

"If we have a sunny day, the batteries will be fully charged, so I don't see why not."

"Awesome," she said as she used the washrag on my back. I stood there a moment in front of the mirror and looked at myself. At six-feet, three inches and somewhere around two-twenty, my physique was lean and toned without an ounce of fat. The effects of farm fresh food and hard work was showing. I vowed to make sure my kids never lacked and grow up to be healthy and strong. Kelly tossed a towel in my face, indicating I needed to stop gawking and help dry off the kids.

"Alright, let's get breakfast going, I'm hungry."

"You know, after breakfast, they'll be needing a diaper change."

"Yeah, it's time to potty train him," I said, pointing to Frederick, who was inspecting our toilet and was about to stick his hand in it before Kelly grabbed him. She picked him up and handed him to me.

"Yeah, it's way past due. You would have thought those people who claimed to be so fond of them would have taken the time to do that," she remarked. She was right, of course. There were a lot of things they could have done differently, but I kept telling myself to focus on the here and now and said as much.

"Yeah, there's been so much bad stuff in the past we'll drive ourselves crazy if we dwell on it." She then grinned. "So, why don't you focus on the present and start by bringing some firewood inside."

"Zach, we couldn't help but notice this house is a little bit different than most other houses," Ruth remarked. We had all gathered for breakfast, with the exception of Major Parsons. He was not allowed inside my house and was currently sitting in a chair outside, although Kelly had taken him a plate. "It doesn't look like a typical home."

"We built it about a year after," I said. "The thought process behind its style of construction was an emphasis on strength and practicality rather than aesthetics."

"I like the thick concrete walls," the sergeant said.

"Designed for protection against small arms fire," I replied. "It was a little difficult fitting windows but Fred and I figured it out."

"Where did you find those metal shutters?" he asked.

"We fabricated them. There's a factory in La Vergne that has a pretty good machine shop. The bad part of that is, we had to use a generator and only use one piece of machinery at a time." I gestured around. "We've got a septic tank system, well water, solar power, and a fireplace, along with some other things. It's more or less zombie proof." But that's about it, I thought. I didn't show them the basement or where I had started working on creating an escape tunnel.

"Unfortunately, the insulation values aren't as good as a regular house. During the winter, the bedrooms get a little chilly. It's something I need to work on." I also didn't tell them about all of those nights Kelly and I slept naked in front of the fireplace. Kelly gave me a subtle, knowing smile.

"Did you build it?" Justin asked.

"It was a collective effort. Fred originally lived here, who as you know was murdered in cold blood. By the way," I casually asked while gesturing with my fork. "Fred and Konya, he was another friend, were both shot by a sniper. Who was the sniper in your unit, Sergeant?" He glanced at Ruth before looking back at me.

"All Marines receive rifle marksmanship training," he replied warily. "Back before, we logged a lot of time on the gun range." I shook my head in disagreement.

"Yeah, well, I'm certain this particular soldier had some formal training beyond basic rifle marksmanship." I kept eating, but watched out of the corner of my eye while they fidgeted with their food. I didn't mention my thoughts about one of them possibly surviving, I hadn't even discussed it with Kelly. No need getting her hopes up for nothing.

"For a man who never served, you seem to know a lot about military doctrine." Justin observed.

"I had two very good tutors," I replied. They both listened attentively as I told them about Rick and Terry.

"Rick was a good teacher, even when he was drunk. He had several dozen military manuals he used to train me with," I said, and pointed toward the bookshelves in the den. "There they are." Ruth stood and walked to the shelves, scanning all of the books.

"This is quite a collection," she observed and pulled out a hardback copy of poetry by Poe. "Very diverse."

"I've raided a few libraries."

"Something tells me you've read every one of them," she said with a smile.

"A few of them I read more than once." I pointed at the book she was holding. "I like that one. You can borrow it, if you want." Sergeant Smithson joined us in the den.

"Those manuals leave a lot out," he remarked.

"Yeah, they don't replace practical application. When Terry and I became friends, we'd spend hours discussing each one. He was good about helping me fill in all the blanks that the manuals left out."

"This Rick fellow, and Terry, they sound like two pretty good guys," he remarked. I nodded.

"They were. And Fred. They were the best friends you could hope for." The sergeant gave me a short look before focusing back on the books.

"So, neither of you have an idea who this sniper is?" There was no answer. "Seems odd," I continued. "You guys lived together, you ate together, trained together, killed zombies together, but you don't seem to know which Marine in your unit who would have been assigned sniper duty." Justin looked at Ruth and cleared his throat.

"When we got back to Fort Campbell that day, everyone was pretty quiet. Well, Solonowski was his usual self, but everyone else was pretty subdued, and at that time Ruth and I weren't…"

"Close," Ruth said.

"Yeah, we weren't an item at that time, so we didn't talk a lot. It took a couple of days before I got the whole story from everyone."

"I'm listening."

"When we snatched you, one of those people who dropped a dime on you also told the Colonel about your kids. So, he made the decision to snatch them too and issued a FRAGO.

"Well, they drive up to the house and the colonel got on the loudspeaker. When he announced his intentions, someone fired a shot from inside the house. It went downhill from there. A corporal by the name of O'Neil was the team sniper. He advised us later he took out two men." He looked at me steadily.

"If you're looking for revenge, I'm not certain any of them who were directly involved are left alive. We think they were all killed when the CDC was overrun, although I can't be certain."

"You've said a few times there were no other survivors, are you sure?" I asked.

"It's hard to say, Zach. Have you ever been there or seen pictures of the place?" he asked. I shook my head. "It's a sprawling complex and is surrounded by other large office buildings. We were set up in the Arlen Specter Headquarters, and although we had defensive fortifications, they were able to gain entry through the third floor windows."

"Tell them about the head butting," Ruth said.

"Yeah, I didn't really give that one credit when I explained it before. One of the last radio transmissions from personnel on the third floor was the zombies were breaking out the windows by head butting them. It was amazing, one of them would butt the window like a ram. It'd bust his skull open and he'd die, but the window would be cracked and another one would immediately take his place. It'd take three or four of them before they had the window smashed open."

"I see, I think." I paused a minute. "Did y'all have any human contact on the way back up here?" Justin nodded.

"Not coming back," Justin replied. "But, we did when we originally went."

"When we left Fort Campbell, we encountered a motley group of about a dozen people who had erected a roadblock on I-24 right at the top of that mountain, what is it called?"

"Monteagle Mountain?" I guessed. He nodded.

"Yeah, that's it. Anyway, they were trying to demand payment for allowing us to pass. Long story short, words were exchanged and they opened fire on us. They killed two of our Marines."

"What did y'all do?" I asked, but I probably already knew the answer.

"What choice did we have, we shot back. I'd say we took most of them out, maybe all of them. On the way back, we were worried they might retaliate against us, but there was nobody and the roadblock seemed to be untouched from the time we cleared it. Some of the bodies were still there, but not all of them." He paused. "There were zombies here and there. I guess the largest group we saw after we left Atlanta was about a hundred of them just outside of Chattanooga." He looked at Ruth for confirmation. She nodded. "Being totally out of ammo, we avoided them like the plague, no pun intended. Other than that, as we drove we'd see an occasional column of smoke, but we didn't have any contact with anyone."

Ah yes, the telltale smoke. Columns of smoke were like a big arrow pointing out your location. When the world first went into turmoil, there were so many things on fire it wasn't an issue. Now it was. Try as I might, I couldn't figure out a way around it. I tried to be nonchalant as I reached for my notepad and began writing. I paused only long enough to ask a question here and there. Frederick, who loved to sit on my lap while we ate, became amused by my writing and started hitting my pencil with his little hand. The result was a lot of messed up penmanship, but I didn't mind.

"Zach, would you mind if the major can come inside?" Ruth asked. I shook my head. Justin chuckled.

"You don't like him very much," he commented.

"You're absolutely correct. I'm not so sure I like you either."

"Yeah, I'm aware of that. I was certain you'd try to kill us as soon as we made an appearance, but Ruth was confident you wouldn't," he remarked with a hint of questioning in his tone.

"I guess she knows me well enough, but truth be told, I was within a breath of opening up on y'all until I saw my kids."

"So, that stopped you."

"Yeah. I'll admit though, while we were standing there eyeballing each other, I was still considering it." As the two Marines stared at me, wondering how serious I was, I saw Kelly looking at me out of the corner of my eye.

"But I didn't do it. Let's just leave it at that. Besides, like you said, that man outside is the only doctor around here. I don't like it, but someone around here will eventually need his skills. But, it would be wise advice if you told him to tread carefully."

"Fair enough," he said. "I'll try not to make you regret your decision." He stood.

"I'll guess we'll get out of your way." I stopped him by holding up a hand.

"It's time the three of you started earning your keep." I stood up and motioned for them to follow me outside. Major Parsons stopped eating and looked up questioningly.

"You three are going to do farm chores today," I said and pulled a sheet of paper out of my pocket. "These are your chores," I said to Parsons while handing the paper to him. "It mostly involves cleaning shit out of the chicken coop and barns." I gestured at Ruth.

"You'll be helping Kelly." Ruth nodded in acceptance.

"What about me?" Justin asked with a wry grin.

"I'm going to be working my ass off doing farm chores and you're going to be doing them right beside me." I waited for anyone to balk or argue, but the three of them nodded in silence. "Alright, let's get to it."

"You mean to tell me you've never ridden a horse?" I asked Justin. He grinned and shook his head.

"Walk me through it, I catch on quick."

"Alright, the first step before putting a saddle on a horse is to brush and comb out any dirt, burs, and whatever else." Justin watched as I brushed Sate. I gestured at the big stallion.

"You have to watch this one close. He'll bite the hell out of you if you're not careful. His name is Sate, which is short for Satan. Bo named him after a horse in a Louis L'Amour novel. He's a mean one, but he's tough as nails and can run like the wind." I nodded at Hank as I handed him the curry comb. "Hank is a gelding. He's much more docile. You'll be riding him."

"Why are we going to use horses?" Justin asked as he looked over at the two ATVs parked in the barn.

"The name of the game is conservation. There used to be an ample supply of fuel around here, but no more." I told him the story about the tanker explosion.

"There is another fuel reservoir near the old Titan's football stadium, but when the Cumberland flooded, it caused a lot of damage. The last time I went down there, it looked like the reservoirs were FUBAR'ed. There's like ten feet of mud piled up, it'd take a lot to get to them, and even then the fuel is probably no good."

"All of downtown is flooded?" he asked.

"Not anymore. The water table has adjusted itself, but a lot of damage was done. So, fuel is at a premium and it's hit or miss these days. Most storage tanks are empty, some of them have fuel still in them but you never know if it's going to be contaminated or not. Okay, now I'm going to clean and check the hooves. Normally, you wouldn't have to do this every time, but nowadays it's a necessity. Now, when you do this, you have to be careful you don't get kicked."

I took my time and made sure Sate didn't try anything. He stood still and let me do my work up until the last hoof before he tried to bite me. I ducked out of the way while Justin chuckled. I showed him the proper way to put on the blanket, saddle and attach the cinches. After showing him how to put on the bridle and bit, I grinned.

"Now you get to mount Hank," I said and pointed. "Always mount a horse on the left side."

The sergeant mounted Hank easily and grinned like a kid as I handed him the reins and gave him a rundown on how to steer a horse. Sate was a different story. He waited until I was barely in the saddle and then reared up. It took a little scolding before he settled down, but I could tell he was full of energy and wanted to go on a run.

"Follow me," I said and nudged Sate. He took off like someone had poked him in the ass with a cattle prod and shot out of the barn at a full gallop. I let him have his head and guided him toward the far end of the farm.

When he started running out of steam, I slowed him to a trot and began checking the fence lines while I watched Justin bouncing up and down in the saddle as he finally caught up with us.

"Man, that horse is fast as hell," he exclaimed.

"Yeah, he hasn't been gelded, that's what makes him so full of piss and vinegar. This is the routine for him if you ever ride him. Get the pent up energy out of him with a quick run and he's mostly fine the rest of the day. Hank is much calmer." Justin nodded thoughtfully. "Okay, the first thing we're going to do is check the animal traps."

"You trap for food?" Justin asked. I suppressed a derisive chortle and motioned for him to follow me. When we got within eyesight of the first trap, Justin gasped. I dismounted, secured Sate to a nearby tree and directed Justin to do the same with Hank.

"Okay, watch my back. Sometimes there're others lurking around."

I walked over to the snarling zombie whose hand was gripped tightly by the trap and barely still attached. He lunged at me as I approached, causing his hand to finally separate from his arm. I sidestepped and brought the machete down on the back of his neck, severing the spinal cord. He went down, now paralyzed, and I finished up by stomping on his head until I heard the satisfying sound of his skull being crushed.

"Is this normal?" Justin asked. I looked down at the now motionless zombie.

"Usually it's a coyote or a 'possum, but I get one of these a couple of times a week." I pointed at the fence line. "Sometimes, they'll get hung up in the barbed wire too. Alright, let's have a look at this one." I used my boot to roll him over. Its face was badly damaged from my attack. This one was wearing a heavy Army surplus jacket, jeans, and some thick leather boots.

"Alright, based on the clothing and his general appearance, I'd say he became infected during the original outbreak. You see all of the scabs and scarring?"

"Yeah, I've seen a lot of 'em looking like this," Justin said. "They're healing up, aren't they?"

"Yep. I don't know how, but they are. They're getting smarter too, but they'll still stick their hand in a bear trap if they see some raw meat. A couple of weeks ago, one of them stuck their whole head in this same trap."

"I bet that ruined your day." I looked at him questioningly. He chuckled. "You didn't get a chance to use your machete."

"We refrain from using ammunition when we can, but yeah, I like using it." Justin nodded in understanding and then frowned.

"So, I've got to ask you, I've seen carcasses of coyotes hung up and you must have two or three crows hanging up by your gardens."

"It scares them off." He continued frowning, so I explained. "Crows and coyotes are surprisingly smart. They see their dead buddies hanging up, they tend to stay away. I've not caught a coyote in a trap for several weeks now." He nodded as he rubbed his face.

"I obviously still have a lot to learn. So, I've been thinking, would you be willing to help us hit up some of the gun stores in the area so we can restock our ammo?" I scoffed.

"Those places were emptied out long ago. No, the best places to find guns and ammo now are in people's houses, but it's hit or miss." I pointed at the shotgun in my scabbard.

"I found some twelve gauge reloading supplies back a few months ago, but shotguns are loud. I only use it when I have to."

"And the zombies are attracted to sound," he added.

"Exactly." Justin crouched down and worked the zombie's jacket loose, exposing a web belt with an empty holster attached.

"Dang, I thought I was going to get lucky for a second." He pointed at the boots.

"Those are some Danner combat boots. I'm tempted to take them."

"Help yourself, but I sure wouldn't wear them." Justin looked up at me before standing.

"Yeah, I guess you're right. So what do you do with them?"

"Drag 'em to a nearby sinkhole and burn 'em. C'mon, let's check the rest of the traps and then we'll take care of him."

"So, what's next?" Justin asked as we watched the corpse burn.

"We need to check the fence lines, make a count of the cattle and make sure none of them are injured, and then we're going to get the two-man crosscut saw out of the barn and cut up a big old tree." I looked at the corpse and threw another old tire on top of him. Satisfied, we mounted up.

As we rode, I pointed out various things on the farm. "We had a little over fifty calves born this past winter. Ten of them died, those aren't good odds."

"What'd they die of?"

"Cold weather mostly. Coyotes got a couple of them. Back when there was a full crew of us, we'd go out every morning, find the newborns and get them into the barns, but it's just me and Kelly now." I pointed to a spot on the far side of the farm. "I found one that looked like it had been eaten by zombies over there, but I never found the culprits, which was weird."

"Why's that?"

"They usually hang around if there's a food source." I paused a minute and stopped Sate. Justin stopped as well.

"What's up?" he asked.

"Kelly and I have discussed the situation with you three. The only reason I could think of for you three to not live here is the possible threat to my kids. But, y'all brought them back. I don't see how you could be a threat after you did that, unless there's some kind of diabolical plot going on."

"That's a negative," Justin said. "I'm just a gunnery sergeant, hatching diabolical plots is beyond my pay grade."

"Yeah, figured as much. So, Kelly and I are not opposed to you guys staying here. You can stay in the homestead if you want. If that's what y'all want to do, I wouldn't mind the extra help." Justin nodded thoughtfully.

"We've talked about it. When we made the decision to go AWOL, we didn't have a specific destination. We were just going to drive and see where it led us. Then, she decided we needed to rescue your kids. That led us here." He shrugged.

"I'm not opposed to finding a place around here and settling down. Ruth likes this area. She likes you too." He made an expression that was hard to decipher.

"We never treated her very well back in the unit. When we were in Atlanta, she confided in me one night that you'd treated her with more respect than anyone else."

"She's a good person," I replied. "It wasn't hard to see."

"Yeah, well, I ain't that smart. It took me a while to figure it out." I headed over to the large fallen tree and stopped.

"Let's break for lunch and talk about it. I've got some beef jerky, canned yams and hardtack."

"The zombie population around here seems pretty sparse," Justin commented as he chewed on the hard jerky. "That one in the trap is the only one I've seen in a couple of days now."

"We've managed to kill most of them off in this immediate area, but there're always the wanderers, not to mention evil humans. You can't ever let your guard down." I sat, watching the sergeant as he chewed his food.

"I'm curious, Justin, if you were in the team that raided the house instead of with the team that snatched me, would you have shot and killed everyone like they did?" He took a long time to answer.

"I don't know, Zach. I honestly don't." He coughed and took a swig out of his canteen. "All I ever wanted to be was a Marine. I enlisted right out of high school and even when I was in basic getting my ass chewed out and pounding sand, I knew I'd found a home. I'd just re-upped when the shit started. The Marines are all about duty and honor, and especially obedience to orders. So, if I were with team one instead of team two on that day and the order was given to open fire – I don't know. I would like to say that I would have refused, but – I probably would have followed orders."

I quietly digested what he said as I finished my lunch. Taking a long drink of water before putting my canteen away, I stood and pointed at the tree. Justin looked at it.

"It's a big one," he said. "I'd bet it's at least fifty-years-old."

"Yep. Let's see if those Marine muscles can handle some good old fashioned farm work," I said with a challenge in my tone. Justin grinned and stood.

We worked on the tree for the next three hours. We began with a steady pace on the two-man saw, but soon started trying to outdo the other. We were both winded within minutes and I'm sure his arm muscles were burning as much as mine, but neither of us complained and neither of us was going to be the first one to stop.

"You're pretty damn strong," Justin grudgingly said between breaths after the first hour. I grunted in acknowledgement, repositioned the saw for a new cut, and started again. When we finally had it cut up in two foot sections, we each sat on the ground catching our breaths and rubbing our arms.

"I have a feeling I'm going to be sore as hell tomorrow," he lamented. I chuckled and watched as he pulled his gloves off and inspected the blisters on his hands.

"Yeah, me too," I admitted and gestured at the cut up tree.

"This tree fell back around December, so we'll stack it in one of the woodsheds and let it season for a year."

"You let wood season a whole year?" he asked.

"Yeah, you can burn it sooner, but it's not as efficient. The bottom line is, you plan a year ahead on your firewood. Those knuckleheads at the school don't seem to understand this." I gestured at logs.

"Okay, now we need to split them, that'll let them dry out a little quicker." We didn't really need to, I could split them at a later time, but while I had the help I was going to get as much labor out of him as I could.

"I try to get eight cords cut every spring," I explained.

"Always plan ahead, right?" Justin asked.

"Yep."

We went at it for the next two hours. I finally relented and used one of the ATVs with the trailer to haul the wood back to the house. Justin admired my woodshed as we stacked.

"Isn't this fancy," he commented.

"Yeah, Fred built this one."

"I like it. He put a pitched roof on it to keep the water off and the floor is elevated and open so air can circulate." I nodded.

"And here I thought you were just a dumb Marine." Justin gave me a look at that comment. I suppressed a smile and looked at my watch.

"I think this is a good stopping point and we've got plenty of daylight left. I've been thinking about where you guys should live. My house is too small for all of us. You guys can stay at the homestead, or there's another house nearby that could work, unless you'd rather go live at the school."

"Yeah, I've been meaning to ask, why didn't you guys ever move in there with the rest of them?"

"At first, I saw no reason to. We had a house and a working farm. The school was meant to be a place for people who had been displaced to relocate to. I probably would have moved in there after what your people did to us, but I don't exactly get along with the woman who is running things over there." He looked at me questioningly and I explained the whole incident with Anthony and the ensuing fallout with Tonya as we rode at an easy gait.

"And this Anthony dude was Tonya's little brother?" he asked. I replied with a nod. "Damn." After a minute, he spoke again.

"So, the radio, how come nobody broadcasts on it anymore?"

"Two reasons; the main reason is the generator for the radio uses a lot of diesel fuel. In fact, those knuckleheads have broken it somehow. The second reason is it hasn't worked out how I had originally hoped."

"How's that?"

"I had envisioned using radio broadcasts to reach out to wayward survivors and bring them together to form a community. If you know anything about history, societies were built around a geographic location which usually started with some type of commerce, like a trading post or a watering hole, for instance. But, most of the people who showed up were only looking for a free handout. The people at the school aren't bad people, but after Fred killed Anthony, our relationship with Tonya soured."

I noticed Justin still bouncing up and down in the saddle and admonished him. "Your ass is going to be sore as hell tomorrow. You've got to learn to let your body move with the horse's movements." He grinned as I looked him over. He was sweating as much as I was, but my hair was all matted down.

"It looks like you have a fresh haircut."

"Yeah, Ruth does a good job. Besides," he said, gesturing at my ponytail. "A Marine can't going around looking like a hippy, now can he?" He thought about what he said and frowned. "Male Marines, that is."

"Well, I've been meaning to cut it. Hair and beards are a plethora for bacteria if you can't wash them every day." Not that I wanted Kelly to shave her head."

"If you want, Ruth can give you a squared-away haircut, and a shave. She's really good at it. She used to shave her dad."

"Yeah, sounds good."

"So, you're done with the school?" he asked as he tried to mimic my riding posture.

"I suppose so. A couple of days ago, Tonya informed me that the school was hers now and I had no say so in how they ran things."

"Well, I haven't seen everything they have going on, but you guys have a pretty decent operation going. I'd say you don't need them."

"I don't, but Kelly is lonely. She's a people person. Having the kids back is definitely going to help, but I think she needs more human contact." I pointed as we made our way through the turnstile in the fence and gestured. "That's the Allen's house." It looked like the gutters were full of leaves, but otherwise there didn't appear to be any discernible damage.

"The Parsons originally owned this house. They were the family who owned all of this property around here. The Riggins owned the other house. They were all related, Mrs. Riggins was the little sister of Old Man Parsons."

"Parsons?" he asked. I nodded. "Do you think the major is related to them?" Justin asked with a grin. I looked at him sourly.

"I sincerely hope not. Anyway, they disappeared during the outbreak. Julie and I met a family named the Allens. They were good people and we moved them in, but they eventually relocated. The place seems to be in pretty good shape still, I winterized the place, so none of the plumbing is busted."

"Where'd they go?"

"We'd encountered a group of soldiers from the Army. They informed us that they'd secured Fort Campbell and were relocating survivors. They worded it like it was an order and we had no choice in the matter. Me, being the smartass that I am, had a little bit of a heated conversation with their commanding officer. At first I thought he was an arrogant prick, but he actually turned out to be a pretty good guy. His name was Captain Jack Steen and his First Sergeant's name was Santiago." It suddenly occurred to me that I never learned Santiago's first name.

"Did you ever have contact with them?" I asked hopefully.

Justin shook his head. "There were a few civilians living nearby when we arrived at Campbell. They said there used to be a large group of people living there, but there was some kind of riot, lots of people were killed, and the survivors packed up and left."

I nodded. "Yeah, well, the Allen family accepted their invitation. The rest of us stayed here. We met with Captain Steen once more about a month or two later. That was our last contact with any of them."

I thought about that last meeting. It was when Captain Steen informed me Howard had been killed, the result of an accidental shooting by one of his preteen sons. I wondered what had happened to them.

I shook those thoughts away and gave Justin a walk-through of the house while we discussed life in general. We ended in the kitchen and took a seat at the table, a nice walnut veneer with a moderate layer of dust on it. I explained more about our interaction with the Fort Campbell soldiers.

"That's how I met Terry. He'd had some trouble up there so he came to live with us. He was a good dude," I said quietly. "He was vague about his life before. I always wondered about that, but never pried."

"Well, as for me, I lived in a rundown house with my mom, aunt, uncle, and their three ugly kids," Justin said with a sour expression. "I was thirteen when my dad left my mom, he decided he was going to make his fortune digging for gold in Alaska. He and my older brother took off with the promise they'd come back for me when they got settled, but I never saw either one of them again. The house was foreclosed on, that's how we ended up living with Uncle Butch. He was my mom's older brother. He owned a seedy dive bar and mom was a bartender there, which suited her just fine because she was an alcoholic." He looked out of the dirty window.

"When I stepped off the bus and entered the wonderful world of Parris Island, the difference was like night and day. I've never had any desire to go back. It's the same with Ruth. She's said some things once or twice which makes me suspect her father molested her, but she hasn't gone into any detail other than to say she's never going back home either. I've no idea about Major Parsons."

"Well, it's not an easy life around here, but it could be a lot worse."

"Yeah, it could be." He looked at me. "Would you mind if we go visit the people at the school?"

"Not at all," I replied and stood up. "We've got plenty of daylight left. Let's get back to the house and get cleaned up." I stopped for a minute and held my finger up.

"What?" Justin asked.

"Oh, I just thought of the perfect revenge against Parsons." Justin looked at me curiously. "I'm going to fix him up with Tonya."

CHAPTER 14 – CUTTER AND SHOOTER

Everyone, well, the original group, were overjoyed to see my kids. Marc, Ward, Rhonda, Tonya, even Gus. And especially the little urchins. The newcomers looked on indifferently. Floyd wasn't anywhere around.

"Tonya, this is Major Grant Parsons, Corporal Ruth Bullington, and Sergeant Justin Smithson. They were a part of Colonel Coltrane's Marines," I said plainly.

She cut her eyes at me with sudden suspicion, kind of like a dog that suspects you slipped some medicine into the bowl of Alpo. She pointed at Parsons.

"I remember this one, I can't say I'm pleased to see you people again," she said sourly and then returned her stare in my direction. "Zach, I'm having a little issue with the boiler. Could you come look it over with me?" I figured something like this was going to happen, so I played along and followed her outside. When she was sure nobody else was around, she turned and faced me.

"What's going on, Zach?" she asked stiffly. "Aren't these the same people who murdered everyone?"

"Yes and no," I replied. "It is my understanding when they received the original mission briefing from Colonel Coltrane, he emphasized nobody was to be harmed and to only fire in self-defense. They split up into three separate teams. Sergeant Smithson's team is the group who snatched me.

"All three claim they had nothing to do with the murders and were only following orders." I was going to leave it at that, but she continued staring at me.

"Yeah, well, I'm not so sure I believe them, and I can tell you the only thing keeping Parsons alive is because he's a medical doctor and you know as well as I how badly we need him, although I wouldn't tell him that."

"What's his specialty, do you know?" she asked.

"Pathology."

"I'm surprised you didn't kill them outright," she quipped.

"If I kill them outright at this point it'd be murder, no?" She frowned at me a long moment and took the opportunity to check the gauges on the boiler.

"You have something in mind, I'm thinking," she queried.

"They're looking for a place to live. I'll let them tell you the story, but the short of it is, they left Fort Campbell and relocated to the CDC in Atlanta. The zombies massed together and overran the place. According to them, they narrowly escaped by the skin of their teeth. They made a group decision and felt the right thing to do was to bring my children back home." She shook her head.

"That's very nice, but you have something else in mind."

"I'm only trying to help them out." I didn't, at least, not at this time, but if I did have something else in mind it was none of her business.

"Are you trying to dump them off on me?" she asked pointedly. I shook my head.

"It's entirely up to you. I showed Justin the house the Allens used to live in, but he wanted to check you guys out first. It's only a suggestion, but why don't you talk to them, they might be able to fill a niche in your group, or you may decide you don't want them. It's up to you." She didn't comment, merely stared at me with folded arms, and then glanced at the gauges once more before the two of us went back inside.

Everyone was in the cafeteria drinking tea or something and chatting. Little Frederick was playing with Rhonda's girls and had an enormous shit-eating grin on his little cherubic face. Ward and Marc were chatting with the Marines. One of the men whom I had never met was trying in vain to chat with Kelly, but she was mostly ignoring him and chatting with Rhonda. I walked over and joined them.

"Hi, Rhonda," I said and gave her a hug. I then turned to the man who was obviously interested in Kelly. "I don't believe we've ever met," I said while extending my hand. "I'm Zach."

"Yeah," he replied nonchalantly. His hand wasn't baby smooth, but it wasn't overly calloused either.

"I'm Cutter. I've heard some things about you." He released his flimsy grip and pointed at the scar on my cheek.

"It looks like you've already been on the wrong end of a knife," he said with a smirk. I looked at him curiously, wondering if he was posturing for Kelly's benefit or was he just your average everyday prick with ears.

"Yeah," I responded.

"How'd it happen? You smart off to the wrong person?" he asked while continuing to smirk. He probably expected it to embarrass me.

"He was a piece of garbage who claimed to be Special Forces, but it turned out he was nothing more than a jailer who told a lot of lies. He got me good, but it was a fatal mistake for him." Cutter's smirk changed to a little bit of disbelief.

"He's dead?"

"Not only is he dead, but all of his friends are dead too, and I set his house on fire to boot." His buddy walked up before he could respond with some kind of stupid retort.

"Yeah, you're Zach," he said without waiting to be introduced. "I'm Shooter." He looked at me with one of those half-smiles that made you wonder if he knew something you didn't. I shook his hand with as much pleasantness as I could muster. The two of them were obviously brothers. They were both about six feet tall, had the same average facial features, hazel eyes, and each had a slight dimple in their chin. They appeared to be in their mid-to-late twenties. The absurd nicknames convinced me they were both arrogant and stupid. I knew them for less than five minutes and already I didn't like them.

"Where did you guys come from?" I asked.

"Until recently, we were living over on River Road," Cutter said. Ah, I thought. I remembered what those two married travelers, Charlie and Mary, had said. We'd met them last March. They didn't have any pleasant things to say about that group.

"What happened? Did y'all get flooded out?"

"Yeah," Cutter replied and looked at me questioningly. "How did you know that?"

"Easy enough to figure out," I replied. "When the Wolf River dam gave way, everything close to the river flooded. So, where did the rest of your people go?"

"Who cares," Shooter said with a snort and walked off. I looked at Cutter who merely shrugged his shoulders. I wasn't going to get any more out of them. Maybe Ward or Marc would know. Maybe I'd ask them about it later.

"Well, it's good to meet you," I lied and looked over at Kelly, who had paused in conversation and now eyeing me amusingly. "Let's plan on leaving in about thirty minutes," I said to her. Before she could respond, Cutter piped up.

"Damn dude, do you always boss her around like that?" he asked with feigned disapproval. I shrugged.

"She's her own boss and she knows it." I gave Kelly a wink and walked over to where Marc and Ward were sitting. They were engaged in an animated conversation with the three Marines. Justin looked up as I pulled up a chair.

"Your two friends seem to think we've done you a terrible injustice," he said with a frown.

"You have," I said and pointed at the major. "Especially him." He started to reply, thought better of it, and instead pursed his lips.

"But anyway, I'm done with it. Maybe we'll talk about it some more at a later time. So, guys, these three are looking for a place to live."

"Yes, we are," Ruth said. Marc and Ward frowned in unison. I could see them thinking it over and the contradictory feelings flashing across their faces.

"Well, there is certainly room enough here," Ward said cautiously.

"But our food supply is tenuous," Marc rejoined. "Maybe something could be worked out, we'd have to discuss it with Tonya, of course."

"Where's Floyd?" I asked. Marc looked up.

"What? Oh, he went hunting earlier." He looked around indifferently. "I thought he'd be back by now. Maybe he has guard duty."

I didn't see anyone guarding anything when we drove up, but that didn't mean very much around here. We talked some more before Kelly walked over with the two kids in tow. "We need to go," she said with an underlying sense of urgency. It seemed odd, but she didn't have to tell me twice. I stood, picked the little guy up and gestured at the Marines.

"Are you guys ready, or would you like to stay a while and get to know everyone?" I asked. Before anyone could reply, Kelly spoke up.

"I think they should go with us." I saw worry in her face now. "There might be a surprise waiting." I had no idea what had her worked up, but she'd used our code word for duress. Something was definitely going on.

"Okay, how about it guys?" I asked them. I guessed they sensed Kelly's worry too, because they readily agreed. We bid everyone goodbye, which took about five minutes longer than was necessary and walked out to the truck.

"What is it?" I asked.

"Floyd's missing," she said.

"Who's Floyd?" Major Parsons asked. I ignored him and looked at Kelly.

"They said he went hunting this morning, he's fine. I'm sure he'll be home before supper gets cold." She shook her head.

"No, he left to go hunting *yesterday* morning, not this morning. He's in trouble, I know it." It was my turn to frown.

"They haven't gone to search for him?" Ruth asked. Kelly shook her head. "What a bunch of pricks," she exclaimed.

"Yeah, they're different," I responded. "Okay, let's think. Where the heck would Floyd have gone hunting?" Kelly and I stared at each other a moment and then realization hit us at the same time.

"The golf course," Kelly exclaimed.

"Yeah," I said. "Everyone load up." I jumped in the driver's seat and started the truck.

"What about the golf course?" Justin asked.

"Floyd rode with us one day when we went to scavenge at a country club with a big golf course," I said as we took off out of the parking lot.

"He kept talking about all of the squirrels and rabbits and deer running around and how he would love to come back and hunt," Kelly added. "It has to be where he is."

I couldn't go fast, the roads were too rough, but it didn't take long to find him, and it looked like it didn't take long for other things to find him as well.

CHAPTER 15 – HUNTING GONE AWRY

Floyd's vehicle, a beige-colored Toyota FJ Cruiser, was stopped on the side of Franklin Pike, sitting at an odd angle, like it had a flat tire. It was also surrounded by a dozen or so zombies. I turned our truck sideways in the road and stopped it approximately fifty feet away. Justin started to exit the truck.

"Hold up," I said as I reached into the glove box, grabbed a packet of ear plugs and handed them out. "Stay in the truck," I said to Kelly. She nodded and held the kids tightly. "Head shots only," I reminded the Marines. "Don't waste ammo." Justin frowned at me as if to say, you think I don't know that already?

I stepped outside and used the hood of the truck to steady my aim while he and Ruth took up positions at the back of the truck. We had no problem dispatching all of them in less than a minute. The last one died and fell against Floyd's door. He struggled to push on the door before finally getting it open with a heavy, one-armed heave. The dead zombie was knocked backwards, landing with a dull thud as its head hit the asphalt. Floyd gingerly stepped over it and jogged down to us. He looked tired and frazzled.

"I sure appreciate y'all. I ran out of ammo about eight hours ago."

"No problem, buddy. Do you have a spare tire?"

"What?" he asked and looked back at his vehicle. "Oh, yeah, but it ain't the tire, I think I broke one of the front struts," he started to explain but stopped and gratefully accepted a canteen from Ruth. I waited as he drank from it sloppily.

"What happened?" Kelly asked. He shrugged with a pained, apologetic expression.

"I was going to go down there to that golf course to shoot a few rabbits and squirrels. I was excited about it and I guess I was going a might too fast. I hit a pothole and messed up the front end." He pointed at the bodies lying in the roadway.

"I started walking back home when them things came out of nowhere." He kept staring and shook his head ruefully. "I barely made it back to my car and it was a good thing I locked the doors because they was pulling on the handles and trying to open 'em. I ain't never seen 'em do that before. They was trying to smash out the windows too, but they was just too weak, I guess."

I looked him over carefully to ensure he hadn't been bitten and waved a hand at the Marines. "I'll let them introduce themselves. Let's get you back to the school."

I made the major ride in the bed of the truck on the way back. He didn't like it, I guess he thought his rank dictated he be allowed to ride in front, but he wisely kept his mouth shut.

"Floyd," Justin said with a little bit of harshness in his tone. "I just met you, but what in the hell were you doing out here by yourself? Your friends back at the school didn't even know where you were, they just said you went hunting somewhere."

Floyd didn't say anything and looked down at his feet. I thought he was going to cry. Justin must have seen it as well and tried to make amends.

"I mean, I'm just saying. Ruth and I will gladly go hunting with you next time. Ruth's a natural born hunter, you should see her shoot." I glanced in the rearview mirror and saw Ruth had actually blushed at the compliment.

It was a very interesting bit of information. I didn't let my face betray any emotion as I wondered if she was the sniper and not some other fictional Marine.

We dropped Floyd off at the school and then drove the Marines back over to the old homestead. I put the truck in park and turned toward the back seat.

"Alright, you're options are plain as day. Go live at the school, stay here, or head out to greener pastures."

"We'll talk it over and should have a decision by tomorrow," Major Parsons said and then cleared his throat. "Is there any chance we can join you guys for dinner?" I started to say something derogatory but I caught a look from Kelly.

"Sure," Kelly replied. "Get in your Hummy-thing and follow us."

CHAPTER 16 – VACCINE

I was pretty sure I'd had my fill of the Marines. After all, I'd spent the entire day with Justin, but dinner was not as unpleasant as I thought it'd be. The conversation was mostly about the people at the school.

"They're certainly an eclectic group," Grant remarked.

"The two gay guys are psychologists?" Justin asked.

"Yeah," I replied. "If I had met them way back when and someone asked me what they're chances of survival would be if the world came to an end, I would've answered they'd be dead in twenty-four hours, but they've proven themselves to be survivors."

"What about that Tonya woman?" Ruth asked.

"Nuclear engineer," I answered. "Very smart, but I don't need to tell you that, she'll tell you any chance she gets." I drank some water.

"I can't say much about Gus, he's a little bit on the lazy side. Rhonda is…"

"Rhonda is very sweet," Kelly interrupted and gave me a look that told me not to say anything negative about her. Ruth picked up on it and laughed.

"I got the impression those two brothers are recent additions to the group." I nodded.

"Yeah, we don't know much about them."

"Well, if we're going to be interacting with them I'm going to teach them a lesson or two about taking care of your own," Justin declared. "That screw up with Floyd was a total no-go."

We talked more, and much to my relief they left as the sun was setting, but not before Kelly invited them to breakfast the next morning.

I opted out of my morning workout, got the kids cleaned up and was sitting on the front porch waiting on them as they drove up in their Hummy-thing, which was known to most folks as a Humvee.

"Good morning, Ruth, Justin," I said amicably. "You two go on inside and help Kelly get breakfast ready." Ruth grinned at me as they walked inside. Major Parsons started to walk in as well. "Not you," I said with an icy undertone. The major stopped in his tracks and stared at me. I guess he was thinking I was probably joking, but quickly realized I wasn't.

"Would you mind if I at least sat down?" he asked. I shrugged noncommittally. He sat tentatively in one of the porch chairs, watching me as he did so.

"You know, Zach, at some point you'll have to put this animosity behind you," he said. I stared at him balefully.

"Did you get a look at that private I killed? What was his name, Solonowski?"

"It was a pretty brutal murder," he asserted.

"Call it what you want. I call it an act of survival. My life depended on me getting out of there. Solonowski was in my way. The bad part about it is he was merely following orders. Colonel Coltrane's orders and your orders," I paused and looked over at him. "You know, I dream about doing the same thing to you."

"So, you're blaming me for the fact that you murdered him," he contended, but before I could respond he waved his hands in a placating gesture. "I was following orders as well, Zach. The tests I performed were necessary. I wish you could see that."

"Human rights be damned, right, Major?"

"Zach, I didn't tell you everything about the CDC." He was deflecting, he didn't want to talk about my imprisonment and the tests. I knew it, but he thought if it weren't discussed I'd forget about it. Fat chance.

"I'm listening," I finally said.

"The world is dying, Zach. Humans are dying out. There has been intermittent contact with other nations, but what little Intel we received left no doubt; it's bad, Zach. The latest projections predicted the extinction of the entire human race within fifty years." He had my attention now, but I didn't act like it.

"Once we arrived at the CDC, there was a collective effort. We worked our asses off. And, with the help of the tests on you and your children, we believe we had made a significant breakthrough. And then..." He left the sentence unfinished.

"Significant breakthrough," I retorted scornfully. "You treated my kids like lab rats."

"Say what you will, but we protected your children, and during that time I grew quite fond of them. Janet, Ruth and I cared for them like they were our very own." I grimaced. The mere mention of Janet's name made my colon churn. I saw a look on his face that made me wonder something.

"Were you sleeping with her?" I asked. Major Parsons grunted.

"I was." He emphasized the last word and saw me looking at him questioningly. "I caught her with Colonel Coltrane. I kind of lost interest in her after that." It was another item I wanted more information about, but it could wait.

"Tell me more about this vaccine, serum, whatever it is."

"Normally, there is a very complex set of protocols to be established and followed. Obviously, there wasn't time to follow those protocols, so we tried it directly on a human." I looked at him in disgust. "You don't understand, Zach," he countered. "I was the human." My expression was a mixture of disbelief and skepticism, but then I realized he was telling the truth and had a sudden epiphany of understanding.

"That's why you said it. The other day, at the barn, you said you needed to be exposed." He nodded.

"It's really the only way to be sure the vaccine works."

"I'll be more than happy to arrange that." Before either of us said anything more on the matter, Kelly stuck her head out of the door.

"Breakfast is ready," she said cheerfully. I stood and as Kelly gave me a look I gestured for the Major to follow me in.

"So, what've you guys decided about your living situation?" I asked after we had finished eating.

"Ruth and I are going to move into the radio tower," Justin replied. I was surprised, I didn't think they'd move there.

"Tonya agreed to feed us until we get on our own feet, but she made it clear we would be expected to help out."

"Well, that's really nice. What about you, Major?"

"Tonya has invited me to stay at the school."

Kelly looked at me with a smile. I guess they had already told her while I was sitting outside having a chat with the major.

"Yeah," Justin continued. "Ruth and I talked it over and thought about starting up radio broadcasts again. But, we're going to help you guys out all we can too."

I looked at him in confusion. "Why? I mean, I can always use help around here, but why the radio tower?"

"You had the right idea, Zach," Ruth said. "But you gave up on it too soon. The survivors of whatever is left of this nation need to pull together, just like you envisioned."

"I thought so too, once, but lately I've been thinking it's a futile effort." Justin shook his head.

"No, I disagree. You may not realize it, but you've already made it work, to some degree. In spite of all the adversity you've had, you guys have created something. We need to keep going with it."

I started to tell him it was going to be a wasted effort, but stopped. I found myself at a loss to express my feelings on the matter, especially with all of them sitting there, looking at me expectantly.

"Excuse me," I said, stood up and walked outside. I found myself walking around the barn. Shithead was outside of the corral doing who knows what, saw me and walked over. When I ignored him, he nuzzled me.

"I don't have any carrots for you, buddy," I muttered and scratched him behind his ear. I heard the back door shut and a minute later Justin appeared.

"Hey, if we said something in there that offended you, I apologize." I shook my head.

"No, y'all didn't do anything," I replied and gestured at the donkey. "This is Shithead. He didn't like any of us at first, except for a girl named Jessica. He loved her and followed her around like a puppy dog. Jessica was a beautiful, sweet girl. She was twenty or twenty-one when your friends killed her." I thought about the horrors she had gone through, only to be murdered a few months after being rescued.

"She never got a break," I said softly and continued scratching Shithead while thinking of the right words to explain.

"Back when it all started, I went to live with my buddy, Rick."

"You two lived in the old homestead, right?" I nodded.

"Yeah. It was just the two of us at first. We talked for hours about what was happening in the world and we wondered if anything would ever return to normal. It got me to thinking."

"About what?" Justin asked. "How life was going to be?"

"Yeah." I chuckled without humor. "I saw the need to recreate a society and thought I was the man to do it, even though I was only sixteen at the time. I had such lofty ideals." I'm sure he heard the irony in my tone, but he said nothing.

"I had a grand plan. I even wrote it all out in excruciating detail if you ever want to read it. But looking back, I realize now how naïve, how stupid I was. Very, very stupid. I had no clue." Justin shook his head again and started to speak. I cut him off.

"Oh, no? Let me put it to you this way. If I had stuck to myself and left everyone alone, people like Jessica would still be alive. Julie would still be alive. Hell, there are so many others you don't even know about." Rowdy, Fred, Andie, Terry, Mac, Tommy, Joe, Wanda, Konya, Howard, they'd all most likely still be alive if not for my *grand ideas*.

"Oh, and let's not forget about the people I've killed in the past three years." Let's see, how many? Twelve? Thirteen? "Did they deserve it? Well, at the time I certainly thought so, but there're many times, this particular moment being one of those times, when I wonder."

I felt myself getting worked up, picked up a rock and threw it as hard as I could at nothing in particular. Justin listened quietly, neither offering an opinion or any other commentary. Shithead nuzzled me again before growing bored and slowly walking off. I decided to change the subject and pointed over at the semi parked near the barn.

"That Volvo is a tough truck. We found it at a dealership about ten miles from here. I've got a lot of repair work to do on it."

"Quite a few bullet holes," he observed. I nodded.

"Kelly was being chased and shot at by people I thought were friends, you met them, the ones who set me up."

"Yeah, I met them. They tried to kill her, huh?"

"Yep, but she managed to escape and then drove around until she somehow found me." Justin looked at me in surprise.

"Did she know where you were?"

"Nope, she didn't have a clue, she just relied on her intuition."

"Wow," he said. "She looks so... what's a proper word, unassuming." I managed a short chuckle.

"Yeah, I thought so too when I first met her, but I underestimated her. I tend to do that with all women. Julie, my wife, she was feisty as all get out. Andie was another girl in our group. She was a skinny little girl but she was a stone cold killer.

"There were some people who died in a tanker explosion, one of them was a pretty unique woman. Her name was Mackenzie but everyone called her Big Mac. She could do everything and I'm pretty sure she could have beaten any man in a fair fight. I have to tell you, these female survivors are as tough as any man."

"You got that right," Justin said. "Ruth's a good example." He paused a moment. "She's a good woman." After a minute or two of silence, I turned and looked at him.

"So, when are you guys going to tell me the truth?" I asked pointedly. Justin, AKA Gunnery Sergeant Smithson, faced me and looked me squarely in the eyes.

"Say what's on your mind, Zach."

"Ruth wasn't with your team. She was with the other team, the team that went to my house and killed everyone."

CHAPTER 17 – ACCUSATIONS AND ARRIVALS

Justin didn't flinch and instead continued staring at me and even though his chiseled features gave him an air of rugged manliness, it also betrayed him when he was tense. The tightening of his jaw muscles were plain to see. He even had a vein that ran along the left side of his jawline would protrude noticeably. I doubt he was a very good poker player.

"What makes you think she didn't stay at Fort Campbell?" he challenged.

"Let me tell you a little bit about myself, Justin. I've got a very good memory, maybe even a photographic memory. If I read something, observe something, and especially if I write it down, I never forget it. You understand?"

"Okay," Justin said warily.

"So, I think you know where I'm going with this. I listened, observed, made mental notes. You said there were three teams, but that wasn't true. There were three teams." I counted off with my fingers. "One team went to the school and kept them in check so they wouldn't interfere with the mission, a second team snatched me, and a third team raided my house, ultimately killing almost everyone. Ruth wasn't with the first or second team. Ruth was with the team that went to my house." There was a long moment of the two of us staring at each other. The tension was palpable, as they say in those mystery thriller books.

"I think it would be best if you asked Ruth," he finally said. "But I want to make something clear, if you decide she's committed a wrong against you, I'm not going to stand around and do nothing if you try to hurt her."

"I suppose I understand that. I'm guessing you've grown fond of her," I surmised. Justin nodded his head slowly.

"We've been through a lot together."

The two of us stood there, continuing to stare at each other when I heard the back door to the house open and close. Ruth and Major Parsons saw us and walked over.

"I guess we should be going," Ruth said, oblivious to what was going on. "We have a lot of work to do. Oh," she added with a grin. "Kelly said the kids need some Daddy attention." That usually meant a diaper change was in order.

"Alright, I guess I'll see you guys later," I said and continued staring at Justin as the three of them drove away.

Just as I suspected, both kids had made very impressive boom-booms. Kelly and I had somewhat successfully potty-trained Little Frederick, but only when one of us was paying close attention. When we didn't, he still felt the need to shit all over himself, so we still had him in diapers. I got them attended to and herded them back to the kitchen table where I pulled one of my notepads close. I had Macie on my lap this time while the little guy crawled around under the table.

"What are you writing?" Kelly asked as she sat down across from me.

"The major believes they may have formulated a vaccine derived from mine and the kids' blood," I said. "I want to jot down what he had to say about it before I forget."

"They found a cure?" Kelly asked incredulously.

"Sort of, a vaccine, kind of like a flu shot I guess."

"Do you believe him?"

"I don't know, but he seems sincere. He claims he tested it on himself just a few hours before the invasion. He doesn't have any lab or equipment to monitor his progress, but he seems to be doing okay. He's asked me to go to Atlanta with him and see if anyone is left alive at the CDC, and if there is, continue with the testing."

"Are you going to do it?" Kelly asked. I looked at her and could see she was a little worried.

"Nope, there's no way in hell I'm going to leave you and my kids," I declared. She smiled in relief.

I went back to my notepad and wrote for about twenty minutes. When I stopped, I looked down and saw little Macie asleep in my lap and Frederick wrapped around my leg chewing on my bootlace. I managed to get it out of his mouth and looked up to see Kelly still sitting across from me with her chin resting in her hands. I offered her a smile.

"I guess you're going to be outside doing chores all day again," she said without smiling.

"Yeah, that's the plan. Why, what's wrong?" I asked.

"Zach, why do you think I'm perfectly fine with being cooped up in the house all day with the kids?" I thought about it for several seconds, attempting to come up with a clever reply. I came up empty.

"I'm not sure what to say. The chores have to be done if we want to survive."

"Well then, how about you stay home today and let me ride around in the fresh air and sunshine?" She was messing with me now, she had to be.

"Don't you realize how hard I work every day?"

"Oh? Are you implying I'm lazy?" Well, I stepped into that one.

"Not at all," I replied quickly. She stared at me pointedly. Seeing no logical way out of this, I threw up my hands in surrender.

"Fine, be my guest." She accepted gleefully. I waited for her to tell me she was kidding, but I knew it wasn't going to happen. So, I tried another tact and went over what had to be done. Unfazed, she responded with her own requirements of what housework she expected to complete.

Agreeing to terms, I put Macie on the couch, tucked a blanket around her and wedged her in with the cushions so she wouldn't roll off. Satisfied, I hoisted Frederick on my shoulders and walked outside.

Kelly was already in the barn and waited expectantly as I loaded up the ATV with an abundance of tools, hoping it would dissuade her. It didn't. She hopped on and started it with a smug grin. I pointed at the shotgun. She checked it and put the safety on before putting it back in the scabbard.

"Alright, at the first sign of trouble, I want you to hightail it back here. And, check in with me on the walkie-talkie every thirty minutes, okay?" She nodded and kissed the two of us before hitting the throttle.

I watched her ride off and sighed. "Alright, big guy, we're going to muck the barn while Macie's asleep."

It took much longer than normal, I kept getting distracted by my exuberant and overly curious son. He was getting into everything and at one point he decided to see what a horse apple tasted like before I could get to him. He scrunched up his face in disgust, causing me to chuckle.

"I bet you never do that again, right?" He looked at me like he was thinking, don't count on it, Dad.

After that, I decided it would be best to stick with the indoor chores. Macie woke up and Frederick decided he wanted to rest his eyes, which made it a lot easier. She was a perfect angel and watched me quietly with her big blue eyes while I mopped the floors.

She kept her promise and called me on the radio promptly at thirty minute intervals. She sounded like she was having fun, which of course irritated me. Nevertheless, I had no intention of not upholding my end of the bargain and worked diligently on the house cleaning. Promptly at five, Kelly called me with her walkie and advised she was on her way back.

"Oh, and be advised I'm bringing company," she said cryptically. I started and tried to get her to explain, but all she said was wait until she got home. She didn't use any of our prearranged code words, which hopefully meant everything was okay. Even so, I armed myself and was standing by when she drove up.

There was a military Humvee following her, but it was different from Justin's. This one had a slightly different paint scheme and an auxiliary fuel tank jury rigged onto the back. When they got closer, I could make out three women, a child and a dog inside. Kelly led them up the driveway and parked.

"Look what I found," she said with a grin.

"Who are they?" I whispered as they got out and stretched. The dog, a yellow Lab with oversized ears and paws, bounded out of the car and began running around the way excited dogs do, sniffing and finding things to piss on.

"The older one says she knows Fred," Kelly replied. "C'mon, I'll introduce you."

"Everyone, this is my boyfriend, Zach." Kelly pointed to each one as she introduced them. "This is Major Sarah Fowkes from the Air Force, Kate, Kyra, and Sam. Oh, and the dog is Callahan." As soon as Kelly mentioned the dog's name, his ears perked up before bounding over and checking me out.

Ignoring the dog's persistent sniffing of my nether regions, I peered closely at Major Fowkes. She was an attractive woman. Not someone who'd ever win a beauty contest, but the kind you'd see in a gym wearing next to nothing because she could and doing bicep curls with enough weight to cause you to do a double take. I could see why Fred liked her. I guessed her age maybe in her late thirties, although she could have been older. Her features were sharp and her brown hair looked like she had grabbed a handful, pulled it back in a fist and chopped the rest of it off. I got the impression she didn't smile very often. She returned my stare steadily as she watched me giving her the once over.

"Your name's Sarah, right?" I asked. She nodded her head slowly at my recognition. "Fred told me about you."

"He had a lot to say about you as well," she replied. "Where is he?"

"He's dead." When I said it, her features darkened, but she quickly regained her composure.

"I'm sorry to hear that," she said. "He was a good man."

"Yes, he was." I continued staring at her. "Did you come all the way from Oklahoma to see him?" She responded with something of a nod. It wasn't going to be easy to get her to talk, that was obvious.

"I would really like to hear all about it, but let's get you guys settled in first." I looked over at the other two women and the boy. He was obviously shy and clung to one of them tightly.

"Okay," I said. "I didn't get which one of you is Kate and which one is Kyra." One of them partially raised her hand.

"I'm Kate," she responded. She was the tall one, maybe five ten with a typical leanness of someone who'd been on the road a while with very little to eat, long dark dirty hair tied back in a ponytail. Kyra was an inch or two shorter, with the same colored hair, but she let hers flow in a jumbled mess. They both looked like they were in their mid-twenties, but it was hard to tell. The last couple of years had obviously been hard on them, as it had with all of us.

"Are you two sisters?" I asked. They nodded at the same time. I then looked at the kid, a scrawny tow-headed boy with a pale, almost sickly complexion.

"What's your name, big guy?" I asked.

"Sam," he said in a quiet voice barely above a whisper.

"Sam's a little shy," Kate said and put her arm around him. I looked at her and surreptitiously winked.

"Sam, how old are you, fifteen? Sixteen?" I asked.

"I'm ten," he replied, a little louder now. I feigned surprise.

"Ten? Dang, you're big for your age." He puffed up his chest a little at the compliment. I grinned and looked over at Kelly.

"Why don't you take them inside and get them settled? I'll take care of the ATV and see what I can do about getting some hot water available." As usual, the mention of hot water got a combined look of surprise, even from Sam.

I checked the gauges that Tonya and I had mounted. They showed a charge of ninety percent. Nodding in satisfaction, I opened the panel to the circuit box and turned on the breakers for the water heater and the well pump. Unloading the ATV, I hurried inside.

Kelly was chatting amicably with Kate and Kyra at the kitchen table while Sarah sat quietly on the couch, Sam sitting beside her, thumbing through one of my notepads. Callahan had found my kids, and to his delight, realized he had two new play pals. I poured myself a glass of water and sat beside Kelly.

"How was the trip?" I asked. Kate and Kyra looked at each other like I'd asked them the last time they'd wiped their asses, which, judging by a lingering odor, had been a while.

"Shitty," Kate answered. I don't think she intended the pun. "We got into a few scrapes." I got up quickly and went into the den, coming back a moment later with a pad and pencil.

"If you don't mind, I'd like to hear about it."

"Where do you want us to start?" Kyra asked.

"From the beginning."

"From the beginning," Kate repeated. "Well, let's see. We worked in a casino outside of Shawnee, Oklahoma with Sammy's mom." When she said that, my keen observation skills clued me in that they perhaps had some Native American ancestry in their blood. You couldn't get anything past me. Kate continued.

"We're both card dealers. We'd watched the news reports of everyone getting sick, but nobody thought very much about it and work went on as usual. One night, I guess it was Thanksgiving…"

"November thirtieth," Kyra added.

"Yeah, it seemed to happen quickly. We had about a tenth of the usual number of customers. Kyra and I were dealing at the blackjack tables that night and let me tell you, our tips sucked. Sammy's mom had gotten off work earlier, but she came back with Sammy to eat dinner."

"Employees got to eat for half price," Kyra explained. Kate nodded and continued.

"We all went on dinner break together and all of a sudden we started hearing a lot of screaming out in the main casino area. We figured some drunks were fighting or something. We were going to see what was happening but one of the security guards ran into the back room and locked the door. He had his gun out and he looked scared. Really scared."

"And then the gunfire started," Kyra said. Kate nodded again as she brushed a loose tuft of hair out of her face.

"Yeah, the only people that are supposed to be armed are our security, so we didn't know what the hell was going on."

"We thought maybe it was a robbery or something so all of us ducked into the kitchen and locked ourselves in." Kyra took a deep breath. Reliving the event was obviously bothering her. Kate was more nonchalant about it.

"So, I guess you can imagine what was happening. People were turning into those infected zombie things and attacking other people."

"What happened then?" Kelly asked.

"We tried calling 911," Kate said. "But nobody answered. When the shooting stopped, one of the other security guards came in and got us. Needless to say, it was pretty shocking when we walked through the main area."

"That's an understatement," Kyra said. "It was horrible, gory. There was blood and guts everywhere."

"We did okay for a while," Kate said wistfully. "After security had regained control, there were about thirty people left that were alive and not infected.

Some of them insisted on leaving immediately. Dale, he was the head of security, he tried to convince them to stay, but when they started arguing he didn't force the issue. Anyone who wanted to leave could. Some people stayed for a day or two and then couldn't stand it. They had to go wherever they thought they had to go. By the end of the week, we were down to a dozen people, which actually worked out okay. We were making a go of it and were just waiting for everything to get back to normal. It wasn't easy, but we actually were doing okay for a couple of years, all things considered."

"Then it all went to hell," Kyra said.

"How?" I asked.

"It was over a cunt," Kate said. Kyra stared at her sister in consternation.

"Kate! S-A-M," she scolded.

"I can spell," Sam said from the den. "I'm not stupid." Kyra looked out into the den and smiled at him.

"Well then, you should know that your Aunt Katie has a potty mouth and shouldn't talk like that," Kyra said with a wink and then glared at Kate, who ignored her sister's chastisement and continued.

"One of the women, who I might add was friends with my sister even though I never liked her," she declared with a dramatic roll of her eyes, "began having, shall we say, indiscretions with more than one of the men in the group. As you can imagine, it snowballed out of control. There was a big fight. If that wasn't bad enough, there was this one guy who was off in the head."

"He became obsessed with someone," Kyra said and grabbed my pen and pad. She wrote down that the man had raped and killed Sam's mom. I nodded in acknowledgement as Kelly looked over my shoulder.

"He ran off before anyone found out and was never caught. We were a tight group up until that point," Kyra said. "And then it all came apart. My boyfriend loaded up a car, we grabbed Sammy, and the four of us took off." Kyra stopped then, stood suddenly and went out of the back door. Kelly and I looked questioningly at Kate.

"His name was Burton Rainwater. He was cute, a pretty nice guy, but not very smart. He said he had some relatives that lived near Fort Smith, so we jumped in the car and headed out.

"We were running on fumes when Burton spotted a truck stop. He was convinced we could siphon gas from some of the cars in the parking lot." Her face darkened.

"There were some people there. Burton tried the friendly approach, but they weren't buying it. So, he got the bright idea of pulling a gun on them. It was a big mistake. He was shot. They let us drive off, but we only made it about another ten miles before we ran out of gas. Burton died somewhere along the way. We didn't even have a shovel to bury him. We wrapped him in a blanket and had to leave him on the side of the road. As you can imagine, Kyra didn't handle it very well." I nodded and wrote quickly. Kate waited until I caught up.

"So, there we were, stuck with no gas."

"Yeah, most of the later model cars have this plastic ball in the neck of the gas tank. Its purpose is to keep gas from spilling out if the car is in a rollover accident." I'd figured that one out the hard way and had modified my siphon hose so it would work, but it was still difficult. Kate looked at me oddly. Yeah, there I went again, speaking like a know-it-all.

"Yeah, okay. So, there we were. Stuck. We were about to start walking when Sammy spotted some of those things on the interstate, and they were coming our way. We locked ourselves in our car and ducked down in the seats, but they spotted us and crowded around the car."

"That must have been terrifying," Kelly said. Kate nodded.

"Yeah, we were stuck like that for two days. They made a meal of Burton, but that wasn't enough for them. Those men at the truck stop had taken Burton's gun, so we had no way of killing them." Kate shuddered at the memory.

"We didn't think we were going to make it, but here comes Sarah." Sarah briefly looked up at the mention of her name and then went back to reading the notepad. I wasn't sure which one she had but she apparently found it very interesting.

"So, have you ever heard the expression, bad-ass-bitch? There were ten or fifteen of those things and Sarah killed them all in a little under a minute."

"She shot them all in the head," Sammy said loudly from the den.

"Yeah, she did, and then she asked us if we wanted to join her. And here we are."

"Did you guys encounter any other live people?" I asked.

"Yeah, outside of Little Rock. They seemed like nice people, but Sarah was having none of it. She only wanted to reunite with Fred." I looked through the doorway into the den. Sarah acted like she wasn't listening. "She gave us the option of staying with them or going with her. We chose to go with her. Same thing in Memphis. Some people tried to wave us down, but Sarah never even slowed down." I looked into the den again. Sarah must have sensed it.

"There was no reason to stop," she said without looking up.

"You guys don't happen to have any cigarettes, do you?" Kate asked hopefully. Kelly stood and fished out a carton from a drawer.

"We found these a while back. Neither of us smoke, so you're welcome to them, but not inside, please." Kate looked at Kelly like she'd just bestowed manna from heaven. Kelly motioned toward the door.

"Let's go outside and let Zach fix us dinner," she said with a facetious grin. They walked out, but Sarah elected to stay with me and help me struggle with preparing something edible.

Eight people were currently occupying Fred's house, much more than it was designed for. Kelly and I were snug in our bed with the kids, the rest were either in the spare bedroom or laid out in the den.

"I fear my superb house cleaning is going to be negated," I commented. Kelly laughed quietly.

"I'll have to admit, it was spotless, at least for thirty minutes. Maybe you should be the full time maid."

"Yeah, you should have seen me. I cleaned from top to bottom. I even emptied all of the kitchen drawers and wiped them down." I felt Kelly involuntarily flinch. "Yep, I found them." I don't know where she got them from, but she had enough to last for at least five years. "Why were you hiding them?"

"Because I don't want to get pregnant and I wasn't sure how you were going to react if I said as much," she said plainly. I sighed.

"I thought you knew me better than that. I would have, and do respect your decision."

Kelly snuggled close. "I'm sorry, Zach. I just thought, well, you know, with your kids missing and not knowing if you'd ever see them again you might have wanted to get me pregnant." I was about to object, but then it thought over. When we started having sex, I gave no regard to taking protective measures. Hell, considering the number of times we'd done it and she hadn't gotten pregnant, I should've already figured it out. Maybe she knew me better than I thought. I moved the hair off of her face and kissed her cheek.

"Okay, point taken. So, anyway, the little shit-factory figured out how to bypass those so-called child proof latches."

"He did?"

"Yeah, I'm doing dishes and the next thing I know he's opened one of the doors and is crawling around inside the cabinet under the sink. So, I moved all of the cleaning supplies to the barn and your birth control pills are on the top shelf of the medicine chest."

"Thank you, sweetheart," she murmured tiredly. We lay there in peaceful silence for a few minutes. It was nice. I'm glad I didn't overreact and we had cleared the air.

"You know, I've been thinking. I think we ought to rebuild the Riggins house, or maybe build a series of houses like this one. It looks like our population is going to keep growing, whether we want it to or not." I waited for a response, but after a few seconds of silence, I realized I was talking to myself. Kelly had already fallen asleep.

CHAPTER 18 – SARAH

I woke at my usual time. The house was quiet, nothing but the rhythm of breathing from Kelly and the kids. Sarah and company had been here for two days now, and while I considered them nice people, there were far too many living here for my comfort. I made it outside without waking anyone but Callahan, who happily followed me out and headed for a good spot in the yard.

I stretched at the entrance to the barn as I looked at the clear dawn. It was a little cool, but it looked like it was going to be a pleasant day. My plan was to get in a quick workout, grab something for breakfast and get started on chores before anyone else was even awake. If everything went according to plan, I could get a sizeable amount of work done and then have the rest of the afternoon free. Thinking it over, I decided I was going over to the radio tower and talk to Justin and Ruth about finding quarters for the Oklahoma crew. I did some more stretching and I'd no sooner started into my first set when the barn door opened. It was Sarah. She had on some sweatpants and a sweatshirt with Air Force logos on them.

"May I join you?" she asked.

"Sure," I replied. I assumed she wanted to talk while I worked out, but to my surprise, she took off her sweatshirt revealing a slim but muscular torso with perky breasts barely being hidden by a taut athletic bra. She stretched while I completed my first set, and when I set the bar down she took twenty pounds off and began her own set. We stayed with it throughout, matching each other set for set. It took a little longer than I wanted, but she stayed right with me and the two of us pushed each other. When I thought we were finished, she insisted I join her for pushups and then an exercise she called planking. It was harder than I thought it'd be, but my ego prevented me from uttering any complaint.

Kelly had the kids sitting on the kitchen floor and was cooking breakfast when we walked in. She looked at the two of us in concern, which confused me until I realized both of us were covered in sweat and still breathing heavily. And Sarah had not put her sweatshirt back on. I suppose our appearance could have been mistaken for another kind of workout, but I knew Kelly would never think that.

"Good morning," she said a little suspiciously. Uh-oh, I thought, maybe I was wrong.

"Good morning, love," I replied and gave her a big sloppy kiss. "Sarah decided to join me in a morning workout."

"Oh." Although I had no doubt she believed me, I wasn't sure what else was going on in her mind. Like I'd been reminded many times in the past by Julie, in spite of how smart I thought I was, I was clueless when it came to women. Our discussion was interrupted by Kate and Kyra coming into the den. They plopped down at the table and grumbled about it being so early.

"Please tell me there's something to drink with caffeine in it," Kate grumbled.

"I just ignore them until they get out of their moods," Sammy said as he plopped down in a chair. I grinned at him. He was smarter than I originally thought.

"I'm going to wash up," I said to Kelly and motioned with my head toward our bedroom. She followed me in a minute later.

"I have a plan," I said, turning toward her while taking my shirt off.

"What kind of plan?"

"I want to pick Sarah's brain about life in the Midwest. I thought I'd get her to help me with the farm chores and then take her with me to do some scavenging."

"How was your workout?" she asked with an arched eyebrow.

"Really good, that woman is in pretty good shape," I said and quickly got into the shower. I thought it'd keep her from interrogating me further, but I should have known better. Kelly stripped out of her night clothes and got in with me.

"Is she going to be your new best friend?" she asked as she reached for the soap. I frowned and shook my head.

"No, sweetheart," I said. "You're my best friend." She huffed and rinsed off. When we'd dried off she wrapped the towel around my neck and pulled my head toward hers. She kissed me long and passionately.

"I'm not sure I like three other single women living here."

"Are you jealous?" I asked with a grin. She gave me a look. My grin faded.

"Just keep one thing in mind, I'm not into sharing."

"I don't want to share you with anyone either," I said and kissed her again. "You and me, right?" Kelly looked at me a long moment before smiling at me in a way that made me giddy and I felt myself getting aroused.

"How about this, while we're out scavenging, I'll talk to her about the living arrangements, maybe find them a house nearby. Sound good?"

"If you say so," she replied, gave a certain appendage a good squeeze, and left the bathroom giggling.

"I try to vary my routine every day," I said to Sarah. She looked at me quizzically.

"I figured you for the anal retentive type," she replied. "The kind of person who has to do things a certain way every time, not that I'm criticizing."

"I used to be, but one day I almost got ambushed. The person told me my behavior patterns were very predictable while pointing a gun at me." I thought of Carla and how she'd ultimately killed herself.

"So, what happened?"

"Thankfully, she didn't shoot me and I learned my lesson."

"Someone I know?" she asked, probably wondering if it was Kelly.

"Nope." She looked at me, waiting for me to explain. "Alright, it goes something like this. Tonya had a little brother named Anthony, who was married to a woman named Carla." Sarah listened attentively as I explained everything.

"So, Fred killed him?" she asked when I was finished with the story.

"Yeah."

"Good."

"Yeah. So, anyway, after Fred killed him, Tonya and Carla became very angry with us. Not too long after is about the time that Carla decided it was all my fault. She stalked me, learned my patterns and confronted me one day while I was checking the fence lines. She told me I always checked the fence lines at the same time."

"She blamed you for her husband's death."

"Yeah, she acted like she was going to shoot me for a minute, but she didn't." I paused a moment. "I think things had been building with her for a while. It became too much for her I guess. She ended up killing herself." Sarah nodded in understanding. "It was sad. She wasn't a bad person."

"Yeah, well, shit happens," Sarah replied. I expected her to ask more questions about her, but I don't think she was all that interested.

"Okay, so, now you vary your routine."

"Yeah."

"How much farm do you have?"

"We essentially have two different farms, Fred's farm and a farm collective originally owned by the Parsons family. That's who I worked for when the plague broke out."

"How many acres?" Sarah asked.

"Fred's farm is about fifty acres, the next door neighbor had another fifty which they had combined and worked together, and the Parsons farm is a collective of roughly fifteen hundred acres. So, after my run in with Carla, instead of doing the same things on Monday and the same things on Tuesday, I break it up. Sometimes it's not very efficient though."

"That's a lot of farm for just a couple of people to manage," she commented. I sighed heavily.

"Back when Fred and the rest of the crew were alive, we had a handle on it." I paused for a minute while I made a head count of the cattle. "We were prosperous even. We could've easily kept a hundred people fed. After they were killed, I've downsized considerably. I maintain all of the fence lines but we're now only working a fraction of the land. It's been tough," I said quietly, knowing she understood the multiple meaning.

I told her about the massacre while we rode the fence lines. She listened in silence as I went over everything, starting when Fred arrived back home. I found a couple of places that needed some mending and then showed her the old houses and the resulting damage.

"So, those three Marines were with the same group that did all of this?"

"Yes."

"And killed Fred and your wife?" I nodded.

"And they're the same Marines who abducted you and your kids, and conducted tests on you and your kids like you were lab rats?" I nodded again. I expected her to say something, something derogatory, something insulting, something supportive, anything. But, she had no further commentary on the matter.

"The only thing left for now is to feed the chickens and clean out the coop. Kelly did it last time, so it's my turn. Once we get that done, I thought I'd head out and do some scavenging. Kelly usually goes with me, but now that we have the kids back someone needs to watch them." What I didn't say was that there was no way in hell I was going to leave my kids in the care of Kate and Kyra, people I barely knew. I think Sarah sensed it and understood.

"Are you asking me to join you, Zach?"

"If you want to," I answered. "It's always good to have back up, especially when scavenging, but if you say yes, I'll have to insist on making sure you're knowledgeable about guns and we rehearse room clearing tactics before heading out." She stretched a kink out of her back and brushed herself off.

"Let's get to it," she said and walked to the chicken coop.

"Alright," I said as we drove down Trousdale Drive. "I've been working this area on and off for over a year now and there're still plenty of houses and businesses to check out."

"Why this area?" Sarah asked.

"Are you asking why am I driving all the way over here when there are so many houses and businesses all around the Nolensville area which is so much closer to my house?" I asked sarcastically. Sarah caught the tone.

"Let me guess, it has something to do with the people at the school."

"Bingo," I replied. "Tonya and her buds are either too scared or too lazy to venture out more than a five-mile radius of the school and they get all butt hurt if I work the same area."

"So, instead of causing conflict, you chose instead to scavenge other areas," she concluded. "Very considerate of you." I shrugged.

"It seemed more prudent," I said and gestured. "I've been all over Nashville, but this particular area seems bereft of humans. I haven't seen one around here in quite a while and only a few infected here and there." I pointed at one of the side streets.

"I've not been down this street, let's try it out." We started at the house on the corner. I drove into the yard and backed up to the front door. After a minute of not seeing anyone peeking out of the windows, I went to the door and did the standard knock and announce.

"Do you do that every time?" Sarah asked.

"More or less. There's always a chance that survivors still live here. I don't want to get into a shootout with someone who's merely protecting their property." I gestured at the door.

"I give it a good listen, and then try to make entry without making too much noise." I demonstrated by putting my ear close to the door before forcing it open with a pry bar.

"Hello?" I stood there a minute, waiting for any human to challenge us. There was nothing and I got the distinct musty odor of a home that'd not been occupied in a while. "Okay, let's clear it."

"I look for telltale signs," I said as I pointed out various things. "There's a lot of undisturbed dust on the furniture and some of the water pipes have busted. Those are indicators no human has lived here in a while, which is good. But, you've got to watch for any zombies that've been trapped in a closet or bedroom." She nodded in understanding and we began rummaging through drawers and closets.

We worked through four different houses with minimal results and then took a break for lunch.

"Tell me about Oklahoma," I suggested. She took a long drink of water.

"I guess you know how Fred and I met," she started. I nodded.

"I got a brief summation. You know Fred, he was never one for a lot of prattle." Sarah grinned for the first time since I'd met her.

"Yeah, that's Fred. Well, let's see. He shows up out of nowhere driving a vintage, bright yellow Volkswagen Beetle, says he's going to LA in search of his daughter, and then asked if I would be kind enough to fly him the rest of the way." She smiled wistfully at the memory. "I looked at him like he had lost his ever-loving mind and said as much."

"But, you flew him there."

"Yes, I did," she said. "He had that effect on me. Anyway, after landing, we went to the address where she had lived. She was still there. Unfortunately, she'd become infected. She'd apparently been trapped inside her apartment the entire time. Fred killed her and her roommate, or whoever it was that was with her, and then we flew back to Tinker."

"Why'd you drive here instead of flying?" I asked. "Has all the jet fuel gone bad?"

"Bad enough where I didn't want to risk flying." She pointed at a house down at the end of the block.

"Look, that house has a two car garage and a four-wheel drive truck parked out front. I bet he's a hobby hunter." I looked where she was pointing.

"That truck's covered in grime, even the windows. It hasn't been driven in a while," she observed.

"Good eye," I said and started our truck.

We hit pay dirt in the garage. The owner had converted it to his own personal version of a man cave, complete with mounted bass, deer heads, you name it. He had a gun safe and an elaborate reloading system neatly arranged on a custom work bench. I hastily looked through the drawers and smiled.

"Bingo," I exclaimed as I pulled out box after box of ammunition. The drawers also had several boxes of primers and other reloading material. "Oh, man, this is good," I told her. "We've been really hurting on ammo." I looked over the different calibers and found myself grinning like a fat man at an all you can eat buffet. Sarah's response was a soft grunt; she'd quickly put her emotions back in that hidden little room of hers.

"Try to contain yourself. I know it's a good find, but you're being far too emotional." Her response was to glance at me with an arched eyebrow.

"Fred said you were a little bit of a smart ass," she said glibly. I held my hands out.

"Guilty as charged. Okay, let's get it loaded," I said and started with the reloader. She gestured at it.

"I saw two of these in the barn." I nodded. "But you think you need a third one."

"Yep, this is an excellent barter item. Or maybe we'll give it to Josue. That man is constantly tinkering with stuff."

We loaded everything into the truck, all the while keeping an eye out for hostiles. When we were finished, Sarah gestured toward the garage.

"What about the safe?" I frowned at her question.

"I'm betting they have the combination to it hidden somewhere in the house." My logic sounded good, but after a frustrating search, we didn't find it.

"We can come back later and try to cut it open," I said, but didn't have much hope. Sarah started to say something but we were interrupted by a soft yet distinct sound of something scraping along the asphalt driveway. Sarah looked at me questioningly.

"Company," I whispered. We both raised our weapons and pointed them toward the open garage door. We heard the scraping again, and then a plastic trash bin slowly came into view. I looked at Sarah, who was looking back at me with a look of confusion mixed with disbelief.

One of those things, a middle-aged man, came into view. He was using the curbside recycle bin as sort of a walker. When he saw us, he emitted a raspy guttural groan and started making his way into the garage.

"Where the hell did he come from?" Sarah asked without really expecting an answer.

"I got it," I said, put my shotgun down and pulled my machete out. Sarah watched as I got the bin between him and me, took careful aim, and swung the machete like I was hitting a homerun. I made contact just above his left ear and almost got the machete almost all the way through his head. Working the blade out, I looked at it with a frown.

"I need to sharpen it," I muttered. Sarah walked over and looked at the man, who was now motionless on the garage floor with black ooze seeping out of the gash in his head.

"You seemed to have enjoyed doing that," she opined. "You were grinning." I shrugged and looked around the garage. When I found a scrap of rag, I used it to go through the man's pockets, finding his wallet in a back pocket. When I pulled it out, it was covered in God only knows what.

"What're you doing now?"

"I think this old dude lived here. Let's see if there's anything in his wallet, like a safe combination." I went through it and soon found a folded piece of paper.

"Well?"

"It's possible," I said. "There're several numbers and other writing. I think it's a list of usernames and passwords." The paper was heavily soiled and a lot of it was hard to read. Short answer, after several attempts, we struck out.

"Alright," I said as I doused our hands with sanitizer, "we'll come back to it later. Let's finish up and get out of here."

We pulled down the garage door and she watched as I took a can of spray paint and applied the standard FEMA marking with an abbreviated notation of the safe.

"I saw these markings during the Hurricane Katrina debacle. Is it a FEMA symbol?" I nodded.

"Yeah. It's probably a wasted effort now, but I do it anyway."

"What exactly does it denote?" she asked. I pointed at it.

"You start with a big X. The top quadrant of the X is the date the structure was searched."

"Three-fourteen-zero three?" she asked.

"March fourteenth, third year of the apocalypse. We arbitrarily chose November first as the starting point and we're on year three now."

"Uh, well, I guess you have to start somewhere."

"Exactly." I pointed at the left quadrant. "Here is the identifier of who searched it." I'd put a large Z in there, which I assumed needed no explanation. "The right quadrant is for identifying any hazards that're present, and the bottom quadrant is for notating if there are any bodies inside. I also use the bottom quadrant for any special info, like the safe."

"And you do that with every structure you search?" she asked. I nodded again. "Yeah, I figured," she said with a grin. I glanced at my watch and looked around. "We have time to check a few more houses. Let's just stick with this street." Sarah
nodded in agreement.

"So, you guys fly back from Los Angeles to Tinker. What happened next?" I asked as we worked.

"The base commander, a general, had committed suicide while we were gone. After that, everyone who was left drifted off until it was just Fred and me. I tried to get him to stay, but he wanted to get back home to you guys. He kept calling all of you his adopted family." She paused and frowned.

"I was the one responsible for him staying away for so long. I used every feminine trick I could think of, but one day he announced he was going home and I couldn't stop him."

"Was it a fond goodbye?" I asked, already knowing the answer. Sarah shook her head.

"He asked me to come with him, but I threw a hissy fit and acted pretty badly toward him. I regretted it, of course. We all do things in the heat of the moment that we later regret." I agreed, thinking back to some of the things I'd done in the past I wish I could have changed.

We finished with the last house and were now sitting on the tailgate. Sarah appeared lost in her own memories before realizing I was still there, waiting to listen to the rest of the story.

"I believed I had a duty to stay at Tinker and maintain the base and equipment. I honestly thought I was up to the challenge, but it was too much for just one person. A windstorm swept through one day and destroyed a lot of assets. It was the final straw I guess. I'd been alone for almost two years and found myself missing Fred more and more." She looked over at me.

"I was so stubborn, opinionated, and hot-headed. I never realized what a good man he was. Being totally alone, I had a lot of time to think. Maybe I romanticized him and our relationship a little too much, but no matter."

"I think if I were totally alone for two years, I would've gone crazy."

"Yeah," she replied, but didn't elaborate.

"The storm was most likely a tornado and it did a considerable amount of damage. I hid out in a basement of one of the buildings until the next day. As I walked around surveying everything that'd been damaged, I came across an abandoned car. You see, before Fred left, he took a sharpie and wrote down his home address and a note saying, 'I hope you change your mind.' I ignored it for a couple of months, but one day I walked by that car and saw that the writing was fading, so I wrote it down.

"I carried that scrap of paper in my pocket and I can't tell you how many times I pulled it out and looked at it." She wiped at her eyes before continuing.

"So, even though it'd been almost two years, after that storm I decided to pack up and find him." She paused again and this time a single tear rolled down her cheek.

"Anyway, I fixed up a Humvee and headed out. You know the rest." I nodded in understanding and looked around while she wiped her face. After a couple of minutes, I checked my watch again and noticed she checked hers at the same time.

"Let's head back," I suggested.

"Affirmative, but I'd like to meet those Marines first and have a little talk with them," she said stiffly. I shrugged and began driving us toward the school.

"You two are part of the unit who murdered a group of innocent people, is that correct, Sergeant?"

I had driven Major Fowkes, Sarah, to the radio tower first. Justin and Ruth were outside when we drove up, working a garden plot. They were a little unsettled when I introduced her. Sarah skipped all pretense at niceties.

"I asked you a direct question, Sergeant."

"Yes ma'am, but as we explained to Zach, we didn't murder anyone."

"Yes, Zach said as much. But you two and this Major Parsons have pertinent information about the incident, correct?"

"Well…"

Sarah turned toward me. "Zach, I'll need to make use of that notepad I saw in the truck. Do you mind?"

"Ah, no, not at all. I'll go get it." She turned back to the two Marines.

"The two of you are going to write a detailed statement concerning that mission," Sarah ordered. "Including the names of everyone involved and, more specifically, you will identify every active shooter. Do I make myself clear, Sergeant?"

"Ma'am, I'm not so sure that's a good idea," Justin said.

"I didn't ask for your opinion, Sergeant. I'm giving the two of you a direct order. If you refuse, I'll conclude the two of you were in fact involved in the murder of innocent civilians and summarily execute both of you." She then unsnapped the holster containing her sidearm and grabbed the handgrip. Justin and Ruth looked over at me like this was my fault or something. I gestured at Sarah.

"She had a relationship with Fred. They were friends. If you think she's simply going to let this matter go, you're mistaken. Personally, I think this is a good idea," I opined. "I'd especially like to read your statement, Ruth," I said pointedly as I continued staring at the two of them.

"The two of you have repeatedly said you had nothing to do with the murders. It would be an honorable gesture to memorialize the massacre of my family. Besides," I said to Justin, "you repeatedly emphasized the importance of duty and obedience in the military, and if I understand correctly, she out ranks both of you." Justin worked his mouth, attempting to form a reply, but saw no rebuttal to my logic. He sighed and reached for the notepad.

"Do not leave out any details. If you do, you'll start over," Sarah warned.

When the two of them were finished, Sarah made them swear an oath the statement they wrote was truthful before having them sign it. She signed her name to each statement and then had me sign as a witness.

"Zach," Ruth said. "Please keep an open mind when you read my statement."

"I will, but you could have told me the whole story from the get-go."

"I know. I have no excuse," she said and hung her head. Sarah looked around.

"Why did you decide to live here?" she asked.

"Zach had a plan of using the radio tower to bring survivors together," Justin said.

"He got sidetracked, but we think it would be a worthwhile endeavor to start it up again," Ruth added. Sarah nodded as she looked around.

"You need a storm shelter," she commented and then turned her attention to me. "Let's head over to the school. I'm anxious to meet this Major Parsons."

They had apparently already spotted us when we turned off of Concord Road to the radio tower. There was a group of them waiting outside when we drove up, including Major Parsons. I stopped the truck and started to introduce Sarah to everyone, but she cut me off.

"I'll get to know everyone else at a later time. Right now I'm going to have a private conversation with this person," she declared as she sharply pointed at Major Parsons and then pointed to the far end of the parking lot. She turned and started walking.

"Don't keep me waiting," she threatened without looking behind her. We all watched in rapt silence as Major Parsons hurried to catch up with her.

"So, how's everyone doing?" I asked as we listened to a heated, albeit very one-sided conversation in the background."

"We're doing pretty well, Zach," Ward replied with a nervous smile. "May we ask what the heck is going on over there?" he asked as he gestured toward the two military officers. The two of them were squared off, facing each other, both in the body posture soldiers called the parade rest position.

"Major Fowkes and Fred were very good friends. She's taken it upon herself to get to the bottom of the massacre."

"She's giving him a good ole fashioned ass chewing," Floyd muttered. "Kind of reminds me of my sister-in-law when she got pissed off at my brother."

"A real man wouldn't put up with that shit," one of them said. I looked over and wasn't surprised to see it was Shooter who made the remark. What a dumbass.

"How's everything else going, Zach?" Tonya asked. I turned my attention to her.

"Not too bad. In addition to Major Fowkes, we've got a couple of other arrivals." She frowned and shook her head.

"Our food supplies are stretched a little thin at the moment," she said. I held up a hand.

"Don't worry, I'm not asking you to take them in," I replied. "Kelly and I will take care of them." Then, I decided to have a little fun with them. "Besides, how much can a couple of young slender women eat anyway, right?" I think I saw Shooter's jaw drop.

"You got women?" Cutter asked. I answered with a vague shrug.

"We're going to come visit," he said with a grin. I could almost see his mouth drooling.

"No you're not," I responded. His grin dropped.

"Why not?"

"They've had a rough couple of months. Once they get some rest and sorted out, I'll bring them all over here to visit."

"That'd be wonderful, Zach," Ward said. "We can have a pot luck supper."

"That's a great idea," Marc added excitedly. "We haven't had one of those in a long time." I thought about it. I didn't much care for the prospect of breaking bread with these people, but I knew Kelly would enjoy it, and unlike Shooter, I knew it was always best to have a happy significant other. I looked at the date on my watch.

"Okay, I'm game. Ward, how about three days from now? What do you think, Tonya?"

"Sounds agreeable," she replied. "I certainly hope you'll be bringing steaks."

We agreed and then acted like were weren't listening to the conversation taking place at the other end of the parking lot while we chatted about unimportant things. The only bit of information that caught my attention was when Floyd reported seeing a couple of zombies ambling down Franklin Pike the day before.

About fifteen minutes later, the two majors walked back and rejoined us. Sarah reached inside the truck, removed the other two written statements, and handed Major Parsons the clean notepad. She directed him to sit on the ground. He didn't like it, cast a forlorn glance at me as if to say this was all my fault, and sat. It took him a full forty-five minutes to write out his statement. Sarah had everyone sign as witnesses.

CHAPTER 19 – SWORN

This is the sworn statement of Lance Corporal Ruth Anne Bullington. On 12September of last year, my commanding officer, Colonel Almose Coltrane, called the unit together and issued an OPORD. The mission was, as we were told, to take a person into custody, per the order of the Commander-in-Chief. The unit was split into three separate teams. The location was a small community of survivors located near the town of Nolensville, Tennessee.

Team Charlie's mission was to go to a school located on Concord Road and contain the civilians, preventing them from interfering in the primary mission.

Team Bravo's mission was to coordinate with a group of four cooperating confidential informants who were going to provide access to an adult male hereafter referred to as Target One (Zachariah Gunderson).

Team Alpha's original mission was to provide security, but Colonel Coltrane issued a FRAGO once Target One was acquired. The amended mission was to raid a residence located in the same general vicinity of Nolensville and take custody of two children hereafter referred to as Target Two and Target Three. I was assigned to Team Alpha.

After Team Bravo secured the primary target, they proceeded to a staging area and awaited the other two teams. At 0900 hours, Team Alpha drove onto the property and parked tactically near the house in which Targets Two and Three were believed to be residing in. I was the driver of the third vehicle. The other occupants of this vehicle were Colonel Coltrane and Major Parsons. Colonel Coltrane made an announcement of our intentions with the use of a portable loudspeaker. The occupants of the house refused to come out. One of the occupants shouted an obscenity and fired. The bullet struck Corporal Harold Lamance. He died as a result of this gunshot.

Much to my shock and surprise, Colonel Coltrane ordered an assault on the position. We opened fire and the occupants inside fired back. For several minutes, there was an intense firefight.

Once suppressive fire had been achieved, two Marines were able to set breaching charges on the front door and made entry. I did not enter the house, instead acting as security. I heard sporadic gunfire from inside the house and then there was silence for several minutes. Eventually, Colonel Coltrane and the rest of the assaulting force exited the house with the two children and an adult female who identified herself as the grandmother of the children. Colonel Coltrane ordered all three of them taken into custody. We linked up with Teams Bravo and Charlie and then drove back to Fort Campbell without further incident.

It was only later that I learned the full facts of the mission. The father of the two children, identified as Zachariah Gunderson, was kept secluded in a holding cell for the duration of his confinement. We were advised this action was on direct orders from POTUS, and we were specifically ordered not to tell him about the incident at the house or the fate of his children.

For the record, I want to avow I had absolutely no foreknowledge that lethal force was going to be used on civilians, nor did I participate in shooting said civilians. Instead of stopping it, I sat in the protection of my vehicle like the coward that I am. I swear this statement is true and accurate to the best of my knowledge - Lance Corporal Ruth Bullington.

She'd attached an extra sheet of paper with the ranks and names of everyone on her team, along with a brief, physical description of each one. I read the other two statements and there were no surprises. The other two also denied any foreknowledge there was going to be lethal force used. I sealed the statements in a large manila envelope, quietly walked into the den where everyone was laid out, and placed it in the bookshelf. I was skeptical, but it was better than nothing. Kelly was still awake, the kids snuggled up together on one side of the bed, sound asleep.

"I've been waiting for you," she whispered.

"Yeah, I'm sorry, I wanted to read the statements again." I stripped down to my underwear and carefully crawled in and snuggled up beside her.

"Good thing we have a king-sized bed," I quipped.

"How many times did you read them?"

"The statements? Four or five, I guess." She turned and kissed me.

"Okay, we'll talk about it tomorrow. In the meantime, if we're really quiet, we won't wake the kids," she said very softly. Somehow it made everything feel alright.

CHAPTER 20 – POT LUCK

"There are a total of seventeen people," I told them as we prepared food for the pot luck supper. "Tonya is the de facto leader of the group. She's easy to spot. She's short, kind of shaped like a fire hydrant with a big ass, short gray hair, and constantly glares at everyone over her readers. She had a husband, a brother and a sister-in-law but they're all dead. I'll fill you guys in on the details later." Kelly glanced at me knowingly. I kept going.

"There's Ward and his partner, Marc. They're a salt and pepper couple who were psychologists back in the day. They can be bothersome at times with their 'let's all hold hands and sing campfire songs' attitude, but otherwise they're good people.

"There's Floyd, he's a little bit on the country side with a bad arm and has a raging crush on Kelly. There's Rhonda. She's close to my age with strawberry hair and has become the mother figure for three orphan girls." I thought for a minute and realized I *still* had not learned the names of those little girls, even though they pestered me nonstop whenever I was around.

"There's Gus. He's easy to spot, he's usually sitting on his ass and complaining about something. He has three kids too; two twin girls and his little boy, Vincent."

"Vincent is a little brat who could use a spanking or two," Kelly commented with her nose wrinkled, like she caught a whiff of something offensive.

"There's Grant, he's a doctor and a major in the Marines. Justin and Ruth are the other two Marines and they live across the street at the radio tower. Y'all will see it when we get there. And then there are two brothers about the same age as you two who call themselves Cutter and Shooter."

"Rhonda calls them Butter and Pooter," Kelly said. The women broke out in laughter. I smiled. The two brothers reminded me of boys in high school who desperately wanted to be known as uber cool, craved attention, and would do almost anything to get it. They irritated me and I didn't like either one of them, but kept it to myself. After all, I was hoping Kate and Kyra would develop an interest in them. It'd cause two things to happen; first, that one idiot, Cutter, would stop lusting after Kelly, and second, they would feel like they owed me because I hooked them up. Besides, being in the same house with all of these women was getting bothersome.

"Anyway, I don't think they're bad guys, otherwise Tonya would have booted them long ago."

"Are you trying to play matchmaker?" Kate asked teasingly. Her intuition was spot on, but I shrugged innocently.

"So, there are six kids, not counting your two kids?" Sarah asked. I nodded. "Wow, there may be hope for humanity yet."

"Will Jorge and his family be coming?" Kelly asked.

"I hope so," I said and then looked at the women. "A while back we met a man named Jorge and his sister, Maria. They seem like good people." We chatted for several more minutes before Sarah stood.

"I believe I'm going to jump in the shower," she said.

"Good," I said and looked at my watch. "Let's plan on heading out in three hours."

I waited patiently for my turn, which was last. Even Kelly went before me. Another thing about having four women in the house, by the time I got to the shower, all of the hot water was gone and it looked like four of my disposable razors had been used. All things considered, I didn't complain. I had a particular fondness for Kelly's silky smooth legs and I hoped the two sisters were fixing themselves up for the Butter Pooter boys.

Not surprisingly, the school's cafeteria was decked out with the same colorful crepe paper streamers, balloons, and 3d figures made out of paper scraps they used every time they had an event. The two docs were limited with what they had to work with, so I'm not certain they achieved the look they were hoping for, but it was still colorful.

"What the hell," Sarah muttered when we walked in.

"Marc and Ward love to decorate," Kelly replied with a grin.

"It kind of looks like they hit the crack pipe before putting it up," Kate said with a laugh. I shrugged.

"You work with what you got, I suppose." I looked around and spotted them back in the corner. Ward was on a stepladder, sticking one last streamer on the acoustic tile ceiling while Marc held it steadily and chided his mate to be careful. When he finished, he spotted us and waved merrily. Since my hands were full, I responded with a nod. Sarah scowled as she surveyed the rest of the room.

"Alright everyone," Kelly said and gestured. "Let's take the food over to those tables." We followed Kelly to the tables where Rhonda was busily arranging all of the pots and bowls. I heard a gasp behind me and turned to see Gus fast-stepping our way and his son trying hard to keep up.

"Oh my Lord," he exclaimed and sniffed the Tupperware bin I was carrying. "Do I smell bread?"

"Yep, bread and biscuits," I replied. "Fresh hand ground wheat and not so fresh yeast, but the ladies added some lard to the ingredients and it all turned out delicious." I didn't mention our wheat stores were now almost depleted, no need being a Debbie Downer. Gus helped me unload and stack the loaves on one of the tables. His eyes widened even further when he saw Sarah heading into the kitchen with my large Igloo cooler.

"Please tell me those are some fresh steaks in that cooler," Gus begged. I nodded and he grinned like I just told him he'd won the lottery. He grabbed a serrated knife and started slicing up a loaf.

"I remember Mac trying to bake some biscuits that time we were clearing out all of those houses on Concord Road. They tasted awful," he said. I arched an eyebrow at him. Gus chuckled. "You didn't care much for how I acted back then."

"No I didn't."

"Well, don't worry," he said with a reassuring smile. "I won't say one single derogatory comment today. My mouth is watering too much." I chuckled at him and looked around.

"Where are Butter and, I mean, where are Cutter and Shooter?" I asked. Gus hooked a thumb over his shoulder as he ate a biscuit.

"They're still in the locker room, primping. Man, this bread is awesome."

"Try to save some for the others," I said, patted him on the shoulder and headed down the hallway. I found the two brothers admiring themselves in the mirror. One of them was shaving around his goatee, the other one looked like he'd shaved his chest and was now flexing his muscles.

"How's it going, guys?" I asked.

"Fine as wine," Shooter replied and then popped a double biceps pose. "Are these guns the shit or what?" he boasted. I nodded, as if I cared. Besides, my arms were bigger.

"Did you bring the girls?" Cutter asked as he stroked his face with the razor. I nodded again.

"They're anxious to meet you two, but you men need to play it cool."

"Don't you worry, my man," Shooter replied with that same ever-present smile. "We'll have them wrapped around our fingers in no time."

"Alright, I'll see you out front. Their names are Kate and Kyra. Kate is the taller one. Good luck." They're going to need it, I thought as I headed back to the cafeteria.

To my surprise, the Pooter-Butter duo were polite and mostly minded their manners. Oh, they may have overplayed it a little with their macho behavior and telling tall stories about themselves, but I think the two sisters were more amused than annoyed. Sarah, however, dismissed them as idiots within seconds of meeting them and refused to acknowledge them for the rest of the dinner.

Everyone seemed to be enjoying themselves, even me. Kelly made sure of it by occasionally groping me under the table. Or maybe it was Callahan nudging me for food scraps, I wasn't sure. It didn't matter.

Unfortunately, our festivities were interrupted about thirty minutes into dinner when Floyd burst into the cafeteria. Somehow, he'd drawn guard duty again. His face was flushed and he was breathing hard.

"Someone's coming up the road!" he shouted. Sarah started to jump up, but I caught her by the hand and put my mouth close to her ear.

"I want to see them in action," I whispered. She gave an understanding nod while Kelly looked at me in confusion. I continued eating as I watched how the school group reacted to this supposed threat. Marc and Ward busied themselves with gathering up dirty plates. The Pooter-Butter duo jumped up like we were being invaded by Martians and ran to a closet whereupon they took out handguns. So, that's where they were keeping their weapons. They left the closet door open, which allowed me to do a visual inventory. I only saw less than a dozen weapons, which seemed a little low, all things considering.

I continued watching with mild amusement as they sprinted toward the doors like it was a race and wondered if they thought they were impressing the women. Unlike the Pooter-Butter duo, the three Marines moved with discipline and purpose. I would never admit it, but Justin's mannerisms and coolness made me wish I could have been a Marine.

Wiping my face with one of the cloth napkins that looked like it may have been a piece of curtain once, I stood and walked toward the front entrance. Kelly and Sarah followed close behind. When we made it outside, the dynamic duo had their weapons drawn on the occupants of two vehicles and were yelling at them. One of those vehicles was very familiar looking and my gut tensed.

"Stand down!" I yelled. "Those are friendlies!"

"Who are they?" Tonya asked. Unsurprisingly, she'd waited until everyone had gone outside before venturing out. I made a note to remember that too.

"That's Jorge and his family. I told you about him." She nodded in understanding and we walked over to the two SUVs. Pooter and Butter were still aiming their weapons at Jorge and his family and shouting orders at the top of their lungs. Jorge was looking at me plaintively, like I had invited him into a trap.

"Guys, these are friends," I insisted. "Lower your weapons."

"You heard the man, stand down!" Justin yelled in a very authoritative Sergeant's voice. The two brothers glared at him a moment, and I thought Justin and I were going to have to apply some corrective action, but then Tonya intervened.

"You two, relax." Only then did they lower their weapons. I walked over to Jorge's vehicle then and shook his hand when he exited.

"Man, I thought you guys were going to shoot us," he said and then muttered something in Spanish while making the sign of the cross.

"I told everyone you guys might be coming. Apparently we had a breakdown in communication somewhere," I said while I eyed the two brothers a moment before casting a reproachful stare at Floyd. He's the one that got those two dunderheads all worked up in the first place.

"How are you guys?" Kelly asked.

"Not so good, Kelly," Jorge replied. "Our house burned down."

"Oh, no! What happened?" she asked.

"Bad sparks," an older man said. He was an older version of Jorge with the only difference being a touch of gray in his hair and a few age marks in his face. It was obvious they were related.

"You must be Josue," I said and held out my hand. "I'm Zach."

"Yes, Zach, this is my father," Jorge gestured toward the front seat of his car. "And you remember Maria." Maria was sitting in the passenger seat and there was a young kid sitting in the back seat. He looked like a typical three-year-old.

"That's my nephew, Jose," Jorge said. I eyed him questioningly. "Yeah, it's my sister's son. Okay, so she's not really a virgin." Maria said something to him harshly in Spanish and continued berating him as she got out of the car. It was then I noticed both SUVs were packed tightly with what appeared to be their personal belongings. I could also smell the distinct odor of smoke.

"How'd your house catch on fire?" I asked.

"We put a couple of logs on the fire and went to bed," Jorge explained. "We think some sparks from the embers got onto the couch. Before anyone woke up, the whole den was on fire and the place was full of smoke. We didn't have enough water to do anything, so we started throwing stuff out of the windows until it got too hot and smoky." He gestured at the cars. "This is everything we own, man. While we were loading everything up, that fire attracted all kinds of zombies. We had to leave, man." Tonya interrupted our conversation.

"Well, we can stand out here in the rain, or we can go inside and talk about it over some supper," she said. It was a unanimous agreement and everyone followed her back inside.

Once everyone had calmed down, the joyous atmosphere returned. The Garcia family fit right in and it was soon obvious both Jorge and Josue had a good sense of humor.

"Our house was decorated just like this," Josue deadpanned as he looked at the docs' streamers.

"You're smiling," Kelly whispered in my ear with a grin of her own as we sat in chairs talking to everyone. "Someone's having a good time in spite of himself."

She was right, of course. In fact, everyone seemed to be enjoying themselves, even Jorge and his family, in spite of their recent loss and the harsh welcoming. And, the major. He had his stethoscope out and was letting the kids listen to each other's heartbeat and trying with limited success to explain to them the function of the heart. Kelly nudged me again.

"Your children are on the crest of crashing and burning," she whispered as she stroked my thigh. "And it's getting dark, and I am going to require attention after lights out." I needed no other hints, subtle or otherwise, and made sure a certain part of my anatomy was not going to embarrass me before standing. Kelly followed and went around saying our goodbyes and gathering up the kids. I told Kelly to wait for me at the truck and walked over to Major Parsons. He was gleefully laughing at the kids' antics. When he looked up, his smile disappeared.

"I'd like to speak to you, if you don't mind."

"Certainly," he said, although he was anything but, and stood. I caught Justin eyeing me warily as we walked outside to the parking lot. I stopped a few feet away from my truck so Kelly could hear the conversation from her open window.

"The kids seem to like you," I said. "Do you have any of your own?" The major's face darkened.

"Nieces and nephews," he replied. "I was in love a couple of times, but it never worked out." His brow furrowed more for a moment, and then the moment was gone.

"Your kids call Kelly their mommy," he said with a smile. "It says a lot about her."

"Yes it does," I agreed. There was a momentary pause while the two of us stared at each other.

"What do you want to talk about, Zach?"

"I've been thinking about what you said." The major continued staring, waiting. "About you wanting to expose yourself."

"Yes," he chuckled. "I've been trying to work up the nerve. Perhaps, soon," he said quietly.

"You can't do it," I declared. An eyebrow arched. "I know you've thought about it and have talked yourself into believing it's something that has to be done, but I'm telling you it's the wrong thing to do and very shortsighted."

"Well, if I didn't know any better, I'd say you're actually concerned about my welfare."

"Yeah, in a manner of speaking." I paused for a moment searching for the right words.

"I don't know if I will ever forgive you for what you did. But, your skills are valued, and therefore that makes you a valued member of this community."

"And if I weren't a doctor?" he asked. I started not to answer and turned toward my truck, but stopped.

"I didn't like being a test subject. Setting up a means to have you exposed would make you a test subject, and to encourage you to do so would make me a hypocrite, right?" I got in the truck and drove away while Grant stood there. I looked in the rear view mirror and saw him still staring at us as we drove out of sight.

CHAPTER 21 – JOURNAL ENTRY: APRIL 1ST, 3 A.Z.

The month of March has been a mixed bag of good and not so good. On March 13th, we had four new arrivals: Major Sarah Fowkes, lately of the USAF, Kate and Kyra Redbank (sisters), a ten-year-old kid named Sam Hunter, and a goofy but lovable yellow lab named Callahan. Sarah met Fred back when he went to find his daughter. They had become an item for a short time before Fred came back home. Apparently, ole Fred made quite an impression on her because two years later she came looking for him. She met the two sisters and Sammy by happenstance on I-40 somewhere in Oklahoma. They were stranded and she rescued them.

It's too bad Fred's gone; they could have picked up where they left off.

On the 17th, everybody met at the school for a pot luck supper. It went pretty well, nobody was shot, even though there was a close call when the Garcia family arrived. Jorge and Maria have a father, Josue, and Maria has a little boy named Jose. Their house had burned down and they were effectively homeless, but we've gotten them residence in a house not far from us. They seem to be doing pretty good. Jorge's father is somewhat of a jack-of-all trades and very handy.

Let me address the status of the three Marines who brought my children back. Justin and Ruth, that would be Gunnery Sergeant Smithson and Lance Corporal Bullington, have given me the impression that they are good people. Kelly thinks so as well. They are currently living in the little house at the radio tower and seem to be making a go of it. In addition, they worked with Kelly and me for four straight days planting crops and tending to the livestock.

Major Grant Parsons is a different story. I don't torment him or say anything insulting to him anymore, but I'm not sure I can ever forgive him. As long as he stays away from my kids, I suppose that is all I can ask for. Oh, that man did something totally nuts when he was still at the CDC. He injected himself with a test serum. He's still alive, so maybe those people were on to something. It's too bad they're all dead.

I thought long and hard about what he'd done. He was willing to use himself as a guinea pig, not knowing what could possibly happen to him. So, after the pot luck supper, I pulled him aside and told him that he was a valued member of our community and it was not a good idea to expose himself. He was surprised that I said it, to say the least. Yesterday, he told me he was in fact related to the Parsons who had owned the farm. He grew up in east Tennessee and apparently, Old Man Parsons was his uncle. I told him I didn't give a shit.

Food: It's not where I'd like it to be. We lost too many of our cows this past winter and bad weather had all but eradicated our winter wheat crop. This will hurt us over the coming year. Also, our gardening was meant to feed only a few people. But now, those numbers have increased. The result is our inventory has shrunk much faster than I have anticipated. Suffice it to say, nobody around here is going to get fat. If we have another long cold winter like this past one, we're going to be hurting.

Zombies: We encountered a horde of about twenty of them one day when we were scavenging in the south Nashville area. It's the same neighborhood I'd been working through for the past few months and I'd never seen that many together before. We dispatched them quickly, but I have to report, those things are continuing to show more signs of evolvement. After much thought and discussion on the matter, I've decided to divide them into three distinct categories:

1.   The first category is the weak ones, or as Grant calls them, the first generation. They are mostly decomposed globs now, blind and barely able to move. Most of them in this category have all died off. The only time we find one now is when they've been trapped inside a closet or something similar, where they were not exposed to the elements.

2.   This is the Z14 category – they're evolving. Their bodies are healing (to an extent) and their body mechanics are improving. They are more agile and they can even run. Not very well, but much better than before. They're also drinking water now, something none of us observed during the first year. Whether or not they know how to open a can of soda is unknown, but they will damn sure attack anything alive and try to eat them. So, for all intents and purposes, a normal human becomes infected and turns. They become very violent and attack anything living. Their bodies start decomposing and they become weak. At some point, they either continue to wither and die or they start healing and rejuvenating. What causes this? Even Major Parsons said the brainiacs back at the CDC had no definitive answer.

3.   The last category (for now). For lack of a better term, I call this the 'What-The-Fuck' category. These zombies are living together, communicating, and acting in unison. Kelly and I saw firsthand how a thousand or more of them were travelling together. While we were watching them, there was some kind of silent communication between them; they all stopped at once and turned to look toward us. It was freaky, to say the least. At the CDC, several thousand of them acted in concert to overrun the facility. We've discussed it extensively. How did they all act in tandem and why did they attack? There is no clear answer. It could have been simply assaulting a food source, or they might have even possibly figured out what the CDC is. The thing is, this behavior is downright bizarre. Is the WTF category worthy of another rule? Z15: WATCH OUT FOR THE WHAT-THE-FUCKS! Maybe so, I don't know. Back a couple of years ago when I was a goofy kid, I thought the rules were important, but I view my priorities a little bit differently now. Going around spray painting them everywhere doesn't seem to be all that important anymore.

ZOMBIE RULES BOOK 4

Speaking of important things in life, I must now write about my children. They're doing great and growing like weeds. They are healthy, a handful, and a complete joy. Rick, my first real father-figure, never had any kids and said more than once he had never wanted any. Now that I'm a dad, it seems strange he felt that way. I love my kids and wouldn't trade anything in the world for them.

As for myself, I'm doing okay. I have my kids and I have Kelly. I love them all dearly. It seems kind of odd that I've been in love three times now and I'm only nineteen. I'm sure the docs would just love to sit me down for some therapy sessions to analyze that - among other things.

That isn't going to happen, but if it did, I know exactly what I'd say. I'd say Macie was my first love. Pure adoration, puppy love. I literally ached when I thought of her. After her was Julie, my first true soulmate. I remember the first time she and I met, how we disliked each other at first, and how we later fell in love. Our relationship was a little unconventional by pre-apocalyptic standards (eh, the thing I had with her and Macie at the same time), but it somehow worked for us. Things were a little rocky toward the end, but I have no doubt we would've worked it out, had she lived.

What can I say about Kelly? I've thought about it a lot. The best way I can explain it is she has been my saving grace, my rock, my friend. She is like the first warm day of spring after a cold and turbulent winter. I, love her deeply, count myself lucky, and pray that I never lose her.

CHAPTER 22 – PYTHON

The sound of an insistent horn honking interrupted our breakfast.

"I'll check it out," I told them. I picked Macie up off of my lap and handed her off to Kelly, grabbed a rifle and made my way toward the gate. I recognized Jorge's SUV immediately and broke into a run. Something had to be wrong for Jorge to be making so much damned noise.

"Jose is missing, man," Jorge said breathlessly. "Have you seen him?" I looked at the two men. Both of them were visibly upset, even Josue, who I'd never seen out of sorts.

"What happened? I mean, no, we haven't seen him, do you know what happened?"

"When we got up this morning he wasn't in bed. The back door was standing open." He wiped the sweat off of his brow. "We've looked all over. This is bad, man, this is bad."

"Maria is, what is the word?" Josue asked his son. "Hysterical?" Jorge nodded his head vigorously.

"Yeah, man, she's about to go loco. She's back at the house."

"Okay, let me think," I said. I took a deep breath to clear my brain.

"Okay," I said again after a moment. "Josue, take the SUV and go grab Sarah. Tell her what's going on and that Jorge and I will be out searching east of the farm. She'll know what to do. I'll have Kelly contact Justin and they'll join in." I pointed at Jorge.

"Can you ride a horse?"

"Yeah, man, why?"

"While they're searching in vehicles, we're going to search on horseback. If he's hurt or stuck somewhere, we'll be able to hear him crying out." Jorge seemed a little confused by this.

"We won't be able to cover as much ground," he lamented. I explained my logic.

"We'll have your father and the others searching in vehicles. We have to have someone going slow and be able to hear sounds you wouldn't be able to hear over the autos' noises."

"Yeah, okay, it makes sense." I hurried back to the house, told Kelly what was going on, and then rushed to the barn. Jorge followed. He tried to help me saddle the horses, but I waved him off.

"You better let me do it. You're a stranger to them and they might try to kick you." He nodded and I got them saddled quickly.

"How long has he been gone?" I asked as I watched him get into the saddle. He looked at his wrist, realized he hadn't put his watch on, and looked over at mine.

"About two hours now." I frowned.

"When was the last time any of you actually put eyes on him?" I asked. He looked at me ruefully.

"Maria put him to bed about seven or eight. Last night." I caught myself from letting out an expletive or two and pointed.

"Alright, the first thing we should do is check our traps." Jorge's face paled when he realized what I was suggesting, but he nodded and we headed out.

We kept the horses at a fast walk, even though Sate was dying for a good long run. Jorge rode Hank surprisingly well, and under any other circumstances I would have good naturedly challenged him to a race.

It took another two hours before we spotted anything. The back of their property sloped down to a small creek which was a tributary to Mill Creek. It was where we had set multiple traps.

"Look," Jorge whispered excitedly as he reigned up and pointed toward the far bank.

"Look, man," he repeated as I stared at what he was pointing at. It was an amazing sight, almost surreal.

"Well, that's something you don't see every day," I said and spurred Sate ahead, which was short sighted. When we got about twenty feet away, the big horse stopped suddenly and whinnied in alarm. I held the reigns tightly and rubbed his neck to keep him from bolting. "Easy, boy," I cooed as I backed him away.

"That's a snake," Jorge exclaimed. "A big snake."

He was right. Lying on the opposite bank of the creek was a snake. A very large snake.

"It looks like a Burmese python," I said, mostly to myself. I didn't say out loud the other thing I was thinking.

"It must be fifteen feet long, man." I had to agree with Jorge's estimation, and it also had a considerable bulge in its torso.

"Why is it so fat?" he asked.

"I'd say it's eaten something recently that didn't agree with it, that's why it's having trouble moving."

"Shit, man," Jorge said, and then realization dawned on him. "You don't think it got Jose, do you?" The tone in which he asked was like he thought I was pulling a prank on him. I wasn't sure how to answer.

"We need to kill it," I finally said.

We dismounted and tethered the horses to a tree several feet away. Sate didn't like it and tried to bite me, but I was wise to his temperament by now. When we got close to the big snake, he flicked his tongue at our presence but was simply too engorged to make an escape. Instead, he hissed angrily in an effort to frighten us.

"Let me, man," Jorge said nervously and readied his compound bow. Taking careful aim, he shot it just behind the left eye. The snake jerked with a couple of spasms and then remained still.

"What now?" he asked quietly. I answered by pulling my knife out of my pocket and locking the blade open. Jorge's eyes widened.

"It's got to be done," I said. I saw Jorge shaking now, but he didn't object when I waded the creek and approached the snake. I found a broken tree limb that was a couple of feet long and used it to poke it in the head several times to make sure it was truly dead before rolling it on its side.My knife was razor sharp and sliced open the snake's underside with little effort. Jorge gasped when the contents oozed out.

"Dios mio!" he wailed as he fell to his knees and suddenly began puking. In the mass of gore and ooze was the body of little Jose.

He was dressed only in his underwear and was almost unrecognizable, the snake's digestive acids had already began breaking down the tissue. As I squatted, looking at the remains, his eyes opened and he let out an infantile snarl. I stumbled back and fell into the shallow creek. Jose shakily reloaded his crossbow and put a bolt into his nephew's head.

I got my ass out of the creek and walked over beside him. Tears were falling in buckets down his cheeks. I got my canteen off of my pommel and handed it to him. He rinsed his mouth out and then took several swallows.

"How did he become infected, man?" he asked.

"I don't know." There were many possibilities of how he became infected before being eaten by that damned snake and I had no idea which one was the correct answer.

"I wonder where it came from."

"Well, Burmese Pythons aren't indigenous to the area." Jorge glanced at me. "They're not from around here. It might have been someone's pet or it might have come from the zoo. I don't know." We stood there in silence for several minutes. I was about to suggest a course of action when Jorge started talking.

"When we left Mexico, we lived in Louisiana for a month before we came to Tennessee. That was the first time I saw an alligator. They scared the shit out of me."

"They're definitely scary looking."

"I bet those sons of bitches are eating better than ever these days. They love to eat dead stuff." I nodded my head in agreement.

"We tried to go back to our old house the other day," he said. "We had Jose with us. There were zombies everywhere. We hightailed back here and told each other how we did a good job of protecting the little man."

"Yeah." I paused a moment. "Where's Jose's father?"

"He disappeared shortly after he was born."

"That was sometime around when it started, right?" He nodded.

"About a month before. Jose was born in October."

"He might have gotten killed or something."

"Yeah, maybe." It didn't seem like something he wanted to talk about, so I remained quiet. We sat there for several minutes while Jorge sobbed. When he got most of it out of his system, he turned to me.

"I want you to do me a favor, Zach."

"You name it."

"I want you to leave me alone with my nephew. Go find my father and tell him, but don't tell him where we're at. I don't want him to see his Nieto like this."

"Okay."

"And don't tell Maria. He and I have to do that. I'll clean him up and bring him home. Tell that to my father, he'll understand." He started sobbing again. I nodded and left without a word.

CHAPTER 23 – JOSE

Justin picked me up at the crack of dawn and the two of us prepared a grave on the grounds of a Catholic church nearby. Everyone else showed up about noon and Josue conducted a somber, yet simple service, mostly in Spanish. Maria sobbed loudly the entire time and was literally too weak to stand. Afterward, I asked them to come spend time with us. Jorge shook his head.

"We thank you, Zach, but we're going to spend some time alone." He leaned closer and lowered his voice to barely above a whisper.

"We've got to watch Maria and make sure she doesn't do something to herself. She's feeling very guilty about her hijo's death."

"I understand," I said. "Just remember, Marc and Ward are psychologists, they may be able to help her cope." Jorge nodded in understanding.

"Maybe in a few days," he said. "We'll see how it goes." His father nodded in agreement.

My arms and back were already aching from digging the grave, we dared not use precious fuel hauling a backhoe to the church, but Kelly wanted to spend the afternoon tending our garden plots. She called it therapeutic; all I could think of was how sore I was going to be when I rolled of bed in the morning."So, what I don't understand is how, and at what point, did little Jose turn into a zombie."

"I've no idea," I answered.

"Zach, that's awful. I don't know what I'd do if something like that happened to our kids." She caught her breath. "I mean, you're kids." I stopped hoeing and put an arm around her.

"I liked it better when you said they're our kids." She dropped her hoe and grabbed me in a hug. "They call you mommy after all."

"What about you?" she asked. "How do you feel about me?"

"You know I love you, you're my girl, right?" She responded by hugging me tighter.

"I knew you'd come around," she finally said. "But, since I'm older than you, I think that means you're my boy." I had to laugh.

After an extra-long hug, I held her at arm's length.

"It's only sixteen hundred, let's get the horses out and take a ride around the property, make sure nothing is going on. I'm sure Sarah won't mind watching the kids a couple more hours."

Sarah didn't mind at all and told us to have a good time with a small, knowing smile. I hurriedly saddled the horses and Kelly pulled out some extra blankets and tied them to the saddles. It didn't take long for us to end up at my favorite oak tree.

"Which one of you two picked this spot?" Kelly asked as we laid the blankets out.

"I did. There was a full moon that night."

"Ooh, you're so romantic." I chuckled as I used my binoculars to check the area.

"All good?"

"Yep," I replied and sat beside her.

"So, tell me about her."

"Macie?" I asked.

"Yeah."

"Well, let's see. We had a few classes together during our freshman year and started dating not too long after I got my driver's license. You know the rest."

"And she was your first love." I nodded. "And you lost her virginity to her."

"Right on this very spot." I leaned forward and kissed her.

"I think I'm jealous," she said huskily.

"You like this spot," I replied.

"For some kinky reason, I really do." She pulled me close and we kissed again.

It was dark by the time we rode the horses into the barn. Sarah met us at the door. She gave us a look, but didn't have any smartass remark.

CHAPTER 24 – DREAMS

"I want to talk to you about something and get your opinion," I said to Sarah. She had joined me on a sunrise run, each of us carrying assault weapons at port arms while we ran, and were now walking down the driveway getting our wind back. She looked over at me questioningly. I pointed at the scar that ran along the side of my head. Now that I was wearing my hair cropped Marine close, it was clearly visible.

"About two years ago I was shot upside the head."

"I wondered how you got that scar. Did it happen the same time you got the scar on your cheek?"

"No, that came later." I briefly recapped each incident. "The bullet didn't enter my skull, it only grazed the side of my head. Even so, it messed me up, but I lived through it."

"Are you sure?" she asked with a sarcastic grin.

"Okay, smartass. Anyway, as you can imagine, I had some cognitive issues for a while after that, but I eventually healed up." We stopped at the corral fence and used the top rail to stretch our hamstrings.

"Alright, so the point I'm getting at is about a month afterward, I started having some very vivid dreams."

"Nightmares?" Sarah asked.

"Sometimes."

"PTSD," she declared. "Post-Traumatic Stress Disorder. It happens. You don't seem any the worse for wear."

"No, it's not that. Well, I mean yeah, I probably have a little of that stuff going on up here," I said, tapping at my head. "Marc and Ward definitely think so, but the thing I'm trying to tell you is that sometimes I'd have dreams that would come true." Sarah paused in her stretching and looked at me quizzically, or maybe she was looking for indicators I'd gone off the deep end, I wasn't sure which. I continued anyway.

"At first it was very confusing, but after a while I was able to mostly figure out which ones were going to come true and which ones were just bullshit dreams."

"Do you have them often?" she asked with that look still on her face. I shook my head.

"Nope. In fact, I hadn't had one in a long time and I thought they'd stopped altogether. But, recently I've had the same dream about three times now."

"Alright, I'm game. What've you been dreaming?"

"Colonel Coltrane is alive and well, and he's coming back." Sarah took her leg off of the fence rail and replaced it with the other one.

"Oh yeah?" She said it in a deadpanned tone, and for a second I thought I was talking to Fred.

"He's not going to be alone, and I already know it's going to be an unpleasant encounter." Sarah cast a glance over at me.

"Okay, let's pretend for a moment that you're not, you know, off the deep end, cray-cray, loco, psychotic, looney-tunes—"

"Okay, okay," I interrupted. "Forget it."

"No, wait. Let's pretend you're dreams are perfectly normal. What's going to happen and what should we do?"

"Somehow, he knows my kids are here and he's coming back for them. He'll either try to take me too or kill me outright. What do I think I should do? Kill the son of a bitch, that's what I should do." She was now quiet for a couple of minutes. I couldn't tell if she was seriously thinking over what I said or trying to figure out the best way to placate the crazy guy. She stopped stretching and leaned against the fence.

"He'll most likely have the same armored vehicles he used last time. And, although they may not like him, any soldiers he has with him will instinctively obey him and protect him." I nodded in agreement.

"Unless, of course, in your dream they beam down from their orbiting space ships and you vanquish them with your trusty lightsaber," she added.

"Thanks for the vote of confidence," I replied with mock sincerity along with an eat-shit-and-die look. Now she grinned openly and shrugged.

"I'm a very skeptical person by nature."

"Yeah, no kidding. Well, if you don't believe me, you don't believe me." I finished stretching, lofted my feet up on the top rail and began doing pushups. Sarah, not to be outdone, quickly joined in. When we finished, Sarah wiped the sweat off her brow and looked at me inquisitively.

"Why did you tell me about this dream of yours? I mean, you had to know I'd be skeptical." I shrugged, a little self-conscious now.

"I'm not real sure. Back when Fred was alive, I'd talk to him about these things."

"Am I Fred's replacement for you?"

"I don't know, maybe," I replied. "I never really knew my parents, they both died when I was young. My first real father figure was a gruff old alcoholic. I think I told you about him." Sarah nodded.

"Then Fred came along. He was so much like Rick and yet so diametrically opposite of him, and yet I liked him almost immediately." I paused and looked at her. "He was a smartass too." She started to retort but I kept talking.

"Julie and Macie and I both thought the world of Fred. He became a father-figure to the three of us and he was usually the first person I went to when I needed advice. He was a very wise man and he seemed to think a lot of you, so…" Sarah responded with a short nod, and was quiet for a minute.

"I've got an idea or two about those armored vehicles," she finally said as we walked back to the house. I glanced at her. "The key is to get them to think there is no threat and get them out of the vehicles. The question is, do we kill them all?" She said that last sentence while we walked in the doorway and Kelly overheard it.

"What are you talking about?" she asked.

"The colonel and his soldiers are coming back," Sarah responded before I could say anything.

"But we don't know if they're coming in armored vehicles or space ships," she added. Our conversation was stalled when we heard a vehicle approaching. I cracked the door and peeked out with my shotgun.

"It's Justin and Ruth," I said and waited for a sign. Justin held two fingers out of the open window and I responded with the appropriate countersign.

"Good morning," I said after they'd parked and got out. They weren't smiling. Instead, there was anxiousness plainly etched on their faces.

"We need to talk to you," Justin declared.

"Alright."

"Well," Justin started, but hesitated. Ruth continued.

"We got the radio going."

"That's good," I said.

"The radio station's equipment was designed for transmitting only, not receiving, but long explanation short, we've rigged it so now not only can we transmit, we can receive."

"Let me guess, you made contact with your friends at the CDC," I said. Justin nodded.

"They're not at the CDC anymore, they're coming here. We talked to them not fifteen minutes ago. I had a brief but informative conversation with one of them."

"So, they're coming."

"Yep," Ruth answered. "The colonel has somehow figured out you and the kids are here. They're currently outside of Chattanooga."

I caught Sarah staring at me with a confused frown. At least she wasn't looking at me like I was bat-shit crazy now.

CHAPTER 24 – ALMOSE COLTRANE

"It's going to be tomorrow, I'm thinking," I commented over supper. Kelly looked at me in surprise. After Justin and Ruth's announcement, Sarah and I went with them to the school, filled them in, and we hatched a plan.

"Are you sure?"

"As sure as I can be," I responded. "The feeling is so strong I can practically smell them. So, are you ready?" She looked at me intently and nodded. I reached for her hand and gave it a gentle, reassuring squeeze. "Good. We leave after dark."

"Would you mind telling me where you're going to take them?" Sarah asked. I looked at Kelly.

"I think she needs to know," she suggested.

"It's difficult to explain, but Kelly and the kids are going to be staying somewhere else for a while."

"For how long?"

"It remains to be seen," I answered and looked at Sarah. "Alright, I need to call Justin on the radio to let him know and then we can head out. The truck is already loaded."

"They're all on board?" Kelly asked.

"I believe so." It all depended entirely on the school gang going along with the plan. After hearing me out, they had agreed in principal, but I had nothing but blind faith in them that they'd follow through. Justin seemed confident though.

"There are only a couple of people who know of this location," I explained to Sarah as I drove down Nolensville Pike. Kelly followed me in the Volvo truck. "The Allens were a family who originally lived here. They're gone now. So, the only other people who know about it are you and Kelly," I said.

"This will be the hideout for them?" she asked as she looked around the area.

"Yeah," I responded.

"Doesn't look like much," she observed.

"Exactly," I replied.

"Okay, I understand."

"Alright, sit tight a minute. I'm going to use this night vision gear and check things out." Not waiting for a response, I jumped out, and walked around scanning the area. Satisfied, I unlocked the door to the shop and got the truck parked in one of the service bays. Everyone was quiet except for Frederick. He seemed to think this was a fun adventure which required much verbiage.

When we had the truck unloaded and the kids settled, I gave them a kiss and told them I loved them. Kelly walked me to the door. I turned to her and hugged her tightly. When we separated, I knew it was time.

"I have a present I've been meaning to give you. I started to over Christmas but chickened out. Ever since then I never seemed to find the appropriate time. I was going to do it the other day under the tree, but I forgot it." I reached into my pocket and pulled out the diamond ring. I'd given it a meticulous cleaning and it sparkled from the candlelight. Kelly gasped when she saw it. I gently put it on her finger, kissed her, and hurriedly got in the truck before I ruined it by saying something stupid.

"How long are you going to keep them there?" Sarah asked as I drove the two of us back home. I thought I'd already explained everything and wasn't much in a talking mood, but I went over it again.

"The plan is, if everything works out, I'll come back and get them as soon as possible."

"And if it doesn't?"

"She knows if I don't show up, it means I'm dead or imprisoned. She promised me she'd stay hidden for a minimum of two weeks."

"Two weeks?" She asked. "Zach, that's far too long for a woman to be pent up with two rambunctious kids." She was right, but it didn't stop me from frowning at her in the dark. I tried to explain.

"Hypothetically, if the colonel kills me, I believe he'll stay in the area for a few days trying to find the kids. I don't know his current state of mind, but a worst case scenario is he'll torture people in an effort to find out where they are. That's one of the reasons why nobody knows of this place." I watched her as I said this, trying to gauge her reaction, which was hard to do while wearing the night vision gear.

"I suppose that could be possible," she finally replied.

"She knows it's going to be tough, but she also knows it's for the best."

"Okay, I can see the rationale."

"So, after two weeks, I left it up to her to decide the best course of action. She's gotten pretty good at driving that Volvo. She'll either go back to the school or go elsewhere. We've discussed a few possible alternative locations." I shrugged in the dark. "It'll be up to her. If she comes to you, I hope you'll take care of them."

"Of course I will, assuming that I haven't been killed as well. You're convinced it's going to happen tomorrow?"

"Yeah, I'm pretty sure they're only about eighty or ninety miles from here. I figure they'll be moving somewhere between ten to twenty miles per hour, which puts them arriving in about eight hours. I don't believe they'll travel at night, but make no mistake, they're on their way."

We drove the rest of the way back home in silence. I went straight to bed, but sleeping was not easy. I awoke several times during the night, reaching out a hand in the dark only to find an empty space on the bed beside me. After a dozen or so of these episodes, I finally decided sleep was a futile effort and got up well before sunup.

It was a beautiful May sunrise filled with streaks of crimson and violet hues, and although the morning air was cool, it was nothing a light windbreaker couldn't offset. Everyone was busy setting up tables we'd put in the parking lot of the school. Plus, Sarah's perch on the radio tower offered her an excellent field of fire. When we were finished with our preparations, we waited impatiently. I paced nervously for a while until Tonya finally had enough and motioned toward a chair.

"You're irritating the hell out of me. Sit down and try to relax." She was right, although I didn't say it. I reluctantly sat. She lit one of those things that looked like a cigarette but you filled it with marijuana and offered it to me. I shook my head. I wanted my wits about me, nervous or not.

"I can't tell you how many times I rolled a joint out of toilet tissue or newspaper before I found one of these things."

"I take it you didn't smoke weed until after everything went bad."

"Nope. I thought only idiots smoked it." She gave a lazy chuckle. "If only I knew." She puffed on it for a minute until she'd burned off its contents.

"This should more than redeem ourselves in your eyes," she said as she gestured at everything. I cleared my throat.

"Whatever happens, I want you to know how much I appreciate it." She was silent, but finally responded with a small nod.

"The odds are, I may be killed. If that happens, Kelly will most likely come back here. Sarah said she'd look after her, but I'd be most grateful if you'd help her out, if she needs it."

"You're assuming they don't kill all of us along with you."

"There's only one reason that bastard is coming back here, for me and my kids. As long as you guys sit out here doing nothing more than feeding them, he won't perceive you as a threat."

Tonya grunted. "I hope you're right." Me too, I thought. If this didn't work out the way we'd planned, I'd be killed and these people were going to suffer. Oh, Sarah could probably kill a few of them, but any decent M60 gunner would be able to take her out once they zeroed in on her.

They arrived just after noon. I was surprised. There were only eight of them and instead of riding in those armored vehicles, they were in two dirty Humvees. They turned off of Concord and into the parking lot slowly, almost casually. We all waved cheerfully as they nosed their vehicles toward us and parked. I stood so they'd have no problem spotting me.

"Only eight people out of over two hundred?" Ruth muttered questioningly.

"And no children," I added. "Not good."

We waited expectantly. As rehearsed, none of us had weapons visible. They were instead hidden under the picnic tables, held by makeshift brackets that Justin had hurriedly assembled last night.

While two soldiers manned machine guns mounted on the top of the Humvees, Colonel Coltrane sat in the passenger seat, staring. He somehow looked older, leaner, darker. His coal-colored eyes fixated on me like a malevolent demon. This was not the same man I'd met almost a year ago. It was like he'd transformed, mutated. He eyeballed all of us for a minute, opened the door to the Humvee, and stepped out. He stood there then, square shouldered, gazing intensely, like a Caesar among the plebeians.

Janet stepped out next. I wasn't surprised. She looked no worse for wear. In fact, for a woman in her forties, she actually looked pretty good. It looked like she had even colored and styled her hair; not a gray strand in sight. She made eye contact, and if I didn't know better, I'd swear she was happy to see me.

Sergeant Smithson was the first to meet him. He too was wearing a clean uniform. He stood at attention and saluted. The colonel returned his salute before catching himself, causing him to glare balefully at the sergeant.

"So, my suspicions were right," he growled.

"Sir, when the CDC was in danger of being overrun, we secured the two Gunderson children and escaped."

"And you took it upon yourselves to bring them back here," he said calmly, but there was an underlying anger in his voice. "Why?" he asked.

"Because it was the right thing to do, sir," Ruth answered.

"I must agree," Major Parsons added. The Colonel stared hard at his three Marines for a moment and then a slow, hard smile crept across his face. He then turned to me and placed his hand on his sidearm, which, at the moment, was secure in his holster. I tried to return his smile but it probably looked like I was straining to pass a kidney stone. I held out my hands in a placating gesture, hoping he couldn't see through my deception.

"As you can see, Colonel, I'm not armed. Nobody is armed. So, there is no cause for violence. In fact, we welcome your presence." I hoped I sounded convincing. For all I knew, he'd probably order his soldiers to open fire at any second. None of them were smirking or making any threatening gestures, but just the same, they all looked very tense.

"We shall see, Mister Gunderson, we shall see," Colonel Coltrane said, almost under his breath. He slowly looked around, like a snake looking for prey, and spotted the picnic tables topped with trays of food. Rhonda, Kate, and Kyra were busily waving homemade fans to keep the flies off. We'd taken all of the kids and locked them in one of the school rooms.

"What the hell have you people got going on here?"

"Lunch," I answered.

"Are you people expecting company?"

"Indeed we are," I replied, "you." The colonel now looked surprised.

"You were expecting us?" he asked. I nodded with my best used car salesman smile.

"I bet you're people are hungry, Colonel. Why don't y'all have a seat and dig in before the flies eat it all?" I suggested. He now smiled smugly.

"I believe we will, Mister Gunderson." He turned toward his group and ordered them to exit their vehicles. Based on their clothing, it looked like they were a loose mixture of civilians and soldiers. One of the soldiers, a Marine, didn't dismount. Instead, he stayed put and manned one of the M60s. He was pretty scrawny and looked worried. His finger was not currently on the trigger and I hoped it stayed that way.

"So, you were expecting us," Coltrane repeated again.

"How could you stay away, Colonel? After all, you have only one purpose in this world now, and it involves me, am I right?"

"You *and* your children," he said in a low, menacing baritone. Janet, who was standing beside him, glanced at him before returning her gaze at me. Her expression was unreadable now.

"Where are they?" he demanded.

"They're gone, sir," Ruth exclaimed suddenly.

"And you'll never see them again," I added. His stare was unflinching. It was a cold, evil stare and he smiled without humor.

"I'll deal with you later," he replied menacingly to Ruth and focused back on me.

"You will turn over your children immediately or I will kill everyone here, one by one."

"Just like you did back at my farm? Just like you killed my wife and friends?" I asked. He smiled again. He was smiling too much, and the more he smiled the harder it was for me to keep up the façade.

"So, I see we understand each other," he replied, almost boisterously. "When we arrived at your quaint little home back last September, I tried to deal with them in a reasonable manner."

"If I understand correctly, you ordered my children be handed over, or else."

"I see Corporal Bullington has told you what happened. Did she tell you your petulant little wife had the audacity to call me a vulgar name before firing a shot at me?" he asked. He made it sound like Julie had committed a heinous sin and scoffed in contempt.

"There was nothing more to do but eliminate the obstacle, and as with all obstacles, I remove them and complete the mission." He stared at me dispassionately.

"In the end, I will win again and we will pick up where we left off."

Our plan was working, sort of. He had just admitted to his responsibility for the massacre. He said it loud and clear, everyone heard him. Everyone except Sarah, who was three hundred yards away staring at us through the scope of her sniper rifle, waiting for the signal. Once I raised my hand, she was going to put a bullet in his head.

And then, before any of us could say or do anything, Janet did something that was totally unexpected. Standing close beside the Colonel, a rather small piece of a rectangular metal object appeared in her hand from nowhere. It was seemingly a graceful, innocent act. One might have thought she was wiping a smudge from her lover's face as she reached up to him. The edge of the straight razor caught a sliver of sunlight as it glided across the colonel's neck. He instinctively grabbed his throat and looked at Janet in confusion.

"That's for murdering my daughter, you sonofabitch," she icily declared.

He held his throat with one hand and tried grabbing for her with the other, but he was too slow. She deftly stepped back and watched dispassionately as he slowly fell to the ground, the pulsing blood squirting out between his fingers. Everyone was in shock. The lone Marine manning the machine gun was the first to react and turned it toward her.

"Wait!" I shouted. It was too late, but he was lucky. The bullet hit the Marine's machine gun right at the feed tray. He jerked back in surprise as shrapnel spewed out from the impact. I had no idea if Sarah was that good of a shot or her aim was off. Either way, it worked, it frightened everyone. That was the signal, and most of our group reacted quickly by retrieving their hidden weapons. A couple of CDC people grabbed their assault weapons.

"Don't move!" Sergeant Smithson shouted. "Take your hands off of those weapons if you want to live. That's an order!"

"We have snipers deployed," I quickly added. "Don't do anything that'll get you killed." There was confusion written on all of their faces, but they reluctantly obeyed as Cutter and Shooter aggressively pointed their weapons at them. It was obvious they were eager for action. Marc and Ward, not so much. The women, even Tonya, had opted not to arm themselves when we'd planned this out. It was hoped this would work out to their advantage if we were on the losing end of this goat fuck.

We held them at gunpoint as Ruth and Tonya disarmed them. Thankfully, there was no resistance. Their collective body language was not that of hostility or aggression; I didn't even see an angry sneer.

"Private Mann, stand down and join the others," Justin ordered. The young soldier complied without complaint, looking around nervously as he did so. I guess he was wondering where our snipers were and if he was about to be shot at again.

At about that time, Janet seemed to come out of her reverie. She dropped the straight razor and plopped heavily to the ground. I looked around at this group of people carefully. None of them seemed particularly interested in Janet, or the colonel for that matter. They looked tired; their faces were etched with a greasy mixture of grime and fatigue. The death of the colonel increased their level of anxiety exponentially. I knew I had to do something and made direct eye contact with each of them as I began speaking.

"Listen up, you people. We've no quarrel with any of you," I proclaimed. "Unless you were involved in the massacre of my family." I glanced at Justin, who was now armed with one of the soldier's compact assault rifles and eyed the newcomers closely. "Sergeant Smithson?" I asked.

"Zach, with the exception of Private Mann here, all of these people are from the CDC. Private Mann was on guard duty back at Fort Campbell on that particular day in question." I looked over at the young enlisted man. If he enlisted right out of high school, he was probably around twenty or twenty-one, well under six feet, as dirty as the rest, maybe even more so, and skinny as a rail. I wondered why he was still a Private. Marc spoke up.

"Zach, I don't recognize any of these people either," he said. Ward and Tonya voiced their agreement. "None of them came to the school that day."

Justin walked over and stood in front of one of the soldiers, looking him up and down. He was wearing combat utilities that had a different pattern than Justin's and his nametag said Caswell.

"Do you know that one?" I asked. Justin nodded.

"He's Regular Army and somehow ended up at the CDC. How are you, Caswell?" Justin asked.

"Not so good, Gunny," he replied. "It's been a long, rough road lately, even more than usual." In fact, he didn't look so good. As with the rest of his comrades, his face was in bad need of soap, water, and a shave. Ruth walked over and stood by Justin.

"What happened after we left?" she asked. He shook his head tiredly.

"I've no idea when you guys left," he replied, "but the fight lasted for a full three days and I don't think any of us slept the entire time." He looked over at the colonel's lifeless body. "Well, most of us."

"Damn," Justin muttered. From the look on his face, I sensed he was feeling a little guilty for leaving his comrades.

"Yeah, it was bad." Caswell gestured around. "Some others escaped, they took the LAVs, but as far as I know, this is all that's left." He then pointed over at a freckle-face woman with brown hair peeking out from under her Kevlar helmet. It was hard to tell what her age was, I guessed somewhere around thirty.

"That's Sergeant Benoit." Sergeant Benoit touched her finger to her helmet in the form of a salute. Sergeant Caswell continued. "She's been the ad hoc commo officer for the past couple of months."

"You're the one I spoke to last night," Justin said to her. She nodded.

"Tell them about POTUS," Caswell told her. She cleared her throat and took her helmet off, causing a whole heap of dirty brown hair to fall out.

"After the attack, Colonel Coltrane directed me to contact POTUS with a SITREP." She saw some confused looks and explained.

"A SITREP is a situation report. When we informed them what'd happened, POTUS, the President, ordered us to relocate." She paused and hastened a glance at Colonel Coltrane. The pool of blood continued to grow steadily around him. His face was now only a vacant contorted stare, his brain's fading electrical impulses firing an occasional twitch through his lifeless body. Janet sat motionless on the ground, staring into empty space.

"We were supposed to go directly to his location, but the colonel had other plans." Her voice drifted off at the last and she couldn't stop staring at the now lifeless body.

"Alright, all of you listen up," I said loudly and pointed at the colonel. "Not very long ago, that man ordered the abduction of my children and me, and then ordered the massacre of five people, which he just admitted to in front of all of you. Now I'm no expert on military law, but I've been told what he did is tantamount to a war crime which is punishable by death."

"I don't know what tantamount means," Sergeant Caswell said quickly. "But we had no part in your people being killed."

"I believe you," I said. "That's the only reason you're still alive." He nodded but it didn't stop any of them from looking around nervously. I smiled inwardly, knowing we had successfully planted the belief we had several snipers deployed rather than only one. Our plan was working. Even more so since Janet decided to get in on it.

"Where is the President currently residing?" I asked.

"A place known as Raven Rock," Lieutenant Benoit said. "It's one of those underground bunker facilities located in Pennsylvania." I nodded thoughtfully and looked at Grant. He shrugged.

"News to me, but it seems logical." I didn't see any reason for her to lie about something like that; I'd talk it over with them later. I gestured at her rank.

"I see you have more stripes than Sergeant Caswell." Sergeant Benoit nodded.

"I'm an E-6, a Staff Sergeant. Sergeant Caswell is an E-5."

"That would make you the ranking NCO in charge of your group, am I right?" She reluctantly nodded. "What are you going to do now?"

She looked confused, as if the rank hierarchy of their group meant little. She brushed a strand of hair out of her face and frowned a moment.

"I suppose we'll continue with our original mission and relocate to Pennsylvania." She looked at Sergeant Caswell for confirmation. He didn't look like he had the energy to offer any type of input on the situation and didn't even bother acknowledging.

"Fair enough," I said. "I have a suggestion though. It would be a shame for you people not to enjoy a healthy meal before hitting the road, maybe even get a shower and a good night's sleep first." Their first response was a muted expression of disbelief. Sergeant Caswell finally looked around at his comrades and cleared his throat.

"You're inviting us to stay?"

"Listen up," Justin said authoritatively. "You all know me, so you know you can take my word when I say you can trust these people."

"When's the last time you all have had a good meal?" Ruth asked.

"Not since the attack," Sergeant Caswell replied. "I guess a good meal would help out," he said and looked around again. There were several nods of agreement now.

"What about the colonel?" Sergeant Benoit asked. My expression hardened.

"He belongs to me." There was an open challenge in my tone, but nobody argued.

Justin and I wrapped the colonel's body in an old dirty blanket and loaded him into the bed of my truck. We used some baby wipes that'd expired two years ago to wipe the blood off of our hands and Justin started to get in the truck before I stopped him. I motioned for Tonya and Ruth to come closer.

"Let me talk to you three," I said in a low voice. "If you don't mind, why don't y'all stay here?" I suggested. "You and Ruth know those people. The soldiers might be questioning their duty and obligations right now and you two know how to talk to soldiers. Y'all can straighten them out and calm them down." I looked around.

"Besides, those two knuckleheads might start agitating them into a fight."

"If you're referring to Cutter and Shooter, I'll take care of them," Tonya said. I nodded gratefully.

"Yeah, okay, it makes sense," Justin said. "What're you going to do with the colonel?"

"Rule number eight, Sergeant Smithson. You have to burn the corpses."

Janet insisted on riding with me. That was okay because I was going to finally take care of her, like I should have done a long time ago. I radioed Sarah and brought her up to speed. She replied that she was going to stay on her perch for a little while longer and keep an eye on things.

The church was out of the question. I wasn't going to bury this man on consecrated ground, oh no. Instead, I drove a couple of miles down to an old rock quarry on Nolensville Pike. We'd used it before.

There would be no honorable funeral. I dumped him out of the truck without ceremony, threw a bunch of debris and fuel on top of him, and set it on fire. Janet watched me in silence. As I watched him burn, I contemplated how I was going to kill her. Shooting her would be the most humane, but I wasn't sure I wanted to waste the bullet. I decided I was going to slit her throat just like she did to the Colonel and throw her body on top of him. It would be a fitting end. But, as I started to reach for my knife, she started talking.

"When those armored vehicles drove up the road back on that day, Julie had ordered me to take the kids down into the basement. I hid like a coward while she tried to protect us. When they killed everyone and found us, I begged him for my life," she said. "He was going to kill me anyway until I told him I was the kids' grandmother and I could care for them. He seemed to find something funny about it, but it worked and he took me with them. All I wanted to do was protect the babies, but I also wanted revenge.

"At first, I thought the key was the major. I thought I could recruit him as an ally and he'd help me, so I seduced him." She was staring straight ahead, but hastened a brief glance at me.

"It's not hard to seduce men like him, but it was a wasted effort. It took me a week before I realized Major Parsons was nothing more than a lamb. He was a follower, one doctor among other doctors. " She gave a short, humorless scoff.

"Realizing he couldn't help me, I intended to kill him one night in his sleep, but he really isn't a bad person.

"I thought about it endlessly. I knew the only way to save the kids was to kill Coltrane, and I'd have to do it on my own. So, the first thing I did was seduce him." She gave another short, humorless laugh.

"I was successful the first time I flirted with him, and that was about an hour after I'd slept with the major. You see, I did it because I wanted to gain his trust. At first he just used me as his own personal whore and would throw me out of his room after he had his way with me. But I stuck with it and he soon became comfortable with me. But, every time I had the opportunity, I lost my nerve. Plus, I knew I'd be killed afterward and I still wasn't sure how the kids would be treated."

I listened quietly. Tears were running down her cheeks, but I don't think it was because her recently deceased lover was sizzling and crackling not ten feet from us. She waited as I drug a log over and tossed it on top of the pyre before continuing.

"It was pretty chaotic when those things attacked us. We were trapped for a little over two days. When we made it down to the ground floor, one of those soldiers told the colonel he saw Grant and the other two leaving with the kids. When he heard that, he went nuts."

"So, I was right about him," I said, mostly to myself. Janet nodded. "You were planning on killing him all along?" She nodded again.

"The kids were the only obstacle at that point. I could have done him any number of times while he lay there asleep beside me, but I didn't chance it. I had no idea who was with Grant at that time, but my intuition told me they were going to come back here."

"You decided to wait," I surmised. She let out a long sigh.

"Yes. I didn't know what to do at first, and then I hatched a plan. An ingenious, evil plan that even you would admire."

"You're the one who talked him into coming back here," I exclaimed suddenly. Her lips stretched into a tight thin line; perhaps it was supposed to be a smile.

"Yes. I had to be certain they were okay. When we drove up and I saw you, that's when I finally knew. See, I thought you were dead too. That's what they'd told me. When I saw you, I knew you had the kids and I knew it was time. When you brought up Julie's murder and he..." Her voice cracked and she started sobbing. "He smiled. The bastard smiled about her death. He stood there, smiling like he'd done something wonderful."

She didn't have to explain further. We watched his remains burn in silence.

CHAPTER 25 – JANET

I couldn't kill her.

Janet Frierson, my mother-in-law, the only surviving grandparent of my children, had been an insufferable pain in my butt off and on for a long time now. I'd sworn to myself more than once I needed to kill her, but in the end I couldn't do it.

"We're going back to the school and I'm going to ask if they'll be gracious enough to put you up for the night."

"Zach, what about my grandbabies, are they okay?"

"Yes, they're fine. They're with Kelly."

"Kelly?" I nodded. "I thought she was killed too," she said quietly.

"So did everyone else, but she's alive and well. I'll tell you about it sometime. You should know, she and I are together now." I let that sink in and waited to see if she had some kind of snide remark. If she did, I was going to kick her out of the truck right then and there. Thankfully for her, she kept any opinion she may have had in the matter to herself.

"Can I please see the kids?" she asked pleadingly.

"Not today. Tomorrow, perhaps."

"And then what happens?" Yeah, it was a good question. I sighed deeply as I thought it over.

"I'm going to discuss it with Kelly and I'll ask her if it would be okay if you lived with us." I couldn't believe the words that were coming out of my mouth, nor could I imagine this bitch living under my roof.

"With my grandbabies?" she asked. I nodded. "I'd really like that," she said quietly.

"If she says no, I'm going to respect her decision and I'll get you located somewhere else." I stopped the truck and stared at her.

"I want you to understand this next part very clearly. If she agrees, I expect you to be a positive influence in the family, especially with your grandkids."

"You can count on it, Zach."

"And, I don't want to see any of that old Janet Frierson crap." She looked confused at this statement, so I jogged her memory. "Like the time you plotted to kill Rick and me, remember that?" Her face paled a bit and she looked at the floorboards. "That kind of bullshit is over with. Do I make myself clear?" She swallowed heavily before responding.

"You won't have to worry about any of that, I only want to be with the kids." I stared at her for a long thirty seconds, wondering if I was going to regret this decision. I hadn't realized my left hand was now resting on my thigh, my little finger actually touching the end of my lock-blade knife where it peaked out of my pocket. It stayed there for a moment longer, before I took my foot off of the brake.

When we got back to the school, everyone was eating their lunch in a subdued silence. Justin jogged over to meet me as I got out of my truck, but stopped short when he saw Janet. I walked over to him.

"How's everything?" I asked.

"I believe everyone is going to be alright. I've invited them to stay as long as they needed to rest up and recuperate." He saw the expression on my face. "All weapons are being stored in the radio house, but I promised to return them when they left." I nodded as he eyed Janet, who had not moved from the passenger seat. "What's up with her?"

"I'll explain in a minute." I turned toward Janet.

"Did you bring anything with you?"

"I have a bag in Al's - in the Colonel's Humvee."

"Why don't you go get it and put it in the truck," I suggested. She did so without complaint. I saw Sarah talking to the soldier who identified herself as Sergeant Benoit and motioned her over. When Janet was out of earshot, Justin lowered his voice to just above a whisper. The smartass in me would point out that the proper term is *sotto voce*.

"I thought you were going to kill her." I nodded slightly.

"Yeah, I thought about it." I started to explain why I didn't, but found myself at a loss for words. Justin must have sensed it and nodded his head in understanding.

"I hope you made the right call, bro," Justin said and then stopped talking as Janet walked up and tossed her bag in the back before getting in.

"Is it over, Zach?" I looked at the ground and sighed heavily.

"I think so. At least, it is with Coltrane, but who knows what's down the road. Only time will tell."

"I understand," he said. I wasn't going to go on and on about the soldiers who went to my house and killed everyone. Maybe they were all dead, maybe some, or all of them were still alive. I'd deal with it if I ever found them.

"What's going on?" Sarah asked when she joined us. I briefly filled her in.

"So, I have a favor to ask you." Here it goes. "Would you mind if Janet stayed in the tour bus with you for the night? I'm not so sure it'd be safe for her to stay here with these soldiers. They might take it personally." She stared at me pointedly.

"It's your bus, Zach. Your call."

"It'll just be for one night. I'd like some quality time with Kelly and I'm going to ask her if it'd be okay if Janet lives with us."

"Alright, I understand. Suggest to her that she should behave herself."

"I will." I turned to Justin.

"I'm going to get my family." Justin grinned.

"You do that; I'll take care of everything around here." He reached out his hand and we shook, which turned into a hug.

"We won, Zach," he said as he slapped me on the back. "I thought for certain we were all dead."

"Nah, we had an angel watching over us," I said and quickly grabbed Sarah in a hug. She smiled, in spite of herself.

"Alright, I'm going home. I'll see you guys first thing in the morning, say about seven."

"We're living at Fred's house now," I explained as I drove. "I'm going to drop you at Rowdy's bus for the night. Sarah, that's the Air Force Officer I was talking to, has been staying there and she agreed to let you stay there for the night."

"Oh, she's going to *allow* me to stay there?" Janet asked with a little bit of a haughty tone.

"Yes, she is. I thought it was very nice of her, considering. Now, let me tell you something. Things have changed since you've been gone. You should consider yourself a guest and treat your hosts graciously." She didn't answer, and instead pursed her lips.

"Right?" I admonished.

"Okay, I will."

"I hope so, Sarah has a low tolerance level." A few minutes later, I drove up to the tour bus.

"I'll come by and get you in the morning and have an answer for you."

"Please bring the kids with you."

"I will."

In spite of my anxiousness to see my loved ones, I took a roundabout route back to the old tire shop. I turned onto Old Hickory Boulevard a couple of miles west of the shop and started working my way toward it when I came upon three zombies aimlessly wandering down the road.

"Fuckers," I muttered as I stopped the truck. They were all young men, maybe even my age. I stared at them a moment trying to see if I recognized any of them before remembering I had three very important people I was on my way to pick up. All three pressed their ugly faces up against the protective wiring and one of them attempted to open the door. They made it easy. I used the little Marlin twenty-two and quickly put some rounds into their brain pans.

Per our prior discussion, I briefly flashed my lights, letting her know that it was safe on my end. After a few seconds, Kelly reciprocated with a flashlight through a window. I jumped out and met her at the door as she unlocked it. When she had the door open, I stepped inside and grabbed her in a hug.

"I have quite a story to tell you," I said as my kids began demanding attention. I went over to the couch they were sitting on and gave them each a hug. It looked like they'd been going to town with some coloring books. Even the coffee table had been drawn on. Kelly sat beside me.

"What happened?"

"Let's get out of here, I'll explain on the way." I said. She smiled and we began hurriedly packing up the kids' clothes. "We'll come back for the semi later," I said. Kelly didn't argue.

"She really cut his throat?" she asked.

"Yeah." After getting home, we had an upbeat dinner, with the exception of Frederick wanting to throw some of his vegetables instead of eating them. Callahan ran over and sniffed them, but didn't eat them. Apparently, he didn't like vegetables either. We got them to bed early. Satisfied, Kelly and I made a beeline to our own bed where, after some quiet but intense lovemaking, I filled in some of the blanks that I didn't want the kids to hear.

"Holy shit," she said when I had finished the story. "Where is she now?"

"She's staying the night in the bus with Sarah." Kelly chuckled.

"Poor Sarah."

"Yeah, it's just for the night, but she's going to need a place to live," I said tentatively.

"Are you asking me if she can live here?"

"She could be a big help with the kids, and around the house." Kelly was silent for a long moment. I was afraid of this.

"If you say no, it's no problem. We can put her up in one of the houses around here. I don't think she and Sarah could live under the same roof and Tonya is probably the same way, although I can ask."

"No, she's staying here," she said, although there was no joy in her tone. "I hope she'll behave herself."

CHAPTER 26 – UNANIMOUS

I was the first one up in the morning and I hurried out to flip the circuit breakers, hoping for a nice hot shower with Kelly. It was a little difficult waking her up, but I insisted.

"It feels wonderful," she said.

"Anything for my girl," I responded as I soaped her up. She smiled at my antics.

"You're being awfully attentive."

"I missed you," I replied. "Spending a night without you disrupted my Zen." Kelly chuckled.

"That's a unique way of putting it, but I agree." We kissed each other deeply. "What's on the agenda today?" she asked.

"I promised Justin I'd meet them at seven. Do you want to go?" I asked as I soaped up.

"I'd love to, but do you think the kids will be safe?" She made a good point.

"You and I are going to have our M4s in our hands the entire time. If anyone even looks at them the wrong way…" I rinsed off quickly and hopped out of the shower.

Sarah was sitting outside reading a book when we drove up. She dog-eared a page and stood as we got out and gave Kelly a hug.

"How'd it go?" I asked. Sarah shrugged.

"She ate a little bit and then passed out. She was pretty exhausted. How'd it go with you guys?" she asked Kelly.

"It was a very long twenty-one hours and seventeen minutes without my sweetie, but we're all good now," Kelly said with a grin and casually held up her hand, showing off the diamond ring. Sarah looked at it and eyed me.

"I take it the two of you are engaged?"

"I suppose so," I replied and looked at Kelly, who was giving me one of those looks.

"I mean, yes, we are totally, absolutely engaged." Sarah smiled and tousled my short hair.

"Oh, and we talked last night. Janet's going to move in with us. I'm going to find another bed and move it into the kids' room."

"I think she'll like that," Sarah said. "She talked about it a little last night and was worried you two would reject her." Janet must have heard us. She stepped out of the bus and tried to put on a cheerful smile.

"How'd you sleep?" I asked. She started to answer and then saw the kids sitting in the truck. This time her cheerful smile was genuine as she opened the door and hugged them both. Kelly nudged me.

"Okay, I didn't like it, but maybe it's a good idea after all," she whispered.

"Time will tell," I whispered back and then spoke up.

"We're heading over to the school." Janet's smile immediately disappeared.

"I don't think I can do that," she said worriedly. "Can't I go home?" I felt Kelly touch my shoulder.

"I'll take her home."

"Yeah," Sarah added. "Ride with me, Zach, and I'll bring you home after."

We arrived at the school promptly at seven. Surprisingly, there were two guards on duty. One of them was Private Mann, the other one was Gus. I looked at the Marine warily. He'd cleaned up since yesterday. I suppose Tonya allowed them to shower. He saw me studying him.

"I'm thinking you're not so sure you care for me," he said.

"Yeah, I guess you could say that."

"I don't want any trouble," he said. "Gunny's given us the rundown and told us the rules." I nodded slowly, not having much to say on the matter. I looked around and saw some stakes in the ground off to the side of the drive. It looked like someone was planning on building something.

"I don't believe I've ever seen two guards on duty at one time," I commented.

"Sergeant Smithson is making changes," Gus said with a disapproving frown while the Private looked at us curiously.

"What is this?" I asked.

"We measured it all out about an hour ago. Gunny is going to build a guard tower here," the Private replied and pointed. "He said we're also going to dig a trench along the road all the way to the Interstate and have an LP too."

"Yeah, whatever that is," Gus said sarcastically. The private eyed him before speaking.

"Everyone is inside waiting on you two." I nodded and found a place to park.

The aromas of a freshly prepared breakfast permeated the school and made my mouth water as soon as we walked inside, and even the atmosphere seemed upbeat. Everyone was chatting between mouthfuls. Ruth saw us as we walked in and fast stepped our way.

"We have some big news, but first I want to introduce you two to the rest of the group." She walked us over to a table where all of them were sitting off to the side.

"For all of you who didn't meet them yesterday, this is Zach and Sarah." She pointed at a couple who were sitting together.

"That's Mike and Mary Wagner, they're nurses." Both stood and smiled nervously as they shook our hands. They were a pleasant-looking couple, dark skinned, friendly expressions. Ruth continued and pointed to each as she named them.

"I think you guys met Sergeant Benoit yesterday, her first name is Rachel. Sergeant Caswell's first name is Brandon, and that's Specialist Gentry Franks. All three of them are Regular Army."

"Call me Goober," Specialist Franks said as he stood with a grin. "Everyone else does." He shook our hands exuberantly. He was lanky with an overly long neck which he attempted to abrogate by keeping his head dipped low. "I sure appreciate y'all not killing us."

"You sound like you're a southern boy," I said. Goober nodded.

"Born and raised in a little town outside of Raleigh, North Carolina. It wasn't called Mayberry though," he said, laughing at his own joke.

"And you saw Private Mann outside with Gus," Justin said. "I'm going to go relieve them in a minute."

"But first, we have some news," Ruth said. "We talked long into the night and a vote was taken."

"Oh?"

"And it was unanimous."

"What was unanimous?" Sarah asked.

"All of them want to stay here," Ruth proclaimed. I looked at Justin in surprise.

"We're tired, Zach," Mike, the nurse, said. "All of us have been walking on a tight wire for the past few years and when the colonel arrived, it got even worse."

"We just want a place to live in peace and quiet," his wife added. "We want a place we can call home."

The rest of them nodded in agreement.

"I woke up this morning to children laughing and playing," she continued. "It was a pleasant way to wake up."

"That's wonderful," Sarah said as she eyed Rachel. Kelly agreed. When I didn't reply immediately, she goosed me in the ribs.

"Yeah, sounds good." I know it didn't sound very welcoming, but it was the only thing I could think of at the moment.

"So, counting the colonel and Janet, only eight of you got out?" I asked. I'd chosen to sit with the newcomers, hurriedly ate a plate, and now had my notepad out and asking questions as quickly as I could write.

"There may have been some others who escaped," Mary, a buxom woman with a distinct Jamaican accent, said. "There were some of those big military vehicles missing when we made it down to the garage."

"And the LAVs were gone," Goober added and looked at me. "That stands for Light Armored Vehicles." I already knew that, but I smiled and nodded politely.

"There might have been others on the upper floors," Mike said. "But, we had no way of getting to them. We were communicating with handheld radios, but when the generators died, we had no way of recharging them."

"Yeah, when the generators ran out of fuel, everything went dark except for the battery-operated emergency lights, but that just seemed to add to the eeriness of the whole thing," Mike said.

"It was pretty chaotic," Mary emphasized.

"We could hear gunfire on the other floors," Brandon added and looked around. "But it eventually stopped. We didn't know if that meant they'd killed off the zombies or they'd been overrun."

"What was the issue with the generators?" I asked.

"Them doctors insisted on running those generators all day," Goober said. "Me and a couple others tried to tell them we only had a limited amount of fuel, but they wouldn't listen to us. So, they dried up right at the worst time." He shook his head and rubbed his face.

"The generators were set up in the parking garage," Goober continued. "A group was told to go down there and use the diesel from the vehicles to refill the tanks and get them restarted. They never got them restarted and they never came back."

"We think they're the ones who took the LAVs," Brandon said. "You know, sinking ship and rats, all that stuff." He then realized he was also speaking about Justin, Ruth, and Grant. "No offense."

"Can't say I blame them," Goober muttered.

"Gunny was smart, they left right when it all started," Brandon continued. "We waited a little over three days before the colonel finally gave the order to evacuate." He shook his head in disgust. "A lot of good people died in those three days." That must have been around the time Janet planted the seed, I thought.

"What was the plan?" I asked.

"Work our way to the parking garage, load up the LAVs, and bug out. Getting down to the parking garage was fairly easy, but once we got there we lost ten people."

"They'd found a way in and were waitin' on us," Goober said. I looked at Brandon, who shrugged.

"I don't know if they were expecting us, but there was a bunch of them massed around the doors. I'd say there were about a hundred or more."

"What happened?"

"We took them out, but like I said, it cost us ten in the exchange." He looked sidelong at his companions. "The colonel seemed to think that was perfectly okay. Anyway, the plan was to take the LAVs, but obviously they were gone. So, we took the Humvees, which don't offer much protection. The only saving grace was Goober and Mann; they manned the M60s and cleared us a path. It wasn't until we were clear of Atlanta that Colonel Coltrane told us of our actual destination."

"What about the other doctors?"

"They were all trapped on the third floor," Brandon said. "There were a few attempts to rescue them, but the stairwells were jammed packed after the first day."

"No other survivors?" They all looked at me sadly.

"None that we know of," Mike said.

"And the rest of Atlanta?"

"Gunny can answer that best," Brandon said. "He led most of the patrols around the area."

In fact, Justin and I had already talked about it. He advised all he ever saw was zombies and dead bodies. So, in all probability, any survivors had bugged out of Atlanta long ago. I continued peppering them with questions and wrote down everything they said.

"We were more or less in siege mode," Brandon said. "There were simply too many of those things wandering around the city to do much of anything. We should've gotten out of that place a long time ago," he lamented.

"But, they wouldn't leave because of the labs. They were obsessed with finding a cure and we'd all heard about you," Mike said, gesturing toward me. "The colonel believed you were dead, so your kids were VIPs." I digested what he said and looked pointedly at him.

"I have a question and I want an honest answer." I hooked a thumb at Justin and Ruth. "Don't worry about them, you can speak your mind here without worrying about it."

"Ask away," Mike replied.

"How did Major Parsons treat my kids?"

"Like they were his own," Mary said immediately. "Nobody mistreated your kids, Zach. We believed they were our last best hope for humanity."

"If nothing else, they were spoiled rotten," Rachel, who had been quiet up until now, added. The rest of them chuckled. I glanced over at Justin and Ruth. They looked back as if saying, are you satisfied now?

I caught Tonya eyeing me. I excused myself and walked over to her.

"Are you really going to let these newcomers live in the school?" I asked.

"I think it's a good idea, Zach, but we're going to need more beef cattle. A dairy cow or two would be nice also." I eyed her. "Well, you practically dumped those two sisters and that kid on me." I didn't dump them, they made the choice on their own, but I didn't argue the point. I was frowning, but I nodded.

"We should be able work something out." Tonya smiled in victory.

I sat on the den floor and played with my kids until they could hardly keep their eyes open. They didn't want to go to bed, but when I tucked them in and lay down beside them, their heavy eyelids slammed shut within a minute. I quietly left the bedroom and joined the women in the kitchen. Kelly gestured at the wind-up clock on the kitchen counter.

"What?" I asked.

"It's only six. That son of yours is going to be rarin' to go at about four in the morning. You're on your own with that," she said while smiling sweetly. I chuckled.

"I understand. What are y'all talking about?"

"While you watch the kids tomorrow, we're going to find Janet a bed."

I smiled. "Yeah, okay. I'm going to check around outside before it gets too dark out."

"Shit," I muttered. I saw them as I approached the gate. There were three of them, and it looked like one of them was actually trying to climb over the gate. I took no chances and dispatched them with my shotgun. Kelly met me at the door and I explained.

"I'll burn them tomorrow, but I think tonight I'm going keep watch and make sure there aren't more lurking around."

"You think they're more out there?" she asked.

"Remember the attack on the house?" I was referring to back in April of last year. The zombie I'd captured had somehow led an attack on our house after he'd escaped. Rowdy was bitten as a result and had to be killed. Kelly nodded her head at the memory.

"I'll stay up with you," she said.

"No," I replied. "I'll be alright."

"No more Lone Ranger bullshit, remember?" she chided.

"Fine," I said. "You better fix us a pot of coffee. I'll see if I can raise Justin and give him a SITREP."

I let Kelly use the night vision goggles. They still gave me headaches if I used them for more than ten minutes.

"Nothing," she whispered after she'd made a sweeping scan. "Are we staying up all night?" It was a good question. I looked at the luminescent dials on my watch. They read a little before two.

"I think we should. I've never seen any of them get this close before and I can't stop thinking about that night they attacked the house." Kelly replied with a yawn.

"You can go to bed if you want. I'll be…" I stopped in midsentence when Kelly put a finger to my lips. She'd cocked her head like she heard something before quickly raising the goggles to her face.

"Zach," she whispered urgently. "There's about ten of them walking up the road."

"Alright, go wake up Janet and let her know what's going on. Then get back here and watch my back." I didn't wait for her to respond and made my way toward the edge of the van where I had it parked facing the gate. There was a partial moon out with plenty of stars, so I could make out a few of them. When they got to the gate, they started pushing on it. The gate rattled in the darkness and one of them again made a clumsy attempt to climb it.

As quietly as I could, I opened the door to the van. I rested the fore stock of the shotgun on the window frame of the van's door and turned the headlights on. A couple of them looked up as I took aim. I picked the biggest one first. He reminded me of another tall one I ran into not so long ago. I gently squeezed the trigger. The twelve gauge slug hit him squarely in the forehead and he fell like a sack of day-old shit. I got two more before the rest of them scattered.

"Coming in!" Kelly shouted as she ran up beside me.

"Get the truck," I told her as I fed the shotgun tube with fresh rounds. "We've got to go after them."

We were right beside the van, but I knew we were in all likelihood going to be doing a lot of four-wheeling.

"We've got to hunt them down," I repeated.

"How many are left?"

"I got three. I saw a few more, but I can't be certain." I turned on the CB and tried to raise anyone. Ruth answered almost immediately.

"We're heading that way," she reported.

"Alright," I responded and updated them. "Meet us at November Bravo." It was our code name for the intersection of Nolensville Pike and Burkitt Road. Ruth acknowledged and we headed toward the gate.

There were the two I'd shot earlier, along with the three additional ones I'd just taken care of. Kelly watched nervously as I jumped out and opened the gate. I no sooner than got it closed than one of them emerged from the darkness, charging at me. It was a good thing I was paying attention or else he would have got me.

I sidestepped, ran around the truck. I was attempting to get enough space where I could stop and shoot, but Kelly stuck her rifle out of the window and dispatched him with one shot. I finished securing gate and jumped in.

"That was close," she quipped.

Ruth and Justin were in their Humvee and drove up about the same time we did.

"We've killed six so far." Justin nodded.

"There was one walking down the middle of Concord Road without a care in the world. We took care of it."

"I have a feeling they're going to try the house again. I'd like to get out and sneak back while Kelly drives back in the truck."

"Alright, I'm with you," Justin said.

"Wait, wait," Kelly protested. "That's not a good idea."

"It'll work," I said. "You two ride up front. Justin and I'll ride in back and slip out before you get to the gate. If any of them are lying in wait, we'll get them." Kelly looked at me nervously and then at the Marines.

"What do you two think?"

"I think it'll work if there aren't fifty thousand of them out there hiding in the weeds," Justin said. "If there are, we're screwed anyway."

So, we did it my way. Kelly slowed to a crawl before turning into the driveway. Justin and I slid out, waited until there was twenty or thirty feet between us and the truck, and followed behind. I'd disabled the taillights long ago, so we were practically invisible in the darkness. When Kelly stopped at the gate, I was absolutely certain there'd be a few of them waiting. I wasn't wrong.

As soon as Ruth opened her door, two of them started running toward her. I'm sure Justin felt the same as I did as we dropped to one knee and began to take aim; we were protecting our women. I know, it sounds cheesy, but that's what we were doing.

Well, that's what we thought we were doing. Our protection wasn't necessary. Ruth's sidearm came out quickly and she shot both of them in the head before I could get a good aim. It was damn good shooting. Even Fred would have been impressed.

Justin and I remained in the darkness and watched Ruth open the gate. As soon as she did, I heard loud braying. It was Shithead.

"They're at the house!" I shouted and motioned for Justin to follow me as I jumped in the bed of the truck. Justin was right behind me and Kelly needed no instructions. She gunned it, causing us to lurch backward.

There were more of them, maybe twenty or thirty. Some of them were trying to attack Shithead, but they weren't much of a match for him. These zombies must have been city folks. Donkeys could spin and kick you with deadly accuracy if they felt threatened. We shot the ones Shithead didn't get first, and I paid special attention to any of them who decided to run off. Four of them attempted it, but I was ready for them.

When it was all over, it took a few minutes of coaxing before Janet would open the door, but none of us admonished her. She did her job exactly how I wanted her to.

"Someone from the school called on the radio and asked what was going on," she said. "They asked for you but I told them you were too busy killing people."

"They ain't people anymore," Justin corrected. She gave him a look but didn't respond. He hooked a thumb out the door.

"That mule is deadly with those kicks," he said. I chuckled.

"He's actually a donkey, but yeah, he's a tough one."

"What's the difference?" Ruth asked.

"A donkey is smaller, but can be more aggressive. They're the descendent of an African ass. A mule is a cross between a female horse and a male donkey. You know, a mule is actually superior to a horse in several ways. For instance—"

"Okay, they get the idea," Kelly interrupted. Justin and Ruth chuckled at my expense.

"I'm sure it's a fascinating topic," Ruth said. "One day I want to hear all about it."

"Yeah, me too," Justin said. "In the meantime, I want to know what you think about this, Zach. And by the way, what made you think there was going to be an attack?" Justin was perplexed, as was Ruth.

"Back about a year ago, they'd organized together and made a multi-pronged attack on both houses and the tour bus, which was parked right about where it is now…" I stopped suddenly.

"What?" Justin asked.

"Sarah," I replied.

"Oh shit," Kelly said.

"I tried to call her," Janet said. "She didn't answer."

"Okay, Justin and I will go check on them. You all stay here. We'll keep in contact with the radio." Kelly started to object, but this time I held a finger up. "The kids," I said pointedly. She understood.

It was quiet and dark when we drove up. I flashed the high beams at the bus and even dared tap the horn. After a moment, I saw movement in one of the windows. Ten seconds later, Sarah contacted us on the radio and she came out a moment later. Surprisingly, Rachel exited the bus a few seconds later.

"Any issues?" I asked when they came out.

"We heard some movement, but didn't see anything. We thought it was cows or deer." I walked around the area, using the goggles in an attempt to detect anything. I spotted Sate and Hank out in the field. I wondered what had happened to them.

"Anything?" Justin asked. I pointed out the horses.

"They got spooked and ran. We'll round them up tomorrow."

"So, they pulled a night attack on you guys a year ago?" he asked. I nodded.

"April of last year."

"Damn," he muttered and was silent for a minute or two before speaking again.

"This is an enemy force where you can never let your guard down," he finally said. "You and your people killed over two thousand of them in this immediate area, and yet, they still turn up like roaches."

"Yeah, I was convinced they would have all died off by now."

"At least they're not procreating," Sarah said. "We just have to outlive them."

Yeah, she was right. They both were. We could never let our guard down and we had to survive, we had to outlive them.

CHAPTER 27 — FIREWOOD

In the spirit of camaraderie, everyone joined together for a day of cutting firewood. A mixture of men and women joined in with the axes and saws, and whoever was left over was either assigned guard duty or was back at the school with the kids and the chores.

Tonya had even joined us, but mostly she walked around and watched everyone working, like she was our overseer or something. I made no smart-assed remarks. After all, I owed her big time and the extra manpower assured us all of an abundance of firewood. We stopped for a lunch break and sat around in the shade, enjoying some fresh food.

"Cutting firewood is every bit as hard as it sounds," Ward said with a huff. I chuckled.

"You two are doing fine. You know, it wasn't so long ago when the two of you looked like a couple of powder puffs. Now y'all have calloused hands and hard muscles." I lowered my voice to barely above a whisper. "Those two brothers are having a hard time keeping up." I gestured over to them who were several yards away, lying prone on the bare ground. "Y'all are in better shape, I'm thinking."

The two of them looked over at the much younger, more muscular brothers before looking back at me and beamed at my compliment.

"Well, I for one can say, as a nineteen year old, you're quite strong, Zach," Ward replied.

"Thank you, sir."

"Were you always athletic?" Marc asked.

"No, I had to work at it." I didn't bother telling them what had motivated me to get this way. Nah, the only people who knew about all of that were long dead. Not even Kelly knew.

I smiled pleasantly as I listened to the conversation segue into complaints of blisters and sore muscles. Tonya, Ruth and Justin walked over during the middle of it.

"How much do we have so far?" Tonya asked.

"It looks like about twelve cords," I replied. "That's plenty, but while we have everyone together and pleasant weather on our side, we should keep going until sundown." Tonya nodded thoughtfully. Ruth was looking at me like she wanted to say something.

"We have an idea we'd like to run by you," she said and looked over at Justin.

"Well, yeah," Justin continued. "We've been talking about it and think your trading post idea needs to be dusted off and revisited."

"Justin has an idea that's a variation of the theme," Tonya added.

"Oh, yeah? Like a rendezvous or something?" Justin clapped his hands together.

"Exactly," he said excitedly. "There was a movie I loved watching when I was a kid. Jeremiah Johnson, do you remember it?" I nodded. Justin explained. "Every year, the trappers and the Indians would meet up. They called it a rendezvous."

"And they parlayed and traded," I said.

"Yeah, exactly. I think we can do something similar."

"What do you think, Zach?" Ruth asked.

"We certainly have enough people to pull it off now, and those trailers still have quite a bit of stuff that Mac had collected." I finished my meal and wiped my mouth. "The biggest concern I had was maintaining security. We'd have to have people trained to respond to any threat. If some gang of marauders came in, we'd have to be able to deal with it."

"That's my thoughts exactly," Justin said, and then corrected himself. "Mine and Ruth's thoughts. We've talked it out extensively and with the additional soldiers, I think we can do it."

"Something tells me you've already got the ball rolling. Let me guess, you've been broadcasting it on the radio." Justin nodded apprehensively.

"Did I overstep?" he asked. To his surprise, I grinned.

"Not at all, I admire your initiative," I replied. "I hope you didn't schedule it during the winter wheat harvest." I could tell from the look on their faces they had not even thought of that particular facet. "You do know the harvesting schedules, right?" I got blank stares for an answer. Floyd, who was sitting nearby listening, shrugged one shoulder as if to say, they never ask me anything.

"Did anyone think to ask for Floyd's advice?" I asked. "After all, he knows more about farming than any of you guys."

"Floyd?" Shooter retorted sarcastically. He had walked up during our conversation and felt the need to butt in.

"Yeah." He scoffed at my reply.

"Why would anyone ask Floyd for advice about anything? He's a dumbass gimp."

"Oh? So, tell me, when is the proper time to harvest the sweet corn y'all have planted and what is going to be the expected yield?" Shooter started squirming, so instead of answering, he stood and stretched like he didn't care. I stood as well and looked at Justin.

"If you want to know the correct answer, ask Floyd."

"What's your point?" Shooter asked before Justin could speak.

"My point is, Floyd is a valuable asset but y'all treat him like a cross-eyed stepchild." Shooter responded by rolling his eyes. I started to say something else, but I was cut off by the sound of a distant gunshot. Everyone jumped to their feet. There was another shot, and then another, coming from about a hundred yards east of us.

"That's Kate!" Shooter shouted and took off at a dead run.

"Everyone, form up in your teams!" Justin shouted. "Team one take the left flank!" I was in charge of team one. I didn't want to take the left flank. I wanted to hop in the truck and haul ass back to the school where Kelly and my kids were. But, duty was duty. I gathered my team together as Justin gave me a nod and led his team off.

"Alright guys, follow me. If you see a threat, sing out." I took off at a slow jog on a course slightly left of the source of the now constant gunfire. There was a small copse of trees blocking our field of view, but once we cleared it, we immediately saw what the ruckus was all about.

Zombies, about fifty of them. It was an even larger number than the horde that had attacked us last week. They'd surrounded the Humvee Kate was in, trying to get at her. She was shooting out of the top, but she was in danger of being overwhelmed, real danger. At least one of them had somehow managed to climb onto the hood. And what was worse, Shooter had foolishly run right into the pack and was now fighting for his life. We were about thirty yards away from them, which was a good, safe distance. I ordered my team to stop.

"Cyclic rate of fire, headshots only!" I yelled. "And be careful not to shoot Kate." I really didn't care about Shooter. I pointed to Goober as I took a knee.

"Watch our six!" He acknowledged with a curt nod and took a knee facing behind us, scanning with his rifle as the rest of us began methodically shooting. The sounds of other gunshots told me Justin had set up on the opposite flank and the stinkers quickly began dropping like flies. Only one of them realized what was happening and took off at a loping run. I took careful aim and popped him squarely in the back of his head. It made a satisfying impact like a ripe watermelon being hit by a baseball bat. He fell face first and his face splattered on the road.

It was over in less time than it had taken to run to Kate's aid. Everyone was jubilant and exchanging high-fives, but I was still irritated from the conversation with that idiot Shooter and my ears were ringing from the gunfire.

"There might be more of them hiding, so be careful," I said a little more loudly than I intended and walked over to where Shooter was now hugging Kate. I guess he believed he was the one who rescued her when in fact he was damn near eaten alive.

"They came out of nowhere," Kate lamented, "and I couldn't raise anyone on the radio." Everyone comforted her while I looked around. The reason we put her in this particular location was to afford her a wide open field of view, so it seemed doubtful they came out of nowhere. I glanced in the Humvee and saw a couple of open magazines lying on the passenger seat. Yeah, they came out of nowhere. I reached into the vehicle and raised Kelly on the radio. Thankfully, everything was okay at the school. I told her what'd happened, assured her nobody was injured, and said we'd be there shortly. Justin had walked over while I was talking to her.

"Everything's fine at the school," I said and then lowered my voice to a murmur. "The radio works just fine." He saw the magazines I was gesturing at and nodded at my implication. I kept my temper in check. After all, nobody got killed, bitten, or otherwise injured, so I forced myself to keep it in a positive perspective.

"This is a damn good example of why we went through that training some of you were complaining about," Justin declared while looking at the primary complainers, Shooter and Cutter. "Alright everyone, we need to pile these things together and burn them."

"What for?" Cutter asked. "They're dead now, they ain't gonna hurt anyone." He emphasized his statement by kicking one of the corpses.

"It's the only way to make sure the disease is not transferred to the carrion that are bound to come along and start eating on them," Major Parsons replied. He pointed down the overgrown roadway to a rat up on its hind legs sniffing in our direction. "See? There are rats and other scavengers everywhere, and rats will eat anything."

Cutter responded with a scornful scoff, raised his rifle, and shot at the little scavenger. He missed. Justin yanked the rifle out of his hands.

"We don't have a whole lot of ammo to waste, numb-nuts," he scolded. Several people started chuckling. "Alright, you heard the man. Team one, your job is to take care of the corpses." He pointed at Private Mann. "Grab someone and scout the area. The rest of you police up all of the brass and then help with the burning." He looked over at me. I nodded.

"We can haul the wood back later."

"The brown rat is the most common rat in the cities of America, although the black rat is also prevalent." The doctor had become very talkative on the ride back for some reason. I guess he wanted to show he was a valuable asset. Normally, his manner and the way he spoke irritated me, he reminded me of the actor, Ben Stein, but today I was in a relatively good mood and listened to him with interest.

"If I remember correctly, a rat carries at least eighteen known pathogens that can cause diseases in humans," I said.

"Yes, indeed," he replied.

"I take it y'all conducted tests on them."

"Many, many tests," he responded. "I know what you're about to ask and the answer is yes, we found the virus in several of them."

"Do you think rats spread the plague?" Tonya asked.

"The etiology of the virus was the topic of endless speculation and conjecture amongst my colleagues, but we never reached a unanimous conclusion." I could see him thinking silently. He would start to say something and then stop himself before glancing at me. If I liked the man, I would have encouraged him to speak his mind, but I think I knew what he was about to say. I shook my head ever so slightly. He caught it, and then stared out of the window for the rest of the ride back.

"Let's make one thing perfectly clear, Grant." It was the first time I had ever used his first name. When we parked in the school parking lot, I had asked him to wait behind. After everyone had said goodbye and walked inside, I gave him a cold stare.

"I know what you were about to say a few minutes ago. You don't seem to get it. You've screwed the pooch after what you did with my children and me, so don't even bother suggesting more tests."

"I understand why you dislike me, Zach, but let me say this. Over the last several weeks, I've done a lot of soul searching. In hindsight, I realize how easy it was for us, for me, to rationalize my actions and I know you'll probably never forgive me. But, you're a smart man, Zach. You know that your blood holds the cure and I don't think for a moment that you're selfish enough to keep it to yourself."

"Maybe so, but you don't have the facility nor the equipment to do anything about it, so it's a moot point."

"That could change, if you help," he rejoined. I stared at him questioningly. "We can go back to the CDC and either make use of the labs or retrieve the necessary equipment and bring it back here. There is more than one mobile lab parked down there in the basement, gathering dust." I frowned and shook my head.

"Out of the question. I'm not leaving my children. And before you even think about it, we're not going to take them back down there under any circumstances."

"Fair enough, I understand. But, I want to ask you a candid question." When he hesitated, I motioned for him to go ahead and ask. "If I were to talk a few people into going back and bringing back the mobile lab, would you be willing to resume experiments?" Kelly came out of the school, kids in tow. She was smiling, but it looked like the kids had worn her out. I kissed the three of them and got the kids in the truck.

"What are you two talking about?" Kelly asked.

"The good doctor here wants to recruit people to go back to the CDC and bring testing equipment back here." I motioned for her to get in the truck and I did the same. I thought for a moment and then spoke to him through the open window.

"If you want to get yourself killed going back down there, be my guest. If you're successful and make it back, we'll have a long talk." I started the truck and drove off. I took one last look at him in the rearview mirror before turning onto Concord Road and saw Major Parsons grinning. Bastard.

"Was he telling the truth?" Kelly asked as we drove back home. I shrugged. "You always said he was full of shit."

"Remember that time I was exposed and spent a couple days in that cage?" I explained to her, as best that I could, about antibodies and antigens.

"He is of the opinion that I've developed an immunity, but I'm skeptical."

"But still, if he's right, you have the cure." I wanted to remind her of the time I was held captive and treated like a lab rat, but I didn't.

"Yeah, well, there's nothing he can do about it at the moment. He's going to need – hell, I don't know, a lab and all kinds of equipment in order to synthesize a vaccine out of my blood. Anyway, it's a boring subject. How was your day?"

"We had a great time. I don't think Kate and Rhonda care too much for each other, but everybody played nice. Your son sure does like the girls." I glanced over at him and grinned proudly. "And I had a long talk with the two nurses who came from the CDC."

"Oh yeah? Mike and Mary, right?" I asked.

"Yeah."

"The woman sounds Jamaican. The dude talks like he's from up north somewhere." Kelly laughed.

"Yeah, they met while doing missionary work. They're really nice people, but that hasn't stopped Cutter and Shooter from making a few snide remarks."

"That figures," I muttered.

"Anyway, they confirmed what Grant had said earlier about the vaccinations. All of the kids were inoculated."

"What about the other kids down there, did any of them survive?" Kelly shook her head sadly.

"They said the zombies had cut off the upper floors from the lower floors. They'd killed so many the stairwells were completely blocked." She shuttered. "It sounded horrible."

And Grant is adamant about going back, I thought. I didn't see any good ending to that endeavor.

CHAPTER 28 – SAMMY

"Bingo," Justin said after he worked the portal open and took a sniff. I jogged over to the opening of the underground fuel storage tank he was inspecting. "Diesel," he confirmed, "and it looks to be half full."

It made sense; we were at a UPS hub Jorge had spotted a while back and they had a system in place to fuel up their delivery trucks. I motioned Sammy over.

"Take a sniff, but don't inhale deeply." He got on his knees and did so.

"That's what diesel fuel smells like. It smells different from regular gasoline, right?" He nodded in understanding.

"Okay," I said, pointing. "I need you to go climb up on the top of that truck over there and keep an eye out for anyone or anything, but don't let them see you." Sammy obeyed instantly, hustled over and climbed up the truck faster than any of us could. Justin chuckled.

"He's catching on."

"Yeah, he was a sickly looking kid when he first came here, but he seems to be doing a lot better now."

Ruth got in our truck and Justin guided her as she backed the five hundred gallon tanker up to the open portal. Everyone watched as I dropped the hose into the tank and started pumping the fuel. Jorge emerged from the business and held up a torque wrench.

"They got some good tools in there, man," he exclaimed. His father nodded in agreement.

"That's great," I said. "Anything that'll trade, be sure and grab it." Jorge and Josue needed no further prompting and were soon loading the back of the truck full of various types of tools. We were making a good team.

"It's looking pretty good, so far," Justin commented.

"Yeah, I hope this diesel is still good."

"What else do you think we need for the rendezvous?" Justin asked.

"Anything that'll be good bartering items," I replied. "Besides food, fuel, and ammo, the biggest things will be anything that's useful but hard to find. I don't think I want to barter any fuel or ammo, we need to keep all we find."

"Yeah, I agree. We have an abundance of corn and potatoes, but not much else."

"Tonya's little grow operation might bring in some trade," Justin said. "She has an entire greenhouse dedicated to growing nothing but marijuana."

"A true latent stoner," Ruth quipped.

After we had taken everything we thought would be useful, we tied down our load and stood by the truck.

"It's still daylight out," Justin said. "But there's no room left." I glanced at Sammy. He was still perched atop a semi, dutifully scanning the area with my binoculars. I got his attention and waved him over. He climbed down, ran up to us and stood there anxiously in his loose-fitting tee shirt and jeans that were so long the legs had to be rolled up to fit.

"What's next, Zach?" he asked.

"We're all done here." He looked dejected. No doubt he wanted to do more than just keep watch. I thought about it and gave the men a conspiring wink.

"Sammy," I said, "have I ever told you about Tommy and Joe?" He shook his head.

"Who're they?" he asked.

"They were two young men close to your age. Unfortunately, they died in a freak accident, but when they were alive, they were being trained how to be bad ass survivalists."

"They were?" he asked, wide eyed. I nodded with mock seriousness.

"Yep, and let me tell you, the training wasn't easy."

"What kind of training?"

"There was all kinds of stuff. Some of it was pretty challenging. I'd show you, but I don't know if you're big enough."

"I'm big for my age," Sammy retorted. "You said so yourself." I scratched my chin as if thinking it over.

"Okay, fair enough, but, before we get started, there are things you need to understand. First, you've got to take your training seriously."

"I will," he said earnestly.

"And you have to be able to follow orders from your superiors, can you do that?" He nodded his head even more vigorously this time.

"Alright, let's start with a training exercise right now and we'll see how serious you are about this."

"Okay," he said eagerly. I handed him a flashlight.

"We're going to start with testing your resourcefulness." I pointed out the business we had been in for the past two hours. "I want you to go in there and find three and only three items you can use as a survivalist. Whatever items you find, you have to be able to carry all of them out at the same time, so you must consider the size and weight, right?" Sammy nodded. His eagerness was still there, but it was tempered now as he tried to think through the challenge.

"Okay, there are a couple of other rules. As you know, zombies are attracted to sound and light, so you need to be super sneaky quiet and only use that flashlight when you have to."

Sammy chuckled now. "There ain't any zombies in there. You guys have already checked it out." Jorge groaned and shook his head.

"We didn't check everywhere, man. Those things could be hiding in a closet or crouched down in a dark corner somewhere." Josue said something in Spanish and Jorge nodded. "My father said those things like to hide and wait until someone is alone and then attack. And they like to eat kids, man."

Sammy's grin disappeared and he was now looking a little frightened. Justin and Ruth were each holding their hand over their grins.

"Okay, don't come out until you've found three useful things." I glanced up at the sky. It was a little bit after noon and the sun was shining brightly. "You better get going, it's going to get dark soon."

"Vaya con Dios," Josue said somberly and made the sign of the cross. I thought I was going to shit myself I was trying so hard to not laugh. Sammy walked hesitantly and looked back a couple of times before disappearing through the open door.

"You guys are devious," Ruth said while trying not to laugh. "He watched us clear the business, he knows there's no zombies." I tapped my temple.

"Nothing like the power of suggestion," I said.

"Did you do this with those two boys you mentioned?" Justin asked.

"Oh, yeah. We all had a hand in their training. Corporal Alexander was training them in soldier skills, would you be interested in doing something like that with Sammy and the other kids?"

"Sure, when they get old enough." He looked over at the door Sammy had gone into. "I suppose ten is about the right age to start, depending on the kid. My dad taught me and my brother to shoot a little twenty-two rifle when we were about his age. Yeah," he said, thinking. "Yeah, I think I'd really like doing that. We've got to teach the kids how to survive."

We chitchatted casually, mostly about the upcoming rendezvous. Jorge and Josue listened attentively.

"How's the progress going?" I asked Justin.

"I think we're ready to go."

"So, this rendezvous, is it going to be good?" Jorge asked.

"I hope so," I answered. Justin nodded in agreement.

"You think any women will show up?"

"There might be a few, it's hard to say."

"I hope so, man. Kate has a thing for Shooter, Kyra doesn't want anything to do with me, and my balls are about to explode."

"Kyra no Bueno," Josue said and held his hands out as if measuring something. "Pequeño trasero."

"What'd he say?" Justin asked.

"He said her ass is too small," Jorge replied and shrugged a shoulder. "He likes women with big rear ends." Justin and I laughed while Ruth shook her head in exasperation.

"Well, all I have to say is be wary of Janet. She's no bueno." Both Jorge and Josue nodded in understanding.

"He's been in there a long time," Justin finally remarked. I looked at my watch. It'd been about forty minutes. I thought he would've been out of there long before now.

"Yeah, maybe so. I'll go in and get him." However, before I could act, the door burst opened and Sammy emerged. He ran over and stood in front of us with his hands full and breathing heavily.

"Alright, show us what you got," I said. Sammy held out his possessions.

"I got a hammer, a Bic lighter, and a water bottle," Sammy held out his possessions tentatively. The hammer was a standard machinist's ball peen hammer, the Bic lighter was almost completely full, and the water bottle was one of those plastic ones you bought at a Target store and put in your school backpack. I nodded thoughtfully, somberly, as if making a serious evaluation of his treasures.

"Explain why you picked those three particular items."

"The hammer is for protection and hammering nails and stuff. The water bottle is so I can carry water around with me, and the lighter is for starting fires and for Aunt Kate and Aunt Kyra to smoke their cigarettes." Everyone laughed.

"Alright, good job."

"I passed?" Sammy asked. I looked around.

"Let's see a show of hands of those who think Sammy passed his first training lesson." Everyone raised their hand. Sammy grinned proudly as we slapped him on the back.

I had to drive slowly; we were heavily laden and the roads were rough.

"Roads are shit," Josue commented from the back seat.

"Yeah," I answered, "Unfortunately, they're not going to get any better either unless we start repaving them ourselves." I found myself chuckling at the memory of Big Mac driving one of those huge paving machines home one day. Justin glanced at me but didn't say anything, which was good. Jorge broke me out of my reverie.

"I have a motorcycle back at the barn in our old house," he said. "I'd have no problem riding around on these roads."

"Oh, yeah? What kind?"

"It's a Suzuki dirt bike. It's a two-cycle, so it's a little loud."

"Still, it'd be good to have around, let's go get it." I started to make a detour toward their old home, but was stymied by the sudden appearance of over a dozen infected, standing in the road. I stopped suddenly. They were about three hundred yards away, not walking, just standing in a huddled mass in the middle of the roadway. Justin grabbed the binoculars and scanned them over.

"They're looking this way," he says, "but I'm not sure they know what they're looking at." He stared at them another ten seconds. "They look terrible, I'm actually seeing exposed portions of their skulls on some of them."

"Any kids?" I asked while squinting at them.

"Maybe one or two, hard to tell without getting any closer."

"They're too far away to catch up to us, but I don't want to get any closer." I looked at everyone to see what they had to say.

"I don't want to mess with those things, man," Jorge exclaimed. Sammy, who was sitting beside him, nodded in wide-eyed agreement.

"No bueno," Josue added.

"Yeah, with the truck full of stuff and pulling that tanker, we won't be able to make a quick getaway." I shrugged dismissively. "We'll try for it later then." I steered the truck toward home.

"Maria is really sweet," Kelly said.

"What did you guys do all day?" I asked. Kelly pointed over at the full clothesline. Judging by the amount of clothing hanging, they'd been doing laundry all day. And I doubted they did them all by hand, so the batteries were probably drained.

"She's going to come back tomorrow and pick up all of their clothes."

"That's great," I replied "How were the kids?"

"They played together and even napped together. Little Jose really likes Macie. Maybe they'll get married one day," she said with a mischievous grin.

"You never know," I replied with a chuckle. "Where's Janet?" I asked.

"She rode with Sarah to find a bed," she let out a small sigh. "The woman is a little hard to get along with."

"Yeah, that's for sure. I'll keep her in line."

"Anyway, the girls stopped by.

"How're they fitting in over there?" Kelly grinned.

"Kyra told me Kate and Shooter have their own room now. His real name is Simon, by the way."

"Heh, that's great." One less mouth to feed, I thought. "What about Kyra?" Kelly shook her head.

"She can't stand Cutter. By the way, his real name is Theodore." I chuckled.

"*Cutter,*" I said derisively. "Theodore is a better name than Cutter. Heck, one of the best presidents we ever had was named Theodore."

"She doesn't seem interested in Jorge either. Maybe this rendezvous will bring in some single men who'll catch her eye," she added. "Anyway, she has her own room, which she likes, but Tonya micromanages and keeps assigning her latrine duty, which she hates. She's already said she'd like to move back in with us."

"Oh?"

"Yeah. She said while everyone else is working their asses off, Tonya walks around under the pretense of supervising." I laughed.

"That sounds about right."

I gave her a rundown of our adventures of the day, Sammy's little test, and about the finding of the diesel fuel.

"What are we going to do when we can't use fuel anymore?" she asked. I shrugged.

"We're almost at that point now," I replied. "That's why we need more horses. We're going to need to go back to that golf course soon and round up a dozen or so." I snapped my fingers. "You know what we've been neglecting? Bicycles." I thought a moment before answering my own question. "We need to round up a dozen or so and spare parts too."

"Maybe us women can all go out scavenging in the next day or so while you stay home and watch the kids." I groaned inwardly. We'd had this conversation before. It always worried me, but I had to admit, Kelly had proven herself. Besides, if Sarah and Ruth went with them I had no worries. I nodded amicably and changed the subject.

"I'm going to run up to the Riggins house and check on things and then take Sammy home. I won't be any longer than an hour or so."

"Okay, sweetie. The laundry should be dry by the time you get back," she said with a look. I acknowledged the hint with a grunt.

"Why don't you go get the truck ready, Sammy?" Kelly said. "Zach will be out in a second."

"What's up?" I asked when Sammy shut the door.

"Shooter doesn't want Sammy around and I think the two sisters feel like they're being burdened with motherhood."

"That's stupid," I retorted. "He's a good kid."

"Yeah, I agree. Kyra was kind of implying that maybe Sammy would be better off living here with us."

"What do you think?" I asked.

"You're a good father figure," she responded with a small smile. "And besides, he's an orphan, just like you." I smiled back.

"Well, I've never considered myself a father figure." In fact, I always thought someone like Fred was the epitome of a father figure. Rick too, to a lesser extent. Kelly kissed me on the cheek and squeezed my butt as I walked out.

We found Sarah, Rachel and Janet sitting at a picnic table in back of our old damaged home. There were two dead zombies at their feet.

"They followed us," she said simply. I didn't bother asking the circumstances; they were dead and nobody had been bitten, that's all that mattered. One of them had a backpack on. I searched it and found a roll of toilet paper stored in a plastic Folgers coffee container and a small, rechargeable flashlight. I tossed them to Sarah.

"To the victor goes the spoils," I said with a grin.

"What does that mean?" Sammy asked.

"It's an expression used by a politician a long time ago. It basically means the winner gets the prize."

"Oh."

"I'll explain it in more detail one day. In the meantime, let's clean up Aunt Sarah's mess."

I instructed Sammy how to loop the rope around their ankles and tie it off on the bumper hooks of the truck. The four of us then slowly dragged the corpses over to the sinkhole. I pointed to a tarp covering stuff and held down by rocks.

"I keep a five gallon can of fuel here and some old tires. Once you get a couple of them burning, they'll go for hours. Just dump the bodies on top of them and it'll burn them to a crisp." I instructed Sammy how to do it and he excitedly lit the pyre with his brand new Bic lighter. We talked as we watched them burn. He was standing close and I guided him backwards as I pointed toward the thick black smoke.

"Burning rubber releases a bunch of toxins, so don't breathe any of the smoke." Sammy looked up at me and nodded.

"I see a lot of darkened bones," Sarah commented.

"Yeah, we've had a few unwanted visitors over the past couple of years. The first one was Susan Riggins, the woman who originally lived at the big house.

The second one was Fred's little brother, his name was Franklin." Sarah looked at me questioningly.

"He'd gotten sick and turned. He killed Fred's wife and mother-in-law before wandering off. He came up to the old homestead one night. Julie and I managed to kill him and drug him down here the next morning. A few days later, we met Fred. He wanted to give his baby brother a Christian burial. It was hell getting the remains out of there."

"I remember Julie telling me about that," Janet said and looked at me quizzically.

"Do you miss her?"

"Every day," I replied evenly. I expected more, but she had nothing more to say on the matter. We watched the fire in silence for a few minutes.

"How'd it go with the house hunting?" I asked. Rachel shook her head.

"Busted water pipes, mold, mildew, dead bodies lying around. We couldn't find one that suited us. But we found a bed for Janet. And besides..." She looked at Rachel.

"So, when are you going to move in with Sarah?" I asked Rachel. Sarah looked at me in surprise. Rachel piped up.

"Have you ever heard this one: what does a lesbian bring on her second date?" she asked. I looked at her and she was smiling mischievously. "A U-Haul, get it?" I laughed while Sarah looked embarrassed.

"Okay, I understand. Did you ever get the water tanks in the bus filled?"

"Somewhat," Sarah responded. "But we've used so much I need to refill them again."

"Which house did you live in, exactly?" Rachel asked.

"First it was the old homestead, and then we moved in to the Riggins' house." From the look on her face, I felt it necessary to explain.

"My boss, a man named Rick Sanders, lived in the old homestead. The Riggins lived in the new house. Back when it all started, I moved in with Rick and rode out the shit storm together. He died in his sleep on Christmas night of the first year. Then I started meeting other people, including Janet here and my kids' mother." I thought about Janet's antics at that time and was about to tell them, but decided to hold off.

"At one point, some chuckleheads became displeased with us. They set Fred's original house on fire and were about to do the same with the homestead. We were able to stop them before they did, but they'd poured a bunch of gas in it which had soaked into the floorboards and stuff." My face darkened at the memory. "That's when we moved into the Riggins. Once we moved in, we made a lot of modifications. We had a generator, well-water, a septic tank, a HAM radio tower, wood-burning stoves, most everything to make it self-sufficient."

"Those concrete barricades are a nice touch."

"Yeah, those and the barbed wire were for keeping the zombies out. It didn't help against the Marines though." I sighed. "It was a nice home, once."

"What's the square footage?" Sarah asked. It was an interesting question. I thought about it as I looked over the landscape, watching for any interlopers.

"I never measured it out. Let's see, five bedrooms, three and a half bathrooms, den, kitchen, dining room, plus the basement. I'd guess around four thousand, give or take."

"That's a decent-sized house," she mused. "Are the well and septic tank still working?" I nodded.

"As far as I know."

"Have you ever thought about rebuilding it?"

"Many times," I replied. "But I didn't see any real need when it was just me and Kelly." I saw where she was going. "I think Fred's house is plenty for the two of us and the kids."

"I think it would be safer as a whole if more of us lived together under one roof instead of being spread out," Sarah opined. I looked at her.

"Like at the school."

"Yeah, but I think I understand why you never moved in with them. Between the different personalities and Tonya's abrasiveness, I could never live there."

"Yeah," I replied. I could never live with that group. "So, what are you thinking?"

"We should rebuild it, perhaps even make it larger. The old homestead would be easier to rebuild, but the square footage of the foundation is rather small, and the cellar couldn't hold a great deal. You're going to need more room." I must have made a face or something.

"Think about it. You've got five of you living in Fred's house currently. Rachel and I would like to stay close, so that's seven people. There are likely to be new arrivals we'd be willing to bring into the fold, and you're forgetting one very important thing."

"What's that?" I asked.

"Do you really think a brother and sister will want to share the same bedroom when they become teenagers? Especially with their grandmother? You're kids aren't going to be little forever."

"You make a good point," I conceded.

"I think it could work," she said and then lowered her voice to almost a whisper.

"Plus, I think Sammy would be better off living with you and Kelly. You two make better parental figures." I looked over at Sammy, who had circled around to the far side of the sinkhole and was looking around.

"He's a good kid," Janet said. I nodded in understanding. I got the distinct impression the women got together and hatched a plan to get me convinced Sammy would be better off under my roof. Hell, they didn't need to go through the motions, I was already on board.

"I think you should seriously consider it," Sarah said. "In the meantime, Rachel and I are going to stay in the bus."

"Alright, you women have certainly been doing a lot of planning and conspiring. I guess I shouldn't be surprised."

"Sarah thinks you have a cute butt too, but she likes mine better," Rachel said and then giggled at her own joke. Now Sarah was plainly blushing. I rounded up Sammy and the five of us headed back.

I waited until dinner.

"Sam, I have a business proposition for you."

"You do?" he asked, wide-eyed. I gestured toward Kelly and Janet.

"We'd like to offer you a job."

"What kind of job?"

"I need an extra farmhand. It'll be hard work and it will require you to live here full time. You'll be fed and clothed, and I'll personally see to it that your training continues."

"What kind of work will I be doing?"

"Everything," I answered plainly.

"Will you teach me to hunt?"

"Yep. I'm going to be teaching you many things, including how to hunt. What do you say, would this interest you?" He nodded his head up and down vigorously. Kelly, and even Janet, were grinning from ear to ear.

"It's settled then. After dinner, we're going to the school and give Aunt Kate and Aunt Kyra the news. I'm not sure they'll want you to leave, but don't worry. I'll explain it to them."

"Okay."

"Then we'll get all of your gear and set you up a living area in the den."

"But, I don't have any gear," he lamented. I gave a somber nod.

"Well then, I think that's the first thing we're going to work on."

"He has a grand total of two pairs of underwear," Kelly said after we'd gone to bed. "And he didn't know what dental floss was until I showed him."

"Yeah, well, we'll get him squared away in no time. I hope he doesn't have any cavities."

"So, what's next?" she asked.

"We've got to get ready for the rendezvous."

"And then what?"

"We're going to need to move into a bigger house. Sarah suggested rebuilding the Riggins home. I think the idea has merit and with Tonya's input we can build something bigger and stronger."

"It sounds like a lot of work."

"It will be. Our only alternative is to move into a preexisting structure that's already hardened, to an extent. A parking garage is a good example, but the problem with that is we'd be too far away from the farm itself."

"So, we rebuild then." There was a long pause and then Kelly started giggling.

"What?"

"Maria said the other day she walked in on Jorge masturbating."

"Ohh, T-M-I," I exclaimed.

"I sure hope there're some single women who show up," I muttered after a minute, which caused Kelly to start giggling again.

CHAPTER 29 – RENDEZVOUS PREPPING

"What do you think?" I asked Justin. The two of us were in one of the treehouses. Justin preferred to call them sniper towers, but Sammy called them treehouses and it stuck. Justin jumped up and down, testing the strength of the floor.

"Sturdy," he commented.

"Yeah. It has a good field of fire as well. With the second one on the other side of the church, the shooters will have a good cross projection."

"I wish we could have more than two," Justin commented. I did too, but we didn't have enough personnel to man them all day and attend to the rendezvous duties as well.

"Alright, Sammy. Explain why we built these."

"They're to protect our people during the rendezvous in case someone tries anything." I nodded. I hoped for a more detailed explanation, but it'd have to do. Justin handed him a clipboard with paper and pencil.

"Alright, Private, draw me a range card," he ordered. Sammy scrunched up his face anxiously. I fished into my cargo pants and came up with a compass.

"Start by shooting your azimuths," I directed and the two of us guided him on how to create a proper range card. After we graded his finished product, the three of us walked back to the church.

"I'm proud of our work," Justin said as we stared at them with our binoculars from the church parking lot. "They're well-camouflaged, if I didn't know they were there, I'd never spot them." He glanced at me with a wry grin. "You'd make a decent Marine."

"I'm not sure I'd be very good at following orders," I quipped.

"Point taken," he said with a sigh at my implication and went back to staring at the blinds.

"So, all that's left is stocking them with food and water, and then assigning guard duty."

"Yep."

"I don't think I can hardwire a landline to them due to the distance, but they'll have portable radios. What else do you think we need to do?"

"The school gang is getting the church prepped," I responded. "We'll keep all bartering goods off sight until everyone has arrived, so in the meantime all we need to do is conduct multiple patrols to root out and destroy any nests of zombies that might be inclined to crash the party." Justin nodded.

"I'll handle that," he said. "I hope you'll join in as well."

"I'm always up for killing zombies." I lowered my voice. "Speaking of which..." I inclined my head toward one of the outhouses where Sammy currently was.

"Yeah, about that. On the one hand, he needs to get acclimated to this lifestyle, but still, he's only ten."

"Yeah," I responded. "And no doubt the women will be up in arms if we include him. I don't know, dude, I'm with you, we need to get him acclimated, but if he were to get hurt..." We were interrupted by the sound of a bicycle bell. I knew who it was before I even turned my head. Ward and Marc were peddling up on their tandem bike. I waved and motioned them toward us.

"Alright, guys, we have a question for you." I quickly explained as Sammy rode the bike around the parking lot out of earshot.

"He's awfully young, Zach," Marc said.

"He hasn't even reached puberty," Ward enjoined.

"So, you two think it's too soon."

"Think about it, Zach. You've even admitted you have PTSD. What if he witnesses one of you getting attacked and killed, God forbid, he'd be devastated." I looked at Justin, who shrugged.

"He's already seen people get killed."

"It's like a boxer being punched," Ward explained. "The more times he's punched, the greater the likelihood of brain damage."

"Okay, point taken. But, we can't shelter him forever."

"There'll be plenty of time. Wait until he hits adolescence."

"Like when his voice starts changing and he's bragging about growing hair on his balls?" I asked facetiously.

"Exactly," Ward replied with a big grin.

"Who has hairy balls?" Sammy asked as he peddled up.

"Alright, we need to go over a few things before the rendezvous," Tonya proclaimed. We had all gathered for dinner at the school. They looked at her expectantly as everyone waited on Marc and Ward to finish cooking. She gestured toward me.

"Start us off, Zach."

"First, we don't have an overabundance of food, so everyone needs to help prevent waste."

"We're with you," Rachel said.

"Okay, good. The only food items we're going to trade for are items we have an abundance of; sweet corn, potatoes, and honey. Tonya and I will be in charge of all trading in that area. If anyone asks, refer them to us." I then gestured at Sarah.

"Major Fowkes is coordinating security with Justin and Ruth. If they ask you to perform any type of duties, please help them out."

"Janet and I will be handling the kids, right?" Rhonda asked.

"Yes, so you two will be exempt from guard duty." Everyone seemed to be on the same page, which was the purpose of this meeting. Floyd tentatively raised a hand.

"Yes, sir?"

"Do you people expect any trouble?"

"It's hard to say, Floyd. We've had trouble in the past with some unsavory folks, but we think the plan we have in place will deal with it if that happens." There was a lot of murmuring.

"I bet all of you have been wondering if this is worth the risk. I won't try to throw out a line of," I glanced over at the kids, who were listening attentively, and changed my response. "I won't make any false promises, but we believe it'll work."

"And if it doesn't?" Gus pressed.

"We have contingency plans in place to deal with it," Justin answered. "I seem to recall you bowing out when I asked for volunteers for a reactionary squad, are you wanting in now?"

"Oh, no. I'm sure you soldier boys and soldier girls have it covered." Justin gave him a cold stare.

"Alright, moving on to legitimate matters. Tomorrow at zero-seven-hundred hours, we'll be conducting the first of several search and destroy patrols. It'll be yours truly and Zach leading it off. I'm taking volunteers of who wants to join in." To my surprise, Kelly raised her hand.

"You want to kill zombies?" I asked. "I thought you hated killing them." Kelly wouldn't look at me. I glanced at Justin and shrugged.

"Okay," Justin replied. "Kelly, Sarah, Rachel, Cutter, Shooter, Floyd, Sarah, Rachel, Jorge, Josue. That'll work. I'll see all of you right here in the morning."

I waited until the two of us were snug in bed before talking about it.

"Why the turnaround?"

"What do you mean?"

"You've never liked killing anything, you know that's what we'll be doing on these patrols, right?"

"Yes, I know," she said quietly. "It's something I've got to get used to doing."

"We might encounter unfriendly humans too," I said in the same quiet voice. "You'll be expected to pull your weight if things get hairy."

"I know." She turned and kissed me. "You're being overly protective."

"I can't help it."

"You know the attack the other night?"

"Yeah?"

"What if it happens again? And what if you're not here, or maybe you're injured? I need to do this. I need more confidence."

"Something tells me you've been talking with Sarah and Rachel."

"Well you keep going on and on about what a badass she is." I sighed, knowing I wasn't going to prevail in this discussion. I gave her a kiss and held her closely.

CHAPTER 30 – AMBUSHING 101

We dismounted from the school bus immediately. Our mission objective for the day was to clear Interstate 65 from Concord Road to Old Hickory Boulevard. Floyd kept the bus a half mile back, and when the mission was complete, Justin would give him the word and he'd pick us up. It was roughly four miles, but by the time we'd finished exploring every nook and cranny, I expected we'd have put a good ten miles on our boots.

We planned on doing this for every major roadway leading back to the school until we satisfied ourselves a thousand snarling zombies weren't lurking nearby. Justin ordered Kelly to partner up with Ruth. When I got him alone, I asked why.

"Because if you partner up with her, you'll be watching her so close you won't be worth a shit otherwise." I glared at him. "You know I'm right."

Yeah, he was probably right. I couldn't argue with his logic, but I still didn't like it. I took point and we walked along both sides of the Interstate. After three miles, Justin called a halt and walked over to me.

"Okay, Mister Photographic Memory, has anything changed since the last time you've been through here?"

"Nothing," I answered. Oh, the weeds were thicker than ever, but that's not what he wanted to know. There were no new dead bodies, no signs of any recent scavenging, no cars moved from their original resting spot, and no newly abandoned cars. Nothing. Even all of the zombies trapped inside their vehicles had long since expired, confirming my suspicions that if they went long enough without food, even the virus that festered inside them would die.

"I've got an idea," I said under my breath. "Instead of stopping at the Old Hickory Boulevard exit, let's make our way to the Harding exit and work back along Franklin Pike."

"You're talking about fifteen miles round trip."

"Yep, we should make it back by nightfall, but if anything slows us down we can always jump on the bus and ride the rest of the way home." Justin looked at me quizzically for a moment and then enlightenment spread across his face.

"You think if she gets enough blisters on her feet, she'll never volunteer to go on a patrol again." My response was a very small smile. Justin grunted. "You're forgetting, you're not the only one who has a girlfriend. Ruth isn't going to like this at all."

"Remind her that she's a tough Marine." Justin frowned, but he went along with it.

We reached our original stopping point a little after noon. When Justin informed everyone we were going to continue patrolling and make our way down Franklin Pike, I saw Kelly literally wince at the thought of more hiking. It was bad of me, I know, and I had to fight hard to keep from grinning.

"Alright," Justin said. "We're going to take twenty for lunch. Rest your feet. Zach and I will keep watch."

The two of us took up a position on the Harding Place Bridge overlooking the Interstate and dug into some dehydrated venison and hardtack.

"Damn, this is salty. I hope there's a nice meal waiting for us when we get back," Justin quipped and he washed it down with several gulps of water from his camel back. I shared his hope; this stuff had no flavor other than salt. It would never be mistaken for a gourmet delicacy. Ruth walked over and sat beside Justin.

"Did you tell him?" she asked. Justin gestured with a finger as if he'd casually forgotten something.

"Oh, by the way, Ruth said we're being followed." I looked at him and started to pull out my binoculars, but Justin stopped me. "Don't look; we don't want them to know we spotted them."

"Okay, how about a SALUTE report then, Marine," I suggested.

"I only caught a glimpse of four or five of them. I think they came from the railroad tracks. When we exited the Interstate they moved a little bit closer, but right now they're hiding," Ruth answered. "They looked like zombies, but they could be very dirty humans. I only caught a glimpse."

"It's got to be humans," Justin surmised. "Zombies don't surreptitiously follow you, right?"

"I think we picked them up from the railroad tracks," Ruth added. She was undoubtedly right. Radnor Yards was nearby, on the north side of Harding. It was a huge rail yard, one of the biggest in the south, and I'd never ventured into that area.

"Alright, I've got a suggestion." I was met with quizzical stares. "Whether they're zombies or humans, I think I'd like to see how Marines set up an ambush." Justin looked at me and a big grin crept across his face.

"Oh, this is going to be fun," he said.

Between the Interstate and Franklin Pike is a hill, commonly known as Peach Orchard Hill. I suppose there was a peach orchard there once, hence the name, but it was before my time. Now, there was a subdivision on the north side and a high school on the south side. We made it to the crest of the hill when Kelly stumbled and screamed out in pain. I rushed back to her as she fell to the asphalt and grabbed her ankle. The rest of the patrol circled around the two of us in a defensive perimeter.

"It feels broken," she said loudly. I grabbed it gruffly and she let out another anguished scream.

"If it's not broken, she's got a bad sprain," I said in a loud, disgusted tone. "I told you not to come." Justin put his hands on his hips in frustration.

"Damnit!" he barked. "We'll abort and call for the bus."

"No, don't abort. This area's clear. Y'all Charlie-Mike and I'll wait for the bus with her." We discussed it for a few minutes and there was more than a little yelling back and forth, but Justin cussed me as he relented, rounded up the rest of the patrol members, and headed out. Kelly and I sat in the roadway, and waited.

"Thanks," she said quietly.

"For the record, I absolutely do not like this."

"You're the one who suggested it," she retorted.

"That's *before* you volunteered to be bait. I mean, what the fuck?" Before she could respond, I saw movement. There were eight of them, four men and four women. All of them were wearing the same type of work uniforms, making me wonder if they all had worked for the railroad at one time.

"I'll be damned, they *are* zombies." I would have bet a dollar, if I had one, our stalkers were going to be nefarious humans looking for easy prey rather than zombies that hadn't the state of mind to do anything other than mindlessly charge us.

"Alright, phase two of this goat-fuck is now a go." Kelly frowned at me. "That means it's time for you to suddenly spot them and scream like a hysterical bimbo in one of those stupid horror movies." Kelly responded with a malicious grin before looking toward the zombies and emitted an earsplitting scream. I tried my best to look frightened as I helped Kelly to her feet, draped one of her arms around my shoulders, and the two of us began moving toward the awaiting ambush.

"Alright, get ready," I directed as I moved us between two derelict cars. Kelly hastened a look behind her.

"They're close, Zach," she said urgently. I glanced back. She was right.

"Now!" I shouted and the two of us sprinted into a run toward another group of cars. As we did so, the undead octet loped into the kill zone.

Justin had set it up nicely. There were four derelict cars parked together, all nice and neat like they had parked to go shopping, and then there was an opening in the roadway about fifty feet in diameter before there was a knotted mass of other derelicts. Justin had placed everyone in good positions amongst the second group where everyone was hidden but with overlapping sectors of fire. When the order was given to fire, it was over with quickly.

"They were stalking us," Ruth said in disbelief. "That's not normal, right?"

"No, it's not," I replied.

"So, why were they doing that?"

"Several possibilities."

"Okay," Rachel said. "Are you going to tell us or should we perform a Vulcan mind meld or something?" I looked at her and she smiled sweetly.

"They may have been merely curious, which is doubtful."

"Why?" Rachel asked.

"They're motivated by primal urges. They see us as food, not as a source of amusement."

"So, they were waiting, hoping to catch one of us alone," Sarah surmised.

"Yeah, but there is a third possibility," I said. "They could have been waiting until we encountered some more zombies and had our hands full."

"If that's true—" Justin didn't get a chance to finish.

"There's more of them down the road, somewhere," Rachel interrupted. "Waiting to jump us and eat us all. I bet they like to save the buttholes for last. You know, like dessert."

"Are you sure?" Ruth asked.

"About the buttholes?" Rachel countered. "I'm pretty sure." Ruth shook her head in frustration.

"No, you smartass, not the buttholes." Ruth started to say more but couldn't because Kelly's giggling became infectious. Soon, all of us were laughing. As soon as it died down, Sarah decided to join in.

"So, where are these butthole eaters, Zach?" she asked. I looked at her curiously. She was grinning along with Rachel.

"You realize you two are starting to act more alike every day," I said. Rachel responded by sticking out her tongue and making lurid motions with it. I couldn't help but laugh.

"Alright, if I were to guess, I'd bet there's a bunch of them right over there," I said as I pointed at the nearby high school. Everyone looked at the school as I took a moment to check my weapon.

"Let's go check it out," I said.

"Looks like you're spot on, again," Justin commented as we stood at the front entrance. There were obvious signs; animal remains, dirty footprints, dried blood.

"Should we clear the school?" Ruth asked.

"We have to," Justin replied with a tight smile. "That's what we're here for." I looked pointedly at Kelly.

"I'd like for you to provide rear security," I suggested. She frowned and started to say something, but Justin spoke up.

"Good idea, Ruth, you're with her."

It took us four long, sweaty hours clearing each classroom, but in the end we only found ten more. Everyone, with the exception of yours truly, hurled chunks at least once due to the rancid odor. We were all sitting outside under some shade trees after we had finished, waiting for Floyd to arrive.

"I think I've hurled everything I've eaten for the past three days," Rachel moaned and stared at me. "Why doesn't this shit bother you?"

"I've grown used to it," I answered. She looked at me questioningly and I hooked a thumb toward the school.

"I've seen a lot of this during the past year."

"They're nasty fuckers is what they are," Cutter said. Both he and his brother had been quiet all morning. Ruth had whispered to me earlier that Justin had given them a stern lecture and warned them there would be consequences if they pulled any nonsense.

"I mean, they shit where they sleep," he continued. "And there were bones everywhere. Where did they find all those people to eat?" It was a good question, one I didn't have an answer to. "Even animals don't shit in their nests."

"You got that right," Shooter agreed.

"It's sad," Kelly said. I glanced at her. "I mean, they used to be civilized humans, and now they're even lower than animals."

We sat in silence and waited for Floyd. Justin got an ammo count while everyone else rested. It'd been a long day and we were tired, but it was the way things were now. It never got any easier.

"My feet are killing me," Kelly quipped. I grunted, but held back with a smart assed retort. The truth be told, my feet were sore too, but I was never going to admit it.

"I have to pee," she whispered, stood and coaxed the women to join her. I watched disinterestedly as they walked to a small copse of trees, dropped their pants, and squatted. They weren't hidden very well and their skinny white asses were plain to see, but it certainly wasn't arousing. I was too weary and it smelled too bad for anything to be arousing at the moment.

I glanced over and spotted Shooter. He was about twenty feet from me, leering unabashedly. Picking up a rock the size of my big toe, I hurled it at him, striking him squarely on the side of the head. He yelped in pain as he grabbed his head. Looking around for the source, he spotted me and fixed me with an angry glare, like he wanted to fight about it. I wagged a finger in warning.

"What makes you think you're so fucking tough?" he challenged.

"Feel free to find out," I replied as I got to my feet. To my surprise, he actually started to stand. And he had his assault rifle in one hand. Like I said, it surprised me, but it also excited me. I was finally going to address this issue once and for all. I was going to have to make it quick though, once the women saw what was going on they would most assuredly intervene. I didn't have to worry about Justin; he was lying on the ground with his boonie hat pulled down over his eyes.

Suddenly, Cutter reached out and grabbed his brother by the arm, pulling him back down and whispered to him forcefully. They traded hushed words back and forth, but after a moment Shooter slumped back to the ground in acquiescence. He glared at me briefly, and then pointedly ignored me.

Justin seemed to have magically awakened at the sound of the approaching bus, jumped to his feet, and policed everyone up. He winked as he walked past me.

"Zach," Kelly said, just about the moment I was drifting off to sleep. I muttered a response.

"Don't you ever get upset when you kill those things?"

"Oh, I guess I did a little bit at one time, but not anymore."

"Why not?"

"Because they're not people anymore. They're inhuman. Killing them is the right thing to do." She was silent for a minute or two and I thought that was the end of it, but then she let out a long sigh.

"What's wrong, sweetheart?" I asked.

"After the ambush, everyone was cutting up and laughing, even me. It doesn't seem right."

"Well, let me tell you a story."

"Okay."

"Back when Rick was alive, we killed a few zombies and I was all stressed about it, but Rick was cutting up and joking. He said back when he was in Vietnam, they behaved the same way and that it was a way of relieving stress. So, sometimes people will behave that way after a stressful event. Kind of a defense mechanism so you don't go crazy. Does that make sense?"

"Yeah, I guess so."

"Good, now go to sleep." I was just about to drift off again when I felt her snuggling closer.

"You know," she said huskily, "sex is a good stress reliever too."

"You're insatiable," I muttered. She responded with a giggle and a roving hand.

CHAPTER 31 - THE RENDEZVOUS

"Do you think anyone will show up?" Kelly asked. We'd awakened early and hurried to the school. Everything was ready except for some of the last minute arrangements, and then we hauled it all to the church. Now, most of us were sitting on the Concord Road Bridge over the Interstate, waiting for any arrivals.

"I wonder how many?" Kelly questioned again. It was about the fourth or fifth time she'd said it. It was a habit when she was anxious. I responded with the same answer.

"Hard to say. Maybe a few. They won't all come at once; they'll be trickling in a few at a time." Yep, same answer as the last four times.

Surprisingly, the first arrivals appeared not from the Interstate, but driving down Concord Road. It was a dually truck, much like Rick's truck, but blue in color. And it was hauling a horse trailer. They drove right up to us and stopped. And then, a very, very large man stepped out.

"Damn," Ruth muttered under her breath. The man, who had skin the color of coffee with a dash of cream, had to be almost seven feet tall and well over three hundred pounds. He reminded me of some of the big pro wrestlers I watched on TV back when I was a kid. He stretched as a fair-skinned ginger haired woman exited from the passenger side. Although not as big as the behemoth standing beside her, she was no small sack of potatoes. A smaller, prettier woman with brown hair braided in pigtails exited from the rear. I walked over to them.

"Welcome," I said. "My name's Zach." The man extended his hand, a very large, calloused hand.

"My name is Garland, but everyone calls me Big Country." He eyed me curiously. "I've heard of you."

"You have?"

"Yep," He looked around some more. "I had a nice conversation on the CB radio a while back with a man named Fred. He told me about you. Is he around?"

My facial expression must have answered for him.

"Oh, I'm terribly sorry." He looked uncomfortable at his imagined transgression. One of the women cleared her throat.

"Oh, I got the manners of a hog eatin' slop," he said and gestured toward the two women. "This is my sister, Gigi and my wife, Julie." Gigi was the big one. Julie was the pretty one. All three of them were wearing overalls, but somehow Big Country's wife made it look sexy. I caught Kelly looking at me out of the corner of my eye.

"I know what you're thinking," he said affably. "Gigi and I have the same momma, but different daddies." Well that explained it, I guess. I tried not to imagine how big their mother was.

"I'm very pleased to meet all of you," I said and introduced the others without mentioning anything about Big Country's wife having the same name as my late wife.

"You guys are the first arrivals," Kelly proclaimed.

"Oh, yeah?" Big Country responded, and then lowered his head close to mine. "Are there any single men around here?" he asked in a whisper that probably could be heard for several blocks. He made a subtle motion toward Gigi. "I'm trying to find a husband for my little sis." I glanced over and caught Gigi looking at me with a hopeful smile. I reached up and patted the big man on the back.

"We have one or two wandering around here. I'll do my best to make it happen. Let's head on over to the church and I'll introduce y'all to everyone."

Other groups trickled in throughout the day. We'd greet them and then guide them toward the church.

"I count twelve," Kelly commented.

"Me too."

"I didn't catch the name of the people who brought their kid along."

"Larry and Alma. They're from Spring Hill."

"And I'm betting there are groups out there who won't be coming."

"Why not?" she asked.

"Various reasons," I answer. "They don't have the means to get here, they're paranoid about being set up, or they just don't care. Big Country said they had a group of eight people, but nobody else wanted to come."

Jorge and his family arrived shortly after the last group. They parked beside our truck and scanned the crowd milling about.

"Not a bad turnout, man," he said. "I didn't think anybody would show up."

"Yeah. Oh, by the way," I said and subtly pointed out Gigi. "She's single and looking for a husband. I told her all about you." I watched as Jorge looked. It took about one second for his eyes to widen and his jaw to drop.

"Holy shit, man, she's huge," he whispered in exasperation. "I thought you and me were friends, man."

"Wide hips," Josue, his father said while holding up his hands, much wider than when he was showing us the width of Kyra's backside. "She make a good wife." Jorge shook his head violently in disagreement.

"You two are loco if you think I'm going to hook up with her." I chuckled as I looked at Josue, who winked at me.

Everyone was milling around in the parking lot. There were some friendly conversations going on, but it seemed a little tense, like everyone was wary of each other. Justin had so far avoided any prolonged conversations with anyone. He kept his distance and watched them warily. When I got his attention, I motioned him to join us.

"How's it going?" I asked.

"So far, so good," he said.

"Any surprises?" I asked in our code word.

"I don't think so," he replied. "I've only talked to a few of them though."

"Well, let's get it started." I stood on the tailgate of my truck and held up a hand.

"May I have everyone's attention?" I waited until everyone was looking at me. "On behalf of all of us, I want to welcome all of you to the first annual rendezvous." I paused while there was some polite clapping.

"It looks like the food is going to be ready in just a few minutes. You're all welcome to eat, but our resources are limited. If any of you have something to contribute, please pitch in."

"Here, here," someone in the group shouted. I smiled politely and then pointed at Justin and Ruth.

"Justin and Ruth are the people you've been hearing on the radio. I'm going to repeat some of the things they said, so please bear with me. It's been a difficult three years. Hopefully, we've turned the corner and this rendezvous will be the start of something positive." I pointed over at Major Parsons.

"That's Major Grant Parsons; he's a Marine and a doctor. He's ready, willing and able to treat anyone with any health problems." He looked at me strangely, probably because nobody had bothered to tell him what was expected of him. "Right, Major?" He cleared his throat.

"That's right, I'm here to help."

"I'm betting there are several of you who've brought trade items, or maybe you have a unique skill set." I caught Rhonda waving at me from the open door and gave me the universal okay sign. "So, why don't we talk about it over dinner, what do you say?" There was a loud bellow from Big Country which I assumed was a cheer. A path was cleared for him as he made his way toward the church entrance, much like one of my bulls when I was throwing out hay this past winter. For a big man, he moved pretty quickly.

Dinner was quiet at first, but Big Country had a loud and jovial nature, which seemed to lighten the atmosphere. Soon, everyone was conversing with each other.

"Where's Sarah?" Kelly asked me. Justin answered.

"She and Sergeant Benoit volunteered for guard duty while everyone ate." He nudged me and lowered his voice. "I think they may have something going on," he said. I looked at him in confusion.

"You know, something romantic."

"You just now noticed?" I asked while Ruth and Kelly giggled. Justin looked at the three of us.

"Y'all knew?" We each nodded our heads at him.

"Speaking of romantic connections, look." Kelly subtly pointed across the room. Floyd was sitting beside Gigi and the two of them were merrily chatting away.

"Anyway," Justin continued. "I got a couple of volunteers to relieve them after they have a full belly. And," he glanced at Ruth, "we have a surprise for everyone and it's going to happen promptly at twenty-hundred hours." I started to ask what the surprise was, but he cut me off with an upraised hand.

"Ask me no questions and I'll tell you no lies, but you're all going to be in for a mighty big surprise."

"That was very poetic," I responded. "It doesn't tell me anything though." Justin merely grinned.

"Just be sure to have everyone in the church, or they'll miss out. Sergeant Benoit is going to handle the communications on this end." Before I could pepper him with questions, he patted me on the shoulder and walked out. Ruth shrugged with her hands up in a poorly contrived expression of ignorance and quickly hurried after her lover.

"What do you think they're up to?" Kelly asked me.

"I'm not sure, but they have a radio rigged up to the choir's speaker system and those two are going to the radio tower. I have a feeling he's going to speak to someone and he wants everyone to hear it."

"What do you have going on here?" Julie and her husband had walked over and were looking at the large dry erase board we had mounted on the back wall.

"Ah, I should have mentioned it earlier. Anything you have to trade, write it up here on one of the boards." I pointed. "Here's our list. Also, if you're looking for something in particular, or maybe you have some kind of special post-apocalyptic skill, write that down too." I pointed at a large sheet of plywood mounted on another wall.

"That one is for posting notes or messages." Big Country frowned in confusion. I explained loudly as other people gathered around. "You may have friends or loved ones who you've lost contact with. Maybe they're no longer with us, maybe they're simply displaced. The board is for posting notes, messages, anything for communication. We'll leave them up forever. However, I want to tell all of you now, it's not for posting notes to people who are deceased. I hope that makes sense."

"That's a wonderful idea, Zach," Julie said with a smile. She then elbowed her husband. "Your handwriting sucks donkey dicks, I'll take care of it." Big Country looked at me apologetically as he handed her the dry erase pen.

"She's got a special way of saying things," he said. I chuckled. She reminded me a lot of my Julie. Big Country nudged me.

"Is that your son with your wife?"

"Yeah, I mean, that's my son but Kelly and I aren't married. We hooked up after my wife was killed. She's been great with my kids. If a preacher shows up, maybe we'll do something about it. Oh, I forgot to mention, I named my boy after Fred. His name is Frederick Zachariah Gunderson." He looked out into space and mouthed the name a couple of times.

"That's a damn good name," he finally declared. I nodded in gratitude.

Big Country and I chatted amicably while we watched the dry erase boards quickly fill up. Soon, the haggling began in earnest. The chatting stopped when there was some sudden feedback from the speaker system. Rach quickly adjusted some controls and looked around.

"Alright everyone," she said loudly. "Any second now we're going to be receiving a radio broadcast." At precisely twenty-hundred hours, Justin's voice could be plainly heard.

"This is Tennessee calling, do you have a copy?" Justin said. After a moment, he got a response.

"Standby, please," a woman's voice replied, which was shortly followed by a man's voice.

"Hello, Tennessee."

"Good evening, Mister President," Justin responded. There was a collective gasp in the crowd.

CHAPTER 32 – THE POLITICIAN

"I trust all is going well at the rendezvous?" the President asked.

"Yes, Mister President," Justin replied. "Everyone present is listening to you." I eased over to where Rachel was standing.

"We're on a low band frequency," she said in answer to my unasked question. "So the conversation will frequently have long gaps in it."

"That is excellent, Sergeant Smithson," the President replied and there was a long gap before he started speaking again.

"My fellow Americans down there in Tennessee, and anyone else who may be listening, the cataclysm has happened and we are now among the ruins."

"Oh, my God," Rachel whispered with a chuckle. "The man just stole a line from Lady Chatterley's Lover. Does he really think we're all just a bunch of illiterate rednecks?" I agreed with her sentiment, but remained silent. I wanted to hear what the man had to say.

"America is hurting, the whole world is hurting. We have faced a life changing event. We have been decimated, but we have not been beaten. We have lost loved ones, but we have persevered. Like the mythical Phoenix, we will rise from the ashes and emerge a stronger people. America is wounded, but we are not broken. We need you now more than ever." There were some audible groans now. After a pause, the President continued, and even gained momentum.

"I was elated and encouraged when I was informed of you courageous survivors. You give me hope that there are many others out there, just like you people from Tennessee." I caught a look from Tonya. She rolled her eyes. It's a good thing there were no elections in the foreseeable future.

"Thanks to the hard work of Gunnery Sergeant Smithson, he was able to make possible this means of communication between myself and my fellow Americans. We need more soldiers like him and I am proud to announce I am promoting him, forthwith, to the rank of First Lieutenant." I saw Sergeant Benoit make a masturbating motion with her fist. Rhonda saw it as well and frowned. Kelly giggled. There was an unusually long pause; I suppose the President was waiting until the thunderous applause died down. Just when I thought the radio had lost the signal, he began speaking again.

"I've no doubt many of you have questions. How many survivors are out there? Has a cure been developed yet? What is the government doing? Let me answer by saying this; all of these issues, and more, are being fervently addressed. We are making significant strides. The American government may seem nonexistent to you at the moment, but rest assured we are here, and we hear you."

It seemed as though I remember watching a TV show of another president saying words to that effect after nine-eleven.

"I will close now, but I am encouraged. I am encouraged by the hardiness and true grit of the survivors out there, not only in Tennessee, but everywhere across America. Stay strong, stay tough, and endeavor to persevere."

"That one's from The Outlaw Josey Wales," someone in the audience exclaimed.

"I've counted five now," someone else commented.

The speech lasted for less than thirty minutes and I gleaned absolutely nothing from it. When he signed off, there was some scattered applause, but not everyone was overwhelmed with enthusiasm. Personally, I considered it a tremendous waste of fuel for the tower's generator. Nonetheless, it got everyone talking. I quietly exited the church and checked with one of the guards.

"How's it going?"

"Going good," he replied. "Everyone has just checked in. No threats, no shenanigans."

"Good. Did everyone get to eat?"

"Oh yeah, Justin took care of us." He looked around. "That was some speech, huh?" I scoffed. "Yeah, that's what I think too. Sergeant Smithson, I mean Lieutenant Smithson, has been chatting with them almost every evening. Well, not chatting, Morse code. I don't know why he has to do it in code."

"Morse code can usually travel a greater distance with less chance of distortion." The guard, the one called Goober, looked at me.

"Okay, if you say so."

"Do you need me to spell you?"

"Oh, no. I'm good. Thanks for asking though."

"Alright." I went back in the church and was surprised to see a lot of messages already posted on the plywood. Floyd spotted me and walked over.

"That was some speech, wasn't it?"

"Yeah, I suppose."

"Have you seen the gal I've been talking to?" he asked.

"Yeah, her name's Gigi, right?" Floyd nodded.

"She's something else," he said with a big cheesy grin.

"It looks like she likes you," I said nonchalantly. Floyd looked at me wide-eyed. I thought he was going to wet himself.

"Really?" I nodded. "Oh, golly. I thought maybe I was just imagining things. I like her too."

"Have you met her brother?" I asked. Floyd nodded.

"He's a big 'un, ain't he?" he asked. I chuckled. "Me and him have been talking about farming. They've got a spread over in Dickson." As Floyd spoke, Big Country must have sensed we were talking about him. He ambled over while we were in mid-conversation.

"Floyd says you have a farm in Dickson." Big Country nodded his head and scratched at an unseen flea in his beard.

"A couple hundred acres, give or take. Most of it's for the cattle, the rest is for crops."

"Floyd's a farmer by trade," I said. "I've found him to be a wealth of knowledge, but these people here at the school don't appreciate him." Big Country seemed to take a moment digesting what I said and looked Floyd over.

"I sure could use help around my place. How good are you with a bad arm?"

"He works his ass off," I proclaimed before Floyd could speak and I leaned forward a little. "Your sister seems to have taken a liking to him. You two aren't in cahoots trying to steal our best farmer away from us, are you?" I asked with a grin. Big Country looked surprised at first, but when he realized I was kidding with him he slapped me on the back and let out a belly laugh that sounded like an off-pitch foghorn.

I laughed along with him as I noticed an older man who was standing within earshot openly listening to us. He looked like he was in his late forties with a sunbaked face that only accentuated his gray eyes. I gave him a friendly nod, which he returned and walked over to us.

"This is some shindig," he said.

"We aim to please," I responded. "My name's Zach, this is Floyd, and this here is Big Country." He nodded at each of us.

"Please to meet all of you. They call me Hillbilly." I looked at him in surprise.

"Hold on there, Mister Hillbilly. Have we had some talks with you over the HAM radio a time or two?"

"One and the same," he replied. "I've been meaning to get down this way for over a year now, but things always seemed to happen." He looked around. "I don't mean any offense, but I'd really like to meet Macie in person. We had a lot of pleasant conversations back in the day."

"Unfortunately, she was murdered by a scumbag," I informed him. His features darkened.

"I'm sorry to hear that," he said softly. "I hope you got the bastard who did it." I nodded, but didn't say anything else. I didn't want to rehash it, the memory was still painful, but when I realized he wanted to know more, I told him. Not the intimate details. Not the part where Macie told Julie and I how much she loved us as she lay there bleeding to death and all I could do was watch her die and how it tore me apart inside. Those were memories I was going to take to the grave.

"So, you got them," Hillbilly said when I'd finished.

"Yep."

"Well, we've all lost people we care about." He looked around, a little uncertain what to say. I pointed at Kelly, who was holding my daughter.

"We kept her memory alive by naming my little girl after her." His eyes lit up.

"That's wonderful," he said. "You know, I brought a present for Macie, big Macie that is. I'd like to give it to your little girl, if that's okay with you."

"Sure," I replied. He turned and walked outside.

"Who do I have to get permission from to drink a tad bit of alcoholic beverage around here?" Big Country asked loudly. "I got some fine Tennessee moonshine my sister's brewed up just for the occasion." Needless to say, several ears perked up.

"I don't know why you haven't brought it out already," I admonished goodheartedly.

"I certainly need something after listening to that gasbag," someone commented. Big Country held up a hand.

"Say no more. I'll be right back." He meandered outside in much the same way all big men walked.

I turned back to the boards and saw Big Country's wife had written down they had several bushels of peanuts, which was awesome.

"I haven't had any fresh peanuts in quite a while," I mused. She grinned.

"You got any horses to trade? We could use a couple."

"There are plenty around here, but they haven't been ridden in a while."

"Julie is a genuine horse whisperer," Gigi said. "She's amazing." I looked at them with a smile.

"How many do you want?" Before we got down to specifics, Kelly walked up with Macie and a little puppy. Both of them were all smiles.

"Look what Hillbilly gave to the kids."

"I hope that's okay with you," Hillbilly said to me. I nodded.

"What kind is it?"

"Mostly German Shepherd. If you mind her diet and don't let her get fat, she won't have hip problems when she gets older."

"What are we going to name her?" Kelly asked. I shrugged my shoulders. I had an idea, but I didn't think Kelly would let me name her Moe.

"I've been calling her Zoe, after my late daughter," Hillbilly answered. "Of course, she's still young enough if you want to change it."

"No, I like Zoe," I said. Kelly nodded in agreement. "Zoe it is."

"I couldn't help but notice you're not drinking." After Big Country brought out the moonshine, people became friendlier and louder. I sat politely and listened to everyone tell their stories, trying my hardest to commit them to memory so I could write them down later. Hillbilly sat nearby, equally quiet.

"What?" I asked. "Oh, yeah, I hardly ever drink," I said. "We have some wine stored away for special occasions, but that's it. No moonshine for me." Big Country nodded in understanding and looked at Hillbilly as he held up a jug.

"What about you, friend?"

"I don't drink either. I'm an alcoholic." I looked at him curiously. He saw me looking, smiled, and held up three fingers.

"Scout's honor. I've been sober three thousand, four hundred and twenty-two days now."

"That's a little over nine years," I said. "Very impressive."

"Thank you. I fell in love and she made me see the light, how about you?"

"When I was old enough to understand, my grandmother sat me down and told me how my parents were killed. Short answer, my father was driving drunk. She said he'd had a drinking problem for years. I've read some articles in journals that said alcoholism could be genetic, so I try to abstain." Hillbilly nodded.

"Both my father and grandfather were boozers, so there may be some truth in that article."

"You don't talk like a hillbilly," I remarked. Hillbilly laughed.

"Make no mistake, I'm a hillbilly through and through. I grew up in the mountains and have been farming all my life, but I was also a high school history teacher back in the day."

"Oh, yeah? Who was the greatest president of all time?" I challenged. Hillbilly eyed at me with a wry grin.

"I've got four of them. Washington, Polk, Lincoln, and Roosevelt. Theodore, not Franklin." I frowned.

"I'm with you on three of them, but why Polk?"

"Because he's the last president that kept all of his campaign promises. He only made four, but he kept every one of them." I laughed.

"I bet you were a great teacher."

"I'd like to think so. I'm guessing you were still in school when it all went bad?"

"Yep."

"What was your favorite subject?" His question started a conversation between us that lasted well into the night.

We didn't get home until after eleven. The kids had never stayed up this late and had fallen asleep in the truck before we had even exited the school parking lot. When we got home, they didn't even stir as we carried them into the house. I got Zoe to do her business in the yard before carrying her inside and stuck her in the bed with the kids. She licked my hand, snuggled up between the two of them, and closed her eyes.

"It seems to be going pretty good," Kelly said as we undressed and crawled into bed. "Even Miss Bitch had good things to say." She was referring to Janet, of course.

"It is, for the most part."

"What do you mean?" Kelly asked as she yawned.

"We're going to trade a few horses for some bushels of peanuts, but to be honest, there's not much else being offered that we have a need for." Kelly responded by emitting a tired groan.

"I know, I'm being negative. It's going good. I guess I'm just tired." If we had any further conversation on the subject, I don't know. I fell sound asleep.

CHAPTER 33 – DAY TWO

I awoke well before sunup, left a note for Kelly, and hurried to the church. Everyone was still asleep, even the guards, with one exception. Hillbilly. I found him in the kitchen area.

"Good morning."

"Good morning," he replied. "Where's your family?"

"I let them sleep in. I imagine they'll be here in about an hour or so." I thought about Janet. She'd not yet met Hillbilly and wondered how she was going to act once she did.

"I took the liberty of looking over the kitchen and I have some coffee percolating on that fancy wood stove made out of scrap metal. Who made that?"

"You'd be surprised. Tonya."

"Oh yeah?"

"She's a pretty smart woman," I grudgingly said. "She'll never win an award for Miss Congeniality, but she's smart." Hillbilly nodded in understanding.

"By the way, thanks again for the dog."

"How's she fitting in?"

"She slept with the kids. I took her out shortly after I woke up. She did her business and then scampered back to their bedroom and waited for me to put her in." Hillbilly smiled.

"That's good."

"Awfully quiet around here. Is anyone else awake yet?"

"I don't think so. Even those two guards in the sniper towers are sound asleep." I looked at him in surprise. He smiled and rummaged through the cabinets until he found two mugs.

"Were they that easy to spot?" I asked.

"Oh, no. The towers themselves are very well-camouflaged. It's your personnel. They were a little tipsy last night and argued over which towers they wanted to sit in, right in front of everyone." I mentally went over the guard roster and settled on Cutter and Shooter. Figures. I looked at my watch.

"They were supposed to be relieved an hour ago. I guess their relief is drunk and passed out as well."

"Alcohol does some amazing things to people," Hillbilly commented glibly.

"Yeah, I guess so. Good thing we didn't have any problems."

"Yep," he answered, checked the pot of water, and began spooning coffee grounds.

"This is what's called cowboy coffee. I was reluctant to fire up the generator just to use a percolator, so we're going to have to settle for this."

"Cowboy coffee?" I asked.

"Yep. What you do is boil water in a pot and then throw the coffee in. Let it boil for a few minutes and then use a spoon to scoop off the grounds floating on the top. Some folks throw a little bit of cold water in and the grounds sink to the bottom, but I do it this way." He finished scooping and poured us two mugs.

"Thank you, sir." It was stale, as usual, and I detected a few grounds that Hillbilly missed, but I liked it. God forbid the day when I had to go without caffeine.

"What's the plan for the day?" Hillbilly asked.

"Hopefully, there'll be more trading and socializing. As for me, I'm going to be helping Big Country. There's a fancy horse farm not far from here. The owner, who must have been a bazillionaire, had at least a couple hundred head of varying breeds. After, they were being cared for by a man named Bo, but he's disappeared and the horses have scattered everywhere." I took a sip, and hooked a thumb at the direction of the farm.

"I've worked a deal with Big Country to trade a few horses for some bushels of peanuts. We just have to round them up." Hillbilly digested what I said in silence while he drank his coffee and refilled our mugs before speaking.

"If you don't mind, I believe I'd like to tag along," he finally said.

"You're more than welcome. I hope you have experience with horses."

"I do," he said simply. I figured he did. The man was rugged looking, a no nonsense kind of guy with big, rawboned hands every bit as calloused as Big Country's.

We continued with a quiet conversation while other people awakened and made their way to the kitchen. I liked the man. His demeanor was so much like Fred's they could have been brothers. Sarah and Rachel came in together and accepted our offer of coffee. Both women thanked us and I think I even caught them both eyeing Hillbilly a little bit longer than just a casual glance.

"Why don't you two sit with us," I suggested after I'd made introductions.

"Sarah and Rachel are military," I said to Hillbilly. "Sarah is a pilot in the Air Force and Rachel in in the Army." I thought a second. "I don't really know what you originally did in the Army."

"I was an exotic dancer," Rachel said with a straight face. Hillbilly stared at her before she burst out laughing. "Gotcha." Hillbilly smiled then.

"Yes, you did," he admitted.

"I was a Forty-Six Quebec, which is the Army's way of saying Public Affairs Specialist." Hillbilly nodded.

"I could see you being on television." Rachel blew a tuft of hair out of her eyes.

"I never got that far. I only wrote articles for the base commander and occasionally give him a blow job." She waited for a long five seconds.

"Gotcha."

"Alright, sugar plum," Big Country said to his wife, "which one are we gonna take first?" Julie was wearing jeans and boots this morning with a tight-fitting tee shirt, sans bra, and a Stetson cowboy hat. She looked around and pointed at a big stallion.

"He's a good one. I bet he has lineage." I had no idea about that, he was big though, and since he'd had no human contact in a while, he was going to be a handful.

"Alright," I said. "Let's spread out, separate him from the others, and maneuver him to a corner. With any luck, we'll be able to rope him without too much fuss." Big Country held up a meaty hand.

"Hold on there, friend," he said. "We all are gonna just sit tight and let my beautiful wife work her magic."

"Uh, okay," I said and glanced over at Hillbilly. He glanced back and made a slight shrug with his shoulders.

We watched as Julie separated herself from us and walked out into the field with nothing more than a halter and a rope. All of the horses were grazing, but they stopped and looked at her curiously. She ignored all of them but the big stallion. He looked at her for a moment and then went back to grazing. After a full ten minutes, he looked at her again. Julie produced something from her pocket and held it out.

"She's got a cube of sugar," Gigi whispered to us. I noticed Floyd was standing a little closer to her than normal and smiled to myself. "Horses can't resist her when she does this." I nodded in semi-understanding and wondered where they got cubed sugar from. The big horse stared at her in apprehension, but within a minute he started making his way toward her. The others followed his lead and soon had her surrounded, nudging her for her attention. We watched raptly as the big horse became a big baby in her hands as she stroked and cooed him. Within a minute, she had the halter around his head and tethered a lead to it. She walked him to the horse trailer and gently guided him in without breaking a sweat.

"Ain't that something?" Gigi asked. Hillbilly and I nodded in agreement. Afterward, she walked back to us and pointed out three more.

"I like those three mares. That big stud has already impregnated them, I'm betting. Is that okay with you, Zach?" she asked.

"Yeah, fine by me. Let me ask you, are you going to keep them in the trailer?"

"Oh, no," Big Country interjected. "We've got some barb wire. I'm going to rig up a temporary pen until time to leave."

"Okay, great. So, yeah, the ones you picked out are just fine."

"We're much obliged," Big Country said gratefully.

"That woman sure has a way with horses," Hillbilly commented as we rode back to the church.

"A horse whisperer, just like that movie with Robert Redford," I said. He nodded in agreement. "But much prettier," I added. Hillbilly smile slightly.

"I couldn't help but notice, there aren't any zombies around here." I nodded and gave him the Reader's Digest version of our eradication efforts.

"Sounds a little bit like a military operation," he said. I nodded again. "Very impressive."

"We used a lot of ammo, but it was necessary. Have you and your people done anything similar?" I asked. Hillbilly shook his head.

"No, we had something else working to our advantage."

"Oh, yeah?"

"The second winter was a cold one. Without a few billion people expelling carbon dioxide into the atmosphere, we had a brutal cold snap starting about the middle of January. It got down to twenty below for two nights and the rest of the week it got down to ten below every night. It was hard on the livestock and even harder on those infected things. Every one of them that were outside died."

"Really?" I asked. Hillbilly nodded.

"You didn't have anything similar?"

"No. We saw quite a few freeze solid, but when they thawed out they came back to life." Hillbilly looked thoughtful.

"It sounds like when the temperature drops down to a certain level for a prolonged period, the effects are irreversible."

"Yeah," I said and thought a minute. "If this is not a phenomenon for only the plateau, it means up in the northern areas, the zombies are all but eradicated."

"I certainly hope so," Hillbilly said.

"How many survivors are there on the plateau?"

"The first year was about a hundred that I know of. Now, there's maybe a dozen people left. Some died, others moved on."

"What about your family?"

"All dead," he said. "I've been on my own since almost the first. People up on the plateau are friendly folks but a bit clannish. Once it went bad, people became, shall we say, stand-offish."

"You know, you're welcome to stay here," I said. "Nobody's related and there're plenty of vacant houses around here that'd be easy to fix up." I pointed at the horse farm as we drove by it. "You could even live there, if you're inclined."

"I appreciate that, Zach, I really do. But, I'm fifty-years-old now and pretty set in my ways. I've lived up on the Cumberland Plateau all of my life and I believe that's where I want to die."

I really believed he'd be a valuable addition to our group and wanted to push the sales pitch, but I knew he was too much like Fred. If he said he wanted to live out the rest of his life on the Plateau, that's exactly what he was going to do.

"Zach, I've been meaning to ask you, have you come into contact with any older survivors lately? You know, like over the age of sixty?" I thought about it and shook my head.

"Sadly no." I told him about Bernie the Beekeeper. "He was the last one I know of and he died last year."

"Yeah, the mortality rate isn't very good these days." We drove the rest of the way back to the church in silence.

CHAPTER 34 – FAREWELLS

"Are you sure about this?" I asked. Floyd nodded.

"About as sure as I've been about anything since the world changed." He looked at me as if we knew something he didn't. He asked me as much.

"We just want you to be happy, Floyd," Kelly said.

"They seem like really good people," I added. "If Gigi's the one for you, we're totally behind you." He smiled gratefully.

"Thanks, you two. That means a lot."

"Have you got everything loaded up?" I asked. Floyd nodded.

"Once I get to Dickson, I'll find me another ride, so if you want my Toyota, you're welcome to it." After he'd busted one of the struts, he left his FJ Cruiser sitting on the side of Franklin Pike. It had low mileage and was otherwise in good shape, so, yeah, I had every intention of claiming it. Kelly and I walked with him over to Big Country's truck where a lot of the school group was patiently waiting. Gigi had a grin on her face as big as Cheshire cat's.

"Well now, young Mister Gunderson, this was a mighty fine rendezvous," Big Country declared. "I reckon it's going to be a yearly event?"

"That's our hope," I answered and gave him a folder with papers in it. "Here's some instructions on building a dipole antenna so we can chat more often." We shook hands and hugged and told each other how much we were going to miss each other. I thought Big Country was going to start crying. All four of them waved vigorously as they drove away.

"I'm going to miss Floyd," Rhonda said as they drove off. "He was a sweet man."

"Me too," Marc and Ward said in unison. Gus didn't have much to say, but he nodded at Rhonda's statement. I noticed throughout the rendezvous the two of them had always stayed close to each other and idly wondered if they had started some kind of relationship. I looked over at Tonya.

"He had his uses," she finally admitted. I guess that was the closest thing she could come to saying she was going to miss him as well. She looked around.

"That's the last of them. Quite frankly I'm ready for some peace and quiet around here."

"They sure did eat a lot of food," Gus commented.

"Yeah, so did you," Tonya retorted. Gus glowered at her but said nothing.

"I think it went rather well," Ward said. "Except for that one little mishap."

"Cutter's claiming he got sucker punched," Ward continued. "I didn't see what happened, but I've heard a few variations."

"Well, I'll tell you what happened," Ruth answered. "The dumbass got drunk and was making rude comments to Julie. That was stupid when you consider that she's married to Sasquatch."

"So, Big Country got jealous," Marc concluded. Ruth scoffed.

"Julie told him to back off and so he called her a bitch. Jealous might not be the right word, more like defending the honor of his wife."

"Cutter's lucky," Justin said. "If that man had hit Cutter with everything he had, I sincerely doubt he'd be still walking around."

Cutter must have sensed we were talking about him. He emerged from the church as we were walking in. His left eye was blue and swollen shut.

"What are y'all talking about?" he asked.

"We were just saying how much we're going to miss Big Country and his family," I said innocently.

"Yeah, well he's banned from ever coming back around here," he proclaimed. Everyone got a good chuckle out of that. Cutter's face reddened and he walked off.

"Where did Hillbilly go?" Kelly asked.

"He left last night," Ruth said. "He came by before leaving and said he didn't want to say goodbye and he'll try to get back by here soon."

"That's odd," Kelly said.

"He was a little bit aloof the whole time," Marc said. "I think the only person he really talked to was Zach."

"We think the crowd made him a little nervous," Ward added. Marc nodded in agreement.

"I'd say you're assessment is on the money," I said. "He said all of his family are dead and he doesn't have very much contact with other people. He's become somewhat asocial, I'd guess."

"Will he come back?" Kelly asked.

"Probably so, he just needs some time," Ward said.

While everyone chitchatted, I walked in the church and looked around. The sheet of plywood had all kinds of notes tacked to it with messages to the lost. There were even some photographs. I heard the door open and looked to see Tonya walking in.

"I must admit, it went better than I thought it would," she confessed. "I thought nobody at all would show up, or it would be a bunch of freeloaders looking for handouts." She continued staring at the bulletin boards.

"You were right." I glanced at her in surprise. She continued. "This is the way to rebuild a society."

"We're off to a decent start," I replied.

"Do you believe the President?" she asked.

"About what, sending a delegation down here?" She nodded. "Yeah, I suppose they'll do that at some point. Especially now that they know I'm alive."

"Yeah, they'll come down here and screw everything up," she surmised. I chuckled.

"Yeah, most likely."

"So, what's next?" she asked.

"We've got a doctor and two nurses living here now, we need a clinic."

"Where would we put it?"

"Either here at this church or at the school."

"I'd rather it be here. There's more room and I'd rather not have outsiders wandering around where I live."

"Fine by me," I replied. "Let's make it Grant's project. It'll keep him busy."

CHAPTER 35 — FLU

It took a full day to clean up everything from the rendezvous and almost everyone pitched in, some with more enthusiasm than others. At the end of the day, we found ourselves sitting around, discussing the clinic. Someone pulled out a gallon milk jug of moonshine and someone else, I actually think it was Tonya, pulled out some weed. The only ones who didn't imbibe were Sarah and myself. Even Kelly and Justin had joined in. It got everyone good and loosened up and there was a lot of smiling and laughing.

The bad side of it was, what started out as a thoughtful conversation about the clinic slowly but steadily devolved into a lot of silly arguing. Rachel found a partner in crime with Kelly. They drank some moonshine, smoked some of Tonya's weed, and they soon began mimicking everyone and laughing uncontrollably. Sarah had been sitting quietly across from me, and when she saw me looking she rolled her eyes. I smiled in agreement.

"You're not saying much," she remarked. I closed my notepad and set it down.

"I was hoping to get some constructive input. You know, maybe somebody would have thought of something innovative, but in the end, Grant, Mike and Mary are going to build their clinic however they want it built." Kelly, sitting beside me and giggling and who knew what, suddenly focused on us.

"What are you two talking about, pumping your weights?" she asked and started giggling again.

"Naked weightlifting," Rachel added, which caused more giggling from the two of them.

The endless opinions about the clinic became background noise and I amused myself by watching the kids playing with each other. Well, except for Sammy. He was listening attentively to the adults acting like children. I felt a light pinch on my earlobe and turned quickly to see one of Rhonda's little girls running away, screaming.

"Brittany likes you," Kelly said with a grin. I frowned, Kelly noticed it, and began giggling. "He still doesn't know their names," she said to Rachel.

"Uh, well, I always get them mixed up." Rhonda, who had walked up, heard my response and looked pointedly at me. I shrugged apologetically.

"Okay, busted."

"The one who is sweet on you is Brittany. The other two are Clair and Emma. Clair is the one in the pink shirt." The kids were running around the cafeteria playing tag or something, with Callahan and Zoe happily joining in. Clair ran up and tagged Frederick, and as I watched, she chose that particular moment to sneeze all over him. Great, I thought.

By the time we got home, both kids were fussy and complaining of not feeling well. Kelly was having a hard time keeping her eyes open and as soon as we got home, she went straight to the bedroom. Janet tended to the kids while I hurried through some of the chores.

"They're both running a fever," she said as soon as I walked inside. She'd found the thermometer in our first aid kit. "Both of them are reading a hundred."

"Where's Kelly?" I asked.

"Passed out, she drank too much of that moonshine." Damn, I thought.

"Alright, you're a mom, what do you think?"

"They've definitely come down with something. Let's get them in bed and put some wet rags on their foreheads." I agreed and grabbed a bottle of baby aspiring.

"They're expired, but it's all we've got." Janet nodded in agreement and got each child to swallow one with some sips of water.

"I'll sit here with them, I think you need to go get Grant." The worry on her face was obvious and I no doubt looked the same. I nodded.

"Good idea."

I drove as quickly as I dared over the rough roads. By the time I'd arrived back at the school, all of the kids were showing symptoms.

"We're going to quarantine them," Grant said. He had a look of genuine worry and for a moment it made me forget my disdain for him. "I strongly suggest you do the same."

"What is it?" I asked. "Do you know?" He looked at me grimly.

"Could be anything. A common cold, a childhood disease one of the visitors was carrying, or it could be worse." I understood what he was implying.

"We're going to put them in the radio house," he continued. "Justin and Ruth agreed to stay at the school until it's over."

"Okay," I replied. "We can keep them in their bedroom."

"Nobody else should come into contact with them," Grant added. "I myself will be wearing protective gear, but even that may not be enough." I think my face may have paled when he said that last statement. Grant put a sympathetic hand on my shoulder.

"We'll try to come by in the morning, that's all I can do for now."

I sped back to the house in a somber mood. Once I got the gate secured, I knew what I had to do.

"Quarantine," I said to Janet and related my conversation with Grant. "We'll keep the kids in the bedroom. I've got respirators and nitrile gloves we can use when we check on them. I think we're going to need to sterilize everything we can. It'll be a precautionary measure, if nothing else." I heard the sound of retching and hurried into the master bathroom. Kelly was bent over the toilet bowl.

"The next time I take a drink of moonshine, I want you to bend me over and whip my ass."

"That bad?" I asked.

"Oh, yeah." She straightened slowly, a little unsteadily and moved to the sink to rinse her mouth.

"Did Janet say anything?" Kelly nodded and then grabbed her mouth again and bent back over the toilet.

"Grant isn't sure what it is?" Kelly asked. I shook my head. "Could it be...?"

"The plague? It could be. I don't know." Kelly's lower lip started quivering. I didn't know what to say to calm her.

"You know, it could be something else, like, I don't know, the mumps or something." It didn't help.

"I'm sorry, Zach." she said weakly.

"Don't worry," I replied. "Why don't you get back in bed, Janet and I will take care of them." Kelly started to argue, but she realized she was worthless at the moment. I got her tucked in and quietly closed the door.

"It may be a case of drinking too much, or it may be something more," I whispered to Janet. She looked at me steadily and then handed me the thermometer.

"If she has a temperature..."

Kelly protested when I woke her back up, and even went back to sleep while the thermometer was still in her mouth, but thankfully she didn't have a temperature.

We spent the rest of the day fervidly cleaning everything and worrying over the kids. Janet finally drifted off to sleep around midnight. I couldn't. I checked on them throughout the night, making sure they stayed hydrated, cleaning them up when they soiled themselves, and keeping a cold compress on their foreheads. Their temperatures were up to a hundred and two and by morning their sheets were soaked with sweat.

I can't begin to express the torment in my soul, watching my two kids, too exhausted to cry, their bodies being wracked with painful sobs. Kelly peeked in the door as the sun was coming up. I waved her off and came out a moment later.

"Okay, don't come near me," I said when I took off the respirator, headed toward the bathroom and washed up. Kelly watched from a distance.

"They've gotten worse," I said. No need mincing words. "They both have temperatures and they're having a hard time keeping anything down. How are you feeling?"

"Like shit," she said. "I'm sorry, Zach. I shouldn't have gotten drunk."

"No need to be sorry. We had no way of knowing this was going to happen. You were enjoying yourself, that's all."

I sat down and realized I was absolutely exhausted. Kelly began pacing, much like I would do when I was thinking deeply about something. I would have laughed under any other circumstances. When I saw something change in her expression, it didn't register.

"I think they have the flu," she said.

"It's possible," I replied.

"I think I'll try to fix them something to eat, maybe some broth or soup."

"Good idea," I said and then my tired brain finally remembered I had a few books on illnesses sitting on the shelf. I took one and began thumbing through it. I walked into the kitchen and plopped down in a chair.

"This book lists, fever, chills, nausea, and diarrhea as some of the symptoms, as if I didn't know that already."

"You're exhausted, get some sleep."

"I'm too keyed up," I said and watched as Kelly opened the refrigerator for some milk.

"Shit," she muttered.

"What?"

"The milk is warm." She stuck her hand in the fridge. "It's warm."

"Shit," I said a little more indignantly as I realized what I'd done.

"I turned on the water heater and well pump last night and forgot to turn them off. It drained off the batteries, so now we don't have any electricity." I smelled the milk, it was spoiled. I muttered a few more expletives, hurried outside, turned off the circuit breakers and checked the gauges. As I suspected, my error had drained the batteries and they were going to need a full day to recharge. Kelly and Janet met me at the door as I walked back inside.

"I think you're right," Janet added. "They're not the first sick kids I've seen over the years." Our conversation was cut short by the sound of a horn honking.

"Someone's at the gate," I said. "I'll get it." I hurried outside before either woman objected.

I jumped on one of the bicycles and headed for the gate. For the first time, I was actually glad when I saw it was Grant. One of the nurses was accompanying him.

"We tried calling on the radio," Grant said as I unlocked the gate. I nodded, not bothering telling them about how I stupidly allowed the batteries to run down.

"You look as tired as I feel," I said to Grant and looked at the nurse, a handsome, fit-looking man. "It's Mike, correct?" I asked him. He nodded. "How're the rest of the kids?"

"They're all doing about the same. Clair's temperature is higher than the rest of them and she's breaking out in a rash, but we're doing what we can. How're your kids?"

"We think it's a case of the flu," I said and explained the symptoms. Both Grant and Mike nodded.

"Yeah, that's what we think too," Grant replied. "Would you like us to check on them?" I nodded eagerly, closed the gate and followed them on the bike. The cool morning air woke me up and I even broke a sweat. It felt good and my anxiety subsided for ten, maybe twenty seconds. The sun was glowing bright in the east as I parked the bike, telling me it was going to be a hot one today.

"At least the batteries will get recharged," I muttered to myself.

"It's definitely the flu," Grant said. As Kelly, Janet, and I had watched anxiously, he and Mike had given our kids a thorough examination. They used hand sanitizer liberally before putting on gloves and masks. I was grateful for their precautionary measures.

"Keep them in bed and isolated for the next five or six days. Now, it's important to watch for complications such as pneumonia or encephalitis. Mike has volunteered to stay here and help out, if you like."

"Yeah, I'd appreciate it," I replied. Grant nodded and patted me on the shoulder again. It irritated me when he did that, but I didn't say anything.

"I'll check back later."

"I should have the radio back up and running by this evening if you need to talk to us. If you don't mind, lock the gate behind you."

"Of course. I'll see you tomorrow." I nodded to him gratefully. He responded with a tired smile before leaving.

"I've made a decision," I said to them. "I'm going to start the generator. It's going to be a hot day and we've got to have cool air for them." I thought mentally of how much power the air conditioner was going to pull and the fuel it was going to consume. Kelly must have read my thoughts.

"Are you sure?" Kelly asked. "That's going to burn a lot of gas."

"Yes it will, but that's the least of my worries." I caught a glimpse of Mike's expression. I imagine we all looked like hell, but he was gracious enough not to say anything.

"Mike, we haven't eaten yet, would you like to join us?"

"I never turn down a meal," he replied with a friendly smile.

We had a late breakfast, but Mike was the only one who had an appetite. After some subdued conversation, I stood. It felt like I was trying to lift a freight train and I think I actually wobbled a little bit.

"I'm going to check on them," I told them.

"I'll take care of it," Mike said as he stood. "You're about to pass out on your feet. You need some sleep, that's an order." I started to protest, but Mike held up a hand. "If anything happens, I'll wake you. I give you my word."

"I'll be right there beside him," Janet added. Kelly was giving me a stern look and I was just plain too tired to argue. I don't think I remembered my head hitting the pillow.

They were miserable for two days, which meant that Kelly and I, and even Janet, were considerably stressed. It goes without saying that our anxiety caused a few cross words passed among us. Mike unwittingly found himself acting as both a nurse, peacemaker and therapist.

On the third day, they seemed to feel better and neither one of them had diarrhea anymore. And on the early morning of the fourth day, we awoke to Frederick sitting on the porta-potty I'd put in their room with his head in his little hands and Macie sitting on the floor watching him. When she saw me, she immediately held out her arms.

"Well, it looks like you two are feeling better," I said happily.

"I'm hungry," Frederick replied, which caused me to grin from ear to ear.

The two of them had a healthy appetite and I couldn't wait to get on the radio and inform Grant. It was a brief but good conversation. Grant agreed we should wait two more days before we went to the school.

"Clair died last night," Grant informed us somberly before we even made it through the door of the school. "She developed pneumonia."

"Oh, no," Kelly said and went to look for Rhonda.

"We're going to carry her to the church and have a graveside service," Ruth said.

We used the bus to carry everyone to the church. The collective mood was somber, dark. We'd lost a child who was a part of our future and it weighed heavily on all of us. Her coffin was nothing more than a wooden crate.

"It was the best we could do on short notice," Justin had whispered.

Gus read a few passages from the book of Psalms and led us in a prayer. He did it smoothly, like he'd done it a few times before. Surprisingly, Rhonda sang Amazing Grace in a beautiful, lilting voice. Even I teared up.

I volunteered to do the burial honors and insisted everyone go back to the school. Justin elected to stay with me. When everyone was safely out of sight, I looked at him somberly.

"You know what I intend to do, right?" He nodded without speaking. I pried open the lid. Her little body was wrapped in a blanket. I started to take aim, but stopped.

"Oh, wow," Justin said when he saw what I was looking at. Blood had soaked through the blanket around Claire's head.

"Looks like someone has already taken care of it."

"I bet the major did it," Justin guessed. He helped me put the lid back on and we spent the next hour burying her. The thought of burning her remains didn't seem right, somehow.

When we were finished, Justin and I got in my truck and started back. When we started to cross over the bridge, Justin pointed out four or five zombies wandering down the Interstate. He looked at me questioningly. I responded by turning onto the exit ramp and driving the wrong way down to the Interstate.

"No need for wasting ammo," Justin said tersely. He exited the truck armed with a bayonet and an aluminum baseball bat. I grabbed my machete.

The four of them were adult males, all dressed like they were in a militia or something. All of them had camo jackets and pants, boots, and ski masks that'd been torn open around the mouth area, I guess to expedite eating. Justin ran forward and hit one of them in the chest with a lunging side kick before spinning around and hitting a second one with his ball bat before finishing up with the bayonet through an eye socket.

The other two forgot all about me and focused on Justin. That made it easy for me to run up and bury my machete in the back of the head of one of them. The second one turned toward me then and I readied my machete, but Justin beat me to it. He hit the man so hard the bastard's head literally exploded, spraying Justin. He backed off immediately. I ran up to the last one who was struggling back to his feet and stomped on his head until there wasn't much left.

"Come with me," I directed Justin and led him to the back of the truck. I had one of those hard plastic beer growlers lying in back and grabbed it. Unscrewing the top, I had Justin hold his hands out and poured the water over them.

"It's a mixture of water and bleach," I said. "Wash your face off." Justin hesitated. "Quickly, Marine," I chided. Justin did as I said and then I cleaned myself up.

"You've got to figure out a different strategy for killing them," I said. "You get that goo in your mouth or in your eyes, anything like that, you'll get infected." I thought for a second. "Maybe wear a face shield or something."

"What about you?" he questioned, pointing at my machete. I shrugged.

"I'm immune, remember?" Justin eyed me and scoffed.

CHAPTER 36 – THE MISSION

"I don't want to do it, but Major Parsons has convinced me of the necessity of it," Justin said to us.

"Let me see if I've got this straight," Tonya said. "You all are going back to the CDC?"

"Yes," Major Parsons replied. "But it's not a permanent move. In order to properly conduct tests, we're going to need to access the labs down there."

"What's wrong with staying here?" Marc asked. "I bet there's everything you need at one of the hospitals around here. Heck, I bet Vanderbilt has everything and then some."

"I'm sure you're right, Marc, but there is specific equipment down there and most importantly, I'm familiar with all of it." He glanced over at Justin. "Besides, I'm going to attempt to retrieve the data files of the other doctors."

"It seems awfully risky," Marc said in almost a mumble.

"So, the mission is as follows," Justin stated. "Five of us will be leaving tomorrow. It'll be Major Parsons, Private Mann," he pointed at Blake who acknowledged with a halfhearted salute. "Cutter, Sergeant Caswell, and myself. We know the CDC." He gestured at Cutter.

"Obviously, Cutter has never been there, but he'll still be able to help out. We should arrive in Atlanta within twenty-four hours. It may take us an hour or two to get back inside and perhaps a couple of hours to download all of the necessary files. This, of course, is dependent on how many infected are still inside and whether or not the generators are damaged."

"What if they are?" Tonya asked.

"If that's the case, we'll remove the hard drives and bring them back with us, but if the facility is secure enough, and we can get the generators running, Grant is going to conduct tests with the pint of blood Zach is going to donate and maybe even attempt to synthesize a serum."

"How long will that take?" I asked the good doctor.

"As I told you earlier, we'd actually come a long way before we were overrun. The test batch I told you about is in all likelihood no longer good, but with your blood I believe I can work up a new batch. I'll not make a long convoluted explanation. The short answer is, three days or so." There was some murmuring in the crowd.

"We'll be taking the two Humvees. They've already been prepped and ready to go."

"Why two?" Gus asked. "Isn't that a waste of fuel?"

"We'll need both vehicles to haul the equipment back and if one of them breaks down, we'll still have a viable means of transportation." Justin held his hand up to stop the questions. "Listen people, we've thought this all out and have planned for every foreseeable contingency. We'll be back before you know it." He's looking at Ruth as he says this. She's not going with him and her worry is palpable.

"It just seems like you're taking an awful lot of gas and ammo with you." Gus wouldn't let it go, even though it wasn't his gas or ammo.

"Would you like to go with us?" Grant asked him.

"Oh, no," he answered quickly. The other men traded a look. Tonya had walked out of the cafeteria while everyone was talking and had now returned, holding something in her hands. She handed it to Justin. He and Grant looked at it curiously.

"It's a radiation detection device. You'll be traveling through areas that may or may not have radiation fallout. I'll train you how to use it."

"Thank you," Justin said. Tonya smirked.

"Don't thank me, by the time you realize you're in a hotspot, it'll probably already be too late.

"The technical name for it is an ion chamber survey meter with a beta slide." She pointed at the on/off switch.

"It is quite simple to operate. Turn it on, it automatically clears the chamber and takes a reading. There is no sound card with this one, so it won't make any noise like those Geiger counters you see on TV. You have to pay attention and read the gauge. It's powered with batteries, so I would suggest having extras on hand.

"You're only problem is going to be the range. This particular model will only test the immediate area, drive down the road a hundred yards and you'll need to test again."

Justin listened carefully and tried it out. She was right, it was really simple to use.

"I appreciate it."

"Try not to break it," she said with a tone in her voice which indicated she believed that's exactly what they'd do.

I sat in one of those child-sized classroom chairs while Grant prepped my arm and inserted the needle. Lacking a tennis ball, Grant found one of those erasers for a dry-erase board and had me squeeze it.

"Do you really think this is a good idea? Going back to the CDC?" I asked him. His mouth worked while he formed an answer.

"We have to try," he finally said. It was just the two of us in the classroom, everyone else was eating dinner. He leaned closer and lowered his voice.

"There's something I haven't told anyone but Mike and Mary. Clair was infected." I looked at him in surprise.

"She didn't have the flu?" He shook his head.

"The presentation of symptoms are very similar. It's possible the flu virus activated it, I don't know." He continued staring at me somberly.

"So, you see, the plague is still active. We must find a cure."

"I was going to put a bullet in her head after everyone left the church, but you'd already taken care of it." Grant nodded. "What'd you do?"

"I shoved a scalpel into the base of her brain."

"Wow," I muttered.

"I had to be certain she wouldn't infect anyone. That's one of your rules, isn't it?"

"Yep, rule number one." I watched the plastic bag as it slowly filled with my blood.

"I never read up on viruses."

"It's a fascinating topic," Grant said. "Did you know there are over one hundred million known types to exist? And, we haven't even come close to discovering them all." He had a gleam in his eye as he continued.

"They can self-replicate, and if they're attacked by something like an antibiotic, the cells will mutate. That's why there has never been a cure for the common cold, specifically known as rhinovirus." He wagged a finger.

"This particular virus starts with flu-like symptoms, but it attacks the brain. The infection time varies, we had compiled a data base of exposure to full blown infection from minutes to several hours. At the beginning stages, the infected person becomes highly unstable."

"So, that explains the violent behavior," I said.

"Correct. The frontal lobe is responsible for morality, multi-tasking, complex problem solving. It was easy to observe the damage. The amygdala, which is the portion of the brain which triggers the fear mechanism, is virtually wiped out. Their inability to walk and climb stairs is an indicator of damage to the cerebellum."

"The Zee-Fourteens are showing signs that they're healing," I remarked. "They're moving better and some of them have even tried to flee when they realized their lives were in danger. That's a sign of their brain repairing itself, right?"

"Yes and no," Grant replied. "The human brain is remarkable. A part of it can be irrevocably damaged and another part of the brain can take over the functions."

"Will mankind ever become resistant to this virus?"

"To an extent, *if* mankind survives." Grant noticed me frowning.

"What?"

"Alright, I'm no expert in this topic, but it seems to me the survivors, like you for instance, have at least some type of resistance to the infection."

"Yes, we do, but we're not totally immune." He worked his mouth a moment. "Let's compare it to the smallpox epidemic. Are you familiar with it?"

"Haven't there been several outbreaks over the years?"

"Yes, there have. There was a big one in 1862," Grant said. "It was a worldwide infection. Tens of thousands of people died, perhaps even millions. But, it was only a thirty to thirty-five percent mortality rate. The mortality rate for this virus is somewhere around eighty percent."

"I figured as much," I said. Grant continued speaking while I mentally worked the numbers in my head. That left a worldwide population of roughly

1.6 billion. Figure a mortality rate of the survivors at 25%, and that was a modest estimation, the math left a population of approximately 1.2 billion. Worldwide. I wondered where the highest concentration of the survivors were located, but Grant interrupted my thoughts.

"And, in addition, new vaccination techniques were tested," Grant said. He paused a moment and chuckled.

"Did you know, as early as the fourteenth century, the Chinese would ground up pox scabs from infected people and blow it up the noses of the wealthy elite?"

"I read that online back before," I said. "But the article didn't say whether or not it was effective."

"From all of the known writings on the subject, it was very successful."

"And there was no antigen or vaccine made for this virus?" Grant shook his head.

"Several attempts were made, but they all failed. That's why we at the CDC believed that if we found someone who is immune, like you, we could create an antigen."

"It doesn't explain why I got sick when I was exposed."

"If a sample base of one hundred people were to be inoculated with a flu vaccine, a sizeable percentage would experience flu-like symptoms after being inoculated. It is entirely possible you were experiencing the same thing. If only we had known this information back when the CDC was operational," he mused, "perhaps we could have found the reason."

"Coulda, shoulda, woulda," I lamented. Grant chuckled.

"The CBIRF teams were trained for all forms of nuclear, biological, and chemical attack. CDC personnel had trained for every type of possible outbreak as well. Even so, we had our asses handed to us."

"Was there ever a consensus reached on what the hell caused this?" Grant shook his head.

"It's definitely a virus. The genetic markers indicate it's natural, like chicken pox, herpes, HIV, but that's where the similarity ends. It attacks the brain like meningitis and mutates quickly. All of the autopsies we performed showed portions of the brain such as the frontal lobe destroyed and the rest was..." he rubbed his face, attempting to find the right words.

"The rest of the brain was infected, obviously, but the virus had mutated it somehow." He looked at the IV bag and gave it a gentle squeeze.

"The answer to your question; no, we had no idea what caused it. If I were to guess, it's one of those undiscovered viruses."

"Grant, since we're being so friendly with each other at the moment, I have a question to ask you." He looked at me curiously. "Was there any experimentation done on infected subjects?" Grant looked away, and moved his mouth a couple of times. It was a peculiar habit of his when he was trying to think up the best way to say something.

"Just spit it out, yes or no?"

"Yes." After a few seconds, he elaborated. "Even before Colonel Coltrane and I arrived at the CDC, they were capturing zombies of various genders, age, and ethnicity and performing experiments."

"What kind of experiments?"

"Everything you can imagine, Zach. We injected them with every type of serum known. We'd draw fluid samples from one and inject them into another. We performed hundreds of autopsies. We dissected them while they were still alive. I assisted in one experiment where we removed portions of the brain and then would test their cognitive functions. You name it, we did it." He frowned and shook his head.

"We accumulated a vast amount of data, but, the closest thing we've come to a cure was you and the now deceased female from Kentucky."

"Did you meet her?"

"Oh yes. I was the one who tested her. A cute, eighteen-year-old girl straight out of the mountains."

I sat in silence now and watched the plastic bag fill up with my blood while I pondered what he'd said. For some reason, I didn't believe a cure would ever be found.

"Don't ask me why I say this, Grant, but I don't believe she's dead." Grant looked at me in surprise and then offered a nervous chuckle.

"When you say it like that, I feel compelled to ask. Did you know her?"

"I'm not sure."

"You're not sure if you know her or you're not sure how you suspect she's still alive?"

"Both."

CHAPTER 37 - OPERATION CDC

"It looks different," Justin whispered. They'd stopped on the apex of Interstate 24 where it crested over Monteagle Mountain about a hundred yards from where they got into a firefight not so long ago.

"All of the bodies are gone, but that's all I see," Grant opined. Justin squinted at the remains of the roadblock. It was in shambles now and there had been no effort put forth to rebuild it. It took him a moment before he spotted it.

"Does it seem like there are a few more abandoned cars than last time?"

"Yeah," Grant suddenly exclaimed and pointed. "And that dump truck wasn't there before." It was parked in a seemingly random angle. Justin looked it over for a few minutes.

"Alright guys, I believe I see now." He pointed at the truck. "A few people can hide up there in the dump bed and have a good line of fire along the roadway. That thick steel can offer them some protection from gunfire." Justin thought of how a grenade launcher would've negated that obstacle, if only he had one.

"If you look close, you can see a couple of holes drilled into the walls of the dump bed."

"Is it a set up?" Cutter asked.

"Could be."

"You think they're the same people we tangled with last time?" Blake asked. Justin shrugged.

"We killed all of them. At least, I think we did. Nothing's certain."

"What do we do?" What to do indeed, Justin thought. The last thing he wanted was to get into a gunfight with other survivors. Besides, they were going to have to come back this way after they completed the mission.

"Well, it's a good thing we know Zach," he said with a grunt. Cutter frowned in confusion. "He thought we might encounter potentially hostile people and he came up with a plan." Justin explained, and a couple of minutes later he was walking toward the dump truck holding up a stick with a white rag tied on the end. He was unarmed, at least nobody could see a weapon on him. The loose-fitting, camouflage-patterned combat blouse hid the nine millimeter Glock tucked into his waistband in the small of his back. He didn't see anyone, but still, he felt a presence. In for a penny, in for a pound, he thought and kept walking.

The idea was to get as close to the dump truck as possible, out of the kill zone. If it went bad, his only hope was to charge forward, where they least expected. Blake was back at the truck on the M60, watching closely, and

Brandon provided rear security. When Justin got to within ten feet, he saw movement through one of the roughly sawed out holes. He stopped and spoke.

"Hello!" After a long couple of seconds, a man's head slowly appeared over the top of the truck's hood, which, due to the way the truck was parked, was on the far side.

"Howdy," he replied with no hint of warmness.

"You're the first live people we've spotted in a while. My name's Justin."

"I'm Jubal." He was an older man, maybe in his late sixties. His tone and behavior concerned Justin. He was armed with a rifle which he had laid across the hood and made no move to walk around the truck. Justin guessed due to the height of the truck, the old man was either very tall or he was standing on something.

"I hope we're not intruding," Justin probed, trying for civility.

"That depends. What're you fellas doing here?" he asked, or maybe it was more of a demand, Justin couldn't decide. The man was staring at him quizzically, warily. Justin certainly didn't recognize him, but wondered if the reverse were true.

"We're just passing through, heading to Atlanta, but we saw you all and we were hoping maybe you were in a trading mood, so we stopped." There was a spark of interest in his face now. His head dropped out of sight and he stepped around the front of the truck. He was maybe six feet tall, slender but seemingly fit and a full gray beard hanging down several inches from his chin. Even though it was a warm July morning, he was wearing a dirty beige long-sleeved shirt and jeans. The others kept out of sight.

"Ain't nothing in Atlanta but dead people and zombies."

"I believe you," Justin replied. "But we've got a little bit of unfinished business down there. Hopefully, we'll get in and out in one piece." Jubal replied by spitting. There was a long moment of awkward quietness. Justin was about to bid Jubal goodbye when he spoke again.

"What kind of trading did you have in mind?" It was what Justin hoped for. He held up the plastic gallon jug he had carried with him.

"I've got a gallon of premium Tennessee moonshine here." Someone in the bed of the dump truck gasped and started whispering, which Justin took as a positive sign until the older man scoffed and spit again.

"We're in Grundy County, son. We've been making moonshine ever since our forefathers settled this place."

"I got a jug of honey too," Justin added. The man didn't answer, but Justin could see the man was interested. "Besides," Justin said. "My daddy always said a man can never have too much whiskey."

"You make a good point," Jubal finally conceded.

"That went pretty good," Brandon said. Grant nodded in agreement. "They didn't recognize you at all, Justin."

"We were lucky," Justin said. "But I think there were only two or three of them. If there were more, I believe we would have had to shoot our way out of there."

"You gave them that whole jug of shine *and* the honey, and all we got was a couple of gallons of water and some chewing tobacco. We got screwed," Cutter remarked.

"Maybe," Justin said. "But we avoided a shootout which might have ruined the mission before we even got to Atlanta. I have a feeling we'll need all of the ammunition we have when we get there." Grant nodded somberly in agreement.

"Alright men, let's load up and move out. I want to get some distance between us and them before we stop." He didn't have to repeat himself and they were moving down the backside of the mountain within a minute. Justin watched his mirrors closely, as did Grant.

"They don't appear to be following," Grant observed. "You think they might have friends waiting down the road?"

"It's possible, but I've got the CB on scan mode and we haven't heard anything." Justin hoped there wasn't an ambush awaiting them. Although he was sure they had superior firepower with the two M60s, he only wanted to get to Atlanta and back home to Ruth unscathed. He chuckled to himself as he realized he was thinking of that small house as his home.

Justin caught the flashing of headlights from Blake and stopped. He got out as he saw Brandon and Cutter jump out and begin relieving themselves. He looked over at Grant, who began doing the same thing.

"It'll be dark soon," Blake commented. Justin glanced at him and looked around.

"Yeah, we should find a spot. Let's get moving."

They'd only travelled another couple of miles when he saw a bridge about a hundred feet long and pointed it out to Grant.

"This looks like a good spot to spend the night." He stuck his arm out of the window and gave the hand signal for them to stop. Standing in the open hatch, he did a slow three-sixty with the binoculars. Satisfied, he exited the Humvee.

"We'll camp here for the night," he declared.

"Why here?" Cutter asked.

"The bridge gives us protection on two sides," he answered. "All we need to do is cover both ends. That'll be easy with the two sixties." He looked toward the setting sun. "I think we're going to have clear skies tonight, so that'll help too. Let's get our alarm system set up."

The alarm system Justin referred to was a length of rope tied across the bridge on each end and the rope was festooned with hubcaps and other various types of metal objects, mostly soda cans. Cutter looked it over questioningly as he helped Blake tie it off.

"It's not perfect, but it's better than nothing and it'll make pulling guard duty a little easier," Blake said. "Knowing Justin, he'll have us pull the first shifts and he'll take the last couple of hours." Cutter looked around to see if anyone was listening to them.

"Do you like him?" he asked under his breath. Blake grinned.

"He's what you call a lifer. He would've kept reenlisting until they made him retire."

"And you weren't."

"Oh, hell no. I was going to get out after my hitch and go to college. You know, party, bang college girls, and somewhere in between all of that get a degree." Blake emitted a short chuckle. "God had other plans though."

"So, you don't like him," Cutter pressed. Blake finished tying off the rope and checked its tautness before responding.

"I respect him, if that's what you're asking. Since it all went to hell, the man has gotten us out of a lot of close scrapes. He takes care of his troops too; that's what a non-com is supposed to do. So, yeah, I guess I like him." Blake paused a moment.

"You see, in the Marines you go through boot camp and learn the basics of being a Marine. After I graduated, I was assigned to the CBIRF unit and began specialized training."

"Like what?" Cutter asked.

"The unit has a lot of equipment for detecting biological, chemical, and radiological hazards. I was trained to use almost all of them. Now, all that sounds good, but neither I nor the other Marines in my unit knew very much about real soldiering. Gunny did though, and the colonel." He paused and sat up. "The colonel was a good man once. I guess it got to him." He began unlacing his boots. "I'm going to let my feet air out for a little bit. You should do the same."

Cutter didn't respond. For some reason, his brother detested Smithson. Zach too, for that matter. He'd commented many times they should take them out, just on general principal.

After, when it was utter chaos, Cutter and his brother found themselves alone and starving. The first people they killed were two neighbors down the street from them. They were an old retired couple who had a passion for gardening. The brothers befriended them, offering to protect them and help out. Cutter was fine with the arrangement, but one night Shooter killed them in their sleep. He rationalized it by saying they were old and didn't merit all of the food they were eating, even though it was theirs to eat.

After those two, it became easy. They worked their way all around the west Nashville area doing the same thing and eventually ran into the River Road group. At that time, it was only three teenage boys led by an ex-con nicknamed Kiss. He was mean and vicious, but he took a liking to Simon and Theodore, even gave them their nicknames.

Cutter shrugged off those unpleasant memories. A time in his life he was better off not thinking about. His brother always said they did what they had to do. He wondered if his brother thought that way the time they caught a woman and took turns raping her during a drunken spree.

"What're you thinking, dude?" Cutter looked up to see Blake staring at him.

"Oh, nothing much. When are we going to eat?"

Dinner consisted of whatever each man brought for themselves. Each of them had a small gassifier stove made from tin cans and cooked up various food items, supplemented by jerky and hard bread. Cutter looked over to see Blake sipping a can of Coke. He saw him looking and grinned.

"I found a six-pack in a car a couple of days ago." Cutter said nothing but thought about how long it'd been since he'd had a soda of any kind. Blake must have sensed it. He reached into his backpack and tossed a can.

"You owe me." Cutter nodded his gratitude, popped the tab and took a sip of the hot, foaming soda. It tasted like nectar of the Gods to him.

After dinner, the men lay back on their sleeping rolls and chatted.

"Cutter, why'd you volunteer to go with us?" Grant asked. Cutter made a face.

"Because, Tonya has been a real bitch lately. It's like, you can't even enjoy breakfast before she's creating work projects and ordering everyone around. You know that, she's been doing the same thing to you." Cutter didn't mention his latest failed attempt with Kyra. He'd made a couple of passes at her over the weeks and she rebuffed every one of them. This last time she called him creepy. He shook the thoughts off.

"I don't need some old bitch telling me what to do all the time."

Grant smiled in the growing darkness. "I'm afraid it's all necessary work, my friend." He looked over at Cutter. "Like digging the pit for the septic tank. Wouldn't you agree that it's better to have a functioning septic system rather than burning the turds off every day from the outhouse barrels?" Cutter had no answer. He uttered a profanity under his breath and shifted himself around on his bedroll.

"Whatever, I needed to get out of there for a while. I haven't had any time for myself. Besides," he said with a grin and holding up his large Rambo knife, "I'll get to do some zombie killing." Justin grunted. He knew there was indeed going to be some zombie killing; he only hoped Cutter was up to the task. Grant changed the subject.

"What'd you do before you and your brother ended up at the school?" Cutter shifted again and answered guardedly.

"We were living with some other dudes in a place out on the west side of the county. It was a decent setup, a big house out on River Road that used to be a rehab clinic. They had a couple of years' worth of food saved up and one of the dudes was a pretty good gardener. Everything was okay until the damn river flooded and washed away everything we had."

"Oh, yeah?" Justin asked. "How many?"

"It started out with six of us, but at one time we had fifteen people. But there was some trouble."

"Trouble?"

"Yeah, four of them died."

"How so?" Brandon asked.

"One got infected and attacked the others." Well, that's not exactly how it went, he thought, but no need to give them details.

"Do you know how that person became infected?" Grant asked. Cutter replied with a short laugh.

"Sure. He got careless and got bitten one day. He dumped peroxide on the bites and kept it hidden from everyone, but an hour or two later he went ape shit and tore into the others. So, we had to kill them." Actually, Kiss killed them. He killed all three of them while the rest of them looked on indifferently.

"And then the flood happened and wiped us out. My brother and I decided to head out on our own." Yeah, they snuck out in the middle of the night because Kiss was starting to scare them.

Justin looked him over. For some reason he didn't think Cutter was being entirely truthful, but said nothing. He made a mental note to discuss it with Zach and the others later.

"So, why didn't Zach join in on this goat fuck?" Cutter asked in an effort to change the subject.

"He said after what he'd been through, there was no way he was going to leave his kids," Grant explained. "I guess I'm partly to blame for that." Cutter snorted.

"Sounds like he's a coward." Justin gave him a withering stare, but Cutter was unfazed and continued. "And why do you all keep acting like he's some kind of genius?" It was phrased as a question, but his contempt was clear.

"Because he is, or very close to it," Grant responded plainly, as if he were speaking to a child. "And for the record, I don't believe there is a cowardly bone in his body." Justin looked at him in surprise.

"You actually sound like you respect him," he said. Grant nodded.

"I do, believe it or not." He was silent, until he glanced around and saw everyone staring at him.

"Think about it. He was nothing more than a sixteen-year-old kid when the plague broke out. The one person he was with died within a month. So, he was all alone, seemingly helpless. I mean, really, how many of you really think you could have survived by yourself if this shit hit when *you* were sixteen? I sincerely doubt I could have." Grant paused and looked at them.

"But Zach survived. Not only did he survive, he found others and helped them survive. He achieved it through innovation, cleverness, and toughness." Grant pointed at an arbitrary location on the northwestern horizon. "That school you're living in, that was Zach's idea, along with the radio tower, and the crop production, and the livestock care, and the successful eradication of most of the zombies around the school."

"Hey, I've got an idea. You should train him to be a doctor," Brandon said half-jokingly.

"I'd love to," Grant replied. "Unfortunately, he doesn't like me very much, so I don't believe he'd be interested, but he'd be a good one. I believe he'd be good at anything he set his mind to." He chuckled then.

"You guys want to hear a story Janet told me?"

"Sure," Justin replied.

"At one time, Zach was hooked up with two young fillies at the same time."

"Wasn't he married?" Justin asked.

"Yep, to a girl named Julie, Janet's daughter. But he had another young lady as well." Blake sat up.

"Wait, he was banging two women at once?"

"Indeed he was," Grant affirmed. "There's a few pictures of them still sitting on the shelf of the old house. They were both very pretty. Sadly, both of them are dead now, but you have to admit, for a while he was probably having the time of his life."

"That dog," Justin said with a chuckle.

"What do you mean pictures?" Cutter argued. "There ain't any places to go get pictures since it all went to hell."

Grant turned and looked at Cutter. "Haven't you been listening? Not only is Zach intelligent, he's very resourceful. And, you'd do well to avoid any confrontation with him. He can be very dangerous." When Major Parsons made that proclamation, Cutter cackled derisively.

"I'd have to agree," Justin said. "There was a fellow Marine by the name of Solonowski. He made the mistake of tangling with Zach and lost. Tonya told me he's killed others too. If you keep hitting on Kelly, don't be surprised if one day he gets tired of it and takes a piece out of you." When a minute of silence passed, Cutter spoke up.

"So, what happened between Zach and that Polack Marine?" Cutter asked sarcastically. Justin gave him a look before answering.

"Sol was a decent Marine, but he was a hothead and always let his emotions get the better of him. He underestimated Zach and Zach killed him." He paused a moment. "He killed him with his own knife. So, I guess we should be calling him Cutter instead of you." Brandon and Blake burst out in laughter. Cutter scowled and stood.

"Well, all of this talk about Zach makes me want to take a shit." He grabbed some napkins out of his pack, walked over to the guardrail and stuck his ass over the edge. Brandon sighed and stood.

"Alright, I have first watch. You guys try to get some sleep." He looked pointedly at Cutter as he walked back to the rest of them. "I hope you washed your hands."

They made the outskirts of Atlanta a couple of hours after sunrise. Atlanta was a major metropolitan area back before and traffic jams were common. Now, the streets were, unsurprisingly, a logjam of abandoned and wrecked vehicles, the big difference being as they got closer to their destination there was a marked increase of skeletal remains, as if a large group of people had all been killed en masse. Several buildings had burned at some point and were now nothing more than shells of blackened concrete and steel I-beams. Justin recognized familiar landmarks as they approached the Arlen Specter building. He maneuvering through and led the two vehicle convoy onto Clifton Road without any problems.

"Alright, heads up, gents," Justin said, breaking radio silence. "We're almost there." Without the usual Atlanta traffic, they arrived within minutes. But, they had to stop several feet away. Brandon stopped the second vehicle beside him. Justin set the brake and stood out of the top hatch with hands on the M60. If not for the stench, it would have been an amazing sight. Thousands of corpses were stacked on top of each other. But, that didn't mean there weren't any live zombies left. Oh, no. Justin counted at least thirty on the street. They were standing around aimlessly and seemed not to have not yet spotted the five men.

"Oh, my God," Cutter gasped. Justin pointed.

"See over there? They made a ramp with their bodies. First, to get over the fence, and then to get to the third floor windows."

"That's over thirty feet high," Cutter said in amazement.

"I bet you a lot of them on the bottom are still alive," Grant remarked. It was about that time that the wind shifted. Blake gagged, leaned out of a window and heaved up his breakfast. Brandon searched around in the Humvee, frantically looking for a respirator, but it was too late. The foul odor hit him and he started retching too.

"How are we going to get in the building, Justin?" Grant asked. Justin didn't answer for a long three minutes.

"Mann, try to raise them on the radio." The soldier acknowledged and tried for several minutes without success.

"Alright, this is a no-go, we're aborting," he finally said. Grant looked at him in surprise.

"What do you mean?" he implored. Justin waved a hand around.

"There're too many of them," he explained. "Once they figure out we're here, we'd run out of ammo before we could shoot our way out."

"There's got to be some other way," Grant lamented as he retrieved the binoculars. He scanned the windows, all of them, looking for any signs of intelligent human life. Perhaps a sign hung in one of the windows, or someone using a mirror to signal them, anything.

But there was no sign, there was no signal. Nothing. Only zombies. Thousands of them. He suddenly gasped.

"Oh shit," he muttered.

"What?" Cutter asked as Justin realized what was happening. The zombies, all of them, seemed to turn toward them simultaneously and began walking. Slowly at first, but the momentum was picking up.

"Time to go," Justin said urgently and dropped down into the driver's seat. Blake did the same and together they started the Humvees. Only, Blake's Humvee didn't start.

"Shit!" he barked as he desperately tried to start the vehicle.

"Did you flood it?" Justin asked through the window.

"I don't know, maybe." He kept turning the starter, but the engine refused to crank to life. Justin looked at the approaching horde. They were less than a hundred yards from them now. He made a command decision.

"Grab your gear, the sixty and the ammo and get in here," he commanded. The three men didn't hesitate.

"We're going to leave it?" Grant asked.

"You got a better idea?" Justin responded. All of them turned to look. The original group of thirty was getting closer. What's more, the numbers were growing. They seemed to be coming from everywhere.

Five grown men and assorted gear made it a tight fit in the Humvee, but nobody was complaining. They took off just as the leading edge of the horde made it to them.

The vehicle had plenty of torque, but it'd never win any drag races. It accelerated slowly and the men watched anxiously as the zombies grabbed at them.

"Son of a bitch!" Justin yelled to nobody in particular as two of them jumped in front of them. Justin had to slow slightly to run over them, which gave the zombies a slight advantage.

"They're throwing themselves under the wheels to slow us down!" Brandon shouted in sudden understanding and opened fire. Blake squeezed through the open hatch and joined in the shooting. It gave them just enough of an opening for Justin to accelerate and finally speed away from them.

"Shit," Grant muttered.

"Alright guys, shoot only if you have to," Justin ordered. He was worried. The two soldiers went through a lot of rounds very quickly and they didn't have a whole lot to begin with.

They were back on the interstate when they encountered another horde.

"Where did they come from?" Cutter asked nobody in particular.

"Hold on!" Justin shouted as he swerved right and left in an attempt to avoid them. He understood now. These things were working collectively. If enough of them could get themselves caught up in the undercarriage, they could effectively disable the Humvee. It wasn't a pleasant thought. Brandon started firing again, but at least he was only shooting in three-round bursts.

"It could be worse," Grant said while holding on for dear life. Justin hastened a sideways glance at him. "At least they haven't figured out how to block the road with all of these derelict cars." Justin frowned at him.

"Don't give 'em any ideas."

"Are we going to give it another try?" Blake asked. They'd driven five miles down the interstate, and after not seeing any zombies anywhere in sight, they stopped. While everyone provided security, Justin crawled under the Humvee to check for any damage.

"Damn," he muttered and quickly crawled back out.

"What's wrong?" Grant asked. Justin retrieved his protective mask.

"There's pieces of zombie flesh falling out of the undercarriage," he said as he donned his mask.

"I feel safe to say our mission is a failure," Justin said from under the Humvee. "So, no, we're not going to give it another try."

"I don't know, Lieutenant," Grant rejoined. "We've got to do something." Justin saw no damage, crawled out, and pulled the respirator off. He looked at his military top in disgust and took it off. Blake found a rag and wet it down before handing it to Justin.

"What would you suggest, sir?" Justin queried as he wiped his hands off. "I mean, unless we were looking at totally different things, I don't think there is any way in hell we can get in that building and back out in one piece." Justin watched as Grant tried to form some type of cognizant response, but couldn't. Justin sighed as he threw the rag down. "Who has the sanitizer?"

"Alright," Justin said after he'd cleaned up, "it's decided. We're heading back. Let's sort our gear and take an ammo inventory. Brandon, man the sixty and keep watch."

CHAPTER 38 – MONTEAGLE

"Okay, slow down." Grant was driving now, Justin was in the passenger seat with an M4 sitting in his lap. "Let's see what kind of greeting we're going to get."

They were again approaching the crest of Monteagle Mountain. Suddenly, Grant braked to a stop and pointed.

"That looks like Jubal," he said. There was a man lying on the ground beside the dump truck with his head and shoulders resting against one of the tires.

"Edge closer, slowly," Justin said. Grant complied and came to within fifty feet before stopping.

"Yeah, it's him, and there's blood all over him." Justin scanned the entire area, spotting two sets of legs peeking out from behind the dump truck.

"Blake and Cutter, rear security. Brandon, cover us with the M60." Without waiting for an answer, he and Grant exited the Humvee and the two Marines jogged over to Jubal.

"He's still alive," Grant said and started carefully cutting off his shirt. There were four bullet holes in his torso, each of them oozing blood. Grant briefly glanced at Justin somberly. Jubal stirred and struggled to open his eyes. When he was able to focus, he coughed and drew in a breath.

"Well, lookee here, it's the Marines to the rescue." His voice was ragged and pained. He coughed and a bloody froth came out.

"What the hell happened?" Justin asked. With painful effort, he pointed over at the two sets of legs.

"We had a difference of opinion." He watched Grant fussing over him a moment before waving him off.

"It's too late for all that," he said while coughing up a combination of phlegm and blood. "Unless you got one of them life-flight helicopters on the way to swoop me up and carry me to a fancy hospital." He reached out with amazing quickness and grabbed Grant's arm.

"Marine to Marine, I ain't gonna make it, ain't that right?"

"You were a Marine?" Justin asked.

"What do you mean *were* a Marine, son?" More coughing. "I'll always be a Marine 'till the day I die, which ain't gonna be too much longer, I'm thinking."

Justin gestured at Brandon and hooked a thumb toward the two bodies. He nodded and hustled over and disappeared behind the dump truck. He emerged a moment later carrying two pistols and a scoped rifle.

"They're dead," he said. "Both of them shot in the head. Good shooting, old man." Jubal nodded at the compliment and handed his handgun to Justin.

"That's a Colt Nineteen-Eleven. I've had it ever since 'Nam. It's old, but it'll still do the job. Take care of it, please."

"I will," Justin replied.

"They knew," he said in between coughs.

"What?" Justin asked.

"Ole Banjo over there, he may not have looked like much, but he had country smarts. He saw those machine guns of yours and remembered all of them casings lying around his dead kinfolk from a while back. He put two and two together. They were going to set you up and kill all of you." He gestured. "Banjo is pretty good with that deer rifle. He was going to pick you off." He gestured toward Banjo again. "I don't think I ever saw him miss when we went huntin'."

"Why'd you stop them?" Grant asked.

"Why do you think, son?" Jubal questioned. None of them had a response, and instead watched silently as Jubal's breathing faded. When it was obvious the old man was dead, Justin used the Colt to put a bullet in his head.

"Rule number one," Justin said quietly. "Semper Fi." Justin shared a long moment of silence with Jubal before walking going through his pants pockets. He found two extra magazines for the Colt.

"Good job, Marine," he said under his breath. He stood and walked over to Banjo and his friend. He used Jubal's Colt to shoot each one in the head.

"Do they really come back to life?" Blake asked after they'd gotten underway. "People, I mean. After they die, do they really come back as zombies?" Grant shrugged.

"We'd had reports of it happening, but nothing confirmed. We had all kinds of unconfirmed reports."

It was slow going. Cars and trucks in the west bound lanes of I-24 were more numerous, for some unknown reason. Nonetheless, they had no other encounters, with either man or zombies, until the approached community formerly known as Beech Grove. Justin had been half dozing when he saw something down the road. Suddenly, he sat up and slapped Grant on the arm.

"Stop the vehicle," he told him. Grant braked quickly, looked over at Justin questioningly and followed along his line of sight. About three hundred yards down the interstate, a figure was walking along, his back to the men.

"Is that a zombie or a man?" he asked.

"He ain't walking like a zombie. More like a soldier. Look at how his shoulders are square and the deliberate steps. He's carrying a rucksack and a rifle too." Justin pulled out the binoculars.

"His ruck is stuffed as full as it can get. I bet it weighs almost a hundred pounds." And the man doesn't seem too hindered by carrying all of that weight, he thought. He looked over at Blake. "Let's check him out. Don't do anything threatening but be ready." Grant started forward.

"You know, I still outrank you," he said to Justin.

"Yes, sir," Justin replied, "and as a superior officer you wisely know your forte is doctoring and mine is soldering." Grant started to retort, but instead grunted and sat back in his seat.

"Pull up beside him, but keep some room between us." As they started forward the man stopped walking, dropped his rucksack and waited. He held his rifle at port arms. It wasn't threatening, but Justin knew he could bring it up and fire quickly if he wanted.

The major continued driving and stopped when the Humvee was even with him. The man stood motionlessly, staring at them. He was a younger black man, maybe a year or two younger than Justin, lean, wearing a set of ACUs that'd seen better days and his face was fixed in a perpetual scowl.

"How's it going, soldier?" Justin asked. The soldier nodded quietly and looked them over carefully before his eyes settled on Blake, who was standing in the open hatch casually leaning against the M60.

"Expecting trouble?" he asked with a quiet southern drawl.

"Just being careful," Justin replied. "I'm Lieutenant Justin Smithson." He gestured with his head. "The driver here is Major Grant Parsons. That's Private Mann on the sixty." He hooked his thumb at the back seat. "Sergeant Caswell and Butter, uh, I mean Cutter." The soldier gave them all a curt nod.

"My name's True. I was in the Guard at one time, but I don't much bother saluting to anyone anymore." He paused to see if either of the officers had a problem with that statement.

"Where are your people, Private True?" Grant asked.

"Dead," True responded without emotion. Justin paused a moment to see if True was going to elaborate. He didn't.

"Where are you heading?"

"Nashville," True replied. "I met some people there a while back and I'd like to try to find them." Justin glanced briefly at Grant, who shrugged.

"You want a ride?"

Brandon helped him strap down his rucksack on the outside of the Humvee with the others.

"It's going to be a little cramped," he quipped.

"It don't matter," True replied. "Say you're a lieutenant and you're a major?"

"That's right," Justin said. He had turned in his seat and watched Private True. The man had rendered his assault rifle safe and had the barrel pointing down at the floorboard.

"I don't like officers," True casually announced. Justin glanced at Grant a second before returning his attention to True.

"Y'all don't have to worry about me. I'm appreciative for the ride. I couldn't find a car that'd run."

"Why don't you like officers?" Grant asked loudly over the noise of the engine.

"It's a long story full of bullshit and betrayal," True replied.

"We'd still love to hear it," Brandon countered. True shrugged.

"I was fresh back from Afghanistan and we were promised a week's leave. Just before I was going to leave and head home to my family, this butterball lieutenant, fresh out of college, comes swaggering in and tells me I have to pull weekend guard duty."

"That sucks, what happened?"

"I told him in to go fuck himself," True replied. "I got stopped at the gate by the MPs as I was heading out. I spent the weekend in the brig, got an Article Fifteen and busted back to E-1." Justin nodded in understanding. True leaned back and tried to make himself comfortable, which wasn't easy, being squeezed between Brandon and Cutter.

"So, anyway, the only officer I ever respected after that was a lieutenant by the name of Ward, and he's dead." There were a few minutes of silence before he spoke again.

"If y'all don't mind, I've been a few days without sleep. I'm gonna catch up." Without waiting for a response, he pulled his hat down over his eyes. He appeared to be asleep in under a minute.

CHAPTER 39 – TRUE

Kelly found me in the barn with Sammy and Josue, working on Floyd's Toyota.

"They're back," she exclaimed breathlessly. "They just called us on the radio."

With assurances from Janet that she'd watch the kids, we jumped in one of the trucks and hurried over. I was grinning when I saw everyone was present and accounted for, but my grin faded when I saw him. I pulled up close, jammed on the brakes and jumped out.

"It's been a while, Private True," I said hoarsely as I walked up. Before he could answer, I pulled out my Kimber handgun and aimed it at his head. Kelly gasped and Justin stood quickly.

"Whoa, what's going on here?" he demanded and started to walk toward me.

"Step back, Justin," I ordered. Justin froze in place.

"What's going on, Zach?" Others had started to gather around.

"Remember my story about getting shot?" I gestured at True with the business end of the Kimber. "It was his group. His buddies." Private True stared at me quietly, steadily.

"If you really believe I shot you, you need to go ahead and put a bullet in me." He continued staring. "Go on now, put me out of my damn misery."

I stared long and hard at him and realized I was actually putting pressure on the trigger. I forced myself to take a deep breath and lowered the gun.

"Alright, listen up everyone. Back about March, a couple of years ago, we came upon some members of the National Guard. Private True was with them. A few months later, we ran into them again. The one running the show was a particularly disgusting turd by the name of Corporal Leon Hart. I was shot." I pointed at the horizontal scar along the side of my head.

"You really think I was buddies with Hart and his asshole friends?" True asked. He shook his head slowly. "This is the first I'm hearing about you being shot. I left right after he and his boys killed my lieutenant." I stared at him a minute and then turned to Kelly.

"Go get Janet and bring her back here. She'll know if he's lying or not."

"Okay," she said and then whispered in my ear. "We're going to have to bring the kids with us. Please be on your best behavior." She kissed me on the cheek and ran to the truck.

It was a long twenty minutes until they came back. I waited impatiently, sitting on the tailgate of my truck while True sat on his rucksack a few yards away from me, staring at the horizon. As soon as they parked, I motioned Janet over.

"Do you remember him?" I asked her. She looked him over.

"Yeah," she said. "He was the lieutenant's friend. I thought he got killed too."

"So, he wasn't friends with Corporal Hart?"

"Oh, hell no," she responded. I nodded.

"Alright, it looks like I owe you an apology then, Private True."

"Just call me True. I ain't been a Private in a long time." He looked down at the ground.

"What's your first name?" Kelly asked. He looked almost embarrassed now.

"It's Nimrod, but nobody calls me that now, just call me True."

"So, tell me what happened at Houston Barracks," I asked, but before he could answer, I explained to Justin and the others.

"Houston Barracks is the National Guard facility on Sidco Drive. It was where we'd first met him and his fellow Guard members." I didn't bother mentioning that Janet and her son lived with them at one time. True waited for me to finish before speaking.

"Long story short, Hart got some of the other soldiers to side with him and they turned against Lieutenant Ward. They shot him and a couple of others and took over the place. I hid until it got dark and took off." He stared pointedly at me. "I ain't no coward, but they had me outnumbered. Wasn't nothing else I could do."

"Understandable," Justin said.

"Where'd you go?" I asked. True shrugged.

"Around. I tried going back to Manchester, that's where I grew up." His face darkened. "It didn't work out. I took off and that's when you men found me." He looked around at everyone staring at him. "If I'm not welcome here just say the word and I'm out." There were a lot of looks passed back and forth, many of those looks were directed toward me. I was about to respond when Justin stepped forward.

"No need for that," he said. "If there isn't any room at the school, you're welcome to stay with Ruth and me." Justin gave him a wry grin. "That is, if you can stand being in the same house with a military officer." True actually smiled, somewhat. It was more like he stretched his lips a little. I cleared my throat.

"It's settled then," I said. "But, at some point I'd like to talk to you about what you've seen and been through." True nodded amicably. "But it can wait. For now, I want to hear about Atlanta." I looked at each of them and their expressions were grim.

"Was it that bad?"

"We were lucky," Justin replied and began talking. The others joined in the conversation.

"There must have been thousands," Cutter joined in.

"For some stupid reason, I thought perhaps all of the zombies had died or moved on," Grant said with a shake of his head. "I can't imagine why they're staying in there. There can't be any food source." He shook his head again. "There's something else going on with them."

Well, no shit, I thought. I'd been trying to tell them for a while now how those things were changing.

"So, what's next, doctor?" I asked. He gave a small, hopeful smile.

"I still have all of the data on my laptop, but I need a lab. I think we need to pay a visit to Vanderbilt." Cutter scoffed. Shooter had walked up during the conversation and added his own derisive snort.

"That place is full of infected. We tried to get in there a while back, and then we tried Saint Thomas," He shook his head with a scowl. "Same thing. Crammed packed."

"What do you think, Zach?" Grant asked. Cutter and Shooter were looking at me as if they were being challenged.

"I believe the brothers have a valid point," I said. "When people started getting sick, many of them flocked to the hospitals. I'm sure a lot of them are still trapped inside." I thought a moment.

"By the way, did you guys ever try the prisons?" I asked the brothers.

"Oh, yeah," Cutter answered. "It was the same thing. If you saw something wearing orange, they were infected, and trust me, there were a lot of those things wandering around wearing orange." I'd thought as much.

"Well, we'll have to find another way," Grant mused.

"I always knew he was bad news," True said, referring to the late Leon Hart. He, Justin and I were sitting at one of the picnic tables. Everyone else was inside, probably in bed. Kelly had gone back home with Janet and the kids.

"When I got in trouble, I got transferred to Houston Barracks. Nobody knew about it, but the lieutenant was from Manchester too. His family and my family were friends. He pulled some strings, said he wanted to make sure I didn't get into any more trouble."

"He seemed pretty squared away," I surmised.

"He was. You didn't know him before he hurt his back. He was fit as a fiddle. He could run all day and then knock out a hundred push-ups. He took care of me, made sure I didn't get shit on.

"Anyway, I'd heard the talk and told him about that damned Hart and what he was planning. He told me not to worry about it, he'd handle it." He paused a moment and rubbed his face. "Hart shot him in the back of the head in the chow hall. All of his buddies was laughing and high-fiving each other like it was something special. I was unarmed, so I couldn't do much about it. I waited until it got dark and left."

"And you went back home?" I asked. He nodded.

"Yeah, I found a car over at that mall nearby with the keys still in it and drove home, but Manchester had changed. Everything was FUBAR. I never found any of my family." He paused and sighed.

"So, I hooked up with some people for a while. They needed someone who could handle guns." He stared into the quiet darkness.

"I did things I'm not proud of, but don't bother asking, because I ain't gonna say what those things are. Anyway, I decided to leave."

"So, what's next for Nimrod True?" Justin asked.

"I would be obliged if y'all would let me stay here for a little while, let me get my shit together, then I'll be on my way." I looked at Justin who gave me a small nod.

"Welcome aboard," I said.

CHAPTER 40 – THE HOSPITAL

The school cafeteria had become the de facto location whenever we met. All of us were there now.

"Alright, let's get a head count and confirm who's going," Justin said. Cutter, who was currently dressed like Rambo, complete with a large knife strapped to his thigh, looked at Kelly in surprise when she raised her hand.

"You're going too?" he asked. She nodded. "I don't know, girl, this is going to be dangerous work." Kelly glanced at him in annoyance.

"Then maybe *you* shouldn't go," Sarah retorted. There were a few guffaws of laughter from the others. He raised his eyebrows.

"Do you mean me?" he asked. Sarah nodded.

"He's right," Shooter added, who was also dressed in a similar fashion. "No offense, but this is too dangerous a mission for a little girl to be going on." Before Kelly or I could respond, Sarah jumped in.

"You're an idiot," she proclaimed. Shooter rolled his eyes at her.

"Nobody asked your opinion."

"I always value her opinion," I said as I stared at him like he was an annoying fly. Shooter responded with that stupid half-smile.

"Well, I hope the rain lets up for y'all's sake. Your makeup will run," Shooter said mockingly and then smiled again. "Oh, wait. I forgot, dykes don't wear makeup." I started to stand up. Justin quickly got between us.

"That's enough," he said gruffly to Shooter. Shooter leaned back in his chair and continued smiling. I slowly sat back down as Sarah and I stared at him balefully.

"Alright, enough bullshit," Justin exclaimed. "You all know what the mission is, so now I'm going to tell you how we're going to do it." He glanced briefly at his notepad and then made direct eye contact with all of us.

"Team one will be myself, Ruth, True, Cutter, and Shooter. Team two will be Grant, Zach, Jorge, Blake, and Sarah. Kelly will be driving the Volvo, Josue will be driving the bus. They'll be team three and will be pulling security with the vehicles while we're inside.

"Now, there are only one hundred rounds of ammo for each of us, so no wild shooting." Actually, I had the semi stocked full of ammo, around five hundred additional rounds, but they didn't need to know that. Kelly and I had spent a lot of hours doing the reloading and there was no way I was going to let anyone piss it all away.

"Zach and Kelly will be leading the way with their semi. We've decided on Southern Hills since it's the closest hospital.

"Once we get there, we'll make a threat assessment and decide if it's feasible to make entry. If it is, the two teams will make entry together. Major Parsons' list will be the priority, but if we see anything else of value we won't hesitate to grab it." Justin looked over at Grant, who took the cue and stood.

"I took a page from Zach, figuratively speaking, and printed out photographs of the items we need." He held up several sheets of paper and passed around packets to each of us. I looked it over and wondered where he had found all of the printing paper. Justin continued with the mission briefing, covering the route, passwords, communications and contingency plans until he had covered everything.

"Any questions?" He looked around, and seeing none, nodded at me. I stood.

"Okay, Lieutenant Smithson has given you the basic mission. I'm going to go over some other items." I opened a cardboard box and pulled out five items. "Sharpies," I said. "Big fat ones, they're called magnums."

"What are those for?" Cutter asked.

"I'm glad you asked. This is the first time all of us as a group have attempted to go into a large, multi-floor building with numerous rooms and hallways. It'll be easy to get lost." Shooter snorted.

"Is something wrong, dumbass?" I asked.

"Well, I don't know what buildings you've been in, but every modern building I've been in have exit signs mounted everywhere."

"You're correct, Simon, but those exit signs won't tell you which exit you're going out of. It's the middle of July and raining like hell. It's going to be hot and stuffy inside, the flies and mosquitos are going to be buzzing around your head, and if there're no windows nearby, there will be areas that are totally dark. Let's say you turn a corner and bam, there's a couple of dozen hungry zombies coming after you. You'll start running and instinctively follow those signs. You could go out the correct exit, or you could go running out of the wrong exit and find yourself on the other side of the hospital, surrounded by zombies and cut off from your back up." I could see by the look on his face he wanted to argue.

"He's right," Cutter conceded, although rather reluctantly. "That happened to me back when we tried to go through that office building in Bellevue." He looked plainly at his brother and handed him one of the sharpies.

"Don't call me Simon," he finally muttered. Jorge chuckled.

"Alright, let's get back on track. Every time you turn a corner, someone in your team needs take one of these and make a big arrow on the wall, pointing it in the direction from where you just came from. This will help you get back to the proper exit point. Also, put your team number beside it and any other information you believe is pertinent." I paused to make sure what I was saying was sinking in.

"Now, if you go down a hallway and see a bunch of infected stuck in a room, put this symbol on the door." I then showed them the FEMA symbol and how to fill in the data.

"As you can see, once it's explained, it's easy to understand. But, if there is any additional info you think is important, feel free to write it on the nearest wall. We may schedule multiple visits in the future so keep that in mind."

Everyone seemed to understand. I looked pointedly at the brothers, who nodded, albeit reluctantly. Justin stood.

"Okay then, let's load up and move out."

Southern Hills was a mid-sized hospital located in south Nashville a couple of blocks off of Nolensville Pike. Fred and Julie had checked it out once, back when I'd been shot, and they advised it was full of infected and part of it had burned.

"Turn right on Wallace Road," I directed and we soon came to the main drive. I directed us to stop. We could see the hospital from here. I gave it a quick scan.

"It looks like only part of it burned," I said. "I bet the sprinkler system was still working, but that means there's going to be significant water damage." Kelly pointed at a logjam of cars and ambulances blocking the entrance.

"I can hop the curb and ride through the grass," she suggested.

"I don't know. It's been raining pretty hard, we might get stuck." I grabbed the microphone.

"The entrance is blocked and the ground may be too muddy. We better walk from here.

"Roger that," Justin replied. "Everyone but team three dismount and form up."

Once formed up, I led team one up the left sidewalk as team two took the opposite side. There were also a lot of skeletal remains lying around and more than a few black eyes watching us with the zombie equivalent of anticipation.

"They're all staring at us," Ruth commented in a whisper with a little bit of tenseness. I pointed at the entrance to the emergency room.

"Look at that shit." The circular drive was stacked full of ambulances. The crews either abandoned them or became infected themselves. Justin gave the hand signal for the teams to stop as Grant whispered to him. After a moment, he jogged across the street.

"The major says those ambulances could be full of stuff we can use."

"Alright, we can search them afterward; let's see if we can get inside the ER."

It didn't take long to encounter a group of them. There were about a dozen, aimlessly milling about the entrance. I motioned for everyone to halt and take up positions, and then used my Marlin with the subsonic rounds to systematically pick them off. The heavy rainfall muffled what little noise the rifle made and they never knew what hit them. Jorge stood beside me and watched, handing me a fresh magazine when I needed to reload.

"Good shooting, man," he encouraged. "Keep it up."

"They're moving slow, not like some I've seen lately."

After ten minutes or so, I had them all neatly dispatched. Grant jogged along the ambulances and made quick peeks in the windows of each one.

"Lots of ransacking," he reported. "But the larger equipment is still there. So far, so good."

I grunted and was about to respond when something caught my eye. "I keep seeing those," I said, pointing at some strange graffiti.

"Shit, man," Jorge said. "Those are gang signs."

"Let's hope we don't run into any of them," I said. "I'd hate to waste ammo."

We had company awaiting us as soon as we made entry through the broken glass doors. They were everywhere. Rotting, smelling, hungry. It was disgusting. The time for being quiet and sneaky was over. We took cover behind the overturned furniture and started firing. They were coming at us steadily. The ER was full of them, but it was also full of scattered medical equipment. There were even gurneys with zombified patients still strapped to them. It created a bottleneck which worked to our advantage. After a couple of minutes, I stopped shooting, opting to save my ammo and watched the others. Everyone fired with discipline and precision, except for the two brothers. Their shots were rushed and they frequently missed their mark. I caught Sarah glancing at me in between shots.

After finishing the last one, Justin called a cease fire while I made a quick count.

"Thirty-one," I said. "Maybe ten wasted shots, so forty rounds fired."

"I'd hate to think what's waiting for us in the rest of the hospital," Ruth said loudly. I looked and noted she was one of the only ones who took my advice and was using earplugs. I took one of mine out before speaking.

"I'm betting it'll be about the same, maybe worse," I said. "What do you think, Major?"

"It's very possible the place is full of them, but I really need a water bath and a centrifuge."

"What the hell does that mean?" Shooter said with a derisive snort. "Are you into water sports or something?" Cutter chuckled as well while the rest of us gave him a withering stare. I pointed at a set of double doors down the corridor. We moved forward, stepping over the corpses as we proceeded forward. When we went past the double doors, the corridor dead ended and branched off on either side. I looked at Justin, who shrugged. I shrugged as well, pulled out my Sharpie and drew some arrows on the wall.

We never made it past the first floor.

CHAPTER 41 – THE GANG THAT COULDN'T SHOOT STRAIGHT

"We've got incoming," Kelly said breathlessly on the radio. "Two SUVs full of people. Possibly six men. I see at least one long gun."

"Team one, rally at the entrance," I ordered. Justin nodded and gave a hand signal to his team.

"Team two, follow me," he commanded.

We'd discussed this possibility and had planned for it. In the event of any contact with humans, my team would make the initial contact while Justin's team provided cover. We hustled out of the ER's doors just as the two SUVs hopped the curbs and slid to a stop in the mud. Each of us spread out and took up positions. Kelly and Josue were hidden inside the semi, as planned, and this crew had not even seen them as they drove past.

There were six of them, all men, a mixture of races and age, and all of them armed with an assortment of weapons. They lined up in front of their SUVs like it was high noon at the OK corral. Sarah and I walked out into the open and stopped. There was a distance of about fifty feet between us. I gave a halfhearted wave. Two of them walked forward and stopped ten feet away.

"Who're you assholes?" the older one of them demanded. I looked him over. He was somewhere around thirty with long greasy hair and an unkempt beard. He was holding a pump action shotgun that had spots of rust all over it, which told me a lot about this man. He held it casually, but ready for use.

"Who are you?" I countered. He sneered at me with a set of teeth in desperate need of a good dental hygienist.

"I asked you a question," he demanded again.

"Fair enough. My name's Zach and I don't appreciate a dirt bag like you making insulting remarks." He was taken aback, obviously not used to being talked to like I just did. Before he could respond, a teenage boy stepped forward in an apparent attempt to look menacing.

"Don't you be talking shit to King Ro," he said menacingly. Well, as menacingly as a scrawny, pencil-necked peckerwood could sound. "This is our turf."

"King Ro?" Sarah asked. The man grinned proudly, although I have no idea what he was so proud of.

"Yeah, that's me, baby. I see you looking me over. Like what you see?" The peckerwood chuckled derisively.

"You should call yourself King Turd," she replied. "I can smell you from here."

His smile turned back to a sneer and he started to bring his shotgun to bear. I already had my handgun drawn, but King Ro beat me to the punch, in a manner of speaking.

Oh, it wasn't a good clean shot at Sarah or me. The mighty King violated one of those rules of gun safety Rick had hammered in my brain; keep your finger off of the trigger until you're on target and ready to shoot. He accidentally shot his little buddy, who instantly fell to the ground howling in pain and wiggling around on the ground like a dying cockroach.

King Ro stared at his companion a moment and started to rack another round into the chamber, but he was frozen in place when he heard a voice behind them.

"Don't any of you move!" Kelly shouted, causing the rest of them to jump and look behind them. She and Josue had exited the truck and were now pointing their assault rifles at them.

"You people are so stupid you don't even see the rest of our crew," I said. They looked back at me and I pointed behind me with my thumb. It was only then that Justin and his team revealed themselves. They didn't move, but they were anxious, I could see it in their eyes.

"You men are outnumbered," I said sternly as I slowly stepped forward. "Drop your weapons if you want to live. It'd be a shame for all of you to be killed after everything you've been through. Besides," I said and gestured at the kid who was sobbing in pain, "we've got a doctor who can help your friend."

"You'll really help Roman?" one of them asked skeptically. He was about my age and even though he was dirty as hell, he looked pretty tough. I nodded.

"You have my word." He looked at me a long moment and then looked at his friends. King Ro piped up.

"It ain't going to work that way," he said and continued staring at me menacingly.

"Can it, Ro," the tough one said. "Your boy needs help." He looked pointedly at his friends.

"Do what he says," he told them and lay his rifle down in the mud gently, as if doing so would prevent it from getting dirty. The others reluctantly followed suit. King Ro refused and continued staring at me. I knew something needed to be done before he raised that shotgun. I charged forward and struck him in the head with the Kimber. He groaned in pain as he fell to the ground and I quickly took the shotgun away from him. The rest of them remained still.

Kelly and Josue gathered up their weapons while we covered them and then ordered them to have a seat on the muddy ground. Justin's team moved in then and I watched as Grant jogged quickly over to the bus and retrieve his medical bag before jogging over to the kid.

King Ro was quiet now. He rubbed his face anxiously at the sudden turn of events. I watched him warily. He jumped when Roman emitted a shriek of pain. He looked both scared and worried. It seemed like more worry than normal. I made the connection.

"Is he your son?" I asked. King Ro glared at me, but then nodded.

"You shot your own son, what a dumbass," Sarah remarked.

His face contorted to a mask of evil. I poked him in the side of the head with the barrel of his own shotgun.

"Why did you come at us looking for a confrontation?"

"You people are trespassing on our turf," he retorted.

"This isn't your turf, dumbass," Sarah rejoined. I gave her a look.

"The hell it isn't," one of them, the tough-looking one, piped up and pointed to one of the gang signs spray painted on the wall of the hospital. "We marked it." I looked at him closely and it dawned on me that I knew him.

"I recognize you. You're Randy Messina. You were a star linebacker for Overton High."

"Yeah, well I don't recognize you," he said suspiciously.

"Again, my name's Zach, and I grew up here." I paused and pointed. "And if you people had taken the time to look closely at the intersection over there, you would have seen that I marked this area over a year ago."

"You're the one who painted those rules all over the place," he said in realization. I nodded. Grant got my attention. He was crouched down beside the wounded man and waved Justin and I over to him.

"He's got a nicked artery," Grant said. I looked down at them. He had cut off the pants leg of the boy and applied a tourniquet. A hunk of meat the size of a child's fist had been gouged out of his thigh just a few inches above the knee.

"Am I going to die?" Roman asked. Grant gave him a fatherly look.

"No, son, you're going to be fine." He focused back on us.

"I can suture him up, and if infection doesn't set in, he'll be okay, but he'll be walking with a limp for a while." He looked around. "There's no sterile area around here and I need to close up that artery. Let's at least get him out of this mud."

"I suppose you should get started and then…" I was interrupted by the sound of someone being hit and a groan of pain. Turning, I saw Cutter and Shooter standing over King Ro, putting the boots to him. Justin and I ran toward them, but Sarah intervened first when she screwed the barrel of her assault rifle into Cutter's ear.

"What the hell?" he asked indignantly.

"What do you two think you're doing?" I growled and glanced at King Ro's crew. If they weren't angry before, they were certainly angry now.

"He deserves it," Shooter retorted. "You hit him, why can't we?"

"Back off," I warned them. Justin had walked up and was standing beside me for emphasis.

"Sure, no problem," Shooter replied with his dumb smile. "He got what was coming to him." I started to say something else, but I stopped when I saw one of the gang slowly stand up.

"I recognize you two," he proclaimed as he pointed and turned toward his friends briefly. "Yeah, I know them. Those two are part of that River Road crew."

For the first time since I knew him, I saw that damned smile disappear from Shooter's face. It was replaced with – worry.

"You know them?" I asked him.

"Oh, yeah, I know them."

"Well now, I want to hear all about this," I said and momentarily glanced at Shooter before looking back at the man. "Let's hear—" Before I could finish my sentence, Shooter quickly brought his rifle up and fired a three round burst into him.

"Cease fire!" Justin shouted and grabbed Shooter's rifle out of his hands. Shooter tried to grab it back but Justin hit him with a devastating right hook. The impact was so hard, Shooter's feet flew up in the air as he hit the ground. If not for the mud, I'm sure his head would have cracked open from the impact. Cutter gasped and started to raise his own rifle but Sarah kept him from it.

"Don't even think about it," she threatened.

"What the hell?" I implored and ran over to the man. He had a three-round grouping right in the middle of his chest. It was the best shooting I'd ever seen Shooter do.

"Talk to me, Cutter. What just happened here?"

Cutter looked at me, Justin, Sarah, and his unconscious brother nervously before shaking his head. "I don't know, man."

"Bullshit," Randy said. He stood as well. "Y'all just murdered Sparks for no good reason." He then glared at me.

"So, this is how it's going to be?" he asked with contempt. I turned toward Grant.

"Major, a little assistance here, please." Grant hustled over to him and squatted down beside him. Surprisingly, he gasped.

"That piece of trash shot me," he said and coughed up some blood. Grant patted him gently on the shoulder.

"Hold fast, I'm going to give you something for pain." There was no response that could be understood now, only a lot of groaning. I crouched down beside him.

"Tell me what you know about those two," I asked. He looked at me, but there was nothing but agony in his eyes. Grant gently pushed me aside. I watched as he filled a syringe and injected it into the man's leg. The man gave a long sigh as his eyes lost focus.

"I've given him an overdose of morphine," he whispered quietly. "There's nothing I can do for him."

"How's Sparks?" Randy asked. Grant looked at him and slowly shook his head.

We stood there in silence, one group staring at the other group. The only sound was an occasional moan coming from the kid known as Roman. Any chance we might have had in forming some kind of positive relationship with this crew was ruined. They stared at us with thinly veiled hatred. In spite of their original intentions, I can't say that I blamed them.

"What are we going to do with them?" Justin whispered.

"The safest thing would be to kill them all," I whispered back. "These guys are our enemies now." He looked at me; I guess he was trying to get a read on me.

"Is that what you want to do?" he finally asked.

"If I were the colonel, I'd say yes, absolutely. But, I'm not the colonel." I turned and looked at the other four men. They were silent, still staring and yeah, the hatred was as evident as the graffiti they'd painted on the wall.

"We'll let them go, then," Justin said with a hint of reservation in his voice.

There was a lull and a minute or two later Grant stood, ripping off his nitrile gloves as he looked at the remaining five men.

"Would one or two of you help Roman into one of your cars?" he asked. Randy looked pointedly at me and I nodded. He motioned to one of his friends and they carried Roman by his shoulders to one of the SUVs. Grant walked with them, giving them instructions.

"You men will need to take care of your friend and watch him closely. Change the dressing daily and watch close for infection," Grant said, paused and put his hand on Randy's shoulder. "Watch for red squiggly lines emanating from the wound, that'll let you know if infection has set in. If you men don't have a supply of antibiotics, I suggest you search for some." He then lowered his voice.

"You should also watch him closely for symptoms of anything else." Randy looked at him a moment before nodding in understanding. They gently loaded Roman up in the back seat of one of the SUVs and shut the door. Randy motioned at me and I walked over.

"What about Sparks?" he asked.

"He's not going to make it," I replied. "If you leave him here, I'm going to put a bullet in his head and burn him."

"I'll take care of him," he said. "He was a good dude." I nodded in understanding.

"What about our weapons?" I thought for a moment and pointed at one of the ambulances.

"We'll put them in there. Wait until we've left before coming back." There was a silence for a moment and it looked like he was sizing me up. I knew he was only a year older than me, but he was a good-sized man, almost as tall as me, beefy, with big muscular legs that looked like tree trunks.

"Back before, what college would you have played for?" I asked, trying to make conversation.

"I would've liked to have played for Bama, but that's neither here nor there, is it?"

"For what it's worth, I'm sorry it came to this."

"But not sorry enough to do anything to that piece of shit who killed Sparks, right?" He didn't wait for a reply, instead, he walked over to his friend he called Sparks, picked him up easily, and carried him to one of the awaiting vehicles. There was some arguing going on amongst them, but they drove away without any further trouble.

"Alright," I said. "I think we need to change plans." Everyone looked at me expectantly.

"We had the element of surprise on them at first, but that won't work again. I don't want to be caught inside that hospital if and when they come back."

"What do you suggest?" Sarah asked. I pointed at the ambulances.

"Let's salvage whatever we can out of them and call it a day." I looked at my watch. "I'd say we have forty-five minutes. By then they'll work up the nerve and possibly plan an ambush."

Ambulances normally came fully equipped with first responder equipment and medical supplies. Not these. They'd been stripped clean. We discussed it and decided it was worth the risk to get some of the equipment out of the ER. There were some filthy gurneys that were going to need a good scrubbing and a couple of crash carts, which made Grant very happy.

"These will do nicely in the clinic," he exclaimed.

Sometime during this, Shooter had come to and had parked himself in the bus, refusing to speak to anyone. We loaded everything up and gathered together.

"We made some enemies today," Ruth said.

"Bad news," True said.

"Yeah, the next time we encounter them it may get ugly."

"Yeah, probably, but that's not what I was referring to. Look." He was pointing at the far end of the hospital. A swarm of zombies were falling out of a busted-out window, clumsily getting back on their feet, and making their way toward us.

"All the noise we made got their attention," Justin surmised.

"Let's kill them," Cutter said enthusiastically.

"No, let's not," Justin retorted. "We've got a decent haul and those dudes may be planning on coming back with friends. It's time to call it a day and get the hell out of here."

"I agree." I looked at Cutter. "Besides, we've got an issue that needs resolving."

"What do you mean?" Cutter asked.

"He means your idiot brother," Sarah said. "Maybe when we get back we should go ahead and hang him for murder." His jaw dropped and he stared at all of us.

"You can't do that," he exclaimed and pointed at Justin. "And he had no right to hit him."

"I disagree," I replied. "Your brother jeopardized our mission and any future missions we might conduct in this area of town. We'll all have a nice long talk about it when we get back to the school."

True jumped in the Volvo as we prepared to go back home.

"We should have killed them all," he said in almost a whisper. "Or turned that boy over to them. This is gonna come back and haunt us. You know that, right?"

I glanced at him and nodded as Kelly put the truck in gear. I caught her looking at me out of the corner of her eye.

"They would have tortured and killed Shooter if we turned him over to them," she said. "We couldn't do that. Right?"

"They're gonna blame all of us for what that idiot did," he contended. I couldn't disagree. "If they get a chance, they're gonna get some payback." Again, I couldn't disagree. Kelly would occasionally look at us both as she drove.

CHAPTER 42 – COURT

We'd talked long into the night deciding what to do about Simon, AKA Shooter. What was decided, by majority vote, was downright ridiculous. At least, I thought so. I said as much to Kelly during our usual nocturnal bed talk.

"Would you have really killed him outright?" she asked.

"It really wouldn't have solved the problem," I said. "The King Ro gang would have still blamed us. Besides, if we killed Shooter, we would've needed to go ahead and killed Cutter too." I continued. "The most prudent thing to have done at that point was exactly what True said; kill King Ro and his crew. That was the only sure way to eliminate any possible future threat from them." Kelly and I were spooning, but she turned in the bed and faced me.

"Are you serious?"

"Yep." She looked at me a moment longer in the dark before repositioning herself.

"What do you think will happen tomorrow?"

"It could go either way. Hell, I don't even know."

"Me either, but if he's found guilty, I wonder how Cutter's going to react."

"So, here we are," I said to Tonya. "Instead of taking care of this on my own, we're deferring to you and your desire to have some sort of judicial process in place." She looked at me like I'd just farted and asked her to take a whiff.

"I'm detecting sarcasm."

"Possibly."

"I imagine if you had your way, he'd already be dead," she retorted.

"Nobody would've stopped me," I countered. "In fact, I'm pretty sure everyone was expecting me to do just that and they were fine with it. Well, except for Cutter." She had no response. I continued.

"Of course, if I chose that course of action, I would've killed Cutter as well." And that was the only reason I didn't kill Shooter outright. In spite of his dumb-assity, Cutter wasn't a bad guy.

"But what the hell, I'm very interested in seeing the Tonya Lee judicial process in action."

Everyone was gathered in the cafeteria. Ruth and Justin acted as, well I don't know what you'd call them, court bailiffs I suppose, and Tonya acted as the judge. True sat behind Shooter with a sawed-off shotgun, staring a hole in the back of his head with those coal burning eyes of his.

I was the first witness and was directed to sit in a chair positioned in front of the cafeteria tables. I recounted the events starting with the original mission.

"After we'd killed the zombies in the main area of the Emergency Room, we started to go into the rest of the hospital, but we never made it."

"What happened that stopped you?" Gus was acting as the prosecuting attorney. He was freshly shaven and was even wearing a coat and tie. I would've laughed under any other circumstance.

"We received a radio transmission from Kelly informing us of contact." Gus looked at me blankly so I explained.

"She advised there were two SUVs approaching our location and the vehicles were occupied by six men."

"What did you do?"

"Team one, that was the team I was in charge of, went outside to make the initial contact. Team two acted as backup and took up positions around the ER."

"And you were armed."

"Of course."

"Please proceed."

"The gang parked, jumped out of their SUVs and lined up. They were a filthy-looking bunch and all of them were armed. The apparent leader demanded to know what we were doing."

"What did you say?"

"I told him we didn't owe him any kind of explanation. A teenage boy, we later found out his name was Roman, stepped forward and said we shouldn't be disrespecting King Ro."

"King Ro?"

"Yeah, that's what he called himself. And then Sarah said he should call himself King Turd because he smelled so bad." There were a few snickers in the audience. "He got pissed; he seemed to think an awful lot of himself." Cutter started to stand, but then seemed to think better of it, sat back down and started taking notes, which surprised me. Up until now, I wasn't even sure he knew how to read. I continued.

"Like I said, this King Ro character became angry and he started to raise his shotgun."

"So, just to clarify, he was armed with a shotgun?"

"Yes, he was. I believed he intended to shoot one of us, and I was about to shoot him, but before I did, he accidentally shot Roman."

"Please be specific, how did he shoot Roman?"

"Roman was standing to King Ro's left side, maybe about three feet away, and maybe a foot or two in front of him. This Ro idiot accidentally discharged his shotgun and as a result, he shot Roman in the right leg."

"What happened next?" Gus asked.

"The kid fell to the ground and started screaming in pain. When King Turd realized what he'd done, he became even angrier. He was in the process of bringing his shotgun to bear on one of us, but I managed to stop him and get his shotgun away from him."

"Then what happened?"

"Kelly and Josue had snuck up behind them while all of this was going on. When they realized they were outgunned, they obeyed when we ordered them to disarm."

"So, they gave up their guns?"

"Yeah," I replied. "They didn't want to, but when I told them we had a doctor who'd treat Roman, one of them told his buddies to comply."

"So, y'all have now disarmed this gang of marauders?"

"Yes."

"What happened then?"

"Major Parsons began administering first aid to Roman and I started to talk to the rest of them."

"What specifically were you talking about?" I was getting irritated, Gus was asking too many irrelevant questions, but I kept my emotions in check and answered.

"I asked them to explain why they confronted us and why were they hostile toward us. One of them responded that we were trespassing on their territory. As fate would have it, I recognized him. He's a year older than me and went to Overton." Gus looked at me blankly. "It's a high school in south Nashville," I explained.

"Ah, please continue."

"While I was talking to him, Shooter and Cutter started assaulting this Ro character. We stopped them and at some point, one of the men, they called him Sparks, recognized Shooter and Cutter. He said he knew them as being with the River Road group and he didn't seem very happy to see them."

"Did he make some kind of threatening statement?"

"No."

"Was he armed?"

"No."

"Was Shooter, or anyone else in our group in imminent peril?"

"No."

"What happened then?"

"I told the man I wanted to hear what he had to say, but before he could respond, Shooter shot him."

"Unprovoked?"

"That would be my opinion, yes."

"And then what happened?"

"Lieutenant Smithson grabbed the rifle out of Shooter's hands and then knocked him out." Kyra gave a short but loud laugh. Her sister glared at her.

"And then, Cutter acted like he was going to shoot Justin, but Sarah stopped him. That was basically the end of it. Grant went over to check on the man, but there was nothing he could do for him. I talked to the one I knew for a minute, then they left. After they left, we did some scavenging and then left approximately forty-five minutes later."

"Your witness," Gus said with his best imitation of Adam Schiff. Cutter stood quickly.

"Alright, I want to start with what you said at first. You said they were all armed and didn't appear friendly, right?"

"Yes, when contact was first made."

"And then you said that there was a confrontation and King Ro was going to try to shoot one of us, but ended up accidentally shooting a member of his group."

"Yes."

"And during this, Kelly and Josue had gained a tactical advantage on this group of thugs."

"Well, yeah that's a good way of putting it."

"And they were ordered to give up their weapons."

"Yes."

"And now, nobody from this group was armed, including the man you've identified as Sparks."

"Yes, that's what I said."

"How do you know?"

"Because he had no weapons in his hands or on his person."

"But nobody had physically searched any of them at that time, so how did you know at that point in time, when he started standing, how did you know right then he didn't have a weapon?"

"You make a good point," I conceded. "The only way I can answer is, he had no weapon in his hands at that time nor was a weapon visible."

"But he could have been armed?"

"I suppose he may have had a weapon hidden on him, but he didn't have any weapon in his hand when he was shot."

"So, if my brother was acting on the assumption that this gang member was armed, he was acting in self-defense."

"Is that a question?" I asked.

"Sure, that's a question. Are you going to try to put some kind of spin on it?"

"Not at all. I will concede at that time, none of them had been physically searched." Both Cutter and Shooter smiled at the perceived victory. "But, he wasn't armed." He started to ask another question but Tonya cut him off.

"Let's stop all of this nonsense, I want to know something," Tonya asked me. "What do you think about this?"

"I think that man was telling the truth about knowing Shooter and Cutter and it's my belief this man was about to say some things that maybe Shooter didn't want us to know about. He became scared and shot him."

"Objection!" Cutter shouted as he literally jumped up and down. "That's all bullshit speculation." Tonya waved him off and looked over everyone else.

"Let's save some time here, is there anyone here whose testimony will contradict what Zach just said?" Cutter quickly raised his hand. Tonya grunted.

"Okay, swap places with Zach." Once Cutter was seated, Gus started to rise, but Tonya waved him off.

"How did this man know the two of you?" she asked. Cutter shrugged.

"I have no idea. It's possible he'd seen us around; we'd made contact with some people from time to time. People were always coming to our compound trying to get free handouts and shit. " Tonya gave him a hard stare, but it wasn't going to work. He'd rehearsed his story and was sticking to it. Whatever the dead guy knew about Cutter and Shooter, it went with him to his grave.

"It's sounding like your brother may have acted without provocation," Tonya surmised. Cutter shook his head vigorously.

"Those men were looking for trouble," he insisted and pointed at me. "Zach pretty much said so. When that asshole stood up, he was about to charge my brother, I could see it in his eyes, and you heard it from Zach's own mouth, none of them had been physically searched. For all we knew, he could have had a hideout gun." He pointed at me again.

"Zach has a hideout gun on him right now. Just because he doesn't have it in his hand doesn't mean he can't get to it and shoot someone if he wanted." He was right. I had a compact three-eighty concealed in my crotch. I never showed it off or mentioned it, so I was wondering how he knew it. Tonya sat quietly for a minute and then looked at Gus.

"Do you want to cross examine him?" she asked. Gus rubbed his chin before responding.

"I don't think I'm going to get a truthful answer out of him, so no." She looked back at Cutter.

"Shooter, are you going to testify?" Shooter started to reply, but Cutter cut him off with a raised hand and shook his head emphatically.

"My client fully recognizes his Fifth Amendment privilege and will not testify." Shooter started to argue but Cutter stopped him with a harsh look. I had to admit to myself, Cutter was proving to be smarter than I gave him credit for. If Shooter started talking, I think Gus could have gotten him to say all kinds of incriminating things. It would have been interesting, to say the least.

"Alright," Tonya said and looked out at the audience. "Marc, Ward, Rachel, Brandon, Mike, Mary, Rhonda, and Maria. All of you are now the jury. I want you to go to another room and deliberate. Oh, and Rhonda, you'll be the foreperson." Brandon raised a hand. Tonya acknowledged him by staring pointedly over her bifocals.

"We're deciding whether or not Shooter committed murder, correct?"

"That's correct," Tonya replied. The newly appointed jury looked at each other in what could best be described as a reluctant burden, filed out of the room and went to an unused classroom in the back of the school. During all of this, Macie's puppy started circling my feet and whining.

"I'm taking Zoe outside," I said to Kelly and stood.

"I'm coming with you," she replied.

"Me too," Sarah said.

When we first got Zoe, I thought it was going to be many weeks of frustration and pissed on floors before properly training her, but I was surprised at how quickly we got her house broken. She scampered down the sidewalk and squatted in the dirt without even being coaxed to do so. When she finished, I praised her and gave her a knotted rope to play with. Her tail wagged in joy.

I walked over to the newly constructed guard tower, a square structure made with a mixture of lumber and concrete blocks, sitting a few feet above ground level and surrounded by stacked sandbags. But, all that was wasted, as the door was propped open by a concrete block. Goober was sitting inside and waved cheerfully as I walked up.

"Every time I come around, you're pulling guard duty," I said. He smiled a big toothy smile.

"Shoot, I don't mind. I kind of like sitting out here. It's nice listening to the birds singing. Besides," he picked up a drawing pad, "it gives me plenty of time to draw." Goober showed me some of his work, mostly of birds, and to my surprise they were really nice with lots of detail and shading which made the birds look three dimensional.

"Those are great," I said. "Do you do people as well?" Goober nodded enthusiastically and showed me a couple more drawings of some of the school group.

"These are really nice." Goober grinned at the compliment.

"You want me to draw a picture of your two kids?" My eyes widened.

"Would you?"

"It'd be my pleasure," he replied. "I like drawing kids." He then thumbed through his pad and carefully tore out a page of the thick paper. When he handed it to me, I think my jaw dropped open. It was an exquisitely detailed drawing of Macie and Frederick.

"I drew that one back at the CDC, but they've grown some since then. I'll be glad to draw them again."

"I'd be most appreciative," I said. Goober grinned again and bobbed his head.

"Let's plan on the day after tomorrow. You and your missus dress them however you want and bring them on down here." He looked around and pointed toward the creek.

"There's a mighty pretty weeping willow tree down there. I think I'd like to pose them in front of it, and we'll put little Zoe in there with them."

"It sounds great, Goober."

"Consider it a plan then."

After chatting with him a few minutes, I walked over to the picnic tables where Kelly was sitting. She had the length of knotted rope and was playing tug-of-war with Zoe. I showed her the picture and told her about Goober.

"That's beautiful," she said. "I have an idea." I looked at her. "Let's make it a family portrait."

"Good idea. We'll need to compensate him somehow, so think that over." I watched as she played with Zoe.

"She's about ready to start some serious training."

"How do you think it's going to go?" Kelly asked. "The decision, how do you think it'll go?" I chuckled.

"You know, I'm a little surprised at Cutter. He actually did a pretty good job as a defense attorney. He rightfully pointed out that we'd neglected to search them."

"You think he'll get off?" Sarah asked. I shrugged. Kate, Kyra and Cutter came outside and joined us. Kyra fished out a pack of cigarettes and lit one. Kate frowned and motioned for one.

"You hope they find him guilty of murder," Kate said accusingly after taking a deep drag.

"I actually don't give a shit, but I will say this," I said as I stared at Cutter. "Your brother is a loose cannon. He's going to get himself, or someone else hurt or killed one day." Cutter looked at me steadily. "And you follow him blindly."

"You've killed people too," he countered. "I've heard the stories." I didn't respond and grabbed the rope away from Zoe. She barked at me the way puppies do when they want something.

"What happens if he's found guilty?" Kyra asked.

"It'll be up to Tonya and the jury, but he'll probably be banished." I said.

"If he's banished, I'm leaving too," Cutter proclaimed, as if that really mattered. I didn't bother with a response. The opening of the steel double-doors made us all look over. Justin and Ruth walked out.

"Janet's bitching again," Ruth said as she sat.

"What about this time?" Kelly asked. Ruth threw up her hands.

"Everything in general," she replied, to which Kelly rolled her eyes.

"Great, dinner is going to be pleasant this evening," she muttered sarcastically.

"You'd be happy to see Shooter banished," Kate accused, obviously not wanting to let it go. "Go ahead and admit it."

"Let me make something clear to everyone. I don't care what the jury or Tonya decides. What I do care about is there's something more going on here." I gestured at Cutter again. "That man knew something about you two, and Simon was willing to murder him in order to shut him up."

"My brother was protecting us," Cutter maintained. Like we needed his protection, I thought.

"What do you have against him anyway?" he asked.

"I could name several things, but the main one is: he's an eccedentesiast." Cutter frowned and looked at me like I was questioning their parentage. I explained.

"An eccedentesiast is a person who hides their true feelings behind a fake smile. You know, like the way politicians would do, back before. Hard to trust a person like that." Cutter looked away and didn't respond. Justin laughed.

"Eccedentesiast, that's a mighty big word."

"Oh, you should have known him a while back," Kelly said with a grin. "He used to never speak unless he could throw in a few words with a lot of syllables." She grabbed the rope away from me and tossed it at Zoe. "He's gotten better though," she said with a grin. While we were talking, Tonya stuck her head out of the door and motioned at us. All of us hurriedly walked back inside. After everyone was seated, Gus ushered the pseudo jury back into the cafeteria.

"Has the jury reached a verdict?" Tonya asked. Rhonda, who'd sat down a microsecond before Tonya spoke, quickly stood.

"We have a bit of a quandary - judge," Rhonda said shakily.

"What kind of quandary?"

"Four of us think Shooter committed murder, and the other four think he acted in defense."

"In defense?" Tonya asked. "You mean self-defense?" Rhonda shook her head.

"I mean, we mean, Shooter acted in defense of the group." She looked around at all of us. "We all agree Shooter may have acted hastily, but some of us think he was acting in the best interests of the crew and not acting with malice."

"What does that mean?" Kelly whispered to me. I shrugged.

"It means we have a hung jury."

Tonya heard my response and looked at me. I looked back as if to say, what now? The look on her face told me everything. She broke eye contact and looked over at the so-called jury.

"Thank you for performing your duty," she said, got up, and walked out of the room.

"That was weird," Kelly said as we drove home. "Or am I missing something?"

"What do you think, Zach?" Janet asked.

"It means nothing changes," I replied. In truth, I had a lot more of an opinion on the matter. When it came down to Tonya having to make a serious, tough decision regarding the fate of a person's life, she couldn't do it. It made me wonder about the next time something like this happened.

"Nothing is going to happen to Shooter?" Kelly asked.

"It doesn't look that way."

"That's bullshit," she said. "I was right there and watched him murder that man. The world's so fucked up."

"Yeah, well, what's normal these days," Janet quipped. She was right.

CHAPTER 43 – THE DELEGATION

I sat and watched in amazement as Justin worked the key with seemingly effortless speed. I'd made a point of memorizing Morse code, but even so, I had a hard time keeping up. Finally, he signed off and looked over at us with a smile.

"They just confirmed it. POTUS is sending a delegation."

"Wait," True piped up. "What? Who?" The man didn't talk a heck of a lot, but Justin's statement had him suddenly attentive and sitting on the edge of his chair.

"The President, he's sending a delegation down to visit since we won't go up there."

"He's still alive?" he asked incredulously. Justin nodded. True leaned back in his chair. "Well, ain't that some shit," he muttered, causing Kelly to snicker.

"What's the purpose of the delegation?" I asked warily.

"They're calling it the reunification tour. Apparently, they've made contact with other pockets of survivors like ours at other cities and have brought them together." I grunted.

"What?" he asked.

"I don't know what they can offer us."

"When are they coming?" Kelly asked.

"Seven days," Justin said.

"Great," I said. "I suppose I'll need to make the Gunderson clan scarce for a while."

"I guess I'm out of the loop," True said. "Because I don't know what the hell you're talking about." I inadvertently let out a long sigh and told the story. True listened closely, occasionally glancing over at Ruth and Justin.

"Is all that true?" he asked Justin when I was through. Justin nodded somberly.

"I'm afraid it is."

"That's pretty fucked up."

"Yeah," I replied quietly. "But, it's water under the bridge." Kelly, who was sitting beside me, gave my hand a gentle squeeze.

"Zach, whatever your decision is, we'll back you," Ruth said.

"I appreciate that," I said and stood. Kelly stood with me. "We're going to go home and talk about it." We bid our goodbyes and talked in the truck on the way home.

"Are we going to bug out?" Kelly asked as she drove.

"I'm not sure. What do you think?"

"I think maybe, at the very least, we should hide the children again."

Janet had already fed the kids so Kelly fixed a plate for the two of us. I sat at the table as the kids climbed up in my lap and vied for attention.

"How is everyone?" Janet asked. I shrugged as I positioned the two of them on each knee and related everything. Her expression changed from joyfulness to concern as I filled them in.

"They'll try me for murder, Zach," Janet said. I almost said it wouldn't happen, but it was possible. For that matter, they might see Solonowski's death as a murder and put me on trial as well.

"What are we going to do?"

"I'm going to hide these two urchins," I said as I gave them a playful bounce. "I've thought about this. I'm not going to ask Kelly to hide out with them again without knowing what the hell is going on. I'm going to do it."

"Are you sure?" she asked. "I mean, I would think they would want to speak to you more than anyone." Sarah was sitting at the table and was listening quietly.

"I'll be happy to hide the kids," she said.

"I will too," Janet added. Sarah glanced at her without any outward emotion. I raised a hand to head off any possible argument.

"Nope, I'm going to take care of it."

"So, you're not going to have anything to do with this delegation?" Sarah asked.

"Doubtful, but we'll see."

"That's a little vague," she said. "But whatever."

Kelly and I were lying in bed, talking about the day's events when there was a soft knock on the door. Kelly and I exchanged frowns and each of us sat up.

"Come in." The door opened slowly and Janet appeared. Kelly instinctively pulled the blankets up over her breasts.

"I hope I'm not intruding."

"Are the kids okay?" I asked. She nodded.

"They're both asleep." She stared at us and I got the impression she was thinking about Kelly and me in bed together and Julie lying buried in the cold ground.

"I think you should reconsider my offer."

"Why?" I asked, genuinely perplexed.

"Because you're the main person who got all of this started. You might have questions for them and you might be able to extract information from them that nobody else would think about." She paused for a second. "You seem to have a knack for that." I looked at Kelly again.

"Thank you for the compliment," I responded. "I want to talk it over with Kelly and maybe we'll reach a decision tomorrow."

"Okay, good night." She closed the door quietly.

"What do you think?" I asked Kelly quietly.

"They said they'd be here in seven days. I'm going to be ready and watching for them."

"Are you going to go out roaming around in your ghillie suit again?" she asked, somewhat sarcastically. I grunted.

"If that's what you want to call it, but I'm not going to be caught with my pants down."

As expected, they arrived precisely one week later. I had a concealed position and watched them with binoculars, although they were easy to spot as they drove along the state highway. They were in a rugged-looking armored military vehicle equipped with eight wheels and a large caliber machine gun mounted on top. Five gallon jerry cans were lashed down around the vehicle. It looked very formidable. I watched them as they slowly clambered up Bell Road and turned onto Nolensville Pike. From my position, I had a view down Bell Road of over a thousand meters. There was no other vehicle in sight.

As rehearsed, Sarah and Rachel were monitoring the radio. When I called them, they caught up with them before they even made it the first block. I watched through the rifle's scope as Rachel waved them down. They stopped and exited the vehicle. All four of them.

CHAPTER 44 – NEVER-ENDING

They were frazzled, maybe even a little shell-shocked. The surviving four delegates identified themselves as Raymond Easting, Earl Hunter, Earl's wife, Sheila, and Seth Kitchens. All of them were in their late twenties and wearing civilian clothes, identified themselves as Congressional aides in their past lives.

"There were six of us originally," Raymond said. He was what you would call an average Joe. Nothing about him particularly stood out. He was skinny, his brown hair was a little oily but freshly combed and his three-day beard growth was not particularly thick. His demeanor was pleasant enough but he spoke with one of those voices that made you think he grew up in a mansion with nannies and butlers and he only went to the finest private New England schools.

"We started out three days ago. It was pretty slow going, as you can imagine.

"When we got to Mount Juliet it was already late in the day, so we decided to stop, rest up, and make a fresh start in the morning."

"You were on I-40?" Justin asked.

"Yes, that was our route through most of Tennessee. Gerard had shot a deer the day before, so we thought it'd be nice to grill some venison." He looked around at all of us.

"With the exception of an occasional zombie wandering around, we hadn't seen a soul throughout the entire trip. We thought it was safe."

"What happened then?" Ruth prodded.

"They came out of nowhere," the one who introduced himself as Seth said. He was calmer than the other three. A lean but muscular build on a six foot frame, and he had a smooth yet authoritative tone to his voice. I scribbled furiously as he spoke. "I'd estimate the number at around three hundred, maybe a few more." He paused and waited for me to catch up. Another one of them, Earl, chose the moment to speak.

"The trip itself was pleasant enough, considering the condition of the roads." He looked to be a couple of years older than the others, a few inches shorter than his companion, even leaner, with wisps of premature gray in his brown hair.

"The location where we stopped had a scenic view and there was a nice breeze coming from the east. The venison was on the grill and the aromas were mouthwatering. It started out as a very pleasant afternoon." He sighed heavily and his wife, a short brunette who appeared to have been sporting a lot of weight at one time, reached out and grabbed his hand.

"I sure hate to interrupt your reverie, Earl, but I believe they want to hear about the specifics of us getting attacked." Seth looked around. "Where was I? Oh, so there were about three hundred of them. They swarmed us from the west, right at sunset."

"They were running," Earl interrupted again. "We've never seen them run before. Have you guys?"

"Not anything worthy of winning the Olympics, but yeah, we've seen a few of them run."

"Yeah, these weren't fast, but fast enough. They caught Gerard and Clyde before they could reach the safety of the vehicle. They put up a good fight and we shot as many as we could but there were too many. They overwhelmed them and ripped them apart." Raymond shuddered.

"Don't get me wrong, I'd seen similar things, but it doesn't make it any easier when you witness your friends being killed like that."

"What'd you do next?" I asked. Seth pointed at their military vehicle.

"Are you familiar with one of these?" he asked. I shook my head.

"It's an Armored Combat Vehicle, commonly called a Stryker. They're very sturdy, virtually indestructible against small arms fire, zombies, and things like that. When we first started out, we stayed inside it at all times and only got out when we had to answer the call of nature." Earl again spoke up.

"We were very vigilant at first, but we became complacent, I guess you'd say." He looked around at us. "Trust me, when you're stuck inside one of those things for hours on end, bumping up against your friends and smelling their body odors, tempers get short."

"I can imagine," Marc said. Earl looked at him and gave an uncertain smile.

"Long story short, we started out with six good people, and this is all that is left." He focused on a knothole on the picnic table he was sitting at for a moment and then looked around at all of us again.

"They took us by surprise and there were simply too many of them."

"Did you kill all of them?" Justin asked.

"I believe we killed a sizeable number," Seth responded. The other three murmured their agreement.

"But not all of them," Justin pushed. Seth shook his head.

"As it got dark, the ones left alive kind of faded away and left." He looked pointedly at us. "Damned peculiar behavior, if you ask me. We waited until morning before heading out." Cutter snorted. I looked up from my notes and waited for his derisive comment.

"I hope you didn't lead those damned things to our doorstep," he remarked. I glanced sharply at him and then at Justin.

"He makes a good point," I conceded. Justin gave the delegation a hard stare.

"What route did you use to get here, after the attack?" Justin demanded. Raymond looked a little uneasily now and hastened a glance at his three companions.

"We got turned around once or twice," Sheila replied. "But, there wasn't anyone or anything following us." Earl nodded in agreement with his wife.

"Those things aren't that smart," he declared.

"But, you people didn't take any active countermeasures, now did you?" Justin rejoined. Three of them looked pointedly at Seth but didn't respond. They probably didn't even know what countermeasures were.

"They're regaining their cognitive processes," I said. "You can't underestimate them." True stood suddenly, then thought better of it and sat back down.

"What is it, True?" Justin asked.

"Maybe it ain't my place to say," he said to Justin. "But we don't need to be taking any chances. We need to go on a recon patrol ASAP." he said. "We've got to find out if them things are close by."

"Yeah," Justin replied. He stood as well. "Goober, Blake, Ruth, gear up." They nodded and hurried off. Cutter and Shooter stood.

"We're in," Shooter said without being asked. Justin gave him a look before focusing on me.

"Are you going?" he asked.

"Not if those two are." The two brothers glared at me but wisely remained silent.

Justin pointed at Earl. "You'll be driving that fine-looking car." Earl paled as he shook his head nervously. Seth stood and stretched.

"I'll go," he said. "Earl isn't the best driver in the world."

After gearing up and going over the route with us, Justin led his patrol out. Ward volunteered to man the radio in case they got into trouble and needed help.

"Alright, let's get back to the purpose of your visit," I said to the three remaining delegates after the patrol had left.

"Oh, the usual horse-hockey," Raymond said nonchalantly. "Get a census, establish lines of communications, and try to convince Zach here to come home with us."

"Why is that?" Jorge asked.

"Here we go," I retorted under my breath. Raymond heard me, but was unfazed.

"I'm sure you all are aware of Zach and his children apparently having an immunity to the zombie virus. The President and the surviving members of Congress have been told by our scientists they believe they can create a cure, with his assistance, of course."

"What about the rest of us?" she asked. Raymond held his palms out.

"Our directive is simple regarding who's invited and who's not."

"It should be, you're the one who thought it up," Sheila said snidely. Earl chuckled.

"We are to evaluate all survivors we come into contact with. The benchmarks are skills, health, and most importantly, content of character. I believe all of you pass muster."

"You see," Earl interjected. "We've created a paradigm of the best course of action for rebuilding society. We are going to attempt to recruit as many able-bodied survivors as we can, and then reestablish an agrarian and industrial base. You know, get the farms producing, the power-grid operational, the factories online, the oil refineries booming, the usual. Simply put, get the country going again."

"Along with a formal government," Tonya remarked.

"Yeah, and who wouldn't want that?" Gus asked scornfully. Raymond shrugged.

"You better believe they're doing it in Russia and China. If we don't do the same, there will come a day when somebody, be it the Russians, Chinese, or some Muslim country, they'll show up on our doorstep and claim the U.S. now belongs to them. Not a pleasant alternative, if you ask me."

"Why did they send Congressional aides?" Sarah asked. "Are there no military personnel left?"

"We're expendable," Sheila replied after a pause. Earl frowned at her but she ignored him and focused on Sarah.

"In answer to your first question, there are still military personnel, but they're guarding the base, the town, the President, and what's left of Congress."

"How many civilian and military altogether?" I asked.

"Approximately 133 with four more on the way." He saw at least one confused expression and explained. "Four of the women are pregnant."

"There's one other thing," Raymond added, almost as an afterthought. He looked around at us and gave almost apologetic smile.

"We're not at Raven Rock, we're actually located in Mount Weather." Tonya sat up quickly.

"What do you mean?" she asked.

"Where the hell is Mount Weather?" Gus added.

"Any contact we make with the outside world, we tell them what is left of the government is located at Raven Rock, just in case someone with access to nuclear weapons is listening in.

"Raven Rock is basically an underground bunker that is designed for a small contingent. Mount Weather, although it too has a sizeable bunker system, it was also specifically designed to house the executive branch in case of an emergency for a sustained period of time. It has everything you can think of. Fresh water, living quarters, fresh food, stored food, just about everything you can think of."

We conversed with the three delegates at length through the afternoon. They explained they'd had sporadic radio contact with other pockets of survivors all over the United States. Raymond was hesitant, but I pushed him into giving an estimate.

"We believe it to be approximately a half million," he said. "Our ultimate goal is to get the majority of the population within a hundred mile radius of Weather."

"I've heard of Mount Weather," I said. "It's located in northern Virginia, correct?"

"Yes, about seventy miles from DC." He looked at all of us. "Obviously, we don't want everyone stacked on top of each other, but if we could consolidate, it would go a long way to reestablish America's infrastructure." The delegates discussed it at length. I had to admit, it sounded good in theory, but there were a lot of unforeseen variables. It didn't stop me from taking extensive notes though.

The patrol returned late in the afternoon. All of us were anxious to hear about it and gathered around them as they unloaded.

"One hundred and seventeen dead zombie motherfuckers," Shooter proclaimed and looked at Kate smugly, as if he were the one who killed them all by himself.

"There were ten to fifteen malingerers, we took care of them. The rest of them had already been killed by these guys," Justin said, pointing at Seth.

"So, if Seth's count is accurate, there are still a little over a hundred of them wandering around the Mount Juliet area," Tonya opined.

"It would seem so," Justin answered, "but other than the fifteen we killed, we didn't encounter any others."

I started to question Seth, but he wasn't looking very well.

"Would there happen to be somewhere to clean up?" he asked nobody in particular.

"We have a locker room," Marc responded. "Give me a minute to get it going and I can have the shower up and running."

"That'd be nice," he replied quietly and followed Marc inside. Justin cleared his throat.

"Clyde and Gerard were hardly recognizable," he said somberly. "Seth is taking it pretty hard."

"The three of them were very close," Sheila said. She hurriedly wiped away a tear.

"Would it be possible for us to shower too?" she asked.

"Of course," Tonya replied, and motioned for the three of them to follow her.

"We could be wrong, but we're fairly certain none of those other zombies made their way here," Justin said. "I think we're going to head over to the tower and get cleaned up as well." He made a small motion with his head before getting in his vehicle with Ruth and True. After making some small talk, Kelly and I loaded up.

"We're going over to the radio house. Justin wants to talk to us," I said to Kelly as I turned onto Concord Road. The three of them were standing outside, waiting on us.

"There's something odd going on here," Justin said.

"What do you mean?" Kelly asked.

"That Seth dude is military," True declared. "And he's an officer. I can smell an officer a mile off."

"You two are smart people," Justin said to Kelly and me. "But you've never been in the military. Not everything in the military is written in manuals. If you've noticed, everyone around here calls most people by their first name. In the military, we tend to call everyone by their last names, by their rank, or a nickname." He pointed at Ruth's nametag. "We never called Ruth by her first name; everyone called her a variation of her last name."

"Bulldog," she said. She must have seen my expression and grinned. "Don't worry, I don't consider it an insult. They started calling me that in boot camp and it stuck."

"Everyone called me Smitty," Justin said. "It's a military thing, everyone had a nametag and that's what we called each other. We seldom called each other by our first names."

"Like, everyone calling me True," True added. Justin nodded and wagged his finger. "He kept calling his friends by their last names, and there were a couple of other things. When we went out on the patrol, I asked Seth to take us back to the place where they were attacked. The first thing he did when he pulled the map out was orient it toward north. How many civilians do you know who does that?" Well, I did, but that's how Rick taught me to do it.

"I see your point," I said.

"We went to the scene where they were ambushed and found the two dead ones."

"They were all torn up," True said. "But they had put up a hell of a fight. One of them killed three or four with a knife. Now, he didn't look like no outlaw biker or nothing, he had to have had military training."

"Yeah," Justin said.

"You're convinced they're military?" I asked, already knowing the answer.

"But they said they were all congressional aides," Kelly said.

"Exactly my point," Justin replied. "Why lie?"

CHAPTER 45 – Q & A

I stretched the kinks out of my neck. "We're going to need to get to the bottom of this, and I say the sooner the better."

"No time like the present," True said in agreement and did a press check on his handgun, a Glock model 17.

"Alright," Ruth said with a nod.

We found Seth in the greenhouse with Marc and Ward. He was freshly showered and clean shaven, wearing a clean pair of jeans with a blue Polo shirt. His hair even appeared to have been recently styled. Hell, he looked like he just came back from a day at the spa.

"This is nice," he commented. "We have greenhouses back up in Mount Weather, but I've got to admit, you guys have far more varieties of herbs than we do." He inhaled deeply.

"It smells wonderful in here. When I was a kid, my grandmother had a small greenhouse. She grew orchids. I always loved how it smelled."

"They've done an outstanding job," I said. The two psychologists-slash-gardeners grinned at the compliment.

"Seth is a little distraught over the death of his two friends," Marc said sympathetically. "We thought this might be a pleasant respite from the others for a while."

"They're worried about me," Seth said with a tolerant smile.

"Grief counseling and gardening, it's what they do," I said with my own smile. Seth chuckled appreciatively. I turned to Ward and Marc.

"Guys, would you two mind if we had a private word with Seth?" I asked. "We won't be long." Their smiles vanished but they obliged me and walked out. As planned, Ruth and True followed them out and then guarded the door. When the door shut, I turned to Seth. I wasn't smiling anymore. Seth acted as though he didn't notice our change in demeanor.

"What's on your mind, guys?" he asked with no more tenseness than asking what time was dinner.

"What's your rank?" I asked pointedly. "Judging from your age I'd guess you're perhaps a lieutenant or a captain?" He frowned, as if confused by my question.

"I'm an aide to Congressman Weisenstein from New York, I told you guys that." I shook my head.

"I'm not buying it. Neither is Justin."

"You're military," Justin declared. "We can smell it all over you." Seth didn't respond and simply stared. "You didn't think you could fool us, did you?" Seth continued staring at Justin a moment, realizing the gig was up.

"I guess not, but I can assure you there was no ill intent."

"So, why the subterfuge?" I asked. Seth sighed and reached for a bucket sitting in the corner. He turned it over and sat on it.

"The name's we gave are legit, but I'm not a congressional aide. I'm a captain in the United States Army. At the time of the outbreak, my duty assignment was with the Joint Chiefs of Staff at the Pentagon." He saw my look and explained. "My dad had connections so I was an aide to a general. He didn't make it."

"Your father or the general?"

"My father, and all of my family."

"How many did make it?" I asked.

"Very few," he replied matter-of-factly. "When the outbreak started, fewer and fewer people would show up to work. The day of the evacuation, there were only four of us. We had an assortment of senators, congressmen, high-level bureaucrats and their lackeys. We started with approximately five hundred people, but there's been a lot of deaths and desertions. Oh, and a few births. Even an apocalypse can't keep people from having sex."

"Your mission?" Justin pressed.

"Everything we told you people, with the added emphasis of bringing Zach and his children back to Mount Weather."

"And how do you intend to accomplish this?"

"Not by force, if that's what you're thinking," he said quickly. "Lieutenant Smithson brought us up to speed about Colonel Coltrane."

"When did he do that?" I asked. Seth grunted and nodded toward Justin.

"Who do you think he was showing off his Morse code skills to all those nights?"

He sighed and shook his head. "For what it's worth, I am in complete agreement with Lieutenant Smithson. That colonel went too far. That's the reason for the subterfuge. We knew you'd be wary of soldiers showing up. Hell, for all we knew you'd take your kids and disappear, so we came up with a story." I glanced at Justin. In fact, that's exactly what I was considering.

"All of you are military, sir?" Justin asked.

"No, just me and the two who were killed." He made a pained expression and rubbed his face.

"They were a pair of numbskulls, but they were my friends."

"I imagine you've lost a lot of friends and family, just like us." He nodded in agreement. I wondered if he knew how I'd lost mine. "Alright, keep going."

"The delegation was my idea and for safety reasons, military personnel were included." He gritted his teeth a moment before continuing.

"Our primary goal is to attempt to get you to see the importance, the magnitude of finding a cure and convince you this would be best for the country. No, let me rephrase that, if humanity is to survive, we *have* to find a cure." I looked at him like he was trying to convert me to some kind of weird religion.

"I've heard all of this rhetoric before, Captain, and it seemed like it was just a lot of bullshit from people who were more concerned with themselves than with the wellbeing of my kids and myself." I gestured around at our surroundings.

"We've worked hard to survive, and you're trying to tell me it's going to be in our best interests to drop everything and blindly place our trust in the hands of strangers, right?"

"You guys have done wonderful things here, I'll grant you that, but…" he paused and searched for the right words. "You mentioned the word rhetoric. Let me ask a few rhetorical questions. Someone here goes to Doctor Parsons and says they were walking along one day and had a seizure, what does he have at his disposal to properly diagnose and treat his patient? Someone else has an impacted wisdom tooth that's become infected, or maybe someone takes a bad spill off of a horse or has an automobile accident." He hooked a thumb toward the school.

"I talked to Marc and Ward and they told me about a gentleman named Floyd and the freak accident he had that screwed up his arm. What if Doctor Parsons is the person who has one of these things happen to him?

"How about defensive capability? Can you defend yourself against a horde of a thousand or more? How about a band of marauders who've found themselves a tank or an artillery piece? The bottom line is, in spite of what you've accomplished, survival is still precarious. Tell me I'm wrong."

"No," I said slowly, "you're not wrong."

"Mount Weather is ten times bigger than this place, but unlike this place it's a hardened, secure facility with a wide range of health professionals." He gestured again toward the outside of the greenhouse.

"What do you have here? You've got a guard tower, some fencing, sandbags, and a few people with various types of small arms. Both of you know as well as I do you're vulnerable. Gunny, what do you think, I'd say one tank with a trained crew could make mincemeat of this place. Would you agree?" Justin gave a small nod for an answer. Seth continued. "Hell, for that matter, a platoon-sized outfit with a couple of mortars and a crew-served weapon could wipe this place out. Is your house hardened?"

"It is, to an extent, but I see your point."

"And what about the infected? I've seen satellite feeds of large swarms of them. We monitor them constantly, and believe me, they've started travelling." He didn't have to convince me, I'd seen it myself.

"Let me ask you, Lieutenant, how many of them attacked the CDC?" he asked.

"Several thousand, sir," Justin admitted.

"Zach, we have military personnel and military equipment, Mount Weather can handle an attack of that magnitude, how about this place? I'll answer for you. You people will put up a valiant fight, some of you will survive somehow, maybe, but most will die. Just like what happened at the CDC and everywhere else around the world."

"You've got a good sales pitch," I grudgingly admitted. "I bet you spent a lot of time rehearsing it in front of a mirror."

"Indeed I have," he replied with a wry grin. "I've used it to recruit other survivors. In fact, when we first started going out to recruit, we had a total of two doctors. On one of these missions, I found almost an entire ER staff hiding out in Georgetown. I successfully brought them in." He stopped and watched us. Justin and I swapped looks at one another. He made several good points, I'll give him that. Seth cleared his throat.

"I'm sensing your apprehension and I understand, but I'm not going to back off. Here's where I go for the gut shot. What about the welfare of your kids? We have kids at Weather and we're very cognizant of their importance to mankind's future. You should see our education program. It covers a broad spectrum of survival and vocational skills, along with liberal arts. The children are being taught at advanced levels. It's very impressive." He leaned forward on the bucket, rested his elbows on his knees, and stared pointedly.

"The people here, well, with the exception of those two brothers, have had very positive things to say about both of you. I think you two would be in your element with us. We need more people, people who know how to survive."

"And, the cure I supposedly possess."

"Affirmative. I won't bullshit you, that's the entire reason for this mission."

"Would a delegation have been sent here if I didn't exist?" I asked. Seth shrugged.

"I don't know. We've sent out recruiting missions before, but all have been limited in distance to Weather. This is the furthest we've been."

"You mentioned satellite feeds," I commented. He nodded.

"Several of them are still up there, quietly orbiting, but I think only about ten percent are online. Other countries may have a few still working. I'm not sure of the exact number, that's not my bailiwick."

"Does POTUS communicate with other countries?"

"Yes, but don't bother asking me the specifics. Even if I knew, I wouldn't be able to tell you." Seth looked at his watch, rubbed his hands on his pants legs and stood.

"Tonya has declared a formal question and answer session immediately after dinner, which supposedly started ten minutes ago. Why don't the two of you join in?"

Justin and I agreed and the two of us made our way to the cafeteria. They had some box fans running, but it was still stuffy inside. Everyone was wiping the sweat from their brow in between bites. To my surprise, Janet had loaded up the kids and brought them to the school. Frederick was sitting beside her, feeding the two dogs off of his plate when she wasn't looking. She was armed with one of Fred's revolvers too. I walked over to her with the intention of asking about the soundness of her judgement, but she spoke first.

"I see that look on your face, but there's only four of them. If they try something with my babies, I'll kill them myself." She tapped the revolver for emphasis. Well, that was a good answer. I nodded and sat down beside my kids.

There was a lot of small talk during lunch. Everyone was antsy; they wanted to hear what the delegation had to say. Several times, somebody would try to ask them a question, but Tonya would cut them off, admonishing them to wait until lunch was over. Once everyone had mostly finished, Tonya stood and raised her hand, causing everyone to quieten down.

"Alright, this is what we've been waiting for. We're going to have a question and answer session with the President's delegation. Everyone please mind your manners, wait to be recognized, and don't shout over each other." She motioned at Seth who stood. "Seth is going to start it off."

"First, let me thank all of you for your hospitality and the good food."

"And the hot showers," Sheila interjected.

"Yes, absolutely. We have running water back at Mount Weather, but we didn't think we'd get another hot shower until we got back home." There was some appreciative laughter.

"Let me clear the air about something first. I'm a Captain in the United States Army." There was a sudden silence. "I apologize for misleading you, but we were made aware of the recent incidents involving Zach and his children, so we didn't want to alarm everyone. I've discussed it with Zach and he understands.

"These three," he said, pointing at his friends, "are not military. They are indeed congressional aides and are members of a task force whose primary mission is to reconstruct America." Gus quickly raised a hand.

"Is it true you're inviting all of us to go back with you?"

"Affirmative." Raymond then stood.

"We have available housing in the facility and there are also people who live around the immediate area on farms. I believe that would appeal strongly to some of you."

"What about those of us who were in the military?" Rachel asked.

"We are in desperate need of military personnel," Seth answered and gestured at Sarah. "Ma'am, I understand you are a major in the Air Force?" Sarah nodded warily.

"We have a diverse fleet of fixed wing and rotary wing aircraft and only two pilots. You would be a valued member."

"Are they flying?" she asked. Seth shook his head.

"They are currently grounded due to fuel issues, but we're working to rectify that situation." I saw Josue whisper something to Maria, who tentatively raised her hand.

"Yes, ma'am?"

"I don't mean to be impolite, but how would my family be treated?" she asked. "We're not exactly American citizens."

"The status of your citizenship is not an issue," Sheila quickly said. "You are all welcome to join us."

"Will we be required to disarm?" I asked.

"Yes and no. There are certain areas in which firearms are not permitted. All personnel who want to be armed while inside the compound must be able to pass a safety and qualification course."

"I bet they have a rear-echelon hump for a safety officer," Justin quipped under his breath. True grunted in agreement. Seth chuckled.

"I happen to be that safety officer. I'm also the OIC of the armory."

"Sounds like you're wearing a lot of hats, sir," Rachel remarked.

"Too many," he replied in agreement.

"How many military personnel you got?" Sarah asked.

"Not nearly enough, ma'am," Seth replied. "Approximately forty of various ranks and services. There is a group of Marines, two squads, who are currently being supervised by a Navy ensign. Those jarheads don't like it too much, maybe a Marine lieutenant would be a better fit." I could see Justin liked the sound of it. That captain would have been an excellent used car salesman. Earl, who had been mostly quiet, stood.

"I took a look at your greenhouse and gardens, they are very impressive. There is plenty of farmland available around the compound. In addition, we have greenhouses and an active livestock operation. If farming is your gig, we have the land and the equipment to help you out. Also, we have a water treatment facility on premises and our power grid is hardwired directly to a nearby hydroelectric dam."

"What about single women?" Jorge suddenly asked. There were more than a few guffaws directed at him. He grinned sheepishly.

"There are a number of single people, both male and female," Earl replied, to which his wife arched an eyebrow at him.

I had to admit to myself, all of it sounded impressive. My thoughts drifted as Raymond took over answering questions. His oratory was impressive and he was doing a good job of luring everyone in. When the questions had lulled, he held up his hand.

"As I've been standing here answering questions, it occurred to me that it may sound like I'm painting a mighty rosy picture, which wouldn't be entirely accurate. Our situation is tough and we've had set backs.

"A typical workday is long; you can expect some days to be twelve hours or more. You'll be expected to work and be a contributing member to our burgeoning society, but in our opinion it's totally worth it."

When the questions had finally stopped, Raymond paused long enough to drink a glass of water before speaking again.

"I'm sure you people will want to discuss this in private. I've taken the liberty of clearing it with Tonya and we're going to bed down in that nearby church for the night so that you can talk freely amongst yourselves."

Justin and Ruth volunteered to take them to the church and get them settled in. One of the tables was under a shade tree and I motioned toward it.

"It's hot in there," Kelly remarked.

"Not much better out here," Janet quipped. We were in the shade and there was a gentle breeze, but they were right, it was still hot and humid. In other words, a typical July in Tennessee.

"We have a month or two more of hot weather before it starts cooling down," I said. Kelly and Janet nodded in agreement. True ambled up while we watched the kids playing with the dogs. Macie stopped what she was doing and looked up at him in wonder. True responded with a small smile.

"She don't see many black men, does she?"

"Just you and Mike," I said. "What's on your mind?"

"I'd like to know what you think about all of this."

"They make some valid points."

"So, what are you going to do?"

"I want what's best for my family, but I'm also suspicious."

"Of?"

"The government. There's a lot of politicians up there. Now, keep in mind, I've had limited exposure to politicians during my lifetime, but I've read a lot of history books."

"So, what do them books tell you?" True asked.

"They tell me that throughout history politicians have always had a peculiar mindset of what's best for the people."

"Yeah, that usually means what's best for them," True said. I nodded in agreement.

"What if you didn't have a family? What would you do?" he asked, to which I scoffed.

"That's a no-brainer."

"But, what would you do?" he pressed. "Would you stick around here?"

"Good question." I thought for a minute. "Do you mean like, if I had nobody else?" True nodded. I shrugged. "I suppose I'd stay right where I am."

"You've never wanted to get out? See the country?" In fact, I had. I'd never been outside of Tennessee and I'd often wondered what the rest of the world looked like, especially now.

"Yeah, sure, I suppose. But, it'd be dangerous doing something like that by yourself. I'm sure when you were by yourself you had some hairy moments." True looked at me, but he had the best poker face of anyone I knew, with the possible exception of Fred.

"Why do you ask?" At about that time, Brandon walked up.

"Mind if I join you guys?" I gestured toward a chair.

"Did you tell him?" Brandon asked True.

"I was just gettin' at it."

"Tell him what?" Kelly asked. Brandon glanced at True again, leaned forward and spoke quietly.

"Myself, True, and Mann have been talking about heading out on our own," he said.

"Why?" Kelly asked.

"We're done with the military," Brandon replied. "If we go up there, we'll be expected to be a part of the rank and file."

"And that means a life of taking orders," True said.

"Why don't you want to stay here?" Kelly asked again. True shook his head slowly.

"I don't think this place is for me," he said. "I don't much like it here. Tonya has a thing for telling people what to do too."

"Yeah," Brandon agreed. "We've been talking ever since the rendezvous." He nodded at True. "We think alike. We know we can count on each other," Brandon said and the two men exchanged a fist bump.

True said. "Mann too," True said. He then gestured toward Kelly. "I'm thinking if you didn't have her and the kids, you'd probably be wanting to go with us instead of hanging around here." Yeah, I had to admit, I probably would've.

"We've decided we don't need other people giving us orders all the time, deciding what's right for us and what's not," Brandon continued. "We know what's best for us."

"We ain't like those idiot brothers." They exchanged another fist bump. I smiled and nodded in understanding.

"Sounds like you men have already decided," I responded. "When are you leaving?" True glanced at Brandon.

"We're getting things ready right now," Brandon answered.

"And we don't want anyone else to know what we're going to do until then," True said. I understood all too well their reasoning. Kelly started to ask why, but I nudged her.

"They have their reasons," I said. "The military officers may cause a stink if three enlisted men decide to end their military obligations."

"Yep," True said. "I don't want to kill anyone, but I ain't taking orders from nobody anymore."

"If any of them try to pull rank, even Smitty, it could get ugly," Brandon said. "We'd rather just avoid that possible scenario."

"I see your point." I looked the two men over.

"I believe I see why you two have told us this. You want us to help facilitate it." Brandon smiled hopefully as he nodded. Now that I was in on the conspiracy, I subconsciously lowered my voice.

"Which vehicle are you wanting to take?"

"Not sure, but we were thinking of appropriating one of those Humvees," Brandon said.

"Hmm, that might cause a stink. Do you know anything about diesel engines and how they can run on used cooking oil?" Brandon nodded.

"A little bit," he said.

"Alright," I said and sat there with my notepad, jotting a few things in an effort to aid my thoughts.

"This is going to be a covert ops type of mission," I muttered to myself. Brandon and True exchanged glances.

"Have you an idea of how much you're going to carry with you?" I asked. They exchanged glances again.

"As much as three men can cram into a Humvee." I shook my head.

"No, taking a Humvee could cause problems. I got a better idea."

"You do?" True asked

"Of course I do," I answered. "That's why you came to me, right?" Brandon grinned openly. True's mouth stretched a little bit. Our conversation was interrupted by Justin walking over.

"You guys look like you're discussing a major conspiracy," he said jokingly. Both men tensed up.

"You know that big dually truck parked at the house?" I asked him.

"Yeah, that was your friend's truck, wasn't it?"

"It was," I answered. "The guys here are going to use it for the trip. We were just discussing what their loadout should be." Justin looked at me seriously. I thought he detected my deception, but instead he snapped his fingers.

"You know what'd go on that truck? A camper shell. Back when we went to that Volvo dealership, I saw one lying in the back lot. It'd fit perfectly." I gazed at him steadily.

"That's an awesome idea," I said. "Right, guys?" Brandon sputtered out his agreement.

CHAPTER 46 – THE DECISION

All of us talked well past sundown. After all, this was a big event in our quaint little community, at least as big as the rendezvous, which everyone was still talking about. For every question, another ten questions germinated, and for every what-if scenario there was a counter scenario. And discussions. And, discussions led to arguments. It was exhausting. I remained mostly quiet, only answering a question that was asked directly to me. Ruth worked her way over to where I was sitting and nudged me.

"You haven't said much."

"Yeah, I guess I'm a little tired." It was a vague answer, but I didn't want to get involved in any debate on the pros and cons. I already knew what I was going to do.

"Are you two going?" I asked when Justin joined us.

"Yeah, we're going," Justin replied. "It's a no-brainer, really. I'm just a Marine; I don't know any other kind of life."

"Besides, he wants the best for his child," Ruth added. We all looked at her in surprise. She gave a bashful but radiant smile.

"Does this mean what I think it means?" Kelly asked. Ruth nodded. Kelly squealed with delight, jumped up and hugged her.

"Well, congratulations," I said to Justin. Justin tried to look nonchalant, but his face turned red as he nodded his thanks.

"Wow, the big tough Marine is blushing," Kelly said teasingly. Ruth reached out and squeezed his hand as the others started congratulating them.

"Who else is going?" Kelly asked. Sarah spoke up.

"We're going to go as well," Sarah said. Rachel nodded in agreement. "Has anyone else committed?" she asked.

"I'm going wherever my grandbabies are going," Janet declared. I nodded in understanding. I personally was happy with her devotion. Her behavior toward everyone else left a lot to be desired, but she certainly looked after Frederick and Macie.

"I'm pretty sure the sisters and brothers are going," Kelly said as she glanced over at them. They were huddled together on the far side of the cafeteria talking about who knew what. Tonya was chatting with her group of people and had not committed one way or another.

"What about you, True?" Ruth asked. His poker face didn't give anything away.

"Yeah," he answered. They took that as a commitment.

"Brandon and Blake are with True," I added, hoping to keep them from asking any direct questions.

"That's good," Justin said. "The more soldiers we have, the better." Thankfully, the subject was changed when Marc and Ward walked over.

"We're going to go get the delegates and invite them to spend the night here," Marc said.

"We don't want them to feel ostracized," Ward added. Justin stood.

"Yeah, that's a good idea. I've got more questions of them anyway. I'll go with you guys." I looked over at True.

"Why don't you ride back with us and pick up the truck?" He nodded and stood.

We left shortly after and everyone was home in bed an hour later.

"I'm tired," I said as I pulled a sheet over us. It was still too warm for a blanket. "All of that talking wore me out."

"Why aren't we going?" Kelly asked tiredly.

"What makes you think that?" I asked. Kelly scoffed.

"Zach, please. I know you better than anyone." Yeah, I suppose she did at that.

"So, are you going to tell me why?"

"I just don't think it's the right move for us," I answered simply. Kelly was quiet. I half expected an argument, but remembered that was how Julie would respond. Kelly always gave me the silent treatment when she disagreed with me. It was a brilliant tactic, very hard to counter.

"So, what are your thoughts on all of this?" I finally asked. Kelly mumbled something and snuggled closer to me.

"What was that?" I asked.

"I think we should go," she mumbled sleepily. I asked her why, but she'd already fallen asleep. I had at least fifty reasons for not going that I wanted to tell her, but I guess it was going to have to wait.

Sarah and Rachel joined us for breakfast and the conversation picked up where we left off last night. Everyone had an opinion over the pros and cons of staying or relocating. Even Janet voiced her opinions, most of them negative. As the conversation continued, I sat with Macie on my lap. She was unusually quiet this morning and wouldn't stop staring at me with her big blue eyes.

"You've been awfully quiet, Zach," Sarah said during a lull in the conversation. I took a deep breath. May as well let them know.

"I could give a big long speech, but the bottom line is we're staying." Kelly looked at me in a mostly neutral expression, but I could see a tiny sliver of disappointment peeking out. She picked up our plates and put them in the sink before quietly walking outside.

The silent treatment. There were no books or military manuals that discussed how to deal with it. Rick sure didn't know, and if Fred did, he didn't share his wisdom on the subject. After a few minutes, I excused myself and went outside. I found her sitting in one of the swings we'd recently erected for the kids and sat in the one beside her.

"I'm sorry, I know you want to go, but I don't see it the same way as you." I gestured toward the field where some cows were contentedly grazing. "I like it here. In spite of the setbacks we've had, we've made a good home for ourselves."

"But what about all of the things they can offer us?"

"Sure, they can offer things that aren't currently available to us, but is the grass really greener up there in Virginia?" I paused, searching for the words.

"I'm not sure what to say. Everyone else may decide to pack up and go. If that happens, I'd totally understand if you went with them. Of course, that'll mean I'll be stuck with Janet." Kelly gave me a look.

"You know I'm staying with you, no matter what." She held up her hand showing the ring. "It's hell being married to a shithead." I laughed, even though the joke was at my expense.

"If you consider us married, I guess I need to start acting like a dutiful husband." We held hands and watched the morning come to life.

"It's going to be a hot one today," Kelly remarked as we watched the morning dew being converted to shimmering vapors.

"Let's go to the school and give them the news. Then we'll go horseback riding, just the two of us. Janet won't mind babysitting."

"We can fix up a picnic basket and eat lunch under the oak tree," Kelly suggested. I thought of the last time we did that and reminded myself to bring along some mosquito repellent.

"Yeah, that sounds wonderful."

I waited until Sarah and Rachel rode off, insisting Sammy ride with them. After they passed through the gate, I turned to Janet.

"Just in case they don't take the news well and there is a plan-B which includes using force, I want you to load the kids up in the van and disappear for a little while."

"You think they may try something?" she asked.

"I don't think so, but I don't want to take any chances." Janet agreed without argument. She insisted on not one, but two assault rifles and as much ammo as I would give her, which actually seemed prudent. I handed her a map.

"You'll be in radio range if you stay in this area," I said as I pointed. "Once we give them the news and get out of their sight, I'll give you a call." She nodded and I looked at my watch.

"Okay, it's zer0-eight-hundred. We're going to ride over there, tell them of our decision, and leave. It shouldn't take over an hour. Remember the duress password?" She nodded in irritation.

"And if everything is good on your end, you're going to use the word fireworks when you call."

"Got it. Zach, be careful of Smithson," Janet warned.

"Why's that?"

"I know you two have become friends, but back at the CDC a couple of idiots said some rude things toward Ruth. He gave them both a pretty vicious beating."

"Okay, good to know. We'll see you in an hour."

Unfortunately, we didn't get to go on that horseback ride.

CHAPTER 47 – REVERSAL

Kelly gasped at about the same time I hit the brakes. There were hundreds of them. A lot were dead, strewn about Concord Road, from the radio tower to the school. But there were still plenty of them alive.

"See if you can raise them on the radio," I said as I reached into the glove box for ear plugs. Kelly grabbed the microphone and began calling for them as I rolled down the window, stuck the barrel out of the grating and started picking off stragglers before she yelled at me to stop.

"I can't hear anything with you doing that!" I paused in my shooting as I heard Justin speaking on the radio. I took an earplug out.

"What'd he say?"

"He asked for us to drive over to the radio tower. They're out of ammo and there are still zombies around the house."

I was glad we were in our Ford Raptor truck. The enhanced ground clearance and four-wheel-drive capability allowed me to drive over the corpses lying in the roadway and down the drive leading to the tower. There were about twenty zombies crowding the small house, trying feebly to get in. When they saw us, they turned and launched themselves at us.

"Okay, cover your ears," I warned before shooting again. When the last one dropped, Justin emerged from the front door. He had to push some of the dead bodies out of the way to get out.

"Those sons of bitches attacked in the middle of the night," he said. "I didn't think they could see at night, just goes to show you what I know. We ran out of ammo about an hour ago." I gestured toward the back.

"I've got a hundred rounds in here, all five-five-six." The three of them, Justin, Ruth, and True hastily loaded their magazines before inserting them into their rifles.

"We tried calling you on the radio," Ruth lamented. I looked at Kelly. She shook her head.

"We never heard anything," I said and wondered if someone had turned it off.

"We've had contact with the school. They said they were completely surrounded but were holding them off." Before I had a chance to respond, Kelly was on the radio. Marc answered after a few tries. He sounded frightened. I motioned for Kelly to hand me the microphone.

"Have they gotten into the school?"

"I don't think so," Marc responded. "But they're all around outside. We've killed a bunch though."

"Alright, tell everyone we're coming, so don't shoot toward us. Concentrate on the rear of the school only."

"Affirmative," he replied nervously. I swapped seats with Kelly and let her drive.

"These are all the rounds I have left, so let's make 'em count," I said with a grin as Kelly maneuvered down the road and into the school's parking lot.

There were dozens of them lying around. Most had singular headshots, which was a good sign of shooting discipline, but there were several with additional bullet holes in their torsos.

"Looks like around thirty or so, do it," I directed. Kelly began honking the horn, causing several of them to turn toward us. A couple of them even began running. We made short work of them.

"Did you see how they were acting?" Justin asked. "They were trying to get the doors open, just like they were doing at the radio tower."

"Those last few that we killed, they were trying to run away," True observed. "They still stupid, but not as stupid as they was." I chuckled at his unique assessment.

"Well put," I said and spoke into the microphone. "Alright, Marc, tell everyone to cease fire. We're going to circle the school and pick off the remaining." Marc acknowledged, and we found three more attempting to break through the back door.

"It was a simultaneous attack on both the school and the radio tower," Justin contended. We were all walking around outside, surveying the damage.

"What about the church?" I asked. "Were there any issues?" Justin shook his head.

"We went over there yesterday evening and brought them back. No problems."

"We didn't see any when we were there," Seth added and then looked embarrassed.

"I didn't want anyone to feel threatened by us, so we left all of our weapons in the Stryker. Unfortunately, it backfired. When they attacked, we were trapped inside the school." We made our way to the guard tower. There were several corpses stacked against the tower. Goober had put up a hell of a fight. We found him inside the tower and it wasn't a pretty sight. He was literally torn to shreds. A lone zombie, some kind of female in a former life, was straddling his torso, feasting on his intestines. She was so focused on her meal she didn't even notice us.

"Oh my God," Kelly gasped. I didn't know if Goober had turned or was going to turn, but I took no chances. I took aim and put a bullet in both of their heads.

"He never gave an alert," Justin lamented. "True and I split radio duty. Neither one of us fell asleep, I can guarantee that." He glanced over at Seth.

"Yeah, they had the school surrounded as well." He pointed at the corpses. "After we started killing them, the others figured out our kill zones. I guess they were simply going to wait us out."

There was one solitary picnic table that was bereft of blood and gore. I sat on top of it, surveying the grounds. The others joined me. Kelly sat close, sobbing quietly.

"He was a sweet guy," she said. I nodded silently.

"How many, do you think?" Justin asked. I shrugged.

"Two hundred, give or take," I let out a heavy sigh. "I thought we'd cleared this area out." We sat there in silence, dejected silence, for several minutes. True had been walking around the area and came jogging up.

"Them things came up the interstate from Nashville," he said. "They came down the road and then split into three groups. One group went to the church and the other two came this way and split up between the school and the radio tower. Then, the church zombies came down here." He paused a moment.

"I don't mean to speak badly of the dead, but if I were to guess, I'd say they caught Goober while he was sleeping. There ain't no way they could have snuck up on him otherwise." He found a clean spot on the ground and sat.

"Them things are starting to scare me. Are we going to burn them?" he asked.

"Yeah," I answered. "We'll use a backhoe and a dump truck." And it's going to take a lot of fuel, I thought. Seth cleared his throat.

"Forgive me for the inappropriateness of changing the subject, but has everyone decided on whether or not they're going?" I cut my eyes at him. "Sorry to ask, but if everyone is going to go, I say let's give Goober a Christian burial and not worry about cleaning up the rest of this mess." He looked around at everyone. Tonya, who had been standing nearby, spoke up.

"There are a few of us who intend to stay," she said. "But, I can't speak for everyone."

"What have you decided, Zach?" Raymond asked tentatively. Kelly raised her head off of my shoulder and looked at me. It hurt me to see her sad. I squeezed her hand, didn't answer, and changed the subject.

"We've got a hell of a mess to clean up, but first we need to bury Goober."

I called Janet on the CB, and after having to give her the proper password twice, I convinced her everything was okay, told her to keep the kids away from the school due to all of the stinking corpses and advised we'd be home later in the afternoon.

"Don't worry about damaging the bodies," I told Sheila, who had volunteered to run the backhoe. "Just scoop 'em up and dump 'em in the truck. Oh, and if you have any kind of respirator mask, I'd strongly recommend using it."

The soldiers provided security while the rest of us hauled off the bodies. We'd done this before, but I don't think you ever got used to it. The stench was nauseating, and looking at those things and knowing they were humans once made it depressing. We settled on the rock quarry on the side of Nolensville Pike to dump and burn them. Everyone helped out, although there was some grumbling and complaining.

"I don't understand why we're going through all of this trouble to burn them," Kate finally said in a huff. I glanced at her. She was covered in sweat and looked to be in a foul mood. "Well?" she demanded.

"Tell her, Sammy."

"We're burning the corpses to prevent the spread of pestilence and disease." He pointed at the pyre burning. "In order to fully cremate a human body, you have to burn them at a temperature of at least fifteen hundred degrees. Since we have no way of doing that, we use tires, which there are plenty of around here. Tires burn at about seven hundred and fifty degrees, but the smoke is toxic, so you don't breathe it." Kate didn't like the answer.

"You're starting to sound just like him," she quipped.

"Thanks, Aunt Kate," Sam replied proudly. I gave him a wink.

"We really appreciate it," Ward said as we watched the pyre burn. "If we were left with this mess to clean up, it'd take us a month or more."

"You two are really going to stay?" Kelly asked. Ward and Marc nodded in unison.

"We see no need to relocate," Ward said.

"Even after this?" Kelly pressed. They nodded again.

"It's our home," Marc said simply. I understood how he felt.

"At least we'll have company," Kelly said as we lay in bed.

"Yeah. We've got a lot of work to do, but the good news is we'll have a lot less mouths to feed."

"I guess we can do this," she said. "It won't be easy, but nothing ever is, I guess." She snuggled up closer and was asleep within a minute.

I woke up with a start to the sound of a child's laughter. Thinking the munchkins had somehow gotten out of their bedroom and were now getting into who knew what, I sleepily wandered into the den. When my brain registered what I was seeing, the hair on the back of my neck stood straight up.

"Hi," she said quietly, almost a whisper. Julie was sitting on the couch. Little Macie was in her lap and was laughing in the way a small child laughs, without a care in the world.

"Hi," I answered.

"Come sit with us, Zach." As if in a daze I walked over to the couch and slowly sat, not daring to touch her. She sat there, gently stroking Macie's hair.

"She's so beautiful."

"Like her mother," I answered. Julie turned and looked at me then.

"What is your destiny, Zach?" Her question befuddled me. She did that frequently, back when she was still alive.

"I don't understand." God how I wanted to hold her, but I was afraid she'd disappear if I tried. She smiled as if she knew what I was thinking and continued stroking Macie's hair.

"Your destiny isn't here." I tried to touch her now, but I couldn't move. I felt my eyes growing heavy.

The sun's rays shining through the slits of the shutters awakened me and I found myself sitting on the couch. Rubbing the sleep out of my eyes, my brain became alert. It took a good minute or so to realize it was simply a dream. I started to stand but suddenly realized little Macie was curled up beside me, sleeping soundly. I had no idea how she got there, and yet, I did.

I was still sitting there when Kelly walked in. She looked at us in puzzlement.

"What are you two doing?" she whispered. I motioned her to come sit beside us. When she did so, I leaned close and kissed her gently on the cheek.

"We're going," I said. Her eyes widened as I explained.

CHAPTER 48 - PREPARATIONS

"You have to be very careful with your knife when cutting it open," I said as I slowly started making a cut. I glanced over at Sam, who was grimacing while holding his bandanna over his nose.

"Do you know why?" I asked. He shook his head and I explained.

"A cow's intestinal tract contains harsh bile. If any of it gets on the meat, it'll make it unfit to eat, and it smells awful." I gestured downward at the plastic tub lying on the ground immediately below the hanging carcass. "We're going to use that tub to catch the stomachs and intestines. How many stomachs does a cow have?" I asked.

"Uh, I don't know, one?" I smiled and worked my blade down from the neck. After a minute or two of careful cutting, I had the interior exposed. I motioned for Sammy to come closer.

"A cow has four stomachs. These are the first two." I pointed. "When a cow eats, they bite big mouthfuls of grass or hay and swallow it immediately. It goes into these two stomachs. They're full of stuff called microbes."

"What does microbes do?" He was still holding the bandanna over his nose, but he was curious and not shying away.

"They start breaking down the food in kind of a fermentation process. That's why cows fart so much. Now, when these two stomachs are full, cows will find a spot to settle down, like under a shade tree, and then they'll cough it up and chew it. It's called cud, that's where you get the phrase, chewing the cud." Sammy nodded. "Once they chew it up, then they swallow it again and it goes into one of the two other stomachs. That's them right there." I pointed at the omasum and abomasum.

"Those two stomachs contain enzymes, which digests the cud differently from the other two stomachs. Cow stomachs are also edible, but I've never tried it." I gestured with my knife again.

"Now I'm going to, as carefully as I can, cut them out without rupturing them. If you think it smells bad now, you won't believe how bad it'll smell if I cut one open." Sammy responded by holding his nose.

"Normally, we'd keep all of this and use it. The fat can be rendered down for soap, the blood can be used in the compost pile, things like that. But for now, we're only keeping the meat for our upcoming travel. I'll teach you all about it at a later time. So, today we're only going to harvest the meat."

"Oh." Sammy watched me work and I soon had the entire digestive tract removed from the carcass.

"By the way, did I tell you why I picked out this particular gal from the rest of the herd?" Sammy shook his head. "She was getting up there in years and I'd noticed she had less muscle mass than she did last year. It was her time. Always take things like that into consideration, right?" He nodded thoughtfully as he took in my lesson.

"Another thing to consider about the smell." Sammy wrinkled his nose. "Yeah, you never quite get used to it. So, if this odor gets in the wind, there's always a possibility any zombies wandering around nearby can smell it too. If they catch a whiff, you better believe they'll head this way, so you've got to be aware of that, right? After all, it's not going to be too long before you become a full-grown man. You'll have a lot of responsibilities and will be expected to know things like this, right?"

"Yeah, I mean, yes sir."

"Good. Frederick is still a little young, but when he gets to be your age, I expect you to help me train him as well. You think you can handle it?" Sammy nodded excitedly now. I laughed and nudged him. "I think you can too."

"Will we have to train Macie too?" he asked.

"Oh, absolutely," I said and looked around, thankful there were no women around who would've heard my exclusion of Macie. It'd be yet another reason for them to call me a chauvinist. I nudged him again.

"Justin and I have been talking about you." His eyes widened.

"You have?"

"Yes, we have. You're the oldest kid in this group. I don't know anything about those kids up in Virginia, but you're going to be taking up a leadership role one day with this group. Being a leader is hard work, but we think you've got the potential to do it."

"The other day Doc Parsons asked me if I wanted to train to be a doctor." I paused in my work and looked at him. It irked me for a brief moment, but then I realized Grant was merely trying to find a suitable apprentice to pass along his talents to.

"What did you say?" Sammy shrugged his shoulders. I gave him a brotherly smile.

"That's a serious thing to think about, so take your time. If being a doctor is something that would interest you, I'm sure you'd be a good one."

"Zach?"

"Yeah, bub?"

"Are we really going to move?" I stopped working and motioned for Sammy to walk outside with me. There were a couple of stools sitting nearby and I motioned him to sit. Immediately, one of the goats trotted up, expecting a treat.

"Yes, we are."

"Why?"

"It's hard to explain, but back when I was your age the world was moving along at a fairly rapid pace. Now, we're slowly but surely regressing backwards. If it were just me and Kelly and a few of the other adults, that wouldn't be very important, but it's extremely important for you kids that it doesn't happen."

"Why?"

"When you start back to school, they'll explain it a lot better than I can, hopefully."

"When do we leave?"

"Three days." Our conversation was interrupted by a loud slamming of the back door. I walked to the entrance of the barn and saw Kelly making a beeline toward us with Maria following close behind. I groaned to myself.

"Sammy, when you get older you'll find yourself having to deal with adult things that are rather unpleasant." Sammy started to ask me what the heck I was talking about but I quickly motioned for him to be quiet.

"Your mother-in-law is being an insufferable bitch," she growled between clenched teeth. I gave Sammy a knowing look and winked. "You'd think she was the only person who ever cooked a meal the way she's bossing Maria and me around."

It wasn't the first time Janet had angered Kelly and I always invariably suffered. Before I could say anything, Rachel and Sarah stormed out of the house, spotted us, and made a beeline in our direction. This time I groaned aloud.

"My mother and I argued all the time," Kelly continued. "But she was a saint compared to that woman."

"My mother was never that bad," Maria added and then she saw the tub of cow guts. Holding her hand over her mouth, she ran over to the fence rail and wretched.

"You need to take that bitch on a long drive and dump her somewhere," Rachel grumbled angrily. I took my butcher's apron off and handed it to Kelly.

"Alright, why don't y'all help Sammy finish butchering the cow, I'll see what I can do."

"Those little girls could use a lesson or two in the kitchen," Janet declaimed as soon as I walked in. I nudged a chair out from the table with my foot and sat down, careful not to touch anything with my dirty hands.

"You know, Janet, this seems to be an ongoing problem. You're going to have to be nicer to people, especially Kelly." Janet acted like she didn't hear me and stirred a pot of vegetables. "I'm serious. We've had this discussion before. We've all got to get along and you need to start making a conscious effort to be nice."

"Fine," she finally said. "But she needs to learn how to cook." I started to retort. Kelly knew how to cook just fine and Janet knew it. I suspected it had to do more with Janet feeling the need to have some control. I placed my hands on my knees and let out a long sigh. Janet glared at me.

"Is there something else you feel the need to lecture me about?"

"Are you aware in just a few months it'll be four years?" She stopped stirring for a moment until she realized what I was talking about.

"Of course I am," she snapped and started stirring again.

"And you and I are the only two left out of the original group?" She didn't answer this time.

"You're the grandmother of my children. That makes you family. But, Kelly is family too and for the life of me I don't understand why you act the way you do sometimes."

Janet finally looked at me then and I could see her eyes watering up. I had some other harsher things to say, but at that moment, I couldn't do it. She looked sad, lonely, older. The wrinkles on her face seemed more pronounced these days. I softened my tone.

"I don't want everyone hating you, okay?" After a moment, she nodded and turned her back to me so I couldn't see the tears falling. "Well, it looks like you've got everything ready. I'll go round everyone up and we'll set up outside." Janet didn't respond and busied herself with the food.

"All right guys, I've made a checklist of everything that still needs to be done and who is responsible for what," I said as we ate dinner. Everyone who had decided to go was here, sort of a last meal I suppose. We had some Tiki torches for lighting and Josue had found some of those mosquito repellent candles and had them spread out. It helped.

I pulled out a notepad and opened it to the first page. Rachel moved her chair closer and snatched it away from me with a smart-assed grin and began perusing it. They were both in pretty cheerful moods lately. I glanced at Kelly who grinned knowingly. Rachel fanned through the pages and looked up.

"Zach, this so-called checklist is about a hundred pages long," she exclaimed. Seth leaned closer and eyed it.

"One hundred and twenty-two, to be exact," I replied in between mouthfuls. "The mission order is comprised of the last nine pages, of which I made copies for each vehicle." She arched an eyebrow at me.

"You wrote this out in just one day?" Raymond asked. I nodded casually.

"You think you could just give us an overview for the time being, big guy?" she asked amid a few chuckles.

"Sure. We're going to take a total of nine vehicles. That's why I made nine copies, one for each vehicle." Actually, only eight vehicles would be making the trip, but only a few of us knew that.

"Which cars are we taking?" Cutter asked. I glanced at him briefly. I was going to go over all the details, including which vehicles we were going to take as I laid out the mission and being interrupted was irritating, but I held off with a sarcastic retort. Instead, I exercised patience as I counted off with my fingers.

"The Stryker, our full-sized van, our work truck, Sarah's Humvee, Justin's Humvee, my truck, the eighteen-wheeler, the dually, and Jorge's SUV. Captain Kitchens will be leading the convoy in his Stryker." I looked at the two brothers. "I figure you two can ride in the truck and pull rear security, yes?"

"We can handle it," Shooter proclaimed and got a fist bump from his brother. I retrieved my notepad back from Rachel. I had blank spots beside each vehicle and filled in their names for the truck.

"Alright, tell me who wants to ride in what vehicle."

"I want to ride in the Stryker!" Sammy shouted excitedly. I looked at Seth who smiled and imitated the brothers by giving Sammy a fist bump. We went down the list and I dutifully jotted down who was riding in what vehicle.

"Why so many vehicles?" Kate asked. "I mean, I'm not complaining, but it seems like we could fit everyone in half the number."

"You're right, we could," I replied. It was then I noticed she was wearing makeup. In fact, Kyra was wearing makeup too. It seemed foolish.

"Let me explain. First, we have the fuel. Now, it'll be *all* of our fuel, but we must take into account that one or more of the vehicles may break down along the way. If that happens, and we can't fix the problem immediately, we're going to unload it and abandon it. Simple. And then, there is a possibility we may pick up people along the way, or if we're really lucky, we'll find an abandoned vehicle or two full of items we can make use of."

"Alright, Mister Zach, what else?" Seth asked. He was smiling appreciatively or condescendingly, I couldn't decide which.

"All vehicles need a CB radio with sideband capability and shortened antennas."

"Why's that?" Cutter interrupted. I reminded myself to be patient, but it wasn't easy. I imagine I wasn't much different from other nineteen-year-olds when it came to patience; mine had a short life. I held up a finger to signify that he should wait for the explanation.

"Seth and Justin can correct me if I'm wrong, military doctrine is to stagger out the vehicles when travelling in a convoy to reduce the risk of something like an air strike. In this case, the convoy will travel closely; the first vehicle will always be within eyesight of the last vehicle. We'll use the radios to communicate but we don't want their transmission range to extend any further than line of sight. So, the easiest way to do this is with CB radios equipped with a short antenna."

"A short antenna?" Kate asked.

"Yeah, the wattage of a radio and the antenna is what gives a radio range. We want to limit our range." I pointed at Josue.

"Josue has volunteered to take care of this. Jorge and I are going to help him."

"No long talkie-talkie on radios with short antennas," Josue said. "Short words only."

"Why not?" Kate asked. She was being unusually inquisitive and had been argumentative on more than one occasion in the past. I couldn't decide if it was Shooter's influence or if she was a young version of Janet. "I mean, why are we limiting our range and why no long talkie-talkie?" She made quotation marks with her fingers when she mimicked Josue. Only Shooter laughed. Justin cleared his throat.

"I can answer that. First, we must assume there are people out there who are monitoring radio transmissions with their fancy little Bearcat scanners. They may be good guys or they may be bad guys, marauders. So, we limit our transmission range and we only speak when we have to. Second, and this is what I think Josue is worried about, if you talk a lot on one of those radios that has a short antenna, it'll eventually damage the radio."

"Si," Josue replied.

"Oh," Kate said.

"So, reiterating, all radio transmissions should be short and sweet and we'll be changing frequencies often." I saw Kate about to ask another question and I held up a finger.

"There is a pattern we're going to use when changing frequencies. It's all written down in the packet, so read up on it." I'd answered her question, but not to be out done, she rolled her eyes and flippantly tossed some hair back. I had no idea why she didn't like me, I only assumed it was because she was sleeping with Shooter and therefore she *had* to dislike me. Seth nodded and motioned for me to continue.

"Also included in the packet is an inventory list of essential gear. Whatever vehicle you're in, you'll be responsible for the gear, and of course you can bring any of your personal property along. Keep in mind though that space is at a premium." I looked over the passenger list and passed out the copies of the mission order.

"Okay, please take the time to read up on this, and if you decide to switch vehicles, please let me know. Any questions on what we've covered so far?" Nobody said anything, not even Kate.

"Okay, good. Now, we need to address our biggest issue: ammunition. We don't have a whole heck of a lot."

"Captain, what is your inventory of ammunition?" Sarah asked.

"Ma'am, in the Stryker we started out with two thousand rounds for the fifty caliber, one hundred grenades of various types, and fifty mortar rounds. But, we only have approximately two hundred rounds of five-five-six."

"And each vehicle is going to have their own load of ammunition," I added.

"So," Sarah continued. "We don't need to be going on any zombie safaris."

"Agreed, ma'am," Seth said. "We only shoot in defense of life, right, Lieutenant?"

"Absolutely, sir," Justin replied and pointedly made eye contact with everyone to ensure they understood.

"If you have a stash of ammo, don't leave it behind. If there is some type of specialty item you think we'll need and you don't have it, let me know and maybe we can scrounge it up.

"Our departure is in three days. Major Fowkes and Captain Kitchens have agreed that a certain jarhead should be the road commander." There was laughter at this.

"Absolutely," Sarah replied. Seth nodded his agreement.

"Cool. Now, with Jorge and Josue's help, I'll ensure that every vehicle is prepped and ready to go. It is up to all of you to ensure you have your essentials. I'm not sharing my toilet paper or tooth paste, so bring your own. Any questions?" I looked around and waited. Rachel raised her hand.

"How long will the trip take?"

"It took us three days to get down here," Seth responded. "With the eighteen-wheeler and extra vehicles, I'd estimate an additional eight to ten hours. No more than four days, barring any unforeseen catastrophe."

"We're going to assemble at zero-six-hundred hours at the Concord and Nolensville intersection," Justin declared. "That means all vehicles will be loaded up and ready to go the night before. We're going to depart no later than zero-seven-hundred hours. Anyone not present will be left behind." Sheila wiped her mouth and spoke up.

"Zach, if I may ask, you have a lot of livestock, what's going to happen to them?"

"I had considered acquiring a second eighteen-wheeler and hooking a cattle car up to it, but decided it isn't feasible, so I've worked it all out with Tonya. The school group is going to take over running my farm."

"What about that tour bus?" Kate asked. "Why can't we take it?"

"We considered it, but after discussing the road conditions with the captain, I don't think the bus would be a viable means of transportation, so we're going to go with the van instead."

"But the bus has a toilet," she lamented.

"Oh, please," Sarah retorted. Kate's lips tightened, but she didn't say anything else.

"Okay, getting back to the fuel, we have the two tankers, one will be for diesel and one will be for gas."

"How much?" Seth asked. I noticed Raymond had surreptitiously slid my notepad closer to him and was now reading it intently.

"Each tanker can hold up to five hundred gallons, but we only have about two hundred gallons of each, maybe a little less. With each vehicle filled up, we should be okay, but we may need to siphon a few tanks along the way." Raymond looked up.

"It looks like you've thought of everything, Zach. We need to set you up with the logistics team when we get home."

"Ray runs the logistics team," Sheila said.

"It's a lot of work," he lamented. "I could certainly use some help."

I didn't comment. The truth was, the only thing I really wanted to do anymore was run a farm, raise my kids, and chase Kelly around the house. I cleared my throat.

"If you'll note, I'm going to have the semi, work truck, the dually, and the van loaded up and ready to go on the eve of departure. Sergeant Caswell," I said and nodded toward him, "has agreed to assemble a team to guard them that night."

"That's affirmative," he replied. "True and Mann have volunteered." I pretended to look at my notes while I gauged the reactions of Justin and Seth out of my peripheral vision. I didn't detect signs of suspicion.

"Okay, I would like for each of you to read the mission order thoroughly and have a good idea of how this is going to be run. If you find a mistake or have a suggestion, please speak out."

The rest of the evening was spent by everyone discussing what they should bring. Several questions were asked of me, that is, until I kept referring them to specific pages in the checklist and mission order. Everyone slowly ran out of steam and decided to retire to their respective homes. Brandon and his crew lingered behind and were the last ones to leave.

"Do you think it'll work?" he asked.

"Yep. How's your scavenging going?"

"We've been going at it hot and heavy. Tonya's been on our asses for shirking our duties." Blake scoffed and spat.

"I'll be one happy ex-soldier when we get out of that school."

"Yeah," True added.

"Well, anyway, we've found some stuff we can use, the rest we'll give to you."

"We ain't giving it to Tonya, that's for sure," True said. I chuckled.

"Alright, we're still good with the plan?" I asked. The three of them nodded. "Good, I'll see you men in two nights."

I started to walk back inside, but as I did so, their headlights caught the shadow of two figures standing beside the barn. I pulled my Kimber out and started to open fire.

"Wait, Zach." It was Sarah. She and Rachel emerged and walked over.

"What are you two doing?" I asked as I holstered my handgun.

"Being nosy," Rachel responded cheerfully.

"Not cool," I rejoined.

"What's going on, Zach?" Sarah asked. I didn't answer, only stared at her coldly in the dark.

"Does this mean you don't trust me?" she asked in a softer tone.

"The two of you are soldiers; you've sworn an oath, correct?" Sarah didn't say anything this time, she merely stared at me. "The answer is yes, you have, and I think the two of you don't give your word glibly."

"What are you saying?"

"I'm saying I'm not going to answer you. You two are going to have to trust me and honor my request to not say anything about this. It'll all come to light very soon. Afterward, if you feel I've done something wrong, you can criticize me all you want."

"Does Kelly know?" Rachel asked.

"Of course."

"Oh, good, we'll ask her," Rachel said and headed for the door. Sarah reached out and grabbed her by the arm. Rachel scoffed.

"You're no fun."

"I want you two to stay quiet about this. I'll explain everything at a later time." They didn't like it, but they didn't argue and left soon answer.

CHAPTER 49 – DEPARTURE

I was sitting on the tailgate of my truck waiting for them with a thermos of coffee. It wasn't decaf and I'd probably stay awake all night, but I couldn't help myself. They arrived promptly at twenty-three hundred hours in Rick's dually truck. They'd found a camper top from somewhere that fit nicely on the back.

"How'd it go?" I asked. Blake inhaled deeply and let it out slowly.

"She knew we were going to pull guard duty here on these vehicles, but that didn't stop her from assigning me guard duty at the school."

"Well, that wasn't very nice of her, but you really don't have guard duty," I reminded him. Blake scoffed.

"Yeah, but she didn't know that."

"No worries," Brandon said. "You can sit in back and catch some shut-eye."

"Hell, I'm too keyed up to sleep. But I got her back," he said. "At the end of my shift, I fired off a shot and told them I spotted a zombie. All of them are awake now." I couldn't help but laugh. It served them right for doing that to Blake.

"Do y'all have the dually all packed up and ready to go?"

"Roger that," Brandon replied.

"Alright, well, I guess there's nothing left to say. If you get tired of seeing the country, this house should be empty and available."

"We appreciate you, Zach. Are you sure you can handle those officers? They might want to come looking for us."

"Not a problem, don't even worry about it. You guys just promise me to take care of each other," I said and took turns shaking hands with each of them. Without further fanfare, they loaded up and left. I went back to my tailgate and sat.

"You can stop hiding now," I said into the dark. After a moment, a small flashlight came on and the two women emerged from the barn.

"Did you know we were back there the whole time?" Rachel asked.

"How could you not be?" I responded. "You two are a couple of busybodies. Look," I said as I used my own flashlight to point out two cups sitting beside me. "I was so certain you two were going to spy on me, I brought extra cups." I poured each of them some coffee and motioned toward them. "Drink up." They each took a cup and sat down beside me.

"So, what did we just witness?" Sarah asked.

"You just watched three soldiers resigning from their military obligation and going their own way." Sarah took a moment to digest the information.

"And you helped them," she said with an accusatory hint in her tone.

"Yep."

"But, why?" Rachel asked.

"They're tired of taking orders." I told them about the bullshit stunt Tonya had pulled on Blake. "That right there is a good example. They're ready to be their own men."

"But why did they sneak off in the middle of the night?"

"Because they didn't want any officers trying to pull rank and cause problems. They already said if that happened, it was going to turn ugly. I believed them and I prevented any possibility of it happening."

"Lieutenant Smithson is going to take it personally," Sarah said.

"That's why you're going to help me explain it to him."

We couldn't sleep; all of us were keyed up. Instead, we talked the rest of the night. At about four, we opted to surprise everyone with breakfast.

"I know you two don't quite understand, but your mother is buried here." I glanced at Kelly as I said this. She was sitting across from us; it was the first time she'd come up to the mound since she helped me bury everyone.

"But Kelly is your mommy now," I continued. She smiled quietly as she brought her camera up.

"Okay, everyone look at me," she said and snapped a couple of photographs. When we made the decision to leave, she'd scrounged up a digital camera and took pictures of everything and everybody. I wondered if we'd ever be able to print them off once we got to Mount Weather.

I said a few more words, wiped away a tear before Kelly noticed it, and led my family down the hill to Sarah and her Humvee.

"Alright, I've forgotten something; let's ride back over to Fred's house." Sarah glanced at me as if to say, you never forget anything, but she didn't comment. All three of them were standing there expectantly when we drove up. Getting out, I got some carrots out of the Igloo cooler and walked over to them. Shithead was the first to walk over to me.

"Alright you guys, you're on your own now. Take care of each other, okay?" Sate responded by bumping me with his head and sniffing me, looking for more carrots. It was a sad goodbye, almost as bad as a few minutes ago when I was up on the mound. I was tempted to load up a horse trailer at the last minute, even though we'd decided against taking them back when we planned out the trip. I gave each of them one last scratch behind the ears.

"I'm going to miss them more than anyone at the school," I commented after I got back in the Humvee. Sarah nodded in agreement.

"I'm telling you, man, I'll be okay," Jorge declared. He was sitting on his motorcycle, gripping the handlebars while his sister tried to pry his hands off. We had loaded it up in the semi's trailer but last night he apparently got a wild hair and unloaded it. It was obvious he'd washed and waxed it, probably after everyone had gone to bed.

"It's not safe," Maria countered.

"I can scout ahead and I got this walkie-talkie to let you guys know if I see anything. When I get tired, I'll load it up and ride with you." I looked over

Jorge's motorcycle before glancing at Justin and Seth. Both of them shrugged apathetically.

"It can't hurt, I suppose," Justin said. Jorge grinned in triumph. When they walked off, Justin turned to me.

"Apparently, we have three men who're AWOL. It seems like I'm the last to know about it." I took a breath and explained it all to him. Sarah was standing off to the side. Within earshot but far enough away to be out of the conversation. When I was finished, Justin let out a long sigh.

"Why didn't you just tell me?"

"They know how much you believe in duty. They weren't going to take a chance that you'd pull rank on them."

"If I did, would they have listened?"

"Nope, and you better believe they were ready to shoot it out if they felt threatened."

"That wouldn't have happened," Justin claimed.

"So, you wouldn't have tried to stop them?" He didn't answer.

"Yeah, you would have been pissed, and then Captain Kitchens would have felt an obligation to back you, and the next thing you know, it would have been a major cluster fuck."

"Maybe," he conceded.

"Don't get me wrong, I would've loved for them to be with us, but it was their choice, nobody else's."

"They took one of the M60s."

"I gave it to them." Justin stared at me with a frown.

"If I remember correctly, when you first spotted True, you pulled a gun on him and you're still not convinced Mann wasn't involved in the death of your wife."

"I've given them the benefit of the doubt, just like I have with you and Ruth." Justin snorted at this.

"Alright, what's done is done, I suppose." He looked around. "We're wasting time; let's get this goat fuck underway."

We had the convoy of vehicles lined up in proper order almost an hour before departure time. Everything seemed to be going as expected and I hoped it stayed that way. Feeling I had to do something useful, I walked the line and checked the tires on each vehicle. They looked no different from the last time I checked them and was about have everyone check their headlights again when Tonya walked up.

"Looks like everyone's ready to go."

"Alright, if you decide to visit my farm, I've disabled all of the booby traps except for the creek. The bottom is full of sharpened stakes. Oh, and if anyone decides to move in the home, the stovepipes and chimney are full of creosote, they'll need cleaning."

"I'll warn everyone," she replied and changed the subject. "I'm still surprised you decided to go."

"And I'm surprised you decided to stay," I replied.

"They don't have anything I want or need." She looked me over and actually smiled. "I bet one day I'll see you coming back down this road. I'll give it a year."

"Time will tell, I suppose. If it does happen, I hope my family and I will be welcome."

"Of course you will." She lit her little one-hitter and offered it to me. I shook my head, which caused her to snort.

"You're the most straight-laced kid I've ever met." I chuckled as I watched Marc and Ward walking around giving everyone a farewell hug. I gestured at them.

"I kind of thought they'd go too."

"They're scared of the unknown," Tonya replied. "This is their comfort zone. Same as everyone else who's decided to stay." I guess she was right. Marc, Ward, Gus, Rhonda, and the two nurses had decided to stay.

"I heard about the soldiers," she said.

"Oh, yeah?"

"And you knew all about it."

"Word travels fast around here."

"Did they say where they were going?" she asked.

"They said they were going to hit the open road and see the world."

"Dumbasses," she said in contempt. I chuckled, even though I disagreed with her sentiment. I wish they were going with us, but I was happy for them. I didn't tell her that Goober's death was the deciding factor in their decision. True pointed out how Goober had pulled guard duty three nights in a row while others, Tonya specifically, had never pulled a single shift.

I saw Justin giving the hand signal for everyone to mount up.

"Alright," I said. "This is it."

"Yeah, I guess it is." I pulled some papers out of my pocket and unfolded them.

"I made a hand-drawn map of our route and all of the waypoints, just in case anyone changes their mind. Oh, and I have a log of all of the cattle sitting in my desk at home."

She looked at me with a sad smile, took the papers, and put her hands out.

"Give me a hug, kid." Well, that certainly surprised me. I obliged, it was awkward as hell, but I obliged. She finished with a pat on the back.

"You take care of these people and make sure they get there in one piece. Even those two idiot brothers."

"I'll do my best," I said.

"I know you will." She turned and walked away suddenly. I thought I caught sight of her eyes watering up, but maybe it was my imagination. I was about to jump in the truck when Marc and Ward caught me and surrounded me with a group hug. Kelly, not to be left out, jumped out of the Volvo and joined in.

"We're going to miss all of you," Marc said forlornly. Both of their faces were wet and puffy from all of the crying. After the hug, I looked at them sadly.

"Guys, we've certainly had our ups and downs, but I've grown quite fond of you two and I'm going to miss the hell out of you."

"Ditto," Kelly added with another hug. Rhonda ran up and joined in the tears and hugging. At least Gus held his emotions in check and offered a simple handshake. After a lot more hugging and snot filled well-wishes, we managed to get ourselves separated from them and the kids secured in the semi. Kelly got behind the wheel without asking.

"Do you think you can drive this thing with a trailer attached?" I asked with a grin.

"Not only can I drive it, I can drive it better than you," she retorted with a smug wink before going through the startup procedure. I couldn't help but laugh, while Janet, sitting in the sleeper section, grunted. The radio crackled to life

"All units check in with your status," Justin ordered.

"Your scout is ready, man," Jorge replied. Everyone followed suit, with either a ten-four or some kind of simplistic variation, with the exception of Cutter, of course.

"Time to kick ass and take names," he shouted on the radio and then gave a rebel yell. You almost couldn't hear him from the blaring of heavy metal music in the background. I groaned.

"What an idiot," Kelly mumbled. She had put on a pair of Ray-Ban aviator style sunglasses and began checking the gauges. The combination of the glasses and her dark hair was cascading down her shoulders kind of turned me on.

"You're a mighty sexy-looking truck driver," I said. When she looked at me with a smile, I snapped a picture.

"You set me up," she accused with mock indignation and self-consciously ran a hand through her hair.

"It's getting long," I observed.

"I need to cut it. Maybe I'll cut it short, like Sarah's."

"That's a big negative," I replied tersely. She smiled as I took more pictures, and almost as an afterthought I took a picture of Janet sitting with the kids before setting the camera down and looking out the window at the passing scenery.

"Are you nervous?" Kelly asked.

"No," I answered quickly. "Maybe a little," I added after a moment.

"I'm going to miss living here," Kelly lamented.

"Do you ever miss where you lived before?"

"Not really," she answered. "My parents lived in the same house that I grew up in. It wasn't that big, the only decorating they ever did was buy a new TV, and the neighborhood had gone downhill over the years."

"That was in Birmingham, right?"

"Yeah, a working class suburb on the east side." There was a hint of sadness in her voice. "My dad worked in a factory and mom worked at the hotel where I was working at. She got me the job." She'd told me about them. Her mother had gotten infected and she never knew what happened to her father.

I looked back out of the window. It was a little bit sorrowful. I grew up here and it was all I'd known. Hell, with the exception of my involuntary stay at Fort Campbell, I'd never even left the state. The thoughts I had of venturing into something unknown wasn't making me nervous though, for some reason it felt right.

"Yeah, we'll be back one day." I don't know why I said it. It came out without forethought, but the moment I said it, I realized it was true.

Jorge initiated the procession by riding a wheelie. Captain Kitchens and Sammy were the first vehicle in the procession riding in the Stryker. They were followed by Earl, Sheila, and Raymond in the white van Julie and I had found way back when. Josue insisted on driving the work truck that Rick had brought home one evening. With it full of tools, it rattled loudly every time he hit a bump, but he'd fallen in love with that truck the first time he laid eyes on it. Maria was immediately behind him in their freshly waxed SUV. Sarah and Kyra were in the Humvee they'd brought from Oklahoma. We followed in the Volvo. Somehow, the dogs ended up with us and were being very rambunctious, despite Janet's admonishments. Behind us were Cutter, Shooter and Kate in my Ford Raptor truck. I told Cutter in no uncertain terms I expected it to arrive in Mount Weather in one piece. Justin and Ruth brought up the rear in their Humvee.

All of the vehicles were packed, but not completely full. I had to explain to a couple of the slower-witted individuals, specifically the Butter-Pooter duo, that we had to keep room for anything we scavenged along the way or in case one or more vehicles broke down and we needed room to fit everything in.

A lone zombie was walking along the sidewalk as we turned onto Bell Road. The fact that he was on the sidewalk like a normal human instead of walking in the middle of the street seemed odd for some reason. He even stopped and watched as the convoy drove by him. His clothes were filthy, but I could see he had one of those Vietnam-era Boonie hats on his head, held in place by the strings, and he even had a small knapsack strapped on. As I watched him in the side-view mirror, Shooter hopped the curb and ran over him.

"Score one for Shooter!" Cutter cackled into the radio.

"Idiots," Kelly muttered. He better not have damaged my truck, I thought.

CHAPTER 50 – MONTEREY

I'd not been past Mount Juliet since the outbreak and probably looked like a little kid as I pressed my face close to the window, getting an eyeful of everything we passed. Mostly, there was nothing but weeds and that damned kudzu growing everywhere. It was even beginning to swallow up derelict vehicles that were parked a little too close to the shoulders. As we passed through Lebanon and got close to a small community known as Gordonsville, things became a little bit more macabre.

"Holy shit, are you guys seeing this?" Jorge asked over the radio. There were corpses hanging from the overpasses, one had almost a dozen hanging from it.

"Yeah," Seth responded. "It was like this when we first came through, but I believe I'm seeing a couple of fresh ones."

"We're not hanging around to investigate," Justin said. "Maintain our speed." I voiced my agreement.

"It looks so eerie," Kelly remarked. "And desolate. It's sad."

"Yeah," I replied. I had no idea who was operating within the Lebanon area. Nobody from the rendezvous claimed to have lived around here.

"I think they're making a point of telling anyone travelling along the interstate this isn't a good area to stop and look around."

"Like they're staking out their territory," Janet said. I nodded in agreement. I wanted to discuss it with the others, but was mindful of our agreed upon radio discipline. It didn't stop Shooter from commenting about it though. Justin must have read my mind and spoke up, telling everyone to change to a sideband channel.

"Yeah, I'm seeing almost every vehicle salvaged too. We got some rough players around here somewhere, but we'll talk about it later."

And so we kept moving. Everyone was doing a good job of maintaining the proper intervals and I saw Ruth and Rachel in the side view mirror manning their respective M60s. Our trailer was almost fully loaded, and so every bump and pothole on the road seemed to be magnified. At the scheduled check in, Seth asked how the Volvo was holding up.

"A little rough, but no problems."

"The roadways are like this all the way to Virginia, more or less. There is one bridge that's too dangerous to drive over, but we found a detour. I hope you've brought extra tires, just in case." I had. There were multiple sets in the trailer, along with some rims and a tire changer. I was confident the truck would hold up, but I wasn't so certain with the trailer. We'd visited a couple of truck stops and found one that looked to be in better shape than the rest, but there could always be hidden issues.

"How's it looking Jorge?" Seth asked as we left Wilson County behind us and entered the next county.

"Not too bad, man. Lots of potholes. I'm only seeing a zombie or two here and there. Nothing big."

And so it went. Our goal was not to stop and kill zombies. Whenever we came upon one, we ignored them. Jorge expertly drove around them and if they were close enough, they'd try to grab at our passing vehicles. The result was they'd lose their balance and fall. Sometimes they ended up being run over. Our speed was slow but fairly steady. However, sometimes we had to slow to a crawl as we maneuvered through and around the permanent traffic jams. There were only a couple of times we had to use the makeshift bumper on the semi to force other vehicles out of the way; otherwise, it was a peaceful journey. But, leave it to the Butter-Pooter duo to break up the monotony.

"Time to take a crap," Cutter blurted over the radio at about the same time we passed a barely readable sign informing motorists that they were entering Putnam County. Kelly glanced over at me.

"As crass as he is, I need to go too, and I bet the kids could use a break." I looked back at Janet, who nodded. I grabbed the mike.

"Jorge, find a decent spot for the convoy to pull over."

"You got it, man. There's a clear spot about a quarter mile in front of you." Justin keyed up the mike.

"Alright, everyone, you know the drill. Stay with your teams. When you're done doing your business, take a peek in some of these abandoned cars, maybe we can find something, but don't engage with any zombies if you can help it. We'll move out in thirty minutes."

Little Frederick wasn't a problem. As soon as I got him out of the semi, he dropped his pants and relieved himself in front of everyone. Macie on the other hand was a bit fussy and didn't want me to change out her pull-ups, so Janet took over.

Relieved of my fatherly duties, I grabbed Josue and the two of us walked back a hundred yards, checking out the abandoned vehicles. Sadly, all of them had been rummaged through; trunks had been popped open, gas tanks had been punctured and drained. A couple of cars were still occupied. Josue and I made quick work of them with knives, but there was nothing to be gained.

"No good," Josue muttered.

"Yeah," I agreed. We walked back to the main group and explained our findings.

"Is it like this all the way to Virginia?" I asked Seth.

"As far as the roads and obstacles, yes. We didn't take the time to search vehicles though." Our conversation was cut short by the sound of gunfire. All of us instinctively brought our weapons up and crouched, fully expecting an assault of some kind. Justin was the first to spot it.

"Those morons," he growled before jogging over to the westbound side of the Interstate. No surprise, the source of the gunfire were the Butter-Pooter brothers, who were laughing gleefully at their antics. Seth and I followed and caught up with Justin at the moment he was confronting them.

"What the hell are you two doing?" he growled.

"We're killing zombies," Shooter retorted in a tone to suggest Justin had just asked him an incredibly stupid question. I walked over and took a look at their vanquished foes. Two zombies, definitely category ones, trapped in their car. Even with the advanced decomposition, it was obvious they were an elderly couple. I pointed at them and then glared at Cutter.

"They're so rotten they couldn't even get out of their seatbelts. Why in the world didn't you two use your knives?" Cutter stared at me hard, but he couldn't seem to find a response, logical or otherwise. It looked like he was about to concede the mistake, but Shooter spoke up.

"We'll kill zombies any way we see fit," he said defiantly. "You ain't our boss." I ignored him and continued staring at Cutter.

"Here's a good example of what I've been trying to tell you; your brother is an idiot." I gestured at him and his stupid smile. "We have a limited supply of ammo, but shit-for-brains here doesn't think about things like that. He'd rather waste it on a couple of old rotten zombies who'd have to put their dentures in before they could even take a bite out of you." I pointed toward the back seat and looked at the two brothers as if they'd just eaten a turd sandwich.

"For fuck's sake, one of them had to use a walker to get around."

Shooter stared at me loathingly, trying to think of a clever retort, but, like his brother, came up empty. Josue got the back door opened, retrieved the walker and handed it to Shooter, who stared at it as Josue patted him on the back.

"Nice prize," he quipped and walked off.

"Alright everyone!" Justin yelled loudly. "We've made too much noise and wasted too much time, so let's load up and get out of here!" At Justin's gentle urging, as if a career Marine could possibly be gentle when urging people along, everyone hustled back to their respective vehicles. But, we only made it ten more miles before Justin called for us to stop again.

I jogged up to his Humvee just as he raised the hood. A cloud of smoke rushed out of the engine compartment, enveloping him.

"What's going on?" I asked. Justin's expression was a combination of frustration and anger as he crawled under the vehicle. After a moment, he crawled back out.

"Cracked exhaust manifold. It's the same one I welded back when we got back from Atlanta." He looked at me grimly. "I can't weld it again, it's too far gone."

"Alright," Seth said. "I'll get a defensive perimeter formed while you transfer the gear to another vehicle."

"I'll take care of the fuel," I said. Ruth started unloading supplies.

"Do you have a preference?" Justin asked Ruth.

"The van has the most room," she said. He nodded gruffly, still angered about the Humvee.

We were on the road twenty minutes later but had only been travelling a short time when Cutter spoke.

"We've got some company, dudes and dudettes," he said in his best California surfer dialect.

"Do you think you can remember the protocol and be more specific?" Justin growled, obviously still pissed about the Humvee.

"An SUV, four or five people in it. I'd say they're looking for trouble." I wanted to jump on the radio and yell at him to follow procedure but Justin beat me to it.

"Everyone stop in place," he demanded. Before I could get out of the truck, Justin strode past, his jaw clenched and an M4 in hand. I reached back, grabbed a shotgun and quickly followed him. We met up at the Ford truck, where the brothers and the sisters were standing outside. Butter and Pooter were busy looking Ramboesque; the two sisters each had a handgun, but were holding them like they were sticks of dynamite with a lit fuse. As opposed to the brothers, they weren't itching for any type of a confrontation.

"Why don't you two link up with Kelly back at the semi and cover us?" I suggested. They didn't argue.

"They've stopped," Justin said. The dark green SUV, it looked like a Land Rover, had stopped a hundred yards back. Justin peered at them with his binoculars.

"The windows are tinted but it looks like there's five of them. They're just sitting there staring at us." Seth had wheeled the Stryker around and parked beside the Ford. He stuck his head out of the hatch and peered at the SUV with his own set of binoculars.

"I'm going to try them on the CB," I said, reached inside the Ford and switched to channel nineteen. After numerous attempts without a response, I tried channel nine with the same results.

"They've got a radio," Justin said. "I can see the antenna."

"It's not shaping up to be a friendly encounter," I surmised. I was about to suggest the old tactic of one of us walking toward them with a white rag when Seth spoke up.

"Well, I have a suggestion," he said. We all looked at him expectantly. "You guys load up in the Stryker, and we'll drive down there and see what they have to say. I seriously doubt they have the kind of firepower to disable this bad boy."

It sounded like a logical idea. The five of us loaded up and Seth drove toward them, but they didn't react like they wanted to meet us. When we got within fifty feet, the driver put their vehicle in reverse and backed away from us. Seth stopped and I once again tried to raise them on the CB. We tried it a couple of times with the same results. The last time they continued backing up until they were once again a hundred yards away from us.

"I'm getting tired of this bullshit," Justin said.

"Me too," I added. "They may be trying to draw the Stryker away from the convoy and their boys are going to ambush it."

"Or they may just be fucking with us," Cutter said.

"Whatever they're doing, I don't like it," Justin said. "Alright, let's get back to the convoy."

"Yeah, the problem is, once we get underway, they're going to keep following, I'm thinking," I said. Seth looked at me thoughtfully.

"I believe I have a cure, if you gentlemen are agreeable." We all looked at him questioningly. He pointed up.

"One round in their engine block with the fifty will put a stop to this nonsense."

"Do it," Justin responded immediately. I readily nodded. Seth aligned the crosshairs on the monitor, took aim, and popped off a single round. I took my fingers out of my ears and used Justin's binoculars.

"Bull's eye," I said. The radio crackled to life.

"You sons of bitches!" one of them yelled irately. Cutter reached for the microphone, but I stopped him.

"Fuck 'em," I stated. "They had their chance to talk to us like peaceful folks." I could see it in his eyes; he desperately wanted to give those men a bit of Cutter wisdom. I looked over at Justin, who at least wasn't glaring anymore, and he shrugged indifferently.

"Oh, what the hell," I said to Cutter. "Give 'em your best." Cutter grinned and grabbed the microphone.

"Don't let us catch you little shit-birds following us again, or else." Shooter stared at his brother with a disdainful look.

"Dude, that was lame," he said.

"Nah," I rejoined. "Short and to the point, I like it."

We travelled until sunset, never encountering any other people or zombies, and stopped on the outskirts of Monterey.

It was a pleasant night out with a clear starlit sky, so Kelly and I opted to sleep on top of the eighteen-wheeler's trailer.

"It's so beautiful and peaceful," Kelly said as we lay on our backs, staring at the heavens. "It's hard to believe the world is so screwed up when looking at all of those stars." I squeezed her hand in agreement, thinking of a night long ago when I was doing the same thing, lying on my back, staring at the stars with Julie and Macie. Kelly gasped and pointed.

"That's the second shooting star I've seen in the past five minutes. Is that a sign?" I chuckled.

"Could be."

"The trip's going pretty well so far, don't you think?" she asked.

"Yeah, I'd say so. Even the two dumb shits aren't causing too many problems." I glanced at my watch.

"Looks like I have guard duty in five minutes. Either we can try for a quickie or I'll relieve Sarah early." Kelly gave a short laugh.

"Yeah, right," she said. I guess that meant guard duty. I stood and stretched. "Alright, I'll be back in two hours." Kelly smiled in the dark and pulled a blanket over her. I took one last look at her alluring shape before descending down the ladder.

"Three," I whispered loudly as I walked up to the Stryker. Sarah was sitting on the top of it. I stopped several feet away and waited for the counter sign, indicating she wasn't under any form of duress.

"Ten," she answered. I walked up and climbed on top of the Stryker.

"Kate and Shooter are out in the weeds doing the nasty," she said indifferently as she handed me the night vision goggles and pointed. "Outside of the perimeter." I shook my head in disgust.

"It'd serve them right if they got bit." I sighed. "Alright, I'll go rein them in."

I guess I was lucky, they'd already finished and were mostly dressed when I walked up on them. I didn't need the night vision; one or both of them were smoking cigarettes. It was easy to find them.

"Jesus, guys, this isn't safe at all."

"A man has needs," Shooter responded smugly. Kate ignored me and walked back toward the convoy.

"You're not jealous, are you?" Shooter chided as he zipped his pants up.

"The point, Simon, is safety. We don't have to like each other, but we have to watch out for each other – and not do stuff like this without at least telling someone so they could watch out for you. Why didn't you tell your brother? He would've watched your back." Shooter, Simon, whatever, stared at me, the way he did whenever he wanted to reply with a clever, condescending retort but his brain couldn't come up with anything, which was common. Finally, he sighed.

"Alright, whatever." I followed his backside as he walked back without waiting on me. Climbing up on the Stryker, I sat down beside Sarah.

"Alright, Major," I whispered. "You are properly relieved. Grab some sleep."

"I'm not very tired at the moment. I think I'll hang out with you a little while." That was fine with me. Having someone to talk to, even if we had to whisper, made the watch go faster. I stood and did a full scan with the goggles before sitting.

"The first day went pretty well, I'd say." I waited for a response, but got none.

"I had a little talk with Shooter. I don't know if he listened but at least he didn't argue with me."

"Yeah, that's good," Sarah said halfheartedly. Several minutes passed in silence. Sarah was not a talkative type, but I could sense there was something on her mind. It could take days before she'd tell me, so I tried the direct approach.

"Is something bothering you?" I asked. She didn't answer. I prodded a little. "You know, I always feel like if I have a problem and I don't want to discuss it with Kelly, I can always come to you. I hope you feel the same way." There was another long moment of silence and I was going to let the matter drop, but then she spoke.

"I'm scared, Zach," she finally said. I looked at her in surprise.

"You? Scared?"

"Yeah."

"Well, yeah, I guess I'm a little bit scared of the unknown too," I said. She shook her head slightly, I barely saw it.

"No, it's not quite like that. I mean, yeah, it is, but not like you're thinking."

"Uh, okay. Now, I'm confused." There was another long minute or two of silence.

"I spent two years alone. Totally alone. You have no idea how bad that was, Zach."

"After my buddy Rick died, I was totally alone for a couple months. It damn near drove me to suicide, so I can only imagine going through that for two years."

"Yeah, exactly."

"But, you're not alone now. You have us, and you have Rachel."

"That's just it, Zach. Once we get to Mount Weather, who's to say she won't find someone else? I'm a few years older than her and I'm not sure she sees me as anything other than a convenient partner until someone better comes along." She started sobbing then. She was quiet though, not a woman who blathered loudly. I reached out and found her hand in the dark.

"I can't speak for Rachel; I've no idea what the heck she's going to do. But, what I can tell you is that Kelly and I will always be there for you. We're family." She squeezed my hand tightly and sobbed some more. I didn't say anything else, it wasn't necessary. After a few minutes, she gathered herself and blew her nose. I guess this had been building in her ever since we first spoke of relocating. We sat in silence for almost an hour. When I stood to check the area, she stood with me.

"I believe I'm going to turn in," she whispered, reached out, and hugged me tightly. "Thanks, Zach."

CHAPTER 51 – BRISTOL

"I'd always wanted to go to Bristol and watch one of the races," Justin said. We'd taken a break and were about twenty miles from the city, stopped in the middle of the Interstate. "Any of you ever been?" There were shakes of heads.

"When I was a kid, my brother and I begged our father to take us to one of them, but he forbade it," Raymond said. "He felt stock car racing was below our social status." I chuckled.

"I never went to one either, but it had nothing to do with my lofty social status." Raymond looked at me curiously.

"Did you not enjoy auto racing?" he asked.

"Oh, no, just the opposite. I loved NASCAR, but you see, I was what you'd call poor white trash."

"I don't follow," Raymond replied. "I mean, no offense, but I always thought that NASCAR fans were, well…"

"Rednecks," Kelly finished.

"Well, yeah."

"On the contrary. NASCAR had fans all across the social spectrum. We just plain couldn't afford it."

"Zach was an orphan living with his elderly grandmother," Kelly explained.

"Oh, I see," Raymond said, a little awkwardly now. "I didn't mean to be presumptive, I apologize."

"Nothing to apologize for," I said affably. "A buddy of mine had a big screen TV and surround sound. It was the next best thing to being there." I decided to needle him a little.

"I bet you had a huge flat screen in your bedroom, am I right?" He glanced at me again and nodded.

"We had one in every room. I even had one in my bathroom. I could watch it while taking a bath or sitting on the toilet."

"Wow, sounds nice."

"I suppose," he said and quickly changed the subject.

"Well, what do you think is wrong with it?" We were standing around in a loose group, staring at the van's engine.

"Gas," Josue answered plainly. I nodded at him. I liked how the man could say in one word what could be said in one word.

"Yep," I answered. "Regular gasoline only has a viable shelf life of about a year. We've been lucky it's lasted this long."

"Are we leaving it?" Seth asked.

"Yeah, we have to," I replied. "It'd take the rest of the day to clean out the fuel lines." Justin scowled at the van a moment and then spoke up.

"Alright everyone, no need standing around here staring at it. Unload your stuff and split it among the other vehicles." One of them, Earl I think, sighed deeply.

"I guess we should thank you for bringing extras," he finally said. Yeah, I seem to remember a couple of them wondering about my logic with that and this would have been a good time to point that out and say something witty like, 'I told you so' but I didn't. I guess I was getting more mature.

It was going to take some time to get everything sorted out and my stomach had been rumbling for several minutes, telling me I better not hold off very much longer.

"I've got to make a visit to the little boy's room," I told Justin.

"You need me to go with you?"

"Nope, I like a little privacy when I do my business. I won't be long."

"Be careful," Justin said and went back to helping unload the van.

I told Kelly the same thing before fast walking off the Interstate where a lone, dilapidated building stood. Quickly looking around to ensure I was alone, I set my weapons against a wall. Making sure my half a roll of toilet paper was handy, I dropped my pants and squatted. Within seconds, I heard something coming up from behind me. Before I could squeeze my butt cheeks and stand, I was bumped on the shoulder. Startled, I turned quickly, only to see that goofy ass dog, holding a well-used tennis ball in his mouth and looking at me the way all dogs do when they want to play.

"Damn it, Callahan, I'm right in the middle of something here." He panted and sat, dropping the ball at my feet, indicating he was more than willing to wait but I should certainly hurry.

"Damn dog," I grumbled and settled back into position. I was lost in my thoughts, wondering what the heck I'd eaten which was now causing me so much discomfort, and right at that joyful moment of voiding my bowels, Callahan suddenly stood, emitted a short bark and ran back behind me, bumping me clumsily as he passed by. Someone was coming.

"Why in the heck can't I get any privacy?" I muttered and was about to unleash my displeasure with whoever was approaching when I heard that distinctive raspy snarl.

The bastard emerged from around the side of the building and lunged at me. I managed to roll to my side, not an easy thing to do with my pants to my knees and the paperwork not complete, if you know what I mean. The zombie stumbled into my fresh organic deposit before righting himself by flinging his arms up, causing shit to fly everywhere. Somehow, I managed to get to my machete and make short work of him.

"Where the hell did you come from?" I rhetorically asked and looked around for others before inspecting myself.

"Shit," I muttered, not realizing I was making a pun, and tried the best I could to clean myself up. In the end, I sacrificed the rest of my toilet paper, a decent pair of underwear and a half a canteen of water. During all of this, Callahan kept picking up his ball and tossing it at my feet. I was tempted to toss that damn ball as far into woods as I could, but with my luck he would have brought a bunch of zombies back with him.

"Some help you were, you little bastard," I said, picked up the slobbery ball and tossed it in the direction of the caravan.

And so, we were down another vehicle. After Julie's death, I'd developed a special fondness for that van. Whenever I looked at it, it reminded me of her and how the two of us had discovered it. It was like our first date, our first real day together. I hated to leave it. Maybe I'd come back and get it one day. They had finished up repacking everything and after everyone had taken their own restroom breaks Justin gave the command to mount up, but before anyone could act, Sarah spoke up.

"We've got movement coming down the interstate from the north." I looked quickly down the northbound lane. There were five to ten of them, moving toward us at a loping run, snarling loudly as they got closer.

"Get the kids secure!" I yelled at Janet, who didn't have to be told twice.

"They're danger close!" Justin shouted. That meant we were to shoot the front ranks first. I picked the one heading straight toward me and made a clean headshot as the others opened fire. We dispatched them quickly and efficiently, and were about to congratulate ourselves when Jorge yelled.

"Nine o'clock, ten more at fifty feet!" I swung around just in time. Two of them were moving quick and got to within ten feet before I could shoot them. Jorge and Josue made quick work of them just as another one emerged out from behind a burned-out Mercedes. Josue took careful aim and hit him right between the eyes. His son grinned and gave him a pat on the back. When it was over with, we consolidated and caught our breaths.

"Alright, how about a quick debriefing," Justin directed.

"I believe they just tried a flanking maneuver on us," Seth surmised. "They're getting rather clever."

"If they ever figure out how to use weapons, we're really going to have our hands full," Sheila added.

"At least they can't procreate," Rachel said and then snapped her fingers. "I bet all of the zombie men's dicks have rotted off and the women's woo-hoos have withered up…" She stopped as Sarah gave her a withering stare. Everyone else began laughing and soon even Sarah couldn't stop herself from shaking her head and grinning.

It was midafternoon when we rolled into the outskirts of Bristol. It was once a quaint southern city with a population somewhere around thirty-five thousand. Now, it was like every other city across the world; bleak, dismal-looking, a cancerous shell of what it once was. As we slowly travelled along Interstate 81, we saw nothing unusual. Abandoned, wrecked, burned vehicles, overgrown plant life, disintegrating and cracking asphalt was the norm. Even so, I used Kelly's camera to take a few photos.

"Mother Nature is taking back her planet," Janet quipped. "It's not all daisies and lollipops anymore." I looked at her quizzically. It was rare that Janet joked around anymore. She saw me looking and grinned. "Now it's just rotten peters and withered woo-hoos."

"Look at that," Kelly said, pointing out of the window. There was a large commercial plane wreck just to the side of the interstate. The surrounding area around it indicated a large fire had taken place and all of the surrounding vegetation was still dead.

"Do you think there're any survivors here?" she asked. I took another photograph.

"I see several cars that looked like they've been searched, so yeah, probably."

I retrieved the mike.

"Come in, Seth."

"Go ahead."

"Did you guys have any contact with anyone in this area on your way through?" He'd already answered the question back when we talked about it in Nolensville, but I wanted confirmation.

"That's negative," Seth answered. "I don't see any changes either." Jorge interrupted excitedly.

"Man, I see somebody right now!" Kelly looked at me in surprise as I grabbed the microphone, but before I could speak, Justin jumped in and immediately called a halt to the convoy. Jorge sped back to us without waiting to be told to and skidded to a stop. I jumped out as soon as Kelly got the truck stopped. Justin and Seth jogged up to us as Jorge pulled his helmet off and began speaking excitedly.

"It's a man sitting on the side of the interstate. He's beside a van that has the side doors open and a trailer behind it. I don't see anyone else."

Shooter and Cutter, not wanting to be left out, ran up and joined us and demanded Jorge repeat what he had just told us.

"I was about a hundred yards away when I spotted him. He was just sitting there, and then he waved at me, man. Is that bad?" Justin grunted and lowered the binoculars.

"Looks like just one man," he said. "Hard to tell. The van he's sitting by has the side door open and it's full of stuff. What do you think, Zach?" Justin asked as he handed the binoculars to me. We were at a straight, level area of the interstate, very few derelict cars, and the man was about two hundred yards away, sitting without a seeming care in the world. As I watched, he stood up, gave us a wave, and then dropped a piece of paper, seemingly by accident. He looked at it and pointed at it with a stiff arm for a few seconds before picking it up. I smiled grimly as the memory of Rick teaching me that very same trick came to mind.

"Giving the wind speed and direction, huh buddy," I muttered and started scanning.

"Did you say something, Zach?" Justin asked. I focused back on the man, who casually sat back down and scratched his beard. Yeah, he reminded me a little of Rick.

"What're you thinking, Zach?" Justin pressed. I handed his binoculars back to him.

"It looks like he came up from an access road. Since there's nobody else on the interstate, I'd say he's here specifically for us." Justin digested what I said.

"Our route takes us right past him. Seems only prudent we should introduce ourselves," he commented idly. I thought a moment.

"Why don't you two keep the group rock steady and I'll ride up with Jorge and introduce ourselves."

"I'll keep him in my sights in case he tries anything," Cutter declared.

"Oh, no, don't do that," I responded quickly. "I'd suggest not doing anything that might be considered threatening."

"Why's that?" Shooter demanded to know. I looked at him as I got on the bike with Jorge.

"Because he has at least one sniper deployed, maybe more." Justin frowned at my statement and started scanning the area again as Jorge and I rode off.

"Been waiting on you fellas for the past hour," he said as soon as Jorge cut the engine. He was casually sitting on a folding chair under one of those big picnic table umbrellas. Justin was right; he could have been forty or fifty. It was hard to tell with his thick beard, mirrored sunglasses and bandanna tied around his head they way bikers do. A braided ponytail snaked out of the back of it and ended an inch or two below his shoulder blades.

"Yeah, we're a little slow moving today," I responded as I got off of the bike and stood before him. "My name's Zach and this is my friend, Jorge." The man stood easily and offered a closed fist for a fist bump rather than shaking hands. Jorge and I responded in kind. His smile was pleasant, showing a healthy set of teeth, but his wariness was evident.

"I'm Joe, Trader Joe." His manner was casual, although I'm sure he was just as suspicious of us as we were of him. He pointed at his van and the flat trailer behind it. "And this is my mobile trading post."

"So, I'm guessing you saw our convoy and thought you could do a little business."

"You are guessing correctly, my friend." He motioned toward a dry erase board leaning against the van before swinging his arms again.

"I've written down today's specials. If you see something you like, point it out and tell me what you've got to trade for." I looked at him a moment as he smiled good-naturedly. The list, written in small but neat block lettering, filled the entire board, candles, cookware, canteens, hand tools, but all of it was stuff we either had or didn't need. Not surprisingly, there were no essentials like toilet paper listed. He must have sensed it in my expression.

"Like I said, I don't have everything listed. If there's anything in particular you've got an itching for…" he finished with a wave of his hand toward the contents of his van. At his urging, I stepped closer and peered inside. One item jumped out at me immediately. He had bananas, several of them. I pointed.

"Are those real?" I asked. He grinned again, this time like a fisherman who'd just hooked a trophy bass.

"They most certainly are, grew 'em myself." I didn't know how he was able to grow bananas in this climate, but didn't really care. They looked mouthwatering.

"They're for sale," he continued, "but they ain't going to be cheap. A case of ammo ought to do it, any caliber is fine." I frowned at him. His smile continued.

"Mister Joe, if it's okay with you, I'm going to bring my people up. We're friendly enough and will police our own if there are any transgressions, okay?"

"Sure thing, friend."

"Good, please let your snipers know." His smile tightened for a microsecond, but it relaxed again as he once more casually slapped his hands. Jorge and I rode back to the group, who had mostly all gathered around the armored vehicle while Josue provided rear security.

I looked around, trying to make it seem casual, and after a minute I spotted what I was looking for, a slight mound in the bushes directly perpendicular to where our armored vehicle was parked.

"Damn," I muttered, wondering what the odds would be that we'd stopped our convoy precisely at the point where Joe's sniper was hiding.

"What?" Jorge asked.

"Nothing," I responded and waited for him to stop the bike before jumping off. Once he killed the engine, I addressed everyone.

"Alright, his name's Joe and he's running a makeshift trading post. He's got a few things, but he's being totally unrealistic in his valuation." I explained about the bananas and what he demanded in trade.

"So, my suggestion is, we ride up, exchange pleasantries, and then move on." Seth started to say something, but stopped when Raymond raised his hand.

"Ah, Zach, let's not be so hasty about riding off without trying to do some business. Do you know who're the best salesmen in the world?" he asked and then answered his own question. "Politicians of course, and I've been around the best of them and the worst of them most of my life." He looked around at all of us.

"My parents were career diplomats with the state department. If I may be so bold, let me do the haggling, I guarantee we'll come out ahead. Now, tell me, what do we have that we'd be willing to trade those bananas for?" I thought for a moment.

"Since our makeshift refrigerator went tits up, those steaks are not going to last very much longer. And, of course, we have plenty of honey and beeswax." Raymond smiled gleefully in anticipation.

"Perfect. Leave it to me and we'll all be eating bananas within the hour."

"He *is* a pretty good bullshitter," Sheila commented. Her husband guffawed in agreement.

"It couldn't hurt to try," Seth said.

"I haven't eaten a banana in, well shit, since I was in a banana-eating contest at a strip club outside of Fort Polk," Rachel remarked. There was some light laughter as Sarah looked at her questioningly. It was decided.

"Alright, Raymond, let's see what you can do." I motioned to Seth. "Let me borrow those binoculars for a minute, if you don't mind." Seth looked at me inquisitively as he handed them to me.

"Something else going on?" he asked.

"I'm going to give Sammy an impromptu training lesson," I replied and motioned for Sammy to follow me. "Y'all go ahead; Sammy and I will be there in a few." I got a couple of curious looks, but everyone except Seth loaded up and moved the convoy down the hundred yards to where Trader Joe was patiently waiting for us.

"Okay, curiosity has gotten the best of me. You mind if I sit in on this training?" he asked with a grin.

"Sure." I waited until everyone left and then gestured at Sammy.

"Take these binoculars, look down that way and tell me what you see," I directed in a low voice. He brought the binoculars up to his eyes and peered down the interstate.

"I see that Trader Joe man and his van, and everyone gathering around him. He's giving everyone fist bumps; I guess he doesn't like shaking hands."

"Okay, describe him."

"Uh, well, he's older. He's white, he's got a beard that has a lot of gray in it."

"How tall is he?"

"I can't tell."

"That van he's standing beside is a full-size van. A full-size van is about seven feet tall. Use it as a reference. Now, how tall is he?"

"Six feet?"

"Yep. Now, how far away from us is he?" Sammy bit his lower lip as he continued staring through the binoculars. He finally lowered them and looked at me in confusion.

"Remember when I showed you how to estimate distances by imagining the length of a football field?" He nodded in sudden understanding. "How many football fields away are we?"

"Maybe two?" he answered uncertainly.

"Not bad, not bad at all. Now, here's something else to look at." I pointed back down the interstate. "Do you see that orange rock lying on the side of the road about halfway down?" He nodded. "It kind of seems odd looking, doesn't it? A rock with bright orange paint on it, sitting out there all by itself."

"Yeah."

"Okay, good. Now, if you look close you'll see a little flag tied on that CB antenna on the van and another one tied onto the top of his umbrella."

"Yeah, I see them," Sammy replied. "The wind is pretty gusty today."

"We've talked about this before, right?" Sammy nodded in understanding.

"That flags shows a sniper where the wind is blowing from."

"And what about the orange rock?" He furrowed his brow in confusion and looked at it again with the binoculars. I gave him a hint.

"How far away is that orange rock from us?"

"Halfway?"

"Yep, so how far is that?"

"A hundred yards." You could see the wheels turning in his head before his face lit up in understanding.

"Someone put that rock there as a distance marker." He looked through the binoculars again. "And there's another one a hundred yards on the other side of Mister Joe."

"Yep, they're range markers. So, what does that tell you?"

"There's a sniper out here," he exclaimed in hushed understanding. I heard Seth inhale some air. Sammy started looking around intensely. Suddenly, his mouth dropped open and he pointed at the small mound of bushes. I silently nodded, and I think the two of them finally noticed I had my Kimber forty-five out of its holster and holding it down by my side. I gave a tacit warning to Seth, who nodded in understanding, and began speaking out loudly.

"Sniper, I know your duty is to protect Joe, but I'd feel a heck of a lot better knowing you aren't pointing that rifle at my friends. Why don't you stand up and we'll walk down there together and join everyone." He didn't respond, instead, he continued lying perfectly still, the tip of the barrel barely sticking out of the bushes was the only sign he was there.

"I know you can hear me, so let's not sit here all day in the heat." Actually, the steady breeze made it pleasant out, but I knew from experience that lying prone in a ghillie suit hiding in a bunch of weeds and bushes all day was mighty uncomfortable. Yet, there was still no movement or response. I glanced at Seth, who gave a slight shrug. We were at an impasse. I didn't want any violence, but this sniper was trying my patience.

"Well, I guess I'm mistaken. Fellas, I need to pee first and then we'll go down and join everyone. You know what, I think I'm going to piss all over that spot where I'm imagining a sniper is lying down."

"Yeah," Seth added. "I'll join you, my bladder is about to burst." It took maybe two seconds now before the small mound began moving and a figure in a ghillie suit slowly stood up.

"Please keep your weapon pointed down," I said. He did as I suggested, but even through the camouflage I could sense a tenseness. I kept my handgun pointed at the ground, but I wasn't quite ready to holster it just yet.

"I'm Zach, this is Captain Kitchens with the United States Army, and my buddy here is Sammy." I gestured toward the others. "We're travelling through here and not looking for trouble with anyone. I hope you can see that." The sniper reached up and pulled his headgear off. When he did so, Sammy gasped.

"Zach, that sniper's a girl!" I don't know why, but I was as surprised as he was. Her face was painted in various shades of olive drab, but there was no mistaking the feminine features. Her hair was a wild mess of mahogany brown and a pair of bright hazel green eyes glared at us. Seth chuckled.

"Well, this is turning into an interesting day. What's your name, ma'am?" he asked.

"Riley," she answered in a somewhat defiant tone.

"It's a pleasure to meet you, Riley. C'mon, let's join the rest of them," I suggested.

As we walked down the interstate, Seth and I tried to make small talk with her. She wasn't having any of it though and walked along in silence. As we approached Trader Joe and his van, he stopped talking with everyone and started jogging toward us, worry etched on his face. I holstered my handgun and held my hands out in front of me.

"Mister Joe, there's no cause for alarm, right, Riley?" He glanced at me for a microsecond before focusing on Riley.

"What happened?" he asked her.

"They spotted me," she replied and glared at me again briefly. "I'm sorry, Dad." Seth laughed and then caught himself. I spoke up quickly.

"Joe, you can see we haven't done anything to your daughter, so would you do me a favor?" I asked, to which he focused on me suspiciously. "Would you make that hand signal to your other sniper letting them know everything is okay? You know, swinging your arms and slapping your hands together, would you please do that so nobody gets shot by accident?" Joe stared at me a second, frowning.

"Was it that obvious?" he asked before his smile returned and he gave the signal.

"Looks like we need to work on our tactics. Come on, let's go have a seat and jaw at each other a while."

"So, how did you know?" Joe asked Seth. Seth shook his head and hooked a thumb at me.

"Don't look at me; Zach's the one who figured it out." Joe looked at Seth a moment, as if to see if was being bullshitted, before directing his gaze at me expectantly. I saw Kelly looking at me and her expression may have been one of pride at my astuteness or it may have been a silent admonishment not to go acting like a know-it-all. I took both interpretations to heart.

"I guess your casual demeanor was the big tip off." I gestured toward everyone with a wave of my hand.

"I mean, here's a convoy driving up the road with an armored vehicle leading the pack, and yet, you didn't seem particularly antsy about it." The orange rocks, the flags, the hand signals, all of those clues helped, but Kelly was right, no reason to let on that I spotted all of that. There was no need to brag.

"How in the heck did you find Riley though? I had her hidden pretty good, and trust me, I've had a lot of experience in that particular area." I shrugged and glanced at Riley, who had stripped out of her ghillie suit and was now wearing a pair of short camouflage shorts and a skimpy brown tank top.

She was a little on the petite side, skinny but toned. She'd wiped most of the camo off of her face, which revealed a very cute girl in her late teens, but she must have been hunkered down for quite a while because she was covered in sweat and grime and wasn't smelling very pleasant at the moment. In addition, her unshaven legs had several mosquito bites.

And, it was obvious she wasn't wearing a bra. I pretended not to notice, but those idiot brothers were staring unabashedly. Even Jorge was staring, which kind of embarrassed me. After all, Joe was no dummy, he had to have noticed as well, but he ignored it.

"You got lucky," Riley contended in a husky voice. The glare was toned down, but it was still present. I nodded in agreement.

"Yes, we did. Sammy here has good eyesight and he happened to spot the tip of your rifle barrel peeking out."

"Well, my son is undetected as yet and I think I'll leave him out there, just in case. No offense."

"None taken," Seth replied.

"So, you guys never said where you're heading," Joe casually queried. I glanced at Seth.

"Mount Weather," he replied. Joe nodded.

"I had an inkling."

"You know of Mount Weather?" Raymond asked, to which Joe gave another small nod.

"How so?" Raymond pressed.

"My father used to work for the government," Riley said. Joe gave her a look. She ignored him and spotted Kelly, who was over by the Volvo watching as Frederick peed on a tire. Callahan was not to be outdone and hiked his leg on it as well. I hoped I wouldn't need to change that tire anytime soon. At least little Zoe trotted off into the weeds before squatting.

"Who is she?"

"That's my - that's my wife, Kelly, and my kids."

"I think I'd like to say hello." Riley promptly lost interest in us and walked over to her. I watched as Kelly smiled and the two of them immediately began what appeared to be a friendly conversation.

"The key phrase is used to," Joe said. "I've got no desire to be involved with any government of any kind, anymore."

"Do y'all live in Bristol?" I asked. He shook his head.

"We've got a place out in the east end of the county. Bristol was too dangerous. I guess every city was about the same when the outbreak first began."

"How is it now?" Earl asked. Joe shrugged noncommittally.

"It's calmed down some, but you've still gotta be careful."

"Yeah, Nashville is about the same," I said. Joe stretched and smiled.

"Why don't we do some trading?" he suggested.

"Sounds like a good idea," Raymond replied with his own grin and motioned toward the van and trailer.

We watched in amusement as the two men soon became involved in the preliminary verbal jousting and I had to admit, Raymond was indeed a good bullshitter. He used a lot of preamble and foreplay before mentioning what we had available for trade. When he did, Joe actually emitted a small gasp and I could have sworn I heard his stomach growl. He recovered quickly and tried to regain control by throwing out a challenge.

"Well now, I'm not a man to call anybody a liar, but I'd sure like to see some proof of what you're claiming." Justin and Jorge helped me. Soon, we had one of Joe's tables filled with several sirloin steaks and two mason jars of honey. Raymond smiled smugly, knowing victory was his.

When it was all said and done, we had all of the bananas and a goodly amount of strawberries to boot. When the bartering was completed, I suggested we go ahead and grill some of the steaks. Joe and Riley readily agreed.

"Do you want your son to join us?" I asked. Joe thought a moment and then gave a hand signal. After a minute, I saw a figure emerge from the dense bushes on the opposite end of the interstate. He too was wearing a homemade ghillie suit similar to Riley's. He was a little bit shorter than me, lanky, with a ponytail similar to his father's and a scruff of a beard on his chin.

"He's named after me, so we call him Little Joe." Introductions were made all around and then I went back to the trailer to get the fancy Weber grill I'd taken from the farm. I didn't realize Joe and Riley had followed me until I heard a long low whistle from behind me.

"You people have a little bit of everything in there," he remarked. I nodded affably and handed down the grill.

"We're relocating; I didn't see any reason to leave everything behind." I jumped out of the trailer, shutting the doors and padlocking them. Joe seemed a little put off by that. He obviously wanted to look over everything we had.

"If you don't mind my asking, why are you relocating? Is it that bad where you came from?"

"We had a few setbacks with cattle and crops, probably nothing you haven't gone through as well."

"Doesn't seem like that would be the deciding factor," he said as we walked back to the group.

"If I didn't have family, I don't think I would have left, but I have to take their welfare into consideration." Before I could speak further, the little Tasmanian devil ran up from wherever he was and attacked one of my legs in a bear hug. I hoisted him up on my hip.

"This is why," I responded as Janet walked up holding Macie. "These are my two kids and this is Janet, my monster-in-law." Janet glared at me as Joe laughed and introduced himself. Macie hid her face in the cleavage of Janet's shirt, which if I didn't know any better I'd say there were a couple of extra buttons open that normally weren't. Joe laughed again.

"She's a shy one. So, your decision has to do with your kids."

"Yep. There are several things that Mount Weather can offer that I can't provide for," I continued as we all walked back to the main group, which were all gathered around Joe's van.

"Such as?" he asked.

"Medical care, a formal education for the kids," and me, for that matter. "A military presence, and an overall greater access to resources." I glanced at Janet, who was trying, and succeeding, in making pointed eye contact with Joe.

"Hmm," he replied. Whether he was hmming at my statement or at Janet's cleavage, I had no idea.

Jorge had rounded up some kindling, took charge of the grill and started getting a fire going. Josue had gotten our folding chairs out of the truck and everyone was getting comfortable. Little Joe had walked over to the side of his father's van, stripped down to his waist and was doing his best to clean himself up with a washrag. Both Kate and Kyra were giving him the once over too, much to Shooter's displeasure. Kelly pretended not to notice, which was nice.

"How about you guys, what kind of community do you have set up?" Seth asked.

"We have a few farmers, locals and their spouses." He intentionally didn't tell the specific numbers. Seth noticed and looked at me suspiciously, but he didn't push it. Joe picked up on our tacit exchange.

"A couple of winters ago, we had a cholera outbreak. We lost a few people, but I'm not sure I'm trusting enough to tell you our actual numbers."

"We understand," I said. "May I ask how it happened?"

"When everything went bad, a group of us banded together. We had a decent operation going, for the most part. Everyone had job assignments." Joe made a face and shook his head. "We had this one knucklehead, he was a poster child for laziness. We all know the type. Well, unfortunately, he was assigned water duty. Come to find out he wasn't boiling the water we were drawing from a well."

"And the well was contaminated," Grant said. Joe nodded. "It's a wonder all of you didn't die." He then gestured toward me.

"He distills his drinking water." Joe looked at me questioningly.

"Filtering removes sediment, boiling kills bacteria, but only distilling can remove heavy metals."

"That's a lot of time and effort involved. Are you certain there're heavy metals in your water?"

"I don't have any test kits, so no, I'm only guessing, but think about it. The groundwater is contaminated by toxic spills everywhere. I think it's prudent, especially when it comes to my kids." Joe continued staring at me as he grunted thoughtfully.

"How did you people contain the cholera?" Grant asked, his interest now piqued.

"Well, sir, one of the first to get sick and die was our doctor. We quarantined the rest."

"Did anyone who had become sick survive?" he asked. Joe frowned.

"Quite a few died. Riley got pretty sick, but she lived through it." I looked over at her. She smiled demurely. At least she wasn't glaring at me anymore.

"At one point, she'd dropped down to about fifty pounds."

"Now, I'm stronger than ever," she exclaimed and flexed her right bicep. She indeed had muscular arms, small, but muscular. Just like Andie.

"Nice," I said. She smiled again and then I saw Kelly looking at me out of the corner of my eye. I turned to Joe and changed the subject.

"How has it gone with the infected?" I asked.

"About what you'd expect. Once we figured out they can't do shit when it's below freezing, we went on a lot of search and destroy missions. We killed off quite a lot."

"We've killed the shit out of them," Riley declared.

"We lost a few people though," Joe said. "It hasn't been easy."

"Are you people everyone that's left over from Nashville?" Riley asked.

"No, there's a few who decided not to join us and stayed behind."

"Any men?" she asked, and cast a quick glance at Jorge this time. Joe spoke up.

"My little girl is in heat."

"Dad!" Riley scolded. Even through the grime, I could see her cheeks redden. Little Joe, who had emerged from the side of the van wearing a semi-fresh baseball jersey, chortled.

"Yeah, my son is too," Joe added. His son was suddenly quiet and started blushing too. I pointed at the jersey.

"Did you play baseball in high school?" I asked.

"Yeah," he answered, thankful that I changed the subject.

"He loves his baseball," Joe added. "He had the state record for homeruns and was going to have a full ride at Virginia Tech when it all broke out."

"Now he hits homeruns upside zombie's heads," Riley said. "It's gross when their heads bust open."

"At least, he takes his sexual frustrations out with a bat instead of using all of our spare batteries on a vibrator." Most of us laughed loudly now. Riley's cheeks turned even redder. She stood quickly and grabbed the wash rag from her brother before disappearing behind the van.

"Starting about a year ago, we began noticing a distinct change in behavior in quite a few of them," I said and told them some of the stories.

"Have you seen anything similar, Joe?"

"A little bit," Joe admitted, but didn't elaborate.

"What's the largest horde you guys have seen?" Grant asked.

"I suppose the largest was during the initial outbreak. The whole city of Bristol seemed to be infected." He thought for a minute.

"A lot of them died off after the first year. We ventured a little way into the city from time to time and tested the waters. The stench from the rotting bodies is just awful."

"You got that right," Little Joe said. "Riley's BO smells exactly the same."

"Asshole," Riley retorted from behind the van.

"We've killed quite a few as well. Let's see, I'd say in the last year the biggest group of them we've seen together at one time was about five hundred to a thousand. What do you think, son?"

"Yeah, I guess," he answered. "I mean, I didn't take the time to count each one of them and Riley can't count that high."

"Oh, that's rich coming from a dumb jock," Riley retorted as she emerged. She'd wiped most of the grime off of her face and it looked like she'd even brushed her hair a little.

"How did y'all react?" I asked. Joe grinned and held his hands up in a shrug. "We hid."

"They came out of the city," Riley said as she blew a tuft of hair out of her face. "They were all walking together."

"We don't know where they were going but they were walking south," Joe added. I nodded and was about to give my opinion when Cutter spoke up.

"Yeah, we've been studying them," he said with a little bit of puff in his voice. "There are some of them that're evolving and they've figured out they need to travel in order to find fresh food sources." Riley looked at him curiously.

"What kind of studying?" she asked. Cutter obviously wasn't prepared for that kind of question and started stammering.

"Mostly through observation," I said, hoping to stop him from making himself out to look like an idiot. I mean, we all knew he wasn't all that smart, but he was a reflection of us.

"Although, we captured one a while back and conducted some rudimentary tests."

"No shit?" Joe asked. I nodded and pointed at Grant.

"Doctor Parsons and these two Marines were with a unit called the Chemical Biological Incident Response Force when the plague broke out. Later on, they spent some time at the CDC. They'd conducted a lot of research."

"Did anyone figure out the cause?" Joe asked.

"It is a previously unidentified virus, but a lot of data was lost or otherwise compromised. The group of scientists at the CDC had made significant progress."

"I must admit, I'm confused," Joe said. "Doctor, if you were at the CDC, doing research with other doctors. There were other doctors, correct?" Grant nodded. "Then why are you here, now, instead of at the CDC?" Joe looked at us, waiting for an explanation. The three Marines spent the next hour telling the story, but left out the part about my kids and me. When they were finished, the look on Joe and his kids' faces was one of wonder.

"Well, now, that is one hell of a story," Joe said.

"You must be one tough motherfucker," Riley said while looking admiringly at Justin. I suppressed a smile when I saw Ruth's eyes narrow.

"But you never did say if a cure was developed." Grant moved his mouth a few times in that annoying way of his when he was preparing a response.

"Possibly," he finally answered. "But, there have been no clinical trials and it has not yet been manufactured in large quantities. Yet another reason to relocate to Mount Weather." Joe sat up in his seat.

"You said, not in large quantities? What does that mean?"

"Grant is one of those people that when you hear of something he does, you sit back and go hmm," I answered. "One of the crazy things he did was he inoculated himself with a test serum." Everyone who was listening started and I think there was even a collective gasp. Up until now, the only people who knew were Justin, Ruth, Kelly, and me.

"Well, does it work?" Joe finally asked. There were a few nervous chuckles, but even so, everyone was waiting for Grant's answer.

"I administered the dose to myself back last winter. Six months and fourteen days ago, to be exact. I had flu-like symptoms for the next forty-eight hours, but as you can see, I appear to be healthy with no obvious side effects, but the only way to be certain is to be purposely exposed to the virus, under strict conditions, of course."

"Are you going to do it?" Cutter asked. Grant looked at him and smiled ruefully.

"Zach has refused to allow it."

"What the hell does that mean?"

"Simple, Zach said no."

"What a load of bullshit," Shooter declared loudly. "You should do it."

"Pipe down, Simon," Sarah scolded. The others laughed. Grant looked at Trader Joe and his daughter.

"I'll spare you two a longwinded story, but briefly, I'm indebted to Zach, so I'm going to respect his wishes. Perhaps when we get to Mount Weather…" I changed the subject.

"What about gangs and marauders?" When I asked this, Riley hastened a quick glance at her father, who merely shrugged.

"There've been a few here and there."

"I can't imagine a gang coming upon your trading post and not robbing you," I replied questioningly and gestured toward Riley. "Or worse."

"We can hold our own," Riley replied defensively.

"Sure, I can see that." I started to say more, but I didn't think it'd be productive, so I let it go. Joe looked around at everyone as we talked.

"I see a few of you wearing combat utilities," he remarked as he gestured toward Sarah and Rachel.

"We're military," Rachel responded. "I'm with the Army, along with Captain Kitchens, Major Fowlkes here is a pilot in the Air Force, and of course the Marines standing there all serious looking. Lieutenant Smithson spends most of his waking hours looking like he ate persimmons for breakfast." We laughed lightheartedly. Rachel, our self-appointed comedian, especially liked to make digs at the Marines at any given opportunity. Seth gestured at the other three delegation members.

"We're the only ones from Mount Weather. Back a few months ago, we established radio communications with this group from Nashville, along with small pockets of survivors in other parts of the country. The President issued a directive to send out delegations to the known survivors and invite them to come live at Mount Weather until the country stabilizes itself. And before I forget, you and your kids are more than welcome to join us."

"So, he's still alive," Joe commented under his breath. Raymond spoke up.

"Alive and well. Restoring society is our number one goal and it's been hard work.

"How?" Riley asked.

"Several things. One of our duties is to conduct a census among any survivors we encounter. We attempt to get an accurate number, where they're located, and lines of communications reestablished. I'm sure that from your perspective nothing is being done, but I can assure you many positive gains have been accomplished."

"Not to mention a possible vaccine being developed," Sheila said. Joe, who had taken his sunglasses off while we were talking, was silent a long moment. I'd noticed he was looking us over carefully during the conversation, studying us. I got the opinion this man was a lot more intelligent than he appeared.

"It seems like all of you are putting a lot of faith into this." Raymond started to respond but Joe held up a hand.

"Now, I believe I know what you're going to say. You're going to talk about the importance of a hierarchy of government, the belief in the President and the rebuilding of society, all of those post-apocalyptic platitudes." I chuckled.

"Yeah, you're right, but don't get us wrong, we've not been brainwashed."

"That's good, because there's something you should know," he said and gave a sardonic grin. "I went to college with that man."

"The President?" Sheila asked, to which Joe nodded. "You went to Harvard?"

"Yep, we were even in the same fraternity."

"What kind of person was he back then?" Rachel asked. Joe snorted.

"The same as he is now, he was a politician." He paused a second. "I voted for him, but make no mistake, he's a politician and everything that word means."

"I take it you're not interested in Mount Weather." Joe rubbed his face, appearing to be in deep thought.

"I'll admit, there are some valid points to the argument for relocating." He paused again and looked around.

"I assume a few of you went to college. Any of you versed in history?" There was a moment of silence and then Seth cleared his throat.

"A few of us have been to college, yes. I'm an attorney."

"What do you know about the Roman Empire?" There was a collective silence now, and then Janet spoke up.

"Don't just sit there," she said as she gestured at me. "You know good and well you know all about it." Joe looked appraisingly at Janet and her cleavage before focusing on me.

"I know a little bit," I admitted. Kelly grunted.

"He's being modest. What do you want to know? He'll know the answer." Joe scratched at his beard as he gazed at me.

"So, you know a little bit about it?" he asked. "When did it come into being?"

"That seems like a subjective question, Joe. Rome was founded about six hundred BC, but they didn't any kind of major expansion until three hundred years later."

"Not bad, not bad at all. When did it fall?"

"I'll go with the end of the fourth crusade. If I remember correctly, I'll say that was at the beginning of the thirteenth century." Now, Joe looked at me in surprise.

"1204, to be exact. That was the Eastern Roman Empire."

"Also known as the Byzantine Empire," I added.

"I see someone paid attention in school," Joe said as he looked at his two children. "You seem young for a college man."

"I didn't go to college." Joe nodded thoughtfully.

"So, the Empire falls, but for years many Europeans were convinced it still existed." I snapped my fingers.

"You're equating the fall of the Roman Empire with the current status of the U.S."

"You are correct, my young friend. Those bozos up in Mount Weather, or wherever they are, refuse to believe the democratic republic of the USA no longer exists."

"And the option, Joe?" I rejoined. "We can continue living in small communities, mostly isolated from the rest of the world, slowly reverting back to a Stone Age state and eventually dying off." I stood and picked up Macie, who squealed with delight as I kissed her on the cheek.

"I don't want that for my kids." Joe was staring at me intently now as he continued fingering his beard. I couldn't help but notice Riley was now staring at me with renewed interest. I'm sure Kelly spotted it as well.

"You make a good argument, Zach," Joe finally said. "I can certainly see why your friends look up to you."

"Yes, we do," Sarah said. Joe stood and stretched, popping some vertebrae that were out of alignment.

"A good argument indeed," he repeated. "But, before making such a decision, I'd have to talk it over with my people." His gaze wandered back at our trailer, with the kind of look an alcoholic has when staring at a closed liquor store.

"You people have a few hours of daylight left. Are you going to get moving or settle in for the night?" Seth spoke up quickly.

"We still have a little over three hundred miles to go. I think we should take advantage of the daylight." Most of us nodded in assent. Grant started to say something but seemed to think better of it.

"What is it, Grant?" I asked.

"Oh, I was just going to ask if they had any medical problems I might be able to help with."

"Do you have any saltpeter?" Joe asked as he pointed at his kids. "These two are in desperate need." We all laughed as Grant shook his head.

They weren't very forthcoming with census information, but Grant managed to talk them into providing blood samples.

"I'm especially interested in Riley's sample," he confided in me later. "It may have been a case of cholera, or it may have been something else." I couldn't criticize him. He was a doctor, a pathologist whose mission was still clear: find a cure.

Kelly and Sheila took a couple of pictures before we headed out. I was itching to get an idea of what the Stryker was capable of so I opted to ride with Seth and Sammy for this leg of the journey.

"I'm pretty sure we can make it to Roanoke before dark," Seth said.

"Sounds good," I replied. "I'd like to get there as quickly as possible." Seth hit a pothole, causing Sammy and I to bounce around.

"This vehicle rides rough," I commented. Seth laughed.

"Yeah, it was designed for combat not comfort. That's why my three friends don't want to ride in it."

"Tell me about this thing," I asked. Seth looked away from his driving sights for a moment and looked at me.

"The Stryker?" I nodded. "Well, I only have a rudimentary working knowledge of it. Sergeant Martin, that was Clyde, he was the expert. Let me see, it has a diesel Caterpillar engine with a top speed of a little over sixty miles-per-hour, and I can change the tire pressure on the fly to overcome any terrain considerations. It's designed to hold nine soldiers, along with a driver and a commander. It's almost impervious to all small arms fire, the steel cage surrounding the vehicle stops RPGs, and the undercarriage is specifically designed with IEDs in mind." He gestured at the sights.

"As you can see, driving can be done through these viewfinders, or you can open the hatch and stick your head out. You're supposed to have an additional soldier assist you with observing your route, but I've gotten the hang of it. It also has thermal imaging, so you can drive at night in blackout mode and can see up to seventy-eight hundred meters. There are ten different variations; this one is the command version. The weapons platform is a fifty-caliber machine gun and the Mark Nineteen automatic grenade launcher. It's controlled by that." He pointed at a computer screen and a joystick. He pointed at another computer system.

"That's the communications system, it's known as the FBCB2."

"It looks pretty complex," I said. Seth nodded.

"Yeah, Clyde was training us on it, but…" I nodded in understanding as I looked around the interior of the vehicle. There was a stack of cardboard boxes with the familiar MRE labels on them and there were some wooden crates of similar size. I looked at the markings and realized they were cases of fragmentation grenades and mortar rounds. Seth saw me looking at it.

"We also have a sixty millimeter mortar on board."

"Nice," I said and nodded. I had to admit, I couldn't wait to play with it. The Stryker, the mortar, all of it.

"What kind of impression did you get from Joe and his kids?" Seth asked.

"All three of them were healthy looking. Little Joe stayed hidden until his father gave him the signal. That shows a strong amount of discipline." Seth nodded in agreement.

"Did you notice how vague his answers were when we asked about the infected and marauders?"

"Yeah, he was being very guarded, but it was probably just a matter of not wanting to be an open book with complete strangers." I paused a moment. "It's possible he was sizing us up for an ambush later."

"Possible," Seth surmised and patted the bulkhead of the vehicle. "They'd need some heavy hardware to overcome this bad boy though." Our conversation was interrupted when Justin came over the radio.

"All units, status check." We listened as everyone responded. When the last person checked in, Seth checked his watch and nodded in satisfaction.

"Yeah, his trade goods weren't much to speak of, and other than the fresh fruit, he didn't have any canned goods or essentials like first aid equipment or toothpaste. He's smart enough to know you don't trade away things like that."

"Exactly, unless they're already out of those items." After a moment's pause, he glanced over at me.

"If I may pay you a compliment, you seem to be a very intelligent man."

"Thanks."

"No, I mean it. You spotted the snipers rather quickly and you made a good analysis of Joe and his set up. You have very astute observational skills, and that stuff with the Roman Empire was pretty good too."

"I appreciate that, but I'm the first to admit I've still got a lot to learn. What did you do in the Army?" Seth chuckled at the question.

"I was a JAG officer. That's Judge Advocate General in layman's terms. I know quite a bit about military law, very little about actual soldiering. Well, let me amend that last statement. During the past three years, I've learned a lot about soldiering, but I don't think I would have ever spotted Riley."

"You're a lawyer."

"Yep. I've been through a couple of combat arms schools, but the bottom line is I'm nothing more than a fancy attorney wearing a uniform."

"Is there a judicial system in place at Mount Weather?"

"In a manner of speaking. It's more like a civilian arbitration panel to resolve petty disputes. We haven't had to court martial anyone or try anyone for any type of felonious crime." He looked at me questioningly. "Why do you ask?"

"Because there are two of us within this group who have killed members of the military. How do you intend to address that issue?" He took his eyes off of the road for a second and glanced at me.

"I imagine that at some point there will be a board of inquiry," he replied cautiously. He said it in a low tone and it was difficult to hear him over the noise of the engine. I thought about it. I wasn't too concerned about myself. Nobody witnessed the fight I'd had with Sol and I believed I had a pretty good case for self-defense, if it came to that. Janet's act of slitting Coltrane's throat might be another matter altogether.

"So, getting back to Joe and his kids," Seth said, a little louder now.

"I think Joe had two motives. The first one was honest enough, he wanted to trade. He mentioned ammo, so I'm betting they're running short of it, much like we are. He tried to be sly about it, but when he and Raymond were haggling, he mentioned ammo more than once."

"What's his second motive?"

"He was checking us out. If we were marauders, there wasn't much of value we could have stolen from him, other than the fruit. He wanted to see what kind of people we were. If you ask me, I bet there are less than a dozen people in his community and I wouldn't be surprised if it's just the three of them. When you said we were leaving, I caught a very brief moment when he looked downright sad. Riley and her brother too. But, I could have misread them."

"You think they could be a part of a marauder gang?" he asked. I nodded.

"Could be. And I'll do you one better, if they are a gang, I wouldn't be surprised if Joe is the leader. He seemed pretty sharp."

"Riley and Kelly seemed to have had a nice long conversation."

"Yep," I said. "She unknowingly gave up a lot of information."

"How so?"

"She said there were no other women close to who age left in her group and…" I stopped midsentence and snickered.

"What?" Seth asked.

"She asked Kelly about all of the single men because she hadn't been laid in the past two years." Seth chortled, and then frowned.

"She seems a little young."

"Seventeen," I replied. Seth's frown deepened and now he let out a deep sigh.

"Damn."

"What?" I asked.

"I'm ten years older than her and she smelled to high heaven, and yet I was still having nasty thoughts about her." I laughed at him.

"Believe me, I understand."

"Oh well, maybe I'll pay a visit to Bristol in a couple of years and say hello. So, these other women…" I gave him a look. He glanced back with hopefulness.

"Well, let's see. Kelly is with me."

"Obviously."

"Yeah. There's Janet, my mother-in-law."

"She's a little hard on her daughter." I looked at him a second in confusion before it sunk in.

"Oh, no, she's not Kelly's mother." I gave him the reader's digest version of how I first met the Friersons, the ensuing conflict, and how Julie and I had finally hooked up.

"Believe it or not, I was going to kill her at one time, but decided against it. I'm not sure I'd wish her on you. She's – hmm, what would be the proper word."

"Ruth called her a man-eater."

"Yeah, that's one description."

"What about Maria?"

"Maria is single. I don't know if she considers herself available at the moment, but she's very sweet, pretty too. Jorge and Josue are very protective of her."

"That was some shit about her kid."

"You're telling me." The image of little Jose falling out of that snake's belly sprouted up. I rubbed my face heavily, trying to erase it.

"What about those two sisters?" Seth asked.

"Kate and Kyra. Yeah, they're both fine-looking women, they got that, what do you call it? A sultry demeanor. Kate seems to have a thing for Shooter, although I have no idea why. Kyra's pleasant to be around, but she doesn't seem to be interested in men. She had a boyfriend that was murdered not too long ago, so perhaps she's still grieving. And then there's Sarah and Rachel."

"I kind of figured out they're a couple."

"Yeah and I've been meaning to speak to you about that. Is their relationship going to be a problem for them when we get to Mount Weather?"

"No, not for the most part. There are a couple of knuckleheads who refuse to be a part of the twenty-first century, but other than a few sarcastic remarks there hasn't ever been any issues." I chuckled. "What?" he asked.

"I pity the fool who makes a snide remark to Sarah." Seth chuckled.

"Yeah, she seems pretty tough."

"So, there's the rundown of the women of Nolensville, Tennessee." Seth grunted.

"Even in post-apocalyptic America dating is tough," he lamented. I laughed.

"Yeah, I guess so."

"Aunt Kyra farts in her sleep," Sammy said suddenly. "So does Aunt Kate, but not nearly as much." Seth and I looked at each other and burst out in laughter. Sammy seemed nonplussed and pointed at the steering wheel.

"Can I drive?"

CHAPTER 52 – ROANOKE

"The scenery is pretty," Kelly remarked as she drove. Interstate 81 ran alongside the Blueridge Mountains, and as we travelled northward, the trees and other fauna had ignored the apocalypse and were thriving in an almost ethereal beauty.

"Yeah, it's nice." We rode along, admiring the view, when Seth came in on the radio.

"Jorge just gave a hand signal. It looks like we have a single vehicle heading our way, coming down our side of the interstate." There was a pause. "Well, damn. Don't worry, I think I know who it is."

"That doesn't tell us very much, sir," Justin said.

"The two of us need a bio break too," Rachel enjoined.

"Alright, everyone stop and stagger. No, belay that, park in a column." Now that sounded odd. Staggering the vehicles increased our sectors of fire. Kelly pointed out of the window to the semi.

"What the hell?" I looked and agreed with the sentiment. We exited the truck and walked to the front of the column where Seth was talking to a man who was wearing old, worn-out jeans, a flannel shirt with the sleeves cut out revealing muscular arms, and hunting boots. I'd say he was in his mid-thirties or so, but that wasn't what I was wondering, or anyone else I'd say. Seth rattled off everyone's names.

"Everyone, this is Melvin," Seth said. Melvin tipped his hat, a very-worn and sweat-stained Stetson.

"Hello everyone, I'm very pleased to meet you." Nobody answered. He saw what we were looking at. Melvin had a big, four-wheel-drive truck with oversized mudder tires. He'd fixed his truck up much like I'd fixed up my Ford Raptor. He'd caged the windows, rigged a supplementary lighting system on the roll bar, and had a camper on the back. But nobody was paying attention to that; they were all looking at what he had affixed to the front grill.

The grill guard was one of those aftermarket products most off-road enthusiasts and rednecks had on their trucks, but he'd modified it. He had a metal chair bolted onto it, but the most interesting part was that he had a person secured to the chair with duct tape. It was obviously a female; she was wearing jeans and a tight-fitting black tank top that could barely contain an enormous set of breasts. The persons face was hidden by a full coverage motorcycle helmet with a tinted face shield. The face shield was plastered with dead bugs, which told me she'd been there for a while. Melvin saw us all looking at it.

"Everyone, this is my wife, Peggy." He raised the visor, revealing the face of a person with advanced stages of the zombie infection. She hissed. Melvin smiled.

"Peggy said she's very pleased to meet all of you."

"You married a zombie?" Sammy asked. Melvin looked down at Sammy and his grin faltered a little.

"No, son, she was my wife before all of this stuff started."

"Melvin and his wife had what you'd call a tumultuous relationship," Seth informed us. "Isn't that right, Melvin?"

"I suppose that's one way of putting it," he replied with a rueful smile. He glanced at his wife before looking at Seth.

"What's shakin', Captain? You out on another recruiting mission?"

"That'd be affirmative, Melvin," Seth answered and introduced everyone. "They're from Tennessee and are coming to live at Mount Weather."

"What's wrong with Tennessee?" he asked.

"Not a thing," I said. "It's a beautiful state." I gestured at his wife. "Your treatment of your wife kind of seems peculiar."

"Zach, is it?" he asked and I nodded. "Zach, have you ever been married?"

"Yes, he has and is," Kelly said. Melvin quickly doffed his hat revealing a short burr haircut.

"No offense, ma'am. If I remember Seth's introductions, your name is Kelly." His recall of names was pretty good, but still, I was wondering about his level of sanity.

"Yes, and for the record, I'm not so sure I like you," Kelly added.

"Ah, because of your perception of the awful manner in which I'm treating my beloved wife, would I be correct?" Kelly nodded.

"Well then, I feel compelled to tell you all about dearest Peggy," he said.

"Here we go," Seth muttered. Melvin glanced at him for a microsecond and then ignored him.

"Back when I was active duty," he paused and gestured at Seth. "I was Army, just like pretty boy here. Well anyway, I'd been in Afghanistan for an unusually long time without any female companionship, if you know what I mean. So, I think God was conspiring against me when I got back stateside. I went to a…" he paused and glanced briefly at Sammy. "A gentlemen's club one night with my friends, and there she was." He gestured at Peggy.

"She was the prettiest blonde-haired, blue-eyed gal I'd ever seen, with a sexy little gap between her two front teeth. I watched her dance all night and drank almost a whole bottle of bourbon before I got up the nerve to speak to her. I was drunk and most likely said something a little, shall we say, brazen." He chuckled at the memory. "She slapped the hell out of me."

"So, what'd you do?" Shooter asked.

"Hell, man, I slapped her back."

"Nice!" Shooter complimented.

"Yeah, real nice," Kelly said scornfully.

"Well, now, Miss Kelly, it wasn't quite like you think. Sure, I was wrong, but instead of being offended, Peggy here got turned on by it."

"Right," Sarah said. Melvin looked her over curiously.

"I swear to God. So, like I was saying, I slapped her back and the bouncers saw it. There was a big fight, but those bouncers were no match for me and my buddies." He made a hand gesture at Peggy.

"She drug me out the back door and got me out of there before the cops came. We went back to her place and made mad passionate love until the sun came up." He smiled. "We got married a week later." He gestured at her again.

"You see those honkers? I bought 'em for her. Damn, those things were expensive."

"So, what happened?" I asked. I could see by the expression on Seth's face he wished I hadn't asked.

"Oh, the honeymoon didn't last. You folks may not believe this, but she was a little on the crazy side."

"You think?" Rachel asked with a fake look of disbelief.

"Oh, yes ma'am. She did any drugs she could get ahold of and slept around like an alley cat in heat, and that included sleeping with most of my so-called friends. During the middle of it all, she drained our bank account. When I confronted her, she called the police and filed a false police report against me." Seth spoke up.

"She put a restraining order on him," Seth added. "It got him kicked out of the Army."

"Yeah, kicked out of the Army, kicked out of my own apartment, she even took my car and sold it for crack. She wouldn't even let me have my own toothbrush. There was only one of my friends she hadn't been with. He was kind enough to let me sleep on his couch." He looked around to see if we were listening, which was unnecessary. We were collectively infatuated.

"Well, it turns out Felton, that was my buddy, the reason he hadn't slept with her was because he was gay." He laughed at the irony. "He was a good guy though," he said a little more quietly. "He died."

"So, anyway, here I am, out of the Army, out of a job, homeless, and facing some bogus domestic violence charges, but God finally took pity on me."

"Melvin's Uncle is a Virginia Senator," Seth said.

"Yep," Melvin said. "He got me a job at Weather. Since I was facing charges, the only job he could get me was a groundskeeper."

"Bummer," Shooter said.

"Yeah," Melvin replied.

"Whatever," Kelly said. "You still haven't said how she ended up taped to a chair that's bolted to the front of your truck." Melvin looked at Kelly and then glanced over at Peggy.

"Yeah, well, about a year after, I went looking for her. I found her in my apartment. She'd been there the whole time." He looked around at us again.

"You see, this woman drove me to the brink of suicide. When I found her, infected..." he didn't finish. He cleared his throat. "Well, now she's my reason to keep living. She goes with me everywhere."

"He tried to bring her back to Weather, but obviously we wouldn't let him," Seth said.

"Yep, they think I'm crazy." Rachel chortled.

"Those Mount Weather people are pretty smart," she said. Melvin had a sidearm holstered on his left side. I watched his hands closely in case he went for it. Instead, he grinned.

"Yep, I'd say you're right." He looked at his wife, who was staring at him with her black eyes.

"Welp, it was nice meeting all you people. I'm sure we'll see each other again, but Peggy and I've got to be going." He winked at Sammy. "Things to see and people to do. Good to see you, Seth. Tell the general I said hello and go fuck himself, excuse my French." With that, he flipped the visor back down on his wife's helmet, got into his truck and used the open lane to drive off. Now I understood why Seth didn't want us to stagger the vehicles. If we had, Melvin probably would have never left.

"He was a highly decorated soldier," Seth said as we watched the truck disappear down the Interstate. "His last mission was a tough one. A lot of his fellow soldiers were killed. I think it got to him."

"Do you think he's still tapping that?" Shooter asked. I laughed in spite of myself. That is, until I saw Kelly glaring at me.

"Alright, ladies and gents," I said. "This looks like as good a place as any to set up for the night, what do you say?"

We reconfigured our vehicles for defense and got the cooking utensils out. Kelly and Janet argued over what to cook before deciding on pot luck. That meant Jorge and I were going to be peeling a pot full of potatoes. Frederick and Macie played with the dogs and the rest made preparations for us to stay the night.

"It smells good," Earl said as Janet stirred the big cauldron. "Those steaks were delicious as well."

"That was the last of them," I said. "The rest of our meat has been smoke cured, and although it's still good meat, it's not quite the same as a fresh grilled steak." I glanced over at him.

"How well do you know Melvin?"

"Not very well," he said. "He mostly kept to himself, only talked to some of the soldiers. He lives somewhere around Weather." He gestured at Seth. "Seth's been to his house."

"You have?" I asked.

"Yeah, he's a good man, just a little off in the head. He built himself a nice cabin and he's turned out to be a pretty good farmer."

"How many farmers and cattlemen are up there?"

"Maybe ten who actually know what they're doing. There are a few more that dabble at it." Seth paused and chuckled.

"There's this one guy, Harold. Everyone calls him Hog-head Harold because he has a head as big as, well, as a hog's head, and he runs the pig farm."

"Sounds like an interesting dude."

"Oh, yeah, that's one way of describing him. He has a house up on stilts in the middle of the farm. So, he's surrounded by pigs, who stink to high heaven, but he says he's perfectly safe."

"I guess I can see that. Pigs are tough. There's no way zombies could get through them."

"Yep, that's his logic. He's even got a video of a few zombies trying to attack a pig one day. The pigs tore them apart."

"Yeah, I believe that," Jorge said. "Pigs can be mean as hell, man, and they'll eat anything."

"How many acres do y'all have for crops?" I asked.

"They cleared a lot of land around the compound. I don't know the exact number, a couple of thousand I think. Several of us have our own gardens within the compound. We have informal contests. My tomatoes did pretty good this summer, but I somehow managed to kill my cucumbers and squash." Our conversation was interrupted by gunfire. I cursed under my breath.

"If those two are wasting ammo again, I'm going to whip their asses." Earl looked at me in surprise as more gunfire erupted and we each began walking toward the source of the shots. We spotted them at almost the same time.

"Oh shit," Earl lamented.

"Get to a vehicle!" I shouted, grabbed my rifle that had been leaning up against a chair and ran toward the two idiot brothers, and Kate. Kate was running to the safety of the vehicles, but the two brothers were standing in the middle of the interstate shooting toward a horde of approaching infected.

Kate ran by me as I took up a shooting position beside the Stryker, but that's when I noticed Cutter was limping badly and could hardly walk. He was shooting over his shoulder as his brother was trying to drag him along. It wasn't looking good for them; the horde was loping toward them and closing fast.

"Damn," I muttered, loaded a fresh magazine and then ran to them. Cutter paused in his shooting as I ran up beside him.

"We're in the shit now!" I jabbed a finger at Shooter.

"Ride him piggy-back, I'll cover!" I shouted and began firing. Cutter needed no further instruction. He jumped on his brother's back and the three of us began moving. Thankfully, the others were smarter and had jumped in the vehicles. There were individual rounds of gunfire now from our group and zombies started dropping. But, there were a lot of them and they were close, too close.

And I didn't have my machete.

I only managed to reload once before they were on us. It's funny how you think of insignificant things when you're in the midst of an adrenalin-pumped, balls-to-the-wall situation, like fighting for your life from bloodthirsty zombies. There I was, butt stroking left and right and the only thing I was thinking about was these things looked fairly decent, comparatively speaking. They still smelled, but the decomposition was minimal, in some of them it was almost non-existent. Chunks of rotting flesh had completely scabbed over and their blackened eyes actually looked like they had moisture.

The gunfire coming from behind me was almost unnoticed now, like white noise in the background, rain on a metal roof. Instead, I was concentrating entirely on surviving. The only good thing at the moment were the skulls of the infected seemed to be softer than normal. One good whack and they'd burst open like a ripe melon.

"Keep moving!" I shouted at the two idiots. But I was talking to empty air. Once his brother had hopped up on his back, Shooter broke into a run and the two of them were almost back to safety. I applied one more satisfying butt stroke and then turned to make a sprint toward the Stryker. Another one of those random thoughts entered my brain as I realized nobody was shooting anymore. No matter, I had no doubt I could outrun any zombie and I only had a hundred yard sprint.

And then, the unthinkable happened. I tripped and fell. Maybe it was a piece of debris in the roadway, maybe a zombie clutched at my foot, or maybe it was nothing more than my own clumsiness. Like the inept bimbo in a B-horror movie. What I did know was now it wasn't going to matter how immune I was. They weren't interested in infecting me; they were going to eat me alive.

The one closest to me was a big one, a man who looked like he could have been a sumo wrestler at one time. As he bore down on me, I kicked him in the chest as hard as I could. It pushed him back a couple of feet, which momentarily slowed up the others trying to get at me. Suddenly, there was a loud eruption of gunfire. I realized it was Seth; he'd opened up with that fifty caliber machine gun and he wasn't taking any prisoners. The fact that very few of his shots were headshots didn't matter. The kinetic energy of those fifty caliber rounds were literally causing the zombies to explode on impact. It was both terrifying and fascinating.

I spider crawled backwards as fast as I could, not daring to stand up and catch a round by mistake. When my head hit the front of the Stryker, there were five or six left, but they stopped their attack suddenly and attempted to run away. Seth shot them each in the back.

"Don't shoot us, bro!" Justin shouted as he and Ruth emerged from behind the Stryker and crouched beside me. They kept their assault rifles pointed at the wood line, allowing me to get back on my feet.

"Are you hurt?" he asked excitedly. My ears were ringing, my mouth had an acrid coppery taste, and I had quite a bit of black goo splattered on me. It was only then that I saw everyone had driven the vehicles forward and were now immediately behind me.

"Alright, we don't need everyone exposed!" Justin shouted. "Everyone except Zach and me get in your vehicles and reestablish a perimeter, just like we've rehearsed. Move it!" Grant ignored Justin's order and rushed up as we made it behind Stryker.

"Let me check you out, Zach," he begged. I stood still as he donned a pair of nitrile gloves and began closely inspecting me. Looking around, I saw Kelly in the Volvo, looking out at me with a mixture of fear and concern in her expression. The kids were beside her and Frederick even had his face mashed up against the window. I gave her a nod to let her know I was okay. The top hatch of the Stryker opened and Seth stuck his head out. When he saw that I was okay, his worried expression turned ecstatic.

"Thank you, Captain."

"I told you this thing was the shit, but I couldn't shoot until I had a clear field of fire," he explained. "When you fell down, that was the best thing to happen." I nodded in understanding.

"I don't see any bite marks, but you've got some of that stuff on your face," Grant said, went into his medical bag and came up with a plastic bottle of isopropyl alcohol. His other hand had some gauze. He soaked it and started wiping me down.

"So, what the hell happened?" Justin asked. I explained and then pushed the doctor's hand off of my face.

"I'll finish cleaning up later. Why don't you go check on Cutter?" He nodded and jogged off.

"You saved those two idiot's lives," Justin remarked.

"Yeah," I muttered. He sighed deeply at the Butter Pooter duo's latest nonsense and looked around.

"It'll be dark soon, but we probably shouldn't camp here for the night. There may be more around here."

"Yeah, they may come back in larger numbers." Justin digested my opinion, looked up at Seth, who conceded my point with a nod of agreement and slapped the top of the Stryker.

"It's not a problem; this baby is fairly easy to drive at night with the imaging equipment. Everybody just needs to stay close and we can get an hour or two between us and them."

"Alright," Justin said angrily. "We'll head out just as soon as I go have a word or two with those knuckleheads."

"Yeah, most definitely, but first, let me show you two something." They followed me as I worked my way around the fallen bodies until I came upon one, a rather rotund man who was probably African American at one time, although it was hard to tell. I raised my rifle, but realized he was dead. I pointed at his chest.

"I hurried my shot and instead of a head shot I hit him center mass. At first I only thought it disabled him, but look." Both men inspected the wound carefully.

"It killed him," Seth observed.

"Well, that's something new," Justin remarked.

"If that's what killed him, it means their circulatory system if functioning again. Maybe."

"That could be a game changer," Seth said.

"Are you going to cut him open?" Justin asked. Seth frowned and looked at me.

"Nah, we don't have time."

"Have you cut them open before?" Seth asked.

"Yep, their insides are very interesting. They stink even worse when you open them up, but it's still interesting." Seth grunted in thought and then looked pointedly at me.

"Say, Zach," he said as we began walking back toward the group. I stopped and looked at him. Here it comes, I thought. "You know, if something happens to you before we get to Weather, I may as well go live with Melvin and Peggy. Just saying."

"Point taken," I replied and began walking again. I knew that was going to be all he said on the matter, Kelly was going to be a different story, I suspected.

Grant was wrapping Cutter's knee with an elastic bandage as we walked up.

"Hopefully, he just wrenched it," he said. "I'll know more when we get to Weather."

"What the hell happened?" Justin asked them.

"We were scavenging," Cutter replied. "I guess we got a little too far away from the convoy." Shooter joined in.

"When we first spotted them, we took off running, but my idiot brother tripped on his own two feet." He finished his sentence with a reproachful scoff. I looked them both over. Shooter had that same stupid smile he always had; Cutter looked ashamed. I wanted to chew them out, but I just didn't have the energy. I turned to Justin.

"I'm going to wash this crap off of me. Give me ten minutes then we can get underway." Justin nodded and took off to tell the others. I started to walk away when Cutter shouted out to me.

"Hey, man." I stopped and turned. "Thanks," he said. "We would've been goners for sure." I looked at him a long thirty seconds. He seemed sincerely grateful. Shooter, however, just kept smiling that stupid little smile. It made me wonder if Shooter would have stayed with him or when they got too close he would've dropped him and took off.

Kelly watched from the open door of the Volvo as I stripped and used a wet rag she provided to wipe myself down.

"You worried the hell out of me," she said. No silent treatment this time. At least, not yet.

"You did the right thing getting the kids in the truck. They're more important than anything."

"If you really thought that, you would've been inside the truck with us instead of risking your life saving those two." I looked up to see a tear running down her cheek. She quickly wiped it away.

"What will we do if you're dead?" she asked angrily and disappeared into the truck before I could answer. She reappeared a moment later and tossed me some fresh clothes. I changed quickly. I heard the back of the trailer slam shut and a moment later Jorge and Josue emerged from behind it.

"We loaded up the bike. I think I'll ride in a car from here on out." I nodded at his wise decision.

"Justin, this is Kelly," she said into the microphone before I even had a chance to get seated. "We're ready." She stared straight ahead, not saying anything. Even I knew she was upset and I needed to make things right, but wasn't sure what to do about it. I listened as Justin got confirmations from everyone as the sun disappeared below the horizon.

"Alright everyone, code Romeo eight and give me a click." It was a simple code that I had made everyone memorize during the mission briefing. Romeo meant radio. Whatever number of the code, we subtracted one and then went backwards the appropriate number of channels on the CB. When Justin counted the correct number of clicks, he spoke.

"We're going to try for at least one more hour of drive time and then stop. I know everyone is tired, so you need to help each other stay alert and watch your intervals. Once we stop, nobody is to venture more than ten feet away from your vehicle. Copy?" Everyone clicked in acknowledgement.

"Excellent," he responded. "I'll assign guard duty once we stop." I spoke up.

"You drove all day, you must be tired. Why don't you let me drive?" I suggested. Kelly shook her head.

"I'm fine." Her response was clipped as she released the air brakes and started forward. We drove five miles in silence. Yep, it was the silent treatment now. Even Janet and the kids were quiet.

"I love you, Kelly." She looked over at me and her eyes started watering up again.

"I love you too, you – shithead." It was the second time she'd ever called me that. She must have been really upset.

"I'll do better, I promise."

"Bullshit," she said. Frederick chose that particular moment to venture out of the sleeper and jump in my lap, the heel of his foot landing squarely on my groin. I gasped in pain.

"Serves you right," Kelly quipped.

CHAPTER 53 – THE ARRIVAL

"It's not too far now," Raymond said excitedly over the radio as we turned onto State Route 277, and as soon as we made the turn, there were noticeable changes. It was subtle at first, but quickly it became obvious there were humans at work. Seth glanced at me with a grin. He had the hatch open now and was driving with the wind in his face.

"Notice anything different?" he asked.

"Someone's cleared the roads of the derelicts."

"Yep," he replied. "We did that and more. Wait until we hit Blueridge Mountain Road. We repaved it." He nodded in satisfaction. "Now, we had to table a lot of our work while we sent out delegations, but we're going to start back before the cold weather gets here."

"What's on the drawing board?" I asked.

"Well, I think you'll like the answer. There is a detailed report, even longer than your mission report. You'll spend hours joyfully reading it." He laughed at his own joke, which I didn't find very funny.

Soon, we began seeing people. They were in groups of four or more, most of them working the fields. They waved as we drove by. Some even ran to their vehicles and fell into the convoy. It was after five when we turned onto Old Blue Ridge Road and we now had several vehicles following us.

A couple of minutes later, Seth stopped the Stryker. There was a long pause before he spoke.

"Ladies and gentlemen, welcome to Mount Weather." I think all of us were in a state of wonder. The people who were following us had exited their respective vehicles too and had crowded around us, welcoming us and introducing themselves.

A couple of golf carts appeared from around a building. I recognized the passenger in the leading cart.

"I've radioed ahead," Seth whispered as he pointed. "The President is most anxious to meet you."

CHAPTER 54 – JOURNAL ENTRY: AUGUST 4TH, 3 A.Z.

I'm writing this while sitting in a small but rather pleasant suite of rooms three floors underground. We had arrived at Mount Weather about an hour before sunset and were greeted warmly by people we'd never met. Everyone was friendly, but there were no handshakes or hugs, no physical contact whatsoever. Rachel made one of her humorous comments about how it must be because of how we smelled, but then a serious-looking women candidly explained that there was to be no contact until it was proven we weren't infected. Then we were forced to sit and wait at the front entrance making small talk while the medical staff performed blood tests. It was frustrating, but necessary, I suppose. But, I mean, really. You don't need a blood test to spot a zombie. And hell, the medical staff was fully aware of who I was, they even called me by name.

So, after a couple of hours, the doctors declared us plague free (big surprise, right?) and then came the friendly handshakes, the gates were opened, and we were welcomed inside the compound. That's when the second sticking point arose. Somebody, an older man with a pompous air about him, demanded we disarm. Seth spoke up on our behalf and before we knew it, we were being introduced to the President.

He made no attempt to shake a hand or anything physical, and instead greeted us with a preplanned generic speech. He'd probably used it a couple of other times for visiting dignitaries back in the day. I know, I'm being a little cynical about the man. I should reserve judgement until after I get to know him. The Marines, ten of them, watched us warily. After all, we were within ten feet of the man and most of us were armed. Justin had made some small talk with them while we were being tested, but I haven't had a chance to ask him about it.

Afterward we all enjoyed a pleasant dinner, even though every time I got a forkful of food in my mouth someone would invite themselves to sit down and ask about the zombies. It confirmed my suspicions that these people had very little interactions with the world outside. I wondered who cleaned out the infestations around here, the Marines probably. I'd ask about it later.

Finally, we were shown to our living quarters. Like I said, they're quaint, but nice enough. Secure. That's the big thing. All of the living quarters are underground and cordoned off with thick, steel doors and security locks.

There's going to be a debriefing session tomorrow. Seth said it'll start after breakfast and will probably last most of the day. Expect a lot of naïve questions, he said. That's my take of these people; naïve. None of them, with the possible exception of a few of the soldiers, have the hardened expression of someone who's had to fight every day for the past three years just to survive.

These people are a very diverse bunch. There are at least two military generals, senators, congressmen, doctors, university professors, bureaucrats, you name it. I am indeed a small fish in a much bigger pond than quaint little Nolensville, Tennessee. It's a little intimidating.

But, they are, what's the right word - naïve? Yeah, naïve, but also soft. Give them the once over and you can tell most of them had never experienced what we have. They'd never had to wonder where their next meal was going to come from. They'd never gone for days without sleep protecting their loved ones. They'd never engaged in hand-to-hand combat with a bunch of infected things that wanted to eat you alive. When the red balloon went up, most of these people were whisked away to the safety of this shelter, built and stocked with taxpayer money. I overheard one of them saying there was enough stored food to last two hundred people another five years. Five years' worth of freeze dried and preserved food for two hundred people? Damn.

If all that isn't enough to cause a man to develop hemorrhoids, after the debriefing tomorrow they're expecting me to meet with the doctors for "tests." We'll see about that.

I'm going to end this journal entry by saying this; I want this to work, I really do, but I'm also wary, although I'm not sure why. Maybe I've become more like Rick than I've realized; asocial, skeptical, paranoid even.

Well, if this doesn't work out, there's always Nolensville.

CHECK OUT OTHER GREAT ZOMBIE NOVELS

Z BURBIA
by Jake Bible

Whispering Pines is a classic, quiet, private American subdivision on the edge of Asheville, NC, set in the pristine Blue Ridge Mountains. Which is good since the zombie apocalypse has come to Western North Carolina and really put suburban living to the test!

Surrounded by a sea of the undead, the residents of Whispering Pines have adapted their bucolic life of block parties to scavenging parties, common area groundskeeping to immediate area warfare, neighborhood beautification to neighborhood fortification.

But, even in the best of times, suburban living has its ups and downs what with nosy neighbors, a strict Home Owners' Association, and a property management company that believes the words "strict interpretation" are holy words when applied to the HOA covenants. Now with the zombie apocalypse upon them even those innocuous, daily irritations quickly become dramatic struggles for personal identity, family security, and straight up survival.

ZOMBIE RULES
by David Achord

Zach Gunderson's life sucked and then the zombie apocalypse began.

Rick, an aging Vietnam veteran, alcoholic, and prepper, convinces Zach that the apocalypse is on the horizon. The two of them take refuge at a remote farm. As the zombie plague rages, they face a terrifying fight for survival.

They soon learn however that the walking dead are not the only monsters.

 SEVEREDPRESS

facebook.com/severedpress
twitter.com/severedpress

CHECK OUT OTHER GREAT ZOMBIE NOVELS

900 MILES
by S.Johnathan Davis

John is a killer, but that wasn't his day job before the Apocalypse.

In a harrowing 900 mile race against time to get to his wife just as the dead begin to rise, John, a business man trapped in New York, soon learns that the zombies are the least of his worries, as he sees first-hand the horror of what man is capable of with no rules, no consequences and death at every turn.

Teaming up with an ex-army pilot named Kyle, they escape New York only to stumble across a man who says that he has the key to a rumored underground stronghold called Avalon..... Will they find safety? Will they make it to Johns wife before it's too late?

Get ready to follow John and Kyle in this fast paced thriller that mixes zombie horror with gladiator style arena action!

WHITE FLAG OF THE DEAD
by Joseph Talluto

Millions died when the Enillo Virus swept the earth. Millions more were lost when the victims of the plague refused to stay dead, instead rising to slaughter and feed on those left alive. For survivors like John Talon and his son Jake, they are faced with a choice: Do they submit to the dead, raising the white flag of surrender? Or do they find the will to fight, to try and hang on to the last shreds or humanity?

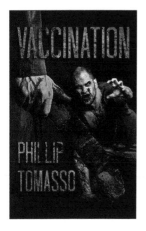

15246711R00189

Printed in Great Britain
by Amazon